THE DAY THE SWISS BANKS CALL THE MAFIA'S BLUFF THERE'S A $2-BILLION SCORE TO SETTLE.

"BABE" VOLPONE, Mafia lover boy, ups the ante with murder and vengeance.

DON GABELOTTI, the rival kingpin, is caught with a fatal hand.

RENATA, the spoiled beauty, pushes her luck.

O'BRION, the syndicate lawyer, goes for bust.

ZAZA, the gang moll, puts up more than her body.

KLOPPE, the kinky banker, plays for sexual pleasure.

INEZ, the high-priced princess, springs a savage surprise on a cheater.

OUT

Pierre Rey

*Translated from the French
by Harold J. Salemson*

OUT

*A Bantam Book / published by arrangement with
Editions Robert Laffont*

Bantam edition / January 1980

ISBN 0–553–13139–7

Published simultaneously in the United States and Canada

*Bantam Books are published by Bantam Books, Inc. Its trade-
mark, consisting of the words "Bantam Books" and the por-
trayal of a bantam, is Registered in U.S. Patent and Trademark
Office and in other countries. Marca Registrada. Bantam
Books, Inc., 666 Fifth Avenue, New York, New York 10019.*

PRINTED IN THE UNITED STATES OF AMERICA

DESIGNED BY MIERRE

When you see a Swiss banker jumping out the window, jump after him. There is surely money to be made there.

—VOLTAIRE

At one end of the chain
The one who is richer than gold;
At the other end of the chain
The one who digs till his death.
Which of the two will die first,
If God should shut his eyes?

—*Pueblo . . . Pueblo . . .*
(Bolivian miner's song)

OUT

Prologue

Coming out of the curve, Roland braked a bit too sharply. His hands, on the control lever, and his spine shook with the heavy vibrations of 750 tons of machinery.

"Staying with us tonight?" Luciano asked.

Roland gradually lowered the throttle to reduce the thrust of the locomotive.

"I'd like to, but . . ."

"Is she pretty?"

"You kidding? My mother!"

"Cut it some more . . ."

The train hissed softly as it glided to a lower speed. For the first time since they started, the parallel tracks before them did not meet in the distance. His hand still gripping the lever, Roland mechanically noted the concrete platforms growing progressively denser with handcarts, packages, and groups of travelers in ranks that tightened as the train moved into the station.

"What's wrong with them?"

"Who?"

"What the hell're they gawking at?"

The locomotive was no more than a hundred yards from the terminal buffers. And the people along the platforms stood gaping at Roland and Luciano in disbelief, grimaces frozen on their faces, even as their heads swung around to watch the engine go by.

"What do you s'pose is wrong?" Luciano wondered aloud. "I got egg on my face or something?"

1

"No. Do I?" said Roland.

The train was doing a bare five miles an hour as it slid beneath the glass-paned marquee under which groups of people stood guard over their luggage.

"Train number one-two-seven, express from Geneva, now arriving. Please stand back!" yelled a man's voice, bouncing out of ten loudspeakers that fed back over one another.

Roland saw a plump woman drop her handbag without bothering to bend down and pick it up; then she pointed a finger at him as she covered the bottom of her face with her other hand in an expression of fright.

"Shit!" Roland swore uncomfortably. "What the hell's wrong?"

Wherever he turned, there were the same looks of surprise. As the train went by, everything fell silent. Platform activity usually generated its own typical din: metallic noises, bumps, rumbles, shouts, but now there was nothing except that sullen movement of withdrawal and those gaping eyes.

"Hit it!"

Roland jammed the brake, and the engine grazed the tip of the buffers. Luciano cut the power. Still no one on the platform moved. Two station employees, heads together, were whispering. Then one of them darted toward the stationmaster's office, and the other climbed up the locomotive ladder and came into the cab. He was obviously embarrassed, glancing first at Luciano, then at Roland, not saying a word.

He cleared his throat. "Where did you pick that up?"

"Pick *what* up?" said Roland.

"What do you mean—*what?*"

"Look," Luciano barked, "we're no geniuses! Why not cut the riddles?"

"Follow me."

The crowd remained as if frozen. All that could be heard was the panting of an antique steam locomotive on a siding. Luciano and Roland hefted themselves down to the asphalt, but only when they were in front of their engine did they understand what was going on.

On the cowcatcher, as if delicately placed there by a ghoulish decorator, was a man's leg—neatly sheared off at

2

the groin. One could just make out a rust-colored blood-stain that came through the dark material of the trousers at the point where the bones had probably been severed. The absurd thought that this was a high-class leg flashed through Roland's mind: the black shoe was made of fine leather, and there was a matching silk sock.

On looking closer, he could see that blood was trickling down the sock, onto the shoe, and ending in a dark brown puddle on the engine's steel cowcatcher.

At that moment, neither Roland nor any of the other witnesses could have any idea that this puddle was going to spread with breathtaking speed over several continents. And turn into a bloodbath.

Part One

GENEVA-ZURICH EXPRESS

1

Morty O'Brion never dared assert himself with his wife. Judith terrified him. The corners of her mouth twisted with a sarcastic bitterness that no makeup could disguise. When she raised her voice, Morty felt like melting away; when she gave him the silent treatment, it was even worse, for it meant she was either repressing her contempt for him or having the kind of migraine headache he would have to handle with kid gloves.

It had been years since Marty had tried to carry on any real conversation with her. Since they had been sleeping in separate rooms, their communication had dwindled to short exchanges, summed up by the words *headache, ridiculous, gimme,* and *how much.* When they were first married, Morty had hoped Judith would take an interest in his work, become proud of his success, but all she ever did was nag him about his failures, taking his triumphs for granted, and they had quickly retreated into a kind of deaf-and-dumb hostility, each remaining alone with her or his own thoughts. Judith didn't bother to complain anymore, except by making faces, and Morty was careful never to mention his professional achievements, for he felt she would take delight in destroying his pleasure with a cruel word or a scornful grimace.

Four years before, as a hotshot financial lawyer, he had wanted to crow to her when he was retained to straighten out some of the Syndicate's business deals. But a sixth sense had warned him not to. Even though it was a potential gold mine, this new connection was not going to mean any change in her life—not for the moment, anyway. Judith's closets were already overflowing with furs, her drawers crammed with jewels, all intended in some way to make up for the lack of communication between them.

Judith lit another cigarette and snuffed the match out in the bottom of the coffeecup on her virtually untouched breakfast tray. Morty went about closing his overnighter.

"You going somewhere?" she asked.

"Yes."

"But you just got back from Europe. Oh, what a headache I have!"

"Take some of your pills."

"Where are you going this time?"

He looked up, surprised. She never pried that way, ordinarily acting as if his goings and comings were beneath her notice. He almost answered, What the fuck do you care? but he simply mumbled, "Nassau."

She poured the rest of her coffee into her half-finished glass of grapefruit juice, then dropped her barely smoked cigarette in after it.

"You're lucky."

Taken aback, he glanced quickly at her eyes, relieved to see that they reflected nothing but her usual sullen boredom.

He challenged her. "Be ready in five minutes and I'll take you along."

"Don't be ridiculous. I've got a headache."

If only she knew. She had not realized how he had grown. To her, he was still the penniless young lawyer who almost had to beg to be taken on as a clerk. And she had thought she could keep him under her thumb by castrating him. Even if he told her about it, how would she be able to comprehend what he was about to pull off?

He coughed "Okay, then . . ." He started to bend toward her, as if to kiss her good-bye, but he stopped. "Well, I'd better be going . . ."

Perhaps he should have been bothered by heartrending feelings of finality, as are all the heroes of books when they're putting an end to twenty years of double harness. But Morty O'Brion was as calm as if he were planning to

8

be back home that evening for dinner. The fact that they had no children suddenly made him deliriously happy. Leaving her like this, all things considered, he was simply dropping off one part of himself, a sticky piece of his life that he was embarrassed to think about because he had waited too long to work up the courage to run out on it.

Forty-eight hours from now, he would be far away, in a dream place of which no one in the world even suspected the existence. And he, Mortimer O'Brion, would be the richest man on earth, richer than any other human had ever been, rich beyond the imaginings of the wildest minds.

He was almost at the door when Judith called out, "Morty! On your way out, ask Margaret to bring me some cold water and my pills."

He nodded. How appropriate, he thought, that the last word he heard from her should be *pills*. He turned his back, so she couldn't see his smile.

The small plane was completing its third loop. Once again it swooped down over the main street of Chiavenna, buzzed the ocher rooftops with its powerful vibration, then righted itself just to the left of the church steeple. Looking up, the people in the small town saw a flock of little pieces of paper dancing on the wind, pirouetting gracefully with the hesitating movements of autumn leaves, to land finally on the street, on the tops of cars, on balconies, or on the brightly colored canvas awnings atop the carts of the market merchants. It was noon, and the market was a once-a-week affair. The street was full of people, and the gentle April breeze off Lake Como outlined the lithe shapes of the younger women who had been the first to take their light dresses out of winter storage.

Two or three boys picked up what they thought to be some kind of advertising leaflet, turned it over between their fingers, then looked at one another in disbelief. One twelve-year-old broke the silence. Tripping over his feet with excitement, he dashed toward his father's bakery, pressing to his chest a handful of folded money. He shouted to his parents, who had rushed out when they heard the noise of the motor.

"It's money! Father! Mother! It's raining money from heaven!"

Suddenly everyone came to life. People were dashing into the merry-go-round of cars occupying the roadway, bending down to get their share of the miraculous catch amid a cacophony of shrieking brakes, cursing drivers, and families yelling instructions to their most agile members. Threats, protests, and shouts of encouragement were suddenly drowned out by the deafening noise of the returning plane. And while a few of the old women chanted "Miracle! Miracle!" as they crossed themselves, more manna came floating down.

Children, held up by sturdier elder siblings, tried to keep their footing on tree branches where early blossoms were flowering into banknotes: real Swiss currency, fine, good bills from the Schweizerische Nationalbank, delicately mauve in shade and worth anywhere from ten to fifty francs. The rush became more violent and people started to fight.

Renata righted her plane and burst out laughing. Seen from above, the view looked something like a chicken coop in which all the birds, suddenly gone mad, had started pecking at imaginary feed.

"You're disgusting!" Kurt yelled at her, raising his voice to be heard over the motor and the wind.

To his utter terror, she let go of the joy stick and slammed shut the Plexiglas cockpit cover. The plane did a flip-flop, which only made Renata laugh harder as she glanced sideways and muttered, "Serves you right for daring me!"

Beneath them they could see a succession of bright green valleys spotted here and there with the darker green of pine trees.

"Hang on! We're diving," Renata called to him.

"Renata!" Kurt shouted back.

The Piper seemed to fall like a stone on the herd of cows Renata had been aiming for, nearly grazing their backs as they spread across the landscape. For a bare second Kurt was able to see the cowherd motion toward the plane and shake his fist at them.

Trying to sound as reasonable as possible, Kurt said, "Just what are you trying to prove to me?"

Leapfrogging over tiny light clouds that were dissipating in the wind, Renata looked serious. "Simply that

10

you're wrong all the way down the line and not honest enough to give a name to your real wishes. Did you see them run and fight when I dropped that money on them? You claimed that it was degrading, that I was insulting the hardworking population! Well, who was right?"

Feeling slightly nauseated, Kurt slunk into his seat as if he had not heard her. If he stood up to her, he was afraid he might drive her to the kind of daring in which a flight in her Piper turned into a roller-coaster nightmare.

"Well, can't you answer?"

To teach him a lesson, she zoomed into a climb that knocked the wind out of him and pinned him back against his seat. After that she treated him to another straight dive, two or three barrel rolls in which earth and sky seemed to be pushing each other around, and a long upside-down glide. "If, as you claim, money were shit," she said, "then people wouldn't get down on all fours to grab after it!"

He gritted his teeth. If she didn't maneuver a crash in the next few minutes, he had a chance of being alive when they got back to Zurich, where at the end of the week, on Sunday, April 26, they were to be married.

Zaza Finney thought she was perfect. Not a shadow, not a wrinkle marred the smooth skin of her face, and she considered her eyes fantastic and mysterious. Naked before her mirror, she swung one of its panels to get a rear view. She was overwhelmed by the harmonious proportions of her narrow waist and ample hips, the satiny velvet of her tanned skin, the daintiness of her ankles, and the soft curve of her thighs. She could almost cry over such breathtaking beauty. Once again she wondered whether she had made a smart move in deciding—for the time being—to latch on to that dull, ordinary little man, even though with every step he took gold seemed to appear as if by magic.

Besides her passion for her own beautiful image, she had a burning ambition to be a star. She was sure that once she got her chance on screen or stage, she would be able to hold the audience captive. But one had to start somewhere, so she had gotten a job posing for a set of pictures for a canned-asparagus-soup campaign.

The photographer, after sleeping with her, got her to

let him take some more revealing shots, which, he swore, were "just to remember her by," even though he had asked her to sign a release. Three months later, she had been beside herself with delight when she saw the photos in the pages of one of those now highly respectable girlie magazines that featured "bedmates of the month." But, even as she was gloating over the pictures, it occurred to her that she might capitalize on his double cross. A small scandal could easily blow up into a media feast, so she had asked a girl friend for the name of the best lawyer in New York.

When she got to Mortimer O'Brion's office, the receptionist wouldn't make an appointment, claiming she didn't know when he would be in. Zaza came back twice. The third time, the receptionist had been interrupted by an undistinguished little man, the kind of guy no woman would look at a second time unless he had a knife stuck in his back or the figure of his net worth plastered on his chest. To her amazement, the receptionist had deferred to him with unexpected servility, saying, "Here is Mr. O'Brion now. He'll be glad to see you."

That was how things had started off between them. She quickly understood that his generosity more than made up for his puniness.

At the time, Zaza was living in a sordid hotel room, one step from being evicted for failure to pay rent. Her worldly goods consisted of a cheap suitcase, a sublime evening gown, a street outfit, and her makeup kit. So Mortimer's gifts overwhelmed her quite as much as his brand of sex failed to—rabbitlike sex that left the exhausted legal eagle in trancelike ecstasy and did nothing for her.

To get her own kicks, Zaza indulged in as many rough secret affairs as she could squeeze in between Mortimer's visits. He set her up in a sumptuous suite in one of New York's best residence hotels, where she was allowed to order anything she pleased from room service. She hadn't been slow to make demands, and within a week she had a wardrobe that would have put a star to shame. Then, to test her lover, she started asking for jewels. He had complied with bashful alacrity, plying her with more loot than she had ever dreamed of. Nothing she asked for seemed to surprise him, and he appeared to dote on fulfilling her wishes even before she expressed them. All he asked for was her company during long, utterly boring, evenings. Sometimes he would take her hand—to her extreme embarrassment, if she thought anyone was watching —hold it in his, and look at her with an expression of unspeakably stupid subjection.

He didn't tell her much about his business, being satisfied to shower her with money and gems, until the day, a month earlier, when he had spoken the mysterious words: "How about you and me living together, alone? Are you ready for that?"

Zaza, who knew he was married, felt a shiver of disgust at the prospect of a permanent shack-up. She promptly went looking for advice from Jimmy, the photographer, whom she had taken to seeing again. Jimmy had not put up much resistance when she had offered him "loans" after her affair with Morty began, but he did wonder why a man like O'Brion would want to take up with this kind of narcissistic hunk of flesh, the likes of which paraded through his studio by the dozen. So he impressed on her what a soft berth she had fallen into.

Only one thing that Jimmy told her really made an impression: "That guy you call a twerp is the top troubleshooter for the whole damned Syndicate!"

She burst out laughing. Morty, a gangster? Yet she could almost see it. And yesterday it had all come to a head. O'Brion had repeated, in more pressing form, his question of a month ago: "Are you ready?"

Remembering what Jimmy told her, she said yes.

Now she opened the drapes and looked out at the street, where a flood of tourists moved along sluggishly in the hot sun. She had always wanted to see Nassau and walk on Bay Street, but now that she was here, it was a fucking bore. Morty wouldn't be back for an hour. Their tickets were all ready, but she didn't know where they were going.

"Where I'm taking you," he had said, "you'll live like a queen. There won't be anything you ask for that you won't be able to have lickety-split."

"An elephant?" she said.

And Morty had come back in his little boy's voice, "I suppose you mean a solid gold one."

She felt ill at ease, and she went back into the bath-

13

room, trying to keep her spirits up by figuring out how many days she'd have to stay with O'Brion before she found a way to latch onto a good hunk of his loot so she could hotfoot it back to Jimmy.

What was most repulsive about Morty was not that she had to spread her legs for him, but that he had the nerve to take her hand and expect her to show him affection.

The military trucks left Geneva, Nyon, Morges, Lausanne, Fribourg, Bern, Lucerne, Zug, and Zurich to drop off their troop contingents. Each man was ordered to explore a three-hundred-meter section of tracks, finecombing the underbrush for a width of ten meters on either side of the right-of-way. For once agreeing on something, the Swiss police and the army had felt that a human corpse, even lacking a right leg, might constitute a jarring note in the happy Swiss countryside. The police were in charge, but the army was supplying the men. The order was to keep searching until the body had been found. As night fell, the engineers' noncoms gave instructions to turn on the searchlights.

As for the leg that had been found on the cowcatcher of the Geneva-Zurich Express locomotive, it had already provided the investigators with a few good leads. The shoe was from Biasca, a well-known New York bootmaker. The Zurich police had immediately gotten on the phone to their American counterparts, who were investigating too, and with a little luck they would quickly know whose shoe it was. In the pants pocket, apart from a roll of American bills amounting to over five thousand dollars, the Swiss officials had found a ticket to Geneva stamped in Zurich. What really threw them was that the leg had appeared in Zurich when it should have been arriving in Geneva at the same time as the other leg, the head, and the rest of the body of its rightful owner.

Seated snugly between Vittorio Pizzu and Moshe Yudelman, Italo ("Babe") Volpone looked sharply at the twelve men around the conference table. That he was sitting in his brother's chair gave him a feeling of quiet authority betrayed only by the constant darting of his eye-balls, two shards of black coal hiding behind half-closed lids. He was concerned about his voice, which had to remain calm and collected, for he knew it was most effective when it was aggressive or threatening.

He tried once again to get into the skin of the character he was supposed to be playing, ordering his hands not to play with his pen, his eyes to keep still.

For reassurance he slipped two fingers into his jacket pocket, next to his heart, to get a welcome feel of the deck of playing cards he always kept there. At times they were his instruments for gambling—he had always lived off gambling, lived only for gambling—and at other times they were the masters of his destiny, tellers of good and bad fortune. When he traveled, he also carried a miniature roulette wheel. When he rolled its ball time after time to work out endless fascinating systems of probabilities and chances, neither day nor night nor time itself existed, and he entered a kingdom in which figures alone were kings. His record had been three days and four nights in a private gaming room at Las Vegas. At regular intervals waiters had set food and drink before him, which he consumed without realizing it, and when he got up from the table and tried to stretch his weary muscles, he collapsed into the deep sleep of the blessed and had to be carried to his room. He hadn't come to until fourteen hours later.

Now, without moving his fingers from the lucky deck, Italo said, "Your representative, O'Brion, has just reached Zurich. Everything is okay. Here's the cable I just got from Don Genco."

He took from his pocket the crumpled piece of paper that he had reread a hundred times before carrying out his brother's instructions to send out invitations and announce the news.

Ettore Gabelotti glanced at it and silently passed it along to Simeone Ferro, who handed it to Joseph Dotto. While Carmine Crimello, Vittorio Pizzu, Angelo Barba, Vincente Bruttore, Thomas Merta, Aldo Amalfi, Carlo Badaletto, and Frankie Sabatini each read it in turn, Italo Volpone was thinking that this was a historic occasion: the peaceful meeting of the two most powerful Syndicate "families"—the Gabelottis and the Volpones—after twenty years of cold wars and murderous feuds. Volpone's eyes slipped from one man to the next, noting the uncontrollable shock of satisfaction that, ever so briefly, cracked the artificial deadpans they sported in public. Having gone all around the table, the cable finally came back to Italo.

"So what else is new?" asked Carlo Badaletto.

Badaletto hated Italo Volpone and never missed a chance to defy him. Five years before, when Italo had come back from London, Badaletto had been a member of the Volpone clan. By way of welcome, he had said, *"Come va, speranzaritu?"* and it had gotten him a double fracture of the jaw as well as the loss of his incisors, one of which, after Italo butted him violently, remained stuck in Volpone's forehead.

Speranzaritu was the scornful Sicilian word for local boys who had had to skip abroad. But if Italo had been forced to spend two years' exile in London, the capo of every family on the East and West coasts knew it was on the express orders of his brother, the don, Zu Genco Volpone, from whom a mere wink was a decree that his younger brother was in no position to challenge.

"Nothing else," Italo snarled at Badaletto.

Babe Volpone would have liked to evoke in Carlo Badaletto the same feeling of inferiority that everyone experienced in his brother's presence, without Genco doing anything to make it so. To be sure, people were afraid of Italo, but Genco had something more: people respected him. His seeming gentleness, his open smile, and his natural gift as a mediator were the perfect front for his grasping, pitiless nature. On the contrary, Italo could not for long contain the rage constantly boiling within him. His murderous impulses drove him to satisfy his desires immediately in every area: private, emotional, or economic. Had it not been for his brother's position, Italo's tendency to resort to brute force would have condemned him to the vegetative life of a punk or a hit man. The capi of the Syndicate didn't trust Italo's lack of self-control or his delight in primitive solutions. Times had changed since the days of Al Capone. Although rough hits might be no less numerous, they were carried out more subtly by nameless characters who were paid off by intermediaries so that the hit men

16

never knew why or for whom they were performing their contracts.

Nowadays each capo had to have the facade of an eminently respectable businessman, so that he could carry on his work without being bothered by the IRS, the police, or the competition. Family investments had the look and the seamless structure of multinational corporations with endless ramifications, and they were directed by an army of lawyers who knew how to put the illegal proceeds of the various rackets into businesses that were beyond reproach. For example, it was not unusual for some of the profits from the narcotics trade to end up, after a mysterious series of twists and turns, financing a hospital for handicapped children, christened by the highest authorities with great pomp and circumstance in the presence of all the local officials, and receiving the deep gratitude of the people.

Zu Genco Volpone's brain trust was made up of the cream of graduates of the best schools of international law, as if buying the top men somehow made up for the fact that, until the age of eighteen, he himself had hardly been able to read.

Moshe Yudelman was the first to speak up. "The first phase of the operation is over," he said. "Within three months all our funds will have been laundered."

Straight out of the Lower East Side, with a brief detour through the Bronx, Yudelman, who had supported himself through school by swiping vegetables from pushcarts and beating the bums on his block at pinball games, could outthink the most cunning head of any international central bank. Born with a God-given gift for figures as some are with eyes of blue, he knew without having to learn, he understood without having to think. He always found the way. This nose for finance was further strengthened by his talent for sharp practice. No contract, however adroitly drawn, could hold him at bay more than five minutes. He could immediately find a chink, the tiny detail, the missing comma that might be used with absolute legality to break off an agreement without anyone even suspecting that bad faith or dishonesty was involved. Better than any computer, his head contained the exact list of holdings, privileges, and profits of all the rival families of the Commissione, that top-level organization consisting of the eleven capi who ran the worldwide business, in which Zu Genco Volpone was not the least important.

When Moshe Yudelman joined Genco's family, Genco had had to put up a fight with his associates to bring Moshe in as consigliere. The proud Sicilians who made up the top group found it hard to accept a Jew among them. With their ferocious attachment to Old World traditions, they had a gut distrust of anything foreign, lumping together the Irish, Negroes, Jews, Chinese, and Protestants. At the beginning, Yudelman had tried to keep a low profile, giving advice only when it was asked for, never taking sides, never saying anything against anyone. He was there, period; like a piece of furniture that gradually became familiar, that you knew would always be on hand when you needed it. He was too smart not to see that some of the clan's unwritten laws were outmoded, but too shrewd to voice the least criticism. The underground world in which he lived was the only one that could ever assuage his lust for power, his yearning to be the strength behind the throne. His amazing accounting and managerial talents had done the rest.

Although the families frequently killed off each other's members over meaningless questions of prestige, Yudelman had succeeded not only in staying alive, but in occupying a place from which none, not even the members of the Commissione, dared try to unseat him. He owed everything to Genco, who had picked him up when he was poor and defenseless, but it was through Yudelman that Don Zu Volpone had been able to reinforce his own prestige and authority. Thereafter, his role as consigliere to one family had been extended to all parts of the activities of the Syndicate, for it had made Moshe a kind of elder statesman, an arbitrator in matters of the greatest delicacy. These responsibilities hadn't kept him from building up his own fortune, day by day increased through careful investments, split-second decisions, the unbeatable flair of the great predator for any weakening prey on the stock exchange, in gambling, slot machines, bars, taverns, real estate, vending machines, bootleg booze, numbers, championship prizefights, blackmail, loansharking, or pimping.

It was on his say-so that Genco had agreed to make an alliance—who knew for how long?—with the man he considered his number one rival: Ettore Gabelotti. Moshe sneaked a sidewise glance at him now. An old Roman face, heavy pouches under his eyes, Ettore weighed over 275 pounds. He kept up a kindly paternal front that was periodically contradicted by terrible rages that often ended in unquestionable condemnations to death.

It had taken inordinate diplomacy for Moshe to get Gabelotti to admit that, over and above whatever separated them, his interests were the same as Genco's when it came to laundering liquid money. To convince him that their money ought to be pooled had been no easy matter, for the two men held against each other the many corpses that each had sown in the other's camp over now-forgotten disagreements. But the accord had been reached, and today it was about to give birth to the greatest financial operation ever undertaken by the Syndicate.

Gabelotti, who had not said a word, must have felt Yudelman watching him. He looked toward him sharply, then covered up with a smile. Moshe smiled back and looked away.

"Lemme see the cable again!" Ettore asked.

From fingers to fingers, it flew from one end of the table to the other. Gabelotti grabbed it and laughed uproariously as he called to the younger Volpone, "Say, Babe, your brother sure didn't waste any dough on Western Union!"

Everybody joined in the raucous laughter. Italo, on the defensive, began to laugh along with the others once he realized that Ettore's words contained no hidden sarcastic criticism.

The cable, beyond the indication of its point of origination—Zurich, Schaffhauserstrasse Post Office—and the address, had just one single word, three letters: OUT. But those three letters represented the code name for the joint operation under which those present at the meeting were bringing home clean and free the net returns from all their criminal activities for the calendar year 1978.

And these net returns came to the sum of exactly two billion dollars.

Inez claimed that as a child she had been raised exclusively on blood and milk. The men in her tribe grew to be seven feet four inches tall, and the women grew to be six foot four. "Normal" warriors, by comparison, seemed like dwarfs. She casually dropped the fact that she was the daughter of a king, and that she had eight brothers, one more handsome than the next. When they went through their rites of passage, signifying their acceptance into the adult world, they had to prove their valor by covering themselves with serious wounds in the genital regions, thus unwittingly duplicating the actions of those young Athenians who slit their phalluses until the puffy scars made them look like sculptured totem poles.

Lando listened to these stories openmouthed, unable to tell where truth gave way to fabrication in the filmy texture of her tale.

"You mean to say your brothers made slits in their pricks with a razor?"

Inez stretched her arm and picked up a tangerine. "Absolutely."

"They gotta be crazy." Lando sighed. "Honest-to-God savages!"

Out of the corner of his eye, he looked at his mistress's immense body, now in repose on the carpet. Barefoot, she was exactly the same height as he, a fact that kept him from getting cramps in his calves when he made love to her standing up. Yet even during his two seasons of professional soccer he had rarely come across guys who were taller than he, either on his own team or the other side.

He turned toward her. "So you really are six foot two?"

"Yes."

"Well, it's funny—you don't look the least bit like a giraffe."

She glanced at him, half amused, half sneering. "Everything is relative, Lando my boy. In my country, even you would be considered a shrimp."

She came from Burundi, from a village called Bujumbura. Several times, pointing with her long, slim chocolate-colored fingers with bright red fingernails, she had shown

Lando the exact spot on the map—a flyspeck stuck between Kenya, the Congo, Uganda, and Tanzania.

"Okay, so what's that river there? Is that near where you live?" he would ask, pointing to a blue line. "Is it big?"

"Just a little stream. About six hundred miles long and about sixty wide. They call it the Tanganyika."

"You're kidding."

"Not so you'd notice."

She said her real name was Kibondo: Princess Kibondo. But how could you tell with people like that?

She had told him an Italian couturier had renamed her Inez before she came to Switzerland. She was a top model in Rome, and well known in London, Paris, and New York. Her figure was so impressive that she even had the guts to wear four-inch heels, yet there was never anything the least bit snide in the way people looked at her, only a kind of surprise one might feel toward something completely unknown, something sublimely beautiful from another planet, without connection to current tastes or standards.

Lando let his hand slide up her long naked thigh, smooth as a pebble buffed by the sea for a thousand years, warm bronze in color, relaxed, muscular yet fleshy, burning in his palm. In a confused way he was proud that so magnificent a creature should be helping to support him, not that he really needed the money—his clandestine profession more than covered all his expenses—but simply for the principle of the thing. The money and gifts she had been giving him since she started whoring were tossed at him like the purse a queen throws to a serf. Without servility, without asking anything in return, without complaint, just because that was what she felt like doing, what she deigned to do as her fancy dictated. Delicately she lifted Lando's hand from her thigh.

"No more time left. I have a seven o'clock date."

"The old man?"

"When we stand facing each other, his glasses come up to my nipples."

"And when you're in bed?"

"In bed, we're all the same. Or just about."

21

"Let him wait a little."

"No, he's a demon for punctuality. And when I work, I'm always on time."

She stretched like a great cat and began to yawn. Aroused by the broad purple-copper circles around the hard jutting tips of her breasts, Lando went on. "Just a minute. Won't you, please?"

This was the limit! He, the man whose tool should have been considered a signal honor by any female, was held at bay by a black woman who was deciding whether or not she was willing!

She glanced at him pensively. "For a white man, you don't make love too badly."

"Would you like it better if I was black?"

"Color isn't what counts, Lando."

"Then what does?"

"What you've got inside your pants."

Lando reared back; he was damn proud of what he had in there. It had been praised to the skies by hundreds of women he had abandoned, broken, exhausted, or worn out after a few high-flying erotic performances. But Inez, in spite of his unshakable confidence in his ability to make anyone come, succeeded in throwing doubt into his soul. The first night, he had had her five times in a row during eight hours of uninterrupted passion play. When she didn't say anything, he fished for a compliment.

"Well, did you like that?"

"Not bad."

"What do you mean, not bad?"

He had felt that he would be able to sleep ten years straight before getting back into shape.

She had nodded that beautiful head, her immense eyes seeming almost pasted on the jut of her cheekbones, and mincingly said, "Not bad for a white man."

Surely she was bluffing. No woman alive could take that kind of treatment without needing a good long rest cure. He had fallen off into a dead man's sleep, revolted by such ingratitude.

The next day she had given him a platinum watch, made by Vacheron; he had dozens more, of all makes, given to him in recognition of his sexual prowess by forgotten women, all of them ready to make even more meaningful sacrifices if only he agreed to go with them again. Even today, he could not comprehend why Inez, Princess Kibondo, daughter of a king, found pleasure in giving him the money she collected from a few filthy-rich lovers. He was a little boy in their relationship, and try as he might he had never succeeded in getting through to that secret place in her makeup for which she alone had the key.

She sat on the edge of the bed and slowly pulled on a pair of fawn-colored boots. One of the parakeets hissed in the cage.

"Did you buy those birds?"

"Someone gave them to me. Do you like birds?"

Orlando Baretto finally got up too, stretching his lean athlete's body. Since he had stopped playing ball, he had been living on nothing but liquor. He consumed a bottle or two a day, depending on his mood, yet he never got drunk.

"I love them," he said.

He went over to the gilded cage, opened the latch door, and fumbled around inside with his fingers. The two parakeets dodged back as far as they could. Tenderly Lando grabbed one of them; it fought back and bit at his fingers, apparently without his feeling it. He took it softly into the hollow of his hands and fluffed its head with a mouthful of warm breath, holding his lips flush against the feathers. He smiled to Inez.

"I'm crazy about all kinds of animals," he said.

Then, in one clamp of his jaws, he bit off the parakeet's head.

2

The secretary made way for the newcomers. Homer Kloppe rose courteously to greet them, ignoring their outstretched hands. Nodding curtly, he indicated the padded leather chairs and returned to his own seat behind his desk. The desk top was empty except for a business card in the right-hand corner: Genco Volpone. Kloppe coolly regarded the impeccably dressed man before him, barely noticing his companion, a nondescript little fellow who seemed swallowed up by the plush chair. Kloppe knew that Volpone, for all his appearance of respectability, was believed to be one of the heads of the Syndicate. The banker politely inquired, "What can I do for you, Mr. Volpone?"

"Open a numbered account."

"You mean, you don't want to use the same one you already have with us?"

"That's right."

"Very well."

"In less than an hour," Genco Volpone said, "you will receive a transfer order from your Nassau branch, where the money was deposited this very morning."

"How much is involved?"

"Two billion dollars."

Homer pretended to clean his glasses. He was accustomed to large figures involving huge, diversified business enterprises over a period of time. This was a lump sum from a single individual!

Genco Volpone calmly added, "I would like this sum to be put to work while it is on deposit."

"Why, of course!"

"What rate of interest would it draw?"

"That depends on how long it is left."

"Give me a daily rate. You'll have the money on deposit for twenty-four hours, forty-eight at the outside."

"Six percent."

"Make it seven."

"The daily rate is only six."

"What do I care? I want seven."

"Done. And after that?"

"The funds will be transferred to Panama, to the Chemical Inter Trust. We both have power of attorney."

Only then did Homer Kloppe pay any attention to the runty middle-aged man who had been introduced as Mortimer O'Brion, financial adviser to Mr. Volpone's partner. Naturally, Kloppe knew better than to ask who that "partner" was. On the other hand, Kloppe did know about O'Brion's law firm, which had a fine reputation in international business circles, and he was somewhat surprised by the unimpressive demeanor of its head.

"What code name will you use for giving us your orders, Mr. Volpone?"

"*Mamma mia*," Genco replied.

"I have that. Now, gentlemen, will you please each give me a sample signature—that is, the signature of *Mamma mia*."

"What for?" Volpone asked. "We'll advise you by phone."

"Oh, it's just a house rule," Kloppe said as he handed them a pen and a blank sheet of paper.

O'Brion and Volpone each wrote *"Mamma mia."*

Kloppe picked it up and said, "Which of you will advise us on transferring the funds—Mr. Volpone or Mr. O'Brion?"

For the first time, Volpone smiled. "I will. But that doesn't really matter, since from now on all you know is *Mamma mia.*"

"You're quite right. Now, all I have to do is give you a number."

"Don't bother. I selected it in Nassau."

25

"Will you give it to me?"

"828384."

"Good."

"Of course, you'll place the interest on our deposit in a separate account."

"Naturally."

"That, you understand, is to cover our costs. Now, what will you charge us for this service?"

"An eighth of one percent."

"Not bad! I should have been a banker," said Volpone.

"The job also has its drawbacks, Mr. Volpone."

"I'll probably phone you tomorrow."

"Whenever you wish." And Kloppe added, "I trust you will enjoy your stay in Switzerland."

"Yes, thanks. I'm staying for forty-eight hours, but O'Brion here is heading right back home."

Then something strange took place. Genco Volpone, who had put his hat back on, found himself nose to nose with Homer Kloppe. Each stepped sideways to let the other pass, but by bad luck they both stepped the same way. The embarrassed banker noted that the American gave him an apologetic smile as his hand went out to slap Kloppe on the shoulder. Then, suddenly, Kloppe found himself gripped in a Sicilian *abbraccio;* Volpone was kissing him alternately on both cheeks and hugging him close. Not knowing what to do with his own hands, Homer automatically brought them to his customer's shoulders. They released each other at the same time and the banker closed the door behind his departing customers, perplexed as any good prim Swiss Protestant would be by the demonstration of Latin affection.

Coming back to himself, Kloppe immediately phoned the powerful financier Eugene Schmeelbling, in Schaan. At Schaan, near Vaduz (Liechtenstein), there is an absolutely colorless five-story building bearing no identification whatsoever. Nothing distinguishes it from the buildings on either side. Each day at five o'clock, its employees head for home as if they had just finished an ordinary day's business. The difference between them and any other clerks is the size of the sums of money that pass through their hands. For Schaan is where the "bankers' bank" is located. Amassed by millions of men and women, each day money is deposited in thousands of banks worldwide that immediately invest it in the various companies whose shares they hold. These companies, in full legality, transfer it to various branches located in countries where all kinds of benefits allow them to expand their activities without being unduly hampered: Switzerland, Nassau, Liechtenstein, Panama, Luxembourg, or one of innumerable tropical islands that have been transformed into independent financial paradises—with the secret blessing of the great economic powers that have every reason to want them to exist. These holding companies complete the circle by depositing their assets in other banks—sometimes the same ones in which the sums originated—in a breathtaking merry-go-round in which money, by the very inertia of its movement, swells like some abstract beast. Finally and inevitably, one day or another, Schaan is the place where, for a shorter or longer period of time, all loose capital has to make a stop on its wild whirligig. So it was at Schaan that Homer Kloppe deposited "on a day-to-day basis" the money that Genco Volpone turned over to him. This had been formalized by an exchange of memos to confirm the "verbal agreement." Then, by methods that he alone knew, Schmeelbling would put that sum to work at a rate higher than the one he gave the banker. And more power to him, thought Kloppe.

Homer mentally went over his figures again. He had given Genco Volpone—Sorry, *Mamma mia,* he smilingly told himself—seven percent. Two billion dollars at seven percent calls for an interest payment of $383,561.643 per day, or, rounded out, $383,562. The same sum, let out at nine percent, would bring him a daily return of $493,150 and change. Net profit for him: $109,588—and that's not chickenfeed, even if it is pocket money for a great financier! To which, of course, there had to be added—on the bank's official books—the service charge on the total deposit involved, which came out to no less than two and a half million dollars!

By the end of the following business day, Kloppe had still not heard from Volpone or his representative. That doubled the $109,588 profit of the day before. "Just let him leave it here with me for a month," Kloppe prayed to some nameless deity—for he dared not use the name of God when dollars were involved.

Behind him the door slammed. "I bet you're dreaming of a woman!" a voice shouted.

Homer jumped as if caught in the act.

"You might at least have knocked before coming in!"

"Okay, I'll tell mother!"

The girl threw her arms around him and swung him about in a waltz step. "I've just invented a game to top them all," she said

"What is it?" he asked. His daughter's escapades secretly delighted him, dangerous though they often were, and he could not deny that Renata held him in the palm of her hand.

Perhaps because she was the living opposite of her mother, because of her full head of auburn hair, her tall, slim figure, her deep, purple eyes. Why, he wondered, among all the fine fellows who had courted her, had she chosen Kurt Heinz, the only one who was not of her social standing, the son of a bank teller. Spotless reputation, to be sure—but thirty-five years a bank teller! And next week, Homer was going to have to dance with Utte Heinz, Joseph Heinz's unappealing wife. And his daughter's wedding, which he had hoped would be as spectacular as the Gauguins and the Fragonards on his walls, would be disfigured by the awkward presence of his son-in-law's parents. To say nothing of the wild-eyed wedding ceremony Renata had selected; people would probably still be talking about it three centuries from now. But there again, Kloppe had given in.

"It's a wonderful, demoralizing game. I call it the flying manna!"

The banker frowned as he repeated, "Flying manna?"

"Yeah, it's on account of Kurt and his cockeyed theories about money being the root of all evil, rotten and all."

"I don't get it."

"He didn't get it either! I took my plane up and flew over Chiavenna, right in the middle of the agricultural show. And I bombed the hicks with folding money! You should have seen them scramble!"

Seeing how badly her father took it, she burst out

laughing. "Don't look like that! Kurt has to get used to being affluent. What good would our dough be to us if we couldn't have a little fun with it once in a while?"

Pietro Biasca was sorry about only one thing: that his old man hadn't lived to see him make good. For it was old Giuseppe, with his advice and his determination to teach his only son to study the profile of a shoe the way you would that of a beloved woman, who was responsible for Pietro's success. "You'll see," he'd say, "all this stuff that bores you now will make your fortune someday." And he was right. At forty-eight, Pietro was rich, no small thing when you've gone hungry as a child. But even better, he was famous and respected. His elegant Fifth Avenue boutique was as prestigious as a private club, frequented only by those whom Pietro deemed worthy of his services.

One of New York's Beautiful People, he was invited to theater openings, cocktail parties, and gallery showings. The secret of his success lay in a loving sense of craftsmanship rare in this technological age. In Biasca's workrooms they didn't manufacture shoes, they hand cut them out of the finest and most expensive leathers. "Gloves for the feet" was the slogan that had won him his fame. Of course, Biasca's shoes went for anywhere from five hundred to a thousand dollars a pair—and up, when customers insisted on things like eighteen-karat gold buckles.

Pietro went into the workshop where a young apprentice, an Italian boy with curly hair, was measuring one of his comrades' feet. Biasca came over, as always slightly heady with the odor of leather that wafted through the place—the same odor as the inside of a Rolls-Royce. As he leaned over, he said to the boy, "Don't forget, the line doesn't count. What is important is the whole. Always think of the foot as a whole. That's what Michelangelo did."

He moved along, glancing admiringly at the shelves of foot molds that were made from each customer after the first two orders placed. "You see these feet?" he said, turning back to the boy. "I know them better than I do the faces they belong to. Even blindfolded, just by touching them, I can tell you whose they are."

The apprentice smiled as a tall blond woman stuck her head through the door. "Signore Biasca," she called.

He raised his chin.

"Two gentlemen to see you."

Pietro stepped out into the shop, and he immediately sensed that they were cops.

"Gentlemen?"

"Mr. Biasca," said the more distinguished one, who was holding a package, "may I ask you a question?"

"If I can be of any assistance," Pietro replied as the second detective showed him his ID.

"Could you identify one of your customers from this shoe?"

"If I made it, of course."

"You made it."

The cop unwrapped the shoe. Biasca didn't even have to touch it.

"It belongs to my friend Genco Volpone," he said.

As if jolted by an electric shock, the two cops exchanged an unbelieving look. "What was that name you said?"

"Volpone! Genco Volpone," Biasca answered condescendingly.

"Are you sure of that, Mr. Biasca?"

"I've been making his shoes for almost ten years," Biasca bragged. "This pair was delivered to him less than three months ago. If you'd like to see his feet . . ." The professional in him hesitated to reveal his secrets.

"His feet, you say?"

"Yes, the molds of his feet are in my workshop."

"Thanks, Mr. Biasca. We may be back in an hour or so."

They were already leaving with their package, nearly shoving each other as they rushed through the door. Why the hurry? Biasca wondered. How did the cops get hold of one of Genco's shoes?

Suddenly excited, he strode toward his office, slammed the door shut behind him, and dashed to the telephone.

When the second hand of his watch was at the figure seven, Homer Kloppe's index finger pressed an electronic remote-control box in his pocket and the service-entrance door swung open. That was where, every morning at eight-thirty sharp, the personnel of the Zurich Trade Bank came in. Within Swiss memory, never had a single bank in the Confederation been robbed. Where could the robbers have gone? Where could they have hidden when the whole population would have immediately pitched in to help the police? And, even assuming they had been able to crack the safe, how could they ever get out of the country? It was just plain impossible.

As the armor-plate door closed behind her, Inez hesitated briefly so that the banker might get the full benefit of her noble stature, impressive in a black floor-length mink coat. Dazzled, Homer looked up, caught Inez's icy stare, and stepped back to let her pass. He pushed the door shut and again pressed the remote control, instantly closing off all the exits. Then, with stiff little dignified steps, like a mechanical turtle trying to keep up with a supple gazelle, he followed her down the long corridor. He couldn't say what he most admired about her—her slender figure or the graceful neck that sprang from her shoulders like the stem of a flower.

They continued their silent walk, going down the stairway that led to the vaults below. Kloppe, walking behind her, was hard put to keep himself from touching Inez. Had he dared, he would have asked her to raise the flaps of her coat and skirt so that he could take in the swivel of her hips and feast his eyes on her long thighs. They finally reached the last door. With trembling hands Homer fingered his remote-control gadget, spelling out the code that would temporarily disconnect all alarm systems.

They were inside the strong room, a rectangular area twenty-two yards long by nine yards wide, where customers requiring isolation could come and meditate. The ceiling, floor, and walls were all made of steel strong enough to withstand an atomic explosion. Inez's perfume invaded the space around them, something warm and living clashing with the deathly cold of the metal.

"Make my bed!" she ordered.

Homer Kloppe took two more keys out of his pocket and went to safe-deposit box 829, his own private depository. Motionless as a statue, Inez watched him, haughty, majestic, inwardly amused by the way she turned him on.

"Dollars?" the banker mumbled.

"Dollars, marks, Swiss francs, and a few ingots!" she commanded dryly.

"Would you please take your coat off?"

"I will when I feel like it."

Homer turned his back to her, dug into the box, and withdrew handfuls of bundled currency. He threw the bundles to the floor and Inez tapped at them with her toes.

"More!"

Awkwardly he removed some ingots, and one of them slipped out of his arms. He immediately apologized in a tone of abject culpability, but she merely shrugged, ogling him like a lizard contemplating an ant. Bundles of bills swam on the floor. Homer got down on his knees to release the individual bills, and Inez carelessly kicked them into a heap that Homer Kloppe smoothed out until they began to form something resembling a pallet on the floor. When this layer of money reached a depth of about eight inches, Inez extended her legs, and Homer, who was kneeling, slipped to the floor. She deigned to smile.

"What does it smell like?"

"You might come down and smell it with me," he mumbled.

"Not yet. Take your clothes off."

"Right away?"

She stepped a few paces away.

"Look, I'm going to show you something."

She dropped down on her back, raised her skirt up high, and lifted her legs in a V—infinitely long, infinitely perfect legs, part of which were still encased in the boots.

Kloppe felt his throat go dry and could barely get out in a hoarse whisper, "Inez—"

"Strip!" she said harshly.

Homer raised himself halfway on his pile of bills and started to unzip his fly. He always wore iron-gray suits, black tie and shoes, and a white shirt. The only incongruous note was his underpants. They were bright red with white polka dots, even though their style, going from his hips to his knees, was quite conventional.

"Take them off!" Inez said.

He suddenly saw the meaning of this scene: a sort of Black Mass, God in this case being Money, and his own action representing its defilement. Ever since he had started seeing Inez—the Devil incarnate!—the same erotic ritual kept taking place. Now, lying on his mattress of dollars in the strong room of his very own bank, under the eye of this fabulous black woman, her legs spread and pointing to the ceiling, he realized that it was he himself who had suggested it, had made it happen.

"Don't move, little white man!" Inez instructed.

In his turn, he slightly spread his thighs. She started to crawl toward his legs, her lips outstretched, her forearms swimming through the money, some of which softly rubbed against her face.

The lobby of the Excelsior Hotel in Nassau was like a village square on market day. Fat mommas in purple shorts and halters, rolls of cellulite on display, laughed uproariously as they stood at the bar, nursing steins of dark beer or gulping them down like men. Their escorts wore T-shirts decorated with gaudy palm trees.

Mortimer O'Brion, sweating profusely, fought his way through the crowd. He had to raise his voice to get the attention of one of the desk clerks.

"Erwin Kelly, Suite 879."

Before he could say another word, the clerk had checked his mailbox and was facing him again, holding a piece of paper.

"Your key isn't here, sir. Mrs. Kelly is upstairs in the suite. But there's a message for you."

Mortimer put it into his pocket without reading it. His heart skipped a beat. He went over toward the elevators and then looked to see if anyone was watching. When he got out on the eighth floor, he took a few steps, saw that there was no one around, and took out the folded paper he had been holding in his pocket. It was addressed to Erwin Kelly, Hotel Excelsior, Nassau, Bahamas. When he unfolded it, he found it had been sent from London, and it had a brief message: PLEASE CALL BACK. JUDITH.

He sighed, made a face, and went toward a stand-up ashtray in the corner. He set the message afire in the ashtray, waited for it to burn, then crushed the ashes with his fingertips. He wiped his face with the back of his coat sleeve, put down his briefcase, tightened the knot of his tie under his soaking shirt collar, and headed for 879 where Zaza was waiting for him. If he had had the slightest hesitation, there was no turning back now. The message cut the last bridge to his past, and, depending on what kind of luck he had, he would shortly either be dead or he would be rich beyond belief. From now on everything had to work on a split-second schedule.

He couldn't phone from the suite, so he decided he'd call from the airport, just before takeoff. With the time difference, it would be around four o'clock in Zurich. He knocked softly on the door of 879, fervently hoping that Zaza was ready and waiting with her luggage.

Italo ("Babe") Volpone impatiently shoved away the naked girl who was soaping his back under the shower. He dried his hands on a terry-cloth robe, reached for the lighted cigar on the edge of the sink, took a drag on it, and spoke into the phone, "Now, say that again!"

Angela, his young bride, was on the other end, calling from New York. He was mad about her, and insanely jealous. When he had to be away from her for a couple of days, he would drive her crazy with phone calls, just to hear her voice.

The mobster mentality divided women into two groups: mothers and cunts. Mothers were mythical, sacred, endowed with every virtue, and in turn consoling and protecting. Objects of the deepest respect among men, who had little respect for anything or anyone else, mothers called forth what little tenderness they knew in childhood. And wives became consecrated mothers as soon as their first baby was born. Then there were the cunts—all other women—to be used and abused, ticked off like numbers on a list and cast aside like filthy animals if they asked for anything in return for the moment's ecstasy they gave.

Then Babe Volpone met Angela, in a place where he had never before set foot, a public library. It must be said in his defense that he was there quite by accident. Not to look for a book, but only to escape from two creeps who been tailing him all over London. He was standing behind the front door, his heart beating wildly, his hand gripping the gun in his pants pockets, when a soft, serious voice inquired, "Can I help you?"

He jumped. But the second he turned around, he knew she was It. The earth might crumble, he might be shot at sunrise, but nothing would be able to undermine his lightning certainty that this woman existed only for him, that they were meant to belong to each other. Their eyes locked, and, sensing the rare and final quality of that moment, Angela had asked with a quaint awkwardness, "What type of book are you looking for?"

She had never met a man like him: athletic and elegant, with a wildness that emanated from him like a scent. Dazzling her with his smile, he quipped, "Do you have anything that tells you how to shake two jerks who are on your tail?"

"This is an academic library, sir."

"Does it have a rear exit?"

She led him to it, and as he stepped out he grasped her hand.

"If you're free this evening, how about having dinner with me? I'll tell you all about it."

"Yes," she whispered.

"I'll pick you up at eight, okay?"

Fifty-eight days later, in New York, Italo Volpone married her, without giving her time to finish the dissertation for her doctorate in English philology. It took her several hours to explain to him what her research was all about, but even now, after six months of marriage, she didn't understand what business her husband was in.

Whenever she pressed the point, he made a wry face. "It's a family business. I work with my brother Genco. We do odd jobs. We sell fruit, vegetables . . ."

But the money he so lavishly spent and their expensive apartment on Park Avenue had left her wide-eyed.

"Angela, *cara mia,* say that again, won't you?" he now asked her.

There was no trouble with the connection from the U.S. to Nassau. When he was sure he had heard what she said, he burst into an uncontrollable fit of laughter, his muscular gut shaking, his index finger mechanically rubbing an old scar from a stray bullet in Puerto Rico that had given him a second bellybutton on the right side of his gut.

But Angela was insistent. "You must listen to me, Italo! They said it was very serious and urgent!"

"Are you kidding? You really think I'm going to call the cops?" The idea seemed so wild to him that he began to laugh once more. "Did they explain to you why I should call them?"

"No, they wouldn't tell me another word. They just said you should call them immediately at headquarters."

Once again Italo burst out laughing. Babe Volpone, calling up those uniformed hoosiers!

"Did you tell them where I was?"

"No, of course not. I told them I had no idea."

The waiting broad pushed the door ajar and smiled meaningfully at him as she cupped her two breasts on the palms of her hands. Wherever he went, the men of his family made sure there was a welcoming committee with plenty of tits and ass, jestingly referred to as "sleeping pills." Italo was always so driven that these sleeping pills were indispensable to his health. Of course, he never felt in any way unfaithful to Angela when he spent a few hours with one of those pigs.

"Angela, I assure you, I have to get dressed now. I have an important business meeting."

With his free thumb he twirled the wheel of his mini-roulette, set the ball in motion, and mentally bet on the nine.

"Italo, please, please! You *have* to call them. I saw them. They meant business."

"You saw them?" he choked out.

"Yes, they came here. How can a phone call hurt?"

"You mean you let them in? To my house?"

"Babe, what else could I do?"

After making several false stops, the roulette ball finally landed on the thirty-one.

"Fuck!" he muttered, more to himself than to her. "Okay, I'll get in touch with them. I'll call you back."

He hung up sharply, rinsed off, got into his robe, took a puff on his cigar and swallowed a gulp of scotch, and picked up the phone again, dialing the operator.

"This is Room 1003. Get me New York. Midtown Precinct North."

Then he went back into the bedroom. The girl, lying on her belly, looked sulkily at him. Absentmindedly, he took a vicious swipe at her fanny, then with sudden delight saw that his hand had left a mark that was turning red.

"That hurts!" she gurgled.

"What's your name?"

"You're too mean! I won't tell you."

"What the fuck do you think I care?" he said as he poured himself another shot of whiskey. "Come on, bitch, do your stuff. Take care of me."

She turned over on her back.

"How about taking care of me first?"

The phone rang. She took the glass from his hand and sipped at it.

"Midtown Precinct North?—I don't know who I want. You're the ones who asked my wife to have me get in touch." He flinched a little. "Italo Volpone—Yes—I'll wait."

He grabbed the broad's hand and closed it around his cock. Then he took her by the back of the neck and pushed her head down until her mouth took him in.

"Yes—Volpone, that's right—What?—Why?"

Suddenly his face was tense, all the muscles of his body contracted.

"What's that you're saying?" he stammered.

He listened for another half a minute. At the change in his tone, the girl pulled back and looked up: his lips had tightened into a hard white line. He kicked her away.

"Get the fuck out of here!" he hissed without looking at her, his hand over the phone.

She stood on her dignity. "You got no right to talk to me like that!"

He slapped her brutally. Nonplussed, she looked at him, gray eyes filling with tears. Italo took a roll of bills out of the night-table drawer and hurled them at her.

"Beat it!" he repeated. "I'll give you twenty seconds!"

She bent over to pick up the money, and for a flash, as he looked at what she was showing him in that position, he was sorry he couldn't make use of her. He said into the phone, "I'm coming in on the next plane," and hung up. Then, to her: "I've got to clean up in the bathroom. Better not be here when I come out."

As soon as he had gone, she counted the money, rubbed her sore cheek, and smiled appreciatively. At those prices, she wouldn't mind if he slugged her even harder! Three minutes later, she was gone.

Italo called his bodyguards, instructing one to have a car ready for him in front of the hotel while the other booked seats on the first plane leaving for New York.

After that, he phoned New York again and instructed his lawyer to meet him at Midtown Precinct North. Finally, he ordered his secretary to find Mortimer O'Brion immediately and make sure he met him at the airport.

Even though he was at the top of the heap, all-powerful and untouchable, Babe still had some of the characteristics of a small-time hood. He knew that some of the highest police officials were on the pad, yet the mere sight of a traffic cop gave him the willies, just as it had when he was fourteen. He was so nervous he tore his shoelace as he tried to tie it, and he thought fearfully of what the fuckin' fuzz told him they had found—without telling him where or how. He knew his big brother was capable of doing just about anything—but not lose his shoes, for chrissakes!

3

Mortimer O'Brion left Zaza alone in the bar at the airport. There were just forty minutes till plane time. No matter how often she asked where they were going, he refused to answer, merely giving her mysterious smiles that didn't hide the nervous tics in his face. Seeing how tense he was, she let the matter drop. But her feelings were evident as she looked down into the glass of lukewarm champagne a sweaty waiter set before her with no more pomp than if it had been a glass of beer.

Mortimer quickly disappeared into the crowd, ready for the next-to-last move in his wild coup. If everything went well, he was sure the final step would present no problems: he could simply disappear off the face of the earth. His heart began to beat heavily as he wandered around retracing his steps. He must have gone past the telephone switchboard two or three times without noticing it.

The telephone operator was carrying on several conversations at once and doing her nails at the same time.

"Miss, could you get me Zurich?"

"In what state?"

"No state! Zurich, Switzerland!"

She glared at him. "What number?"

He told her.

"Booth number three."

"Will there be a long delay?"

"Booth number three."

He closed the door of the booth and wiped his face.

His handkerchief was soaked. Everything stuck to his skin.

At the beginning, his plan had been simply a mental exercise, a what-would-happen-if kind of diversion in which he enumerated causes and effects that meshed perfectly with nothing going awry. Then, to his surprise, what had been purely theoretical began to take shape without his being aware that he was the one carrying it out. His meeting Zaza, which had revealed to him a realm of sensuality he had not even known existed, had made him realize the sexual revulsion he felt for his wife. Now was the time to do all the things he had never dared do when they might have been much less of a danger to him. So what if he was terrified—if that was needed for him to be born again? He sneered inwardly as he thought of Judith lying in her clammy bed, stuffing herself with aspirin and sleeping pills, dead to herself and the world and not even knowing it. Mortimer had made use of her name one last time— to sign a message she had not written.

The ring of the phone made him jump. The receiver almost slipped from his hands as he brought it to his ear. A woman's voice was mumbling something incomprehensible in German. He cleared his throat to speak more firmly, but it did no good. In a quavering voice he said, "Is this the Zurich Trade Bank?"

From halfway around the world a voice said yes and asked, "With whom did you wish to speak?"

Suddenly aware that the whole life-and-death matter was up for grabs right now, he said, "Homer Kloppe. Urgent and personal."

"Certainly. I'll see whether Mr. Kloppe is in. Who shall I say is calling?"

Morty swallowed. Then, in as normal a voice as he could muster, he spoke the magic words: *"Mamma mia!"*

Captain Kirkpatrick's loathing of Sicilian-Americans endeared him to the New York City police force. His bosses knew how to put his prejudice to good use. Every time the Syndicate was involved in anything, Kirkpatrick was assigned to the case. He had a make on every hood, even the least important runners. Unfortunately, getting them locked up was another matter. The bastards paid fabulous retainers to an army of lawyers who were always

on hand to move heaven and earth if the police so much
as touched a hair on any of their heads.

Therefore, Kirkpatrick had felt almost uncontrollable
elation when he was told about a stray leg, found on a
train engine near Zurich, that might belong to no less a
don than Genco Volpone.

No capo ever loses a leg without serious aftereffects,
and, in the case of Genco Volpone, the effect would be
like a tidal wave. If by chance someone had murdered
Volpone, anything might happen!

The captain rubbed his hands with glee and ran them
through his thick red hair. Looking at Finnegan, his assistant, he mused, "Do you realize what's happening? In less
than an hour, we'll have a Volpone sitting in that chair!"

Finnegan made a doubting face. "You really think so,
captain?"

"I can hope, can't I?"

"What did he say on the phone?"

"He said, 'I'm coming in on the next plane.' "

"And what if he does?"

"It's a long shot, but not impossible. After all, it is his
brother, and we've got the shoe."

"If you ask me, his lawyers'll advise him to go straight
to Switzerland to identify the leg."

"Could you identify a leg by itself?"

"If it was a pretty girl's . . ."

"We'll see. Are you ready?"

"Yes."

"Wherever he goes, whatever he does, I want your
men on his tail from the second he steps out of this office."

"Provided he comes."

"Provided he comes . . ." Kirkpatrick echoed hope-
fully, and he shook his head, a warm glow coming over
his face. "Just imagine, Finnegan—if we could get the
goods on him, and he tried to pull a fast one . . . he'd be a
sure thing for the chair. I'd give ten years of my pay to be
able to pull that switch myself."

Whenever Homer Kloppe had sex, that is, once a
week, he brushed his teeth vigorously every hour or so for
the next forty-eight hours. He figured it took at least that

41

long to knock out the billions of microbes in and around his mouth after his lips had come into contact with his lover's unclean skin. He was brushing his teeth for the eighth time today when he finally heard the muffled buzz of his telephone. He spat a mouthful of antiseptic into the sink and dried his lips.

"It is urgent and personal, sir. The gentleman gave the name of *Mamma mia*," the switchboard operator said. "Are you in, sir?"

"Put him on, yes."

There was a click, and for two seconds the banker could clearly hear the strained breathing. Instinctively he got on his guard. Dealing with large sums of money had given him a sixth sense.

"Hello."

"Hello. Mr. Kloppe?"

"Speaking."

"Mamma mia."

The voice was not Genco Volpone's. So it had to be the skinny little one, Mortimer O'Brion, who had his power of attorney. Strange: Volpone had made it clear that he would be calling personally. Prudently, Homer went along.

"What can I do for you?"

"Do you know who this is?"

"Yes."

"You are to make the transfer as arranged."

"Very well."

"But with one slight change."

Kloppe's hand tightened on the phone slightly. He had not been mistaken; there was the stench of something rotten in the air.

"What change is that?"

"The location of the transfer."

"Where is it to be made?"

"To the Banque Centrale in Geneva. As of this minute."

"That presents a small problem."

"I beg your pardon?"

Once again, Kloppe heard O'Brion's hoarse breathing.

"I say it presents a small problem. I can't make the

42

transfer to this new address without a written release from one of the two principals."

"Why not? We're in a hurry, and it had been agreed —"

Kloppe cut in coldly, "Our agreements hold only if all the original terms remain in effect. Now you say I am to change the location we had agreed upon."

"Very well. What must I do?"

"Just a formality. Come in and sign a release."

"But I'm not in Switzerland!"

"I'm sorry. Is the person you came with still here?"

The barest hesitation at the other end of the wire. "I don't believe so. He must be on his way to where I am."

Homer knew the lawyer was lying. His first job was to protect his depositors. In this specific case, although he had no proof, he sensed it was his duty to stall for time. He was not a man to let two billion dollars out of his hands without taking a few elementary precautions.

"I understand your predicament," he said. "Just send me a note signed by you, and your orders will be carried out at once."

"But I'm telling you, this is urgent!" O'Brion shouted.

"It would get here in forty-eight hours."

"That's too long."

Several silent seconds went by.

O'Brion resumed, in a voice that he tried to keep under control, "Listen—considering how urgent this is— you're not making things any easier for us. My client will be most unhappy."

"Believe me, sir, I am unhappy about it, too. But I have no choice."

"Very well. Then I'll come. I'll catch the first plane out and see you this evening."

"This evening? Where are you calling from?"

"Nassau."

"Do you realize, sir, that it is now 5:00 P.M. in Zurich and I am winding up my business for the day?"

"Mr. Kloppe," O'Brion roared, "when you're dealing with sums of this magnitude, the time of day has no meaning."

"I can't agree with you, sir. I have made prior arrangements for this evening."

"Couldn't you see me later tonight?"

"The bank is closed to the public until 9:00 A.M. tomorrow. Even if you were able to fly out immediately, I could not see you outside of the bank's office hours."

"But we have the whole night ahead of us. It would take you only a minute, just to get my signature. You have to do it!"

"I never do business at night, sir. And I make it an absolute rule to be in bed by eleven. I am truly sorry."

"I will be at your office tomorrow morning." O'Brion gave in, desperation in his voice.

"I apologize a thousand times, sir. And I will be looking forward to seeing you."

Homer Kloppe put the phone back into its cradle and suddenly felt an urgent need to brush his teeth.

A stink of dirty feet, stale sandwiches, sweat, and beer hit the three lawyers as they entered the police station. Two uniformed cops did not even seem to notice them. One was hunt-and-pecking on an old typewriter; the other, standing with his hands behind his back outside the lockup, was laughing at the insults a prostitute inside the tank was yelling at him. All the way in back, a bum was sleeping off his drunk on a low cot, snoring symphonically.

"If you please!" Johnny Kieffe called out with scornful authority.

Kieffe had gone forward a couple of steps while his two partners, Hubert Murdle and Chester Henley, stood on either side of Italo Volpone. Kieffe, Murdle and Henley was the most expensive law firm in New York. According to what the traffic would bear, they billed their clients anywhere from $500 to $1,000 an hour. That, of course, was of no import to the Syndicate, which paid them a yearly retainer large enough to have its legal problems take priority.

"Yes?" the cop asked without taking his eyes off his typing.

"We have an appointment with Captain Kirkpatrick," Johnny Kieffe said sententiously.

The cop was not impressed. "Who's 'we'?"

Kieffe shoved his business card under the cop's nose. "Here. How about speeding this up a little?"

The cop took the card, turned it upside down and backward, and then nonchalantly got up.

"I'll see what I can do," he said.

He disappeared through a door behind the counter. When he came back, he said to the lawyer, "The captain is very busy. He has an important appointment. Come see him some other time, or else call him on the phone."

"Just a minute!" Kieffe blustered. "He's the one who called my client in to see him! What do you mean, he's busy?"

"Your client? Who's your client?"

"Mr. Volpone here," Hanley interjected. "Italo Volpone."

"Which one of you is Volpone?" the cop wanted to know.

"What difference does that make?" Kieffe raised his voice. "Go tell the captain that we're here!"

In another half minute, the cop called, "The captain can see you now!" and held the door open for them.

They followed him down a hallway and into Kirkpatrick's office like bulls going into the arena.

The captain got up to welcome them. "I'm sorry about that, Mr. Kieffe. I didn't know you were with Mr. Volpone. The man on duty misunderstood."

"My partners, Henley and Murdle, and Mr. Italo Volpone," said Kieffe, dryly introducing them.

"Please be seated, gentlemen."

"No, thanks, we'd rather stand," said Hubert Murdle.

"As you wish," said Kirkpatrick, again running his hand through his hair. "Mr. Volpone, I'm afraid your brother may have met with a serious accident. Biasca has definitely identified the shoe as belonging to him. It came from an amputated leg found by our Swiss colleagues. Of course that doesn't mean it was your brother Genco's leg, but—would you know—was your brother in Zurich within the past few days?"

"Can we see the shoe?" Kieffe cut in.

"In a moment, sir. Would you answer my question, Mr. Volpone?"

"We will stipulate that Genco Volpone may have been

45

in Switzerland several days ago," Henley answered for him.

Kirkpatrick kept his gaze on Italo, whose eyes in turn whirled rapidly about the room.

"Mr. Volpone?" Kirkpatrick asked again, ignoring the interruption.

Italo cleared his throat. "My brother had a business meeting in Zurich."

"You don't have to volunteer any details," Murdle cautioned.

Kirkpatrick opened a desk drawer, withdrew a package, unwrapped the tissue paper around it, and handed the object to Italo, who carefully examined it.

"This could be my brother's shoe."

"Are you sure?"

"How could he be?" Kieffe cut in. "Would you be sure you could identify something that belonged to a member of your family?"

"Captain," Henley took over, "I don't get the picture very well. Our client here was in the Bahamas for a couple of days' vacation, and you made him come back specially—"

"I only requested him to come back," Kirkpatrick countered, without taking his eyes off Italo, "to help us with our investigation. I had no power to force him to come back. And I must say, Mr. Volpone, I had not thought you would feel you needed three lawyers for so simple an identification."

"When did you find that leg?" Italo wanted to know.

"Thirty-six hours ago. It was lying on the cowcatcher of a railroad engine that came into the Zurich station."

"Let's get out of here," Italo said nervously.

"As far as your brother is concerned, I'm going to have to put out a worldwide all-points missing-persons bulletin. And I may have to call on you if anything we find requires your testimony."

"You know where you can reach Mr. Volpone," Kieffe said.

"Mr. Volpone, are you planning to leave New York City within the next few days?" Kirkpatrick asked.

"I beg your pardon," Murdle replied. "What's the meaning of that?"

"Nothing special, counselor. I just wanted to know where your client might be if I happened to need him."

"I'm taking the first plane to Switzerland," Italo mumbled somberly. "If anything happened to my brother, I'm gonna find out about it."

"I hope for your sake nothing did, Mr. Volpone. But there's another thing that seems to be bother the Swiss police. In the pants pocket of that leg, there was a one-way ticket from Zurich to Geneva, stamped in Zurich only twenty minutes before the accident was discovered."

"So what?" asked Murdle.

"Counselor," Kirkpatrick began, as if the lawyer ought to know better, "an unidentified person got on a train in Zurich to go to Geneva, and twenty minutes later his leg was back in Zurich."

"What are you getting at, captain?"

"That leg should have gone on to Geneva, shouldn't it?"

"What difference does that make? As long as it hasn't been identified . . ."

"Let's get outta here," Volpone said.

"Mr. Volpone," Kirkpatrick concluded, "if you hear the slightest thing from or about your brother, please let me know. And I'll keep you filled in on anything we find out."

There were the briefest nods on all sides by way of good-byes, and Italo and his three mouthpieces had scarcely closed the door when Finnegan stuck his head in.

"Finnegan," the captain exulted, "we got 'em uptight already! Now let your guys make sure this bum gets on the plane to Zurich. I want two of my men on that flight with him. Use Cavanaugh and Mahoney!"

He rolled under her, trying to defend himself, turning his head away as she tried laughingly to kiss him on the lips; and suddenly he pulled away. "They're waiting for us," he warned.

"So what? It could be fun!"

"I don't like being late."

"If you only knew how you turn me on when you pretend you're afraid I'm going to rape you! Or maybe you really are afraid?"

47

Kurt wiped his mouth with the back of his hand. Renata caught the gesture out of the corner of her eye.

"My lipstick is kissproof. You want me to try again?"

Kurt begged off. He was still feeling torn between pride in his humble origins and a craving for luxury.

Renata Kloppe was the incarnation of everything he thought he hated: thoughtlessness, wealth, insolent beauty, and a total lack of interest in global problems—worldwide hunger, ecology, Marxism, the proletarian ideal. In the linguistics courses he taught at the University of Zurich, Kurt Heinz preached sexual freedom and lambasted the family, religion, hypocrisy, the trusts, and the oligarchies and plutocracies.

But in private, Kurt didn't dare put his theories to the test. He never once made the kind of liberating gesture he was constantly urging on others—and that was a shame, for it probably would have put him at peace with himself.

From the day they met, Renata's infallible eye had noted just how his contradictory mechanisms worked. Her unconscious sadism found a happy outlet in the verbal rage she could provoke in Kurt; and she knew that his revolutionary ardor merely hid his lack of sexual daring. So she taunted him at every opportunity, taking delight in shocking him with the crudeness of her vocabulary. She attacked his ideas, his origins, his profession, challenging him in a thousand ways, exulting when she could make him blush by using too vulgar a word, too forthright a gesture.

In order to feed this delicious feeling of power, nothing was beyond her: she would unzip his fly under the table while they were having dinner with the family, walk around naked in front of him when her chambermaid Manuella was in the room, pull her skirt up over her hips in the back seat of a taxi, whose driver, eyes riveted to the rearview mirror, would soon be driving on the sidewalks.

Paradoxically, his very lack of influence with her kept her from breaking off their relationship. Her power over him, instead of turning her off, incited her to make things more binding, and they had gotten engaged, to the great consternation of both families, who saw this union as the wedding of a carp to a rabbit. Naturally, Kurt hated his future father-in-law. To him, Homer Kloppe symbolized the worst of the Establishment, being at one and the same time a power in high finance, a good father, a loving husband, an upstanding citizen, a fervent Calvinist, a giver of alms, a teacher of lessons, and a tabernacle of certainties. In a word, Kloppe was nauseatingly happy! He was the archetype of what Kurt taught his students to detest: the banker, the legal robber, the parasite of the consumer society, the wart on the system.

"I can prove it to you!" he would thunder in class. "The great corporations give their employees their monthly paychecks on the twenty-third of each month. The next day, the money is deposited at the bank. But if you're a worker, just try to draw on it before the first of the next month! The banker will claim it hasn't cleared, that you're overdrawn, or that the computers haven't credited it to your account yet! During that time, he's using *your* money to make himself a personal profit. The bastard is living by the sweat of *your* brow. Do you need any more examples?"

To Renata, his revolutionary ardor seemed sensual. It was she who had made the advances, and Kurt let her.

"Kurt, the zipper on my dress is stuck. Will you help me?"

She was sitting on the bed. The little nothing by Balenciaga that so artfully failed to conceal her body probably cost more than a miner earns in two years.

He tried in his awkward way to undo the zipper. "I can't get it."

"It's a good thing I didn't wait for you to strip my clothes off me! I'd still be a virgin. My poor old Kurt. Manuella!"

"What can I do for you?" Manuella said as she entered the room.

"Kurt just tried to rape me. And the idiot jammed the zipper on my dress. Can you fix it?"

Repressing a laugh, Manuella repaired the damage. Renata, in the mirror, was keeping her eyes on Kurt: the big lug was pretending to look out the window, so they wouldn't see him blushing!

"That dirty rotten little redheaded shit of a cop! Was he ever delighted! Having a Volpone in his office. Genco'll never forgive me for this!"

Yudelman lowered his eyes, embarrassed. Italo was talking to him as if that leg simply didn't exist. Each time Moshe tried to get back to the subject, the younger Volpone shied away from it.

"I'm worried, Babe, very worried. I've had people in Switzerland check it out, and there's no trace of your brother. I'm not looking for trouble, but what if the leg—?"

"Shut up! It's not him, I tell you! You think Genco is dumb enough to fall under a train?"

Moshe Yudelman mumbled as he bit his lip. "What if someone pushed him?"

Italo grabbed him by the lapels and stared into his eyes. "I tell you it's not him! He probably stopped off in Italy for a while to fuck some pig! I know my own brother, don't I?"

But Yudelman couldn't accept that as evidence. This was too serious a problem. He needed to know for sure. Screwing up his courage, he said, "Don't get sore, Babe, but listen to me. You know I've been the family's consigliere for over eighteen years. Genco never made any complaint about me, did he?"

"Oh, cut it out!"

"Just answer my question, just this one."

"What the fuck is it?"

"If it were really Zu's leg, would you be able to recognize it?"

Italo exploded. "What do you think I'm hopping over to Switzerland for?"

"Do you have any way of identifying it?"

"Yes, goddamn it! When we were kids, the old man gave us a bike, just one for the two of us to share. He won it off a pigeon who got drunk and was wiped out in a poker game. He gave the old man his bike to buy back his marker. Genco wanted to ride it right away, so I sat on the baggage rack, and we took one hell of a spill. Genco got cut under the ankle by the pedal. He's still got the scar. But you have to know it's there!"

Moshe was more and more embarrassed. He cleared his throat and asked, "Left or right ankle?"

Babe gave him a killing look. "Right. What time's my plane?"

"You got two hours yet. But there's something else. I was supposed to see O'Brion this morning. He wasn't in."

"So what else is new?"

"Nothing. I phoned his house. He wasn't there either. His wife hasn't seen him since he left for Nassau."

"What the fuck is that to us?"

"Wait a minute. O'Brion has a dame, Zaza Finney."

"Everybody knows that."

"She's disappeared, too."

Volpone looked at Yudelman with renewed interest. "Moshe, what are you trying to tell me?"

"I just think it's strange that somebody who deposited two billion dollars in a numbered account should suddenly fade into the landscape. That's all."

Italo was nonplussed. "If O'Brion wants to disappear, that's no skin off my prick! Let Ettore Gabelotti worry about where he went!"

Yudelman shook his head with extreme patience. "Just a second. You know why Gabelotti didn't go to Zurich with your brother?"

"Everybody knows that jerk is scared to put his fat fanny on the seat of an airplane!"

"Check! So he gave Morty O'Brion his power of attorney. Which means there are only two guys in the world who can collect that bread: Don Genco and Mortimer O'Brion."

Italo started to laugh. A forced, phony laugh.

"Are you telling me that half-pint is trying to make off with the Syndicate's money?"

"I'm not telling you anything of the sort. I'm just saying that there's two billion dollars in that account."

"A dead man can't even use three hundred bucks, let alone two billion."

"O'Brion's not dead. He's just made himself scarce," said Yudelman in a soft voice.

Italo shrugged nervously. "Morty O'Brion! That poor cocksucker is scared of his own shadow!"

"With two billion dollars, nobody calls you a cock-sucker; and you don't have to be scared of a thing!"

Italo glanced at Moshe to see whether he was kid-ding. But he looked dead serious.

"Look, you may be the brain and all, but you seem to be overlooking one thing! Do you imagine Gabelotti is stupid enough not to have gotten the number of the ac-count from Morty?"

"Could be," Yudelman conceded. "Yeah, you must be right."

"So, what's all this big cockamamie scare about?"

"Okay, forget I ever mentioned it. Don't hold it against me. I worked so goddamned hard to bring this deal off. I guess I'm just imagining things. All I can see is fuck-ups all over the place."

"Well, Morty doesn't have the balls. Wouldn't dare! Can't you just see him double-crossing Gabelotti? Moshe . . ." Volpone stopped. "Suppose it was that fuckin' Gabelotti?"

"No, no!" Yudelman shot back. "Gabelotti wouldn't have anything to gain by it. We've been at war with each other long enough. Not Gabelotti! If anything did hap-pen, if by any chance Don Genco—Excuse me, I don't know what I'm saying. But it could only come from O'Brion."

"As long as you feel that way about it," said Italo, "go ahead and talk to Gabelotti. Go ask him. Go ahead."

"I have to confess to you—if O'Brion did try to pull one on us, he'd be stopped before he even raised a little finger. I contacted Orlando Baretto in Zurich. He's watching out for him. Here, I have men spotted outside his house and others watching his broad's apartment. Don't worry about it, Italo, it doesn't concern you. Just go off to Switzerland and let me know where Genco is now. Are you ready?"

"Can I ask you to do me a favor while I'm gone? Put a contract out on Biasca."

"Biasca? Why?" Yudelman asked.

"He's the stupid jerk that got me called in by the cops."

"Maybe he didn't have any choice."

"Screw that. Get rid of him. He could have clammed up and then called me."

"We'll see, we'll see . . ."

Italo gave him an icy stare. "You gonna take care of him or do I have to do it myself?"

"Take it easy. We'll teach him a little lesson. But there are more important things to do."

"No! I like to settle my accounts when they're hot!"

"Okay, but what about our money?"

"It's safe where it is. You just get Biasca knocked off for me. I'll handle the rest."

"Okay," Moshe stalled. "Okay."

The best thing with Italo was never to meet him head on. When he was in a rage, he was capable of anything.

"Italo," Moshe went on, "call me as soon as you get there. If you have the slightest difficulty, I'll follow on the first plane."

When such violent anger showed on Volpone's face, retreat was the safest course. "Okay," Moshe added hurriedly, "okay. I'll just see you to the airport."

4

Pietro Biasca knew immediately that the three men who entered the shop were hoods. They were very young, but there was something hard and cruel in their eyes. The tallest one, as if in parody of an old movie, was carrying a violin case. Biasca wondered what was in it. He was in the clear with the police as well as with the big shots of the various New York families. Besides, his close relationship with Zu Genco Volpone was well enough known so that no one would touch him.

"Gentlemen, can I help you?"

"You're Pietro Biasca?"

"In person," he replied, aware of his power, the usefulness of his high-placed connections, and the many employees around him. At his age, with his success, he was not about to let himself be pushed around by third-rate punks.

"We'd like to order some shoes," said the man with the violin case.

"You'll have to make an appointment. Before we can fill an order, my workers have to have a mold of your feet."

"Here's a sample," the hood replied, swinging Biasca around and kicking him in the ass.

Staff and customers looked on as Biasca blushed with shame to the roots of his hair. But, realizing his reaction would determine what came next, he decided to act tough.

"You don't seem to know who you're hitting," he said.

After taking up a position inside the front door, one of the men took a Colt Magnum out of his pocket and let it dangle nonchalantly from his hand. Another swiftly tore the phone wire out of the wall.

"Okay, you gonna take our molds?" the violin-case guy asked politely, after which he aimed another kick at Biasca, this one missing its target but getting him painfully in the groin.

Biasca was still game. "I don't know who you are, or who was crazy enough to send you after me, but you'll pay for this—and how!"

Another kick. "You gonna start, or do I have to make you?"

"You ever hear of Zu Genco Volpone?" Biasca asked, playing his last trump card.

The one who had torn the phone wires came toward him saying, "Listen, I done a lot of walking. My shoes are all dusty. How about shining 'em for me?"

He put his foot up on the counter on top of a pile of money that the cashier had not had a chance to put away.

"Go on, start shining!"

When Biasca didn't move, the man walloped him across the mouth. Then, grabbing the cashier's blouse without lustful intent, he tore the front of it away and handed it to the bootmaker.

"Rise and shine!"

He placed the muzzle of his Harrington and Richardson .22 against Biasca's temple. Fear and anger in his eyes, Biasca took the piece of blouse and wiped the hood's loafer with its three-inch heel. What phony elegance! Biasca could not help thinking.

"Rub harder! Get down on your knees! You'll do better if my toe is under your nose! I want it to shine good!"

Pietro knelt and rubbed hard at the leather.

"Enough of that," the violin-carrier said after a few seconds. "Now take our molds."

One lady customer started toward the door. "I was just passing by. I've got nothing to do with whatever's going on in here. Let me out!"

"Tut, tut!" said the man with the Colt Magnum, waving her back.

"Can I at least know what you're after?" Biasca asked, his fear taking shape at last.

"We told you. Some shoes. Now, go ahead."

"Hey," yelled the guard at the door, "should we lock up?"

The one who had made Biasca get down on his knees said to the cashier, "Go on over and close the curtains."

Terrified, she came out from behind the cash register, trying her best to make her hands hide the tear in the blouse, behind which the nipple of an overripe breast could be made out. He called her back. "Stick this up where people on the street will be sure to see it."

He pulled a sign out of his pocket that said CLOSED FOR REPAIRS. His two sidekicks were pushing Biasca toward the back room. Not one of the shoemakers made a move; nevertheless Biasca called to them, "Don't try to help me. These men are armed!"

"What are those?" asked the violin guy, pointing to the hundreds of foot molds on the shelves. The other one, his back to the door, had the dozen workmen covered; they were wide-eyed and pale.

"My customers' molds," Biasca answered. "Now, will you tell me—"

"Gimme one of 'em!"

Pietro did as he was ordered.

As he examined it, the hood asked, "You got a lot of 'em?"

"Twenty-six hundred," Pietro mumbled.

"What are they made of?"

"Plaster."

"Why does this one have Paul Newman written on it?"

"Because it's his footprint."

"Well, goddamn," the punk let out. "You don't come cheap, I bet, do you?"

Biasca, shrugging in exasperation, said, "Come on, what's this business all about?"

"You and you!" the man said, ignoring him and pointing to two apprentices. "Take the sticks and knock all those goddamned feet off the shelves."

"No!" Biasca cried out. "You can't do that!"

In two steps, the one who had made Pietro shine his shoes was upon him. Swinging his pistol, he cut open Pietro's cheek. Stunned, Biasca collapsed, groaning, "Don't do that! It's my whole stock!"

"Well, you gonna do it?" demanded the violin-carrier in an icy tone.

The apprentices, after looking at each other helplessly, started sweeping the shelves. The molds fell to the floor with the sound of broken pottery.

"Come on, the rest of you, help them!"

Each of the apprentices went to it, carefully looking away so they wouldn't see the tears and the blood on the boss's cheeks.

"Now, trample 'em. Smash every one of 'em. There's one left, up on the shelf. Knock it down!"

"Not that one," said the oldest of the workers. "That's Marilyn's!"

"Marilyn's? No kidding?"

"Please don't!"

"Okay, you can keep Marilyn. I guess she won't be in very often ordering shoes. Hah! Smash 'em! Go ahead!"

Biasca, still on the floor, his face hidden in his hands, sneaked a peek at his workers, whom he thought of as his own children, trampling those unique molds that had been his treasure. It would take him years to collect them again—if these crooks let him live.

"Now, show me your stockroom!"

Biasca waved his head toward a door at the back. He got up painfully, stumbling over the broken plaster, and caught sight of one shard that said "Henry Kissinger." None of the staff made a move as he turned the knob on the stockroom door. It was full of precious leathers, imported from Italy or England, and shoes that were ready for delivery or partly finished. The hood opened his violin case. To Biasca's surprise, there was no machine gun in it, but an acetylene torch with a half-sized gas tank attached.

"You're not going to burn the place down, are you?" Biasca pleaded.

Without answering, the hood started to shove the shoe boxes around, and then said, "We won't burn anything down. Just singe your crap a little bit."

He turned a button, and the gas started hissing out of the torch. He used a pocket lighter, and the flame spurted forward, setting fire to the first cardboard boxes.

"How much do you want?" Pietro asked as he witnessed the nightmare.

"We don't want your dough!"

"Then what do you want?"

"Nothing. Take your shoes off."

Mechanically, Biasca obeyed. He was no longer afraid. He didn't care. What worse could they do to him?

"Do you have a mold of your own feet?"

"No."

"Good. 'Cause you wouldn't have much use for it."

"Why?"

Unexpected, and with horrible accuracy, the heavy torch came crashing down on each of his bare feet, and he could hear the cracking of his own smashed bones.

"They'll never be the same again," the hood informed him with nice courtesy.

When the wave of pain finally got to him and he was able to scream, Biasca realized he was all alone in his stockroom.

"Come in, my friend. Do come in."

Homer Kloppe was vigorously shaking the hand of his caller, a man of some forty years who looked youthful despite his white crew-cut hair.

"Did you have a good trip?"

"Excellent, thank you."

"Can I give you a drink? Whiskey, perhaps?"

"With pleasure."

Homer took two silver tumblers from a shelf. "Do sit down. How long will you be staying in Zurich?"

"I'm heading back to Detroit in three hours."

"Oh, too bad. I'd hoped you'd come to dinner."

Homer opened a drawer in his desk and took out a bottle of Waterman's ink. He unscrewed the cap and poured a light-colored liquid into two tumblers.

"Don't look worried," he said with a smile. "Even the Swiss don't drink ink. This is Irish Middleton, thirty years old. Taste it."

The man with the white hair smelled it circumspectly.

He was Belvin Bost, chief administrative officer of Intercontinental Motor Cars, an automobile-manufacturing firm set up after the war to launch a new prestige car to compete with Rolls-Royce and Cadillac. In less than ten years the original factory of three hundred workers became a huge complex with six thousand people on the assembly lines. In the interim, the stock went through the ceiling, selling at twelve times its par value. Kloppe was the major stockholder, with a fifth of the total value of IMC.

"I was surprised to hear from you," Kloppe told his guest. "What did you have to tell me that was so secret you couldn't say it over the phone?"

Melvin Bost looked embarrassed, but then he answered, "There's been another accident."

He held his glass out to Kloppe, who poured him another shot of Waterman's.

"Another?"

"The seventh in sixteen months. For the same reason. Break in the steering column."

Homer's little pink mouth twisted slightly. "What did the investigation show?"

"We know very well what it is. Defective tempering of the steel in the steering columns of all our Beauty Ghost P9s."

"Why all of them?"

"We make the parts ourselves. We acquired a three-year supply of steel at a very good price."

"Well, use different steel."

"We've already begun to."

"Have you filed suit against your supplier?"

"The very first day—as soon as the widow of the guy who was killed in the P9 sicced her army of lawyers on us."

"Did she win?"

"Not yet, but she will. It was easy for her to prove that the accident was a clear case of mechanical failure. But that's not the end of it. The estates of the six other victims are suing us, too."

"Well, what do you think we ought to do?"

"I don't know, sir. I came here to ask what you thought."

"How many Beauty Ghosts are on the road?"

"Worldwide, 482,326."

"Are you certain these accidents are not merely co-incidental?"

"Seven accidents for identical causes can't be co-incidence. That's a pattern."

Homer Kloppe sighed deeply.

"We put the problem through the computers. Statistically, there should be one such failure in every ten thousand cars or so. That means roughly forty-eight accidents out of the 482,326 cars in use."

"That's terrifying!"

"Those are just statistics, sir. Nothing proves that all those accidents will actually take place. I'm just saying that the figures show they *may*."

"I won't permit it! We have to forewarn every P9 owner in the world!"

"What are you suggesting?"

"You have to recall them and replace the defective part without charge."

"We've considered that, but it's prohibitively expensive."

"How can you tell? If you make that kind of gesture you'll get such publicity that we may be swamped with new buyers."

"Perhaps, sir, but I still don't think that'll offset the hundred-and-fifty-million-dollar cost."

Homer spilled some of his drink. "I beg your pardon. How much did you say?"

"A hundred and fifty million dollars," Bost repeated in an even tone.

Homer almost choked. Some quick mental arithmetic told him that his personal share of the loss would be thirty million dollars.

"You see, sir," Melvin Bost went on, "I expected you to have this kind of straightforward reaction. But I must warn you that if we do make this honest gesture, it'll be our last. We'll be out of business."

"Still, we can't let forty-eight people ride around risking death."

"Six thousand assembly-line workers fired, five hundred supervisory personnel unemployed, engineers out of work. You can see why I didn't want to do anything before consulting with you."

"I'm appalled."

"And well you may be. There's no halfway measure in this thing. If word about it gets out, we have to go all the way or lose our good name. Unfortunately, if we do go all the way, IMC won't be able to meet its obligations."

"What to do? What to do?" moaned the honest Swiss banker.

"My advice is to do nothing, sir. There may not be any more accidents. If that widow hadn't sued us, we might never even have known about this mechanical defect. We can take our chances . . ."

Kloppe stared at him. "It's not up to us to take our chances, Melvin! We have no right to do that."

"Well, remember, out of the seven accidents, only four involved fatalities."

Homer shook his head. "Only four . . ."

"Two of the others caused rather serious injuries, but the last one only had bruises. If I may, sir, I'd like to suggest something to you. Let's go on for three months, say, and if there's no recurrence, we'll forget about it. In the meantime, I will have had a chance to consider every possible way of staying in business—that is, if there is one—when we order a massive recall for replacement of all the steering columns. How does that strike you?"

Homer Kloppe was pensive.

Melvin Bost waited for a few minutes that seemed like an eternity. Then he resumed his tack: "Under the circumstances, sir, I think that would be the wisest thing to do. Especially since the new P9s coming out in less than a month will have nothing wrong with them at all."

Homer's two shiny incisors appeared and chewed at his babylike mouth as he said, "Do whatever is best, Melvin. Yes, whatever is best . . ."

Chimene Kloppe had two double chins, porcelain-blue eyes, brown hair, and pale, delicate skin. Her life was a series of small quiet pleasures, marked off by teatime, mealtime, prayertime, visiting time, and sleeping time. That there was no longer any time for sex did not surprise her, as if her old urges had dissolved in the unbroken drowsiness of her marriage.

Enclosed in the warm cocoon Homer had spun about

her, she envied no one. She had a reasonably fine collection of jewels and a chauffeur, like everyone else, and she tried to alleviate what guilt she had by generously devoting her time and some of her money to "doing good."

"Homer, are you leaving the table so soon?"

"I have some work to do. Will you excuse me? I have quite a few papers to go through before tomorrow. Where's Renata?"

"Out with Kurt, I believe."

Homer Kloppe made an ill-disguised face which Chimene pretended not to notice. They had already argued a hundred times over their future son-in-law. Chimene thought it charming that he should be considered a revolutionary. Homer questioned the very basis of his revolutionary ideas, calling them childish, unrealistic, and negative—although secretly he was impressed with Kurt's academic status.

"Well, good night, then."

Chimene smiled, then added with a touch of worry in her voice, "You work too hard, Homer. Will I see you at breakfast tomorrow? I'd like to tell you about the final arrangements I've made for the wedding."

Kloppe looked sharply at her, and again she took no notice of it. The scandalous ceremony Renata had decided on for her marriage had tacitly become a taboo subject between them.

As she watched him disappear, she thought what a good husband, a good Christian, a good citizen, and a good father he was to have accepted, in his position in society, his daughter's outlandish whim about the wedding! Nor had Homer ever forgotten Chimene's birthday, or been late to dinner. And even in the days when he was still attractive, she knew he had never been unfaithful to her. Once again she wondered whether she would dare ask him about the pictures of a nude black woman in provocative poses she had accidentally found in his overcoat pocket.

Despite young Volpone's protests, Moshe Yudelman had insisted on two "soldiers" going to Zurich with him. Folco Mori, a simple foot soldier despite his unusual gifts, seemed happiest in this subordinate position, which his

62

high-spiritedness, his disdain for danger, and his inborn ferocity might have gotten him out of. Unfortunately, it was these very qualities, along with dexterity with a switchblade unmatched anywhere in the world, that made his bosses leery of him end kept him unjustly away from any real responsibilities. The *capiregime,* who treated him with affected friendliness, actually feared him. They claimed he went a little heavy on the violent side—striking where threaf would have been preferable, maiming instead of simply breaking reparable bones; therefore, they limited his activities to the handling of people who resolutely refused to conform to the Volpone family code. When Folco Mori went into action, his enjoyment of the job took precedence over everything else.

Pietro Bellinzona was a much simpler case. He carried out the most delicate assignments without complaint, never asking questions. He was fiftyish, but his husky wrestler's shoulders hid the weight he had put on owing to a sweet tooth that had dogged him since childhood. The fact that he also put away a quart of whiskey a day never caused him to miss a target. He had been in the service of Genco Volpone for the past twenty years, and he was satisfied with his fate, delighted not to have to think for himself, simply carrying out orders, no matter what they were. Moshe Yudelman had personally instructed Pietro to stay at all times with Italo Volpone, and that was what he would do. Folco Mori, on the other hand, was supposed to keep a discreet watch and show his hand only if Babe was in imminent danger. Too bad —because Pietro loved Folco's company.

Pietro went through the airport security clearance with Italo Volpone, remembering just in time to wave hello to Folco, who had his nose buried in a news magazine. Volpone had not said a word or even deigned to look at him. As Italo went up the steep ramp into the plane, he reminded Pietro Bellinzona of a dangerously doped fighter climbing into the ring.

Three years before, Carlo Badaletto had bid adieu to Genco Volpone and joined the Gabelotti clan as consigliere. Ettore Gabelotti had all the necessary qualities of an excellent capo—toughness, cruelty, hypocrisy, unscrupulousness, vindictiveness, and outstanding intelligence. After the first phase of Operation OUT, Gabelotti told Badaletto, "Zu Genco is a straight shooter, but his brother is a double-crossing shit."

Carlo ran the tips of his fingers over his jaw at the spot where Italo's head had butted out his front teeth. "Can you tell me what the bastard of a little brother is doing in Switzerland? Especially after going to see Kirkpatrick with a flock of mouthpieces?"

Ettore Gabelotti answered softly, in his best godfatherly tone, "Don't let it upset you, *figlio mio*. After all, Italo Volpone can go anywhere he wants without affecting us. As for that trip to the precinct, maybe they finally found out he's a scofflaw."

Lately, Don Gabelotti had been walking around with a constant chip on his shoulder—quite beyond his customary sudden and often seemingly unwarranted rages. He pretended to make light of Carlo's suspicions, but secretly he shared them, and by mutual accord with his consigliere he had commissioned an out-of-town operator, Rico Gatto, whose face wasn't known in New York, to keep a tail on Babe Volpone. Through one of his contacts at JFK, he had been tipped off that Babe had booked a ticket in his own name on Flight 311 to Zurich. Rico Gatto's assignment was to keep Gabelotti abreast of every move Italo made. And Rico had seemed a little disappointed that that was all there was to it.

Gatto's usual contracts were for hits, and fatal ones. His fees were what the traffic would bear, depending on the importance of the target or the number of people to be rubbed out. Rico had an artist's penchant for putting new twists on the jobs he pulled. It was unusual for him to make two hits in a row in the same way, as some of the unimaginative hit men did, without either enjoyment or revulsion. Before each contract, Rico had the same kind of butterflies in his stomach as a performer about to go onstage.

"Is this Rico dependable?" Carlo Badaletto asked his don.

"Don't worry! I've used him on a lot tougher jobs than this. And if we finally have to shoot it out, he'll know how to handle it."

Gabelotti was delighted that Carlo had reacted the way he did. The jerk had wanted to tail Italo himself, but Ettore had squelched that idea by saying, "Can't you think of any better way to tip our hand?"

Carlo was depressingly envious as he pictured Rico Gatto sitting in a comfortable airplane seat gazing at the back of Italo Volpone's unprotected neck.

Captain Kirkpatrick trusted only cops he had personally trained. That's why he selected Pat Mahoney and Dave Cavanaugh, Irishmen like himself. They were tough guys, dedicated and incorruptible, and they'd stick with Italo Volpone if they had to follow him into hell.

They had looked at pictures of Italo until their minds were full of those hard eyes and raven-black hair. Now they were getting into the 747, having checked in as if they didn't know each other. Cavanaugh was in tourist class, Mahoney in first—the luck of the draw.

Seated in first class, Rico Gatto got up to retrieve the cigarettes he'd left in his trench-coat pocket. Looking forward, his eye took in the back of Italo Volpone's powerful neck.

A young guy with dirty-blond hair, sitting several rows away from Italo, had to be either one of Volpone's hoods or a cop. Rico settled into his seat, stretched his legs deliciously, and waited for his first drink. No chance of Volpone slipping away; next to him sat his bodyguard, a solid giant dressed in a dark suit. Rico opened his favorite book, the Old Testament. There was such a variety of crimes in its pages that his own record, in contrast, seemed almost innocent.

"Boss, how about some champagne?" Pietro Bellinzana was saying to Babe Volpone.

"What's that?"

Italo seemed to be coming up from a deep dream. Bellinzona repeated, "Champagne?"

"No," Italo grumbled.

Moshe Yudelman's doubts had finally gotten to him, and he was sure now that O'Brion was out to double-cross them. He decided he'd put the screws to the fucker real good before rubbing him out. O'Brion had never shown him any respect. The only one Babe could vent his fury on was that tub of lard Bellinzona, but he couldn't do a thing right now. He'd have to put up with Pietro's unpleasant company for several hours.

"Bellinzona!"

"Yes, boss."

"Go take a leak."

"Huh?"

"I said, go take a leak."

"But, boss, I just did."

"Shut up! Go on back to the toilet in the rear and tell me what Folco's up to."

From the rear of the first-class cabin Rico Gatto and Pat Mahoney both watched Pietro Bellinzona get up and lumber back toward the tourist section. Pat Mahoney was enjoying his luck. While big Dave Cavanaugh sat in tourist like a stuck pig, Pat had a roomy armchair and the attentions of the pert hostess who was hanging over him with a bottle of champagne. Mahoney wasn't used to his kind of luxury. Most of his assignments led him up a deadly path. He could boast of shooting a moving target fifty yards away in the velvet darkness of night. But the men who had been his targets were far from his mind at this moment. Mahoney's thoughts were with his wife, Mary. She was probably putting the kids to bed while he sat suspended above the earth debating between the prime ribs and the coq au vin.

A voice came over the PA system: *"Passengers are requested to stay in their seats. Dinner is about to be served. Our cruising altitude is now thirty-five thousand feet. We will be landing in Zurich in five hours.*

5

Three hours before Volpone's Boeing left New York, Zaza Finney and Mortimer O'Brion had taken off from Nassau. Their conversation on the flight consisted of one long argument.

"After Zurich, where?" Zaza pressed.

"Leave it to me. It'll be a wonderful surprise."

She had a sneaking suspicion that something had come up to disturb her lover's usual assurance. When they boarded the plane in Nassau, he announced a detour by way of Switzerland. His sweaty face signaled trouble, although he refused to answer her pleas for explanation. She was beginning to regret this escapade. How could she be sure all the mystery he was creating wasn't just a screen for some dirty work that might backfire on her? When they got to Zurich, she wouldn't let him out of her sight. But they were hardly through passport control and customs in Zurich when he asked her to wait for him at the bar.

"Hell, no! I've had my fill of waiting at airports!"

"Would you rather I took you to a hotel? I'll be busy for two or three hours."

"As if I was some whore you picked up? No, thanks. I'm going with you."

"Zaza, listen, be reasonable. I've got a business meeting."

"What kind of business? That's what I want to know."

"Just wait and be patient one more day."

"I've waited long enough. Now I want to know what you're dragging me into."

He shrugged, discouraged. "You don't trust me."

"I sure as hell don't. Why couldn't you clue me in on what's going on?"

"Listen, Zaza. I have to go to a bank to pick up some money. As soon as the bank opens, I'll be done in five minutes."

"I'm going with you."

He shook his head with resignation. The night flight had not made him look any better. In the postdawn light she could see circles under his eyes and nervous tics that darted across his face as he watched every passing shadow.

"You'd have been better off waiting at the hotel," he said.

She panicked, wondering if he'd changed his mind about her and was planning to dump her in this foreign city. She tried to smile and took solid hold of his arm.

"Oh, can't I go with you, Mortimer?"

"I guess so."

"Where are we going after that?"

Thoughtlessly he answered, "I don't know."

She looked at him and pursed her lips. "You don't know?"

"Of course I know. But I may have to make one more detour."

In order to better cover his tracks after this awful, dangerous stopover in Switzerland, he decided that as soon as he had straightened out that goddamned Kloppe, they'd take the first plane out—for anywhere. Three or four zigzags over different continents would make it that much easier for him to reach his final destination without a hitch. He could feel the weight of Zaza's agile body dragging on his arm.

As they got to the taxi stand, she overcame her feelings and with an affected sweetness whispered in his ear, "Mortimer, the things I do for you, I've never done for any other man."

He felt ten inches taller.

When the doorbell rang, Orlando Baretto already had his topcoat on. He slipped a hand under his jacket, where his holster was, and looked through the peephole. It was Inez. He released the security bolt and let her in.

"Boy, you've been a long time coming. I was just going to leave."

A whiff of perfume had come into the flat with her. She was wrapped in a caramel wild mink coat that came down to her ankles.

"I'm not used to being routed out of bed at 7:00 A.M.," she said, suppressing a yawn.

"You'll have to get used to it!"

"What's up?"

"What's the name of that banker of yours?"

She winced. "Why?"

"Don't worry about that. What's his name?"

"Kloppe. Homer Kloppe."

"Zurich Trade Bank?"

"That's the one. But why?"

He patted her firm buttocks.

"Oh, I just may be wanting to make some investments. Is it a reliable outfit?"

Inez's face twisted in amusement as she thought of the steel coffin, the strongbox room where she made love once a week to her austere pink-and-russet banker on a bed of international currency.

"Very, very solid."

"What kind of guy is this Kloppe?"

"Pasteurized. Immaculate. Fiftyish. Magnificent teeth for a little white man."

"False?"

"No, his very own. I've pulled on them to see."

Lando opened his wide mouth. "What are my teeth? Dogshit?"

"They're all right for a little white man."

"Okay, cover my face with black shoe polish and you'll see how much brighter they shine!"

He slipped his hand under the mink with possessive authority and gruffly grabbed her by the mound. "I'm splitting."

"Was that all you wanted?"

69

"For now, yes."

"Will I see you tonight?"

"Don't know. Stay home. You'll see whether I come by. And now, princess, you beat it first. No need for the jerks in this stupid building to see us go out together."

See her tonight—that was a good one! When Lando was on call for duty, his time was not his own. He got an unusual stipend so that he would be available whenever needed, and his boss, Zu Genco Volpone, the don, was generous. Any work well done was rewarded with fine bonuses over and above his salary, though not necessarily in cash. Genco Volpone was the most thoughtful of men. During his recent stopover in Zurich, Don Genco had honored Lando by treating him to a drink. More important, he had given Lando his dream car, a glistening P9 Beauty Ghost convertible, the prestige model of the International Motor Cars line. Simply because Lando had looked longingly at one—a fact that Zu had duly noted—when they went by a show window.

"You like it?" he had asked. "It's yours." And Genco Volpone, taking care of the purchase on the spot despite Lando's embarrassed protestations, had handed him the keys of the P9.

"That way," Genco said, "you'll be able to drive me to the station."

Overwhelmed with gratitude and respect, Lando had stammered as he kissed the Don's hand. "But, *padrone,* why? *Perchè?*"

"We're well satisfied with you, Orlando. And this gift is to express our personal friendliness."

"I've done nothing to deserve it, *padrone!*"

"Don't worry. You'll earn it, one way or another."

When the don left him with a last affectionate wave of his hand, Orlando had felt as if it was his own father going away. Two days later, at three in the morning, he'd had a phone call from Milan.

"Orlando, you know O'Brion? Mortimer O'Brion, the lawyer?"

"I know who he is."

"Did you ever see him?"

"Once."

"Think you could recognize him?"

"Yes."

The voice had gone on (the same voice that so many times before had given him his orders): "He may be coming your way. Look out for him."

"Where'll he be coming?"

"He's going to a bank, the Zurich Trade Bank. Know it?"

"I can find it."

"He's not allowed in that bank. You understand?"

"Yes."

"Be there before it opens its doors today. And stay there."

"Okay."

"When you see him, grab him."

"What am I supposed to do with him?"

"Put him in a safe place and call me."

"Okay. But what kind of a safe place?"

"That's for you to figure out!"

It was quite a coincidence; he was being asked to keep watch on the bank that belonged to none other than his own mistress's prize weekly trick. Five minutes after Inez left, he went down to the garage, unable to resist using his gleaming P9 for this assignment.

The boss's lieutenants didn't have to worry. O'Brion had no more chance of getting into the Zurich Trade Bank than an excommunicate into the private quarters of the Holy Father.

The 747 deployed all of its braking panels in a wild shrieking of reversing jet engines.

"We have just landed at Zurich. We hope you enjoyed your flight, and that you will fly with us again soon."

Italo Volpone was looking at the flushed face of his bodyguard. Pietro Bellinzona was snoring the innocent sleep of the cutthroat.

Moshe Yudelman had made his instructions crystal clear: "As soon as you set foot on Swiss soil, even before you call your wife, get over to the morgue and see that leg. You can be just about sure you'll be tailed, but Folco Mori will take care of relieving you of the shadow."

Italo remembered these words as he loosened his safety belt. He was irritated at not being able to phone

Angela. By superstition or ancient family tradition, the wife of a capo was to be informed immediately that her man was safe, even though she was never to know the reasons for his travels or the nature of his business.

"Wake up, you fat slob! We're here."

Bellinzona shook himself, a stupid self-satisfied smile on his lips. He said pastily, "My mouth's so dry.. . ."

He had fallen asleep two hours after takeoff, tight on the two bottles of champagne he had guzzled.

Italo snarled at him. "Where the hell you think you are? In a dormitory? I didn't bring you along just to get loaded."

"Sorry, boss. Sorry. I was having a dream—"

"Shit!"

Under the watchful eyes of Pat Mahoney, Bellinzona awkwardly stretched his large carcass. Upon arrival in Zurich, Mahoney was supposed to temporarily turn the job over to Dave Cavanaugh, who would become Babe Volpone's tail. That was the way Kirkpatrick had decided it should be. Mahoney grabbed his briefcase, discreetly took out his weapon, and put it in his holster. At JFK he and his buddy had been passed through without the weapons check. Mahoney donned his overcoat and walked out the front exit of the plane without another look at Volpone or Bellinzona.

In the meantime, at the rear, Dave Cavanaugh was maneuvering to be among the first off the 747. His eagerness did not escape the notice of Folco Mori, who was slowly buttoning his jacket in order to let the bony fairhaired guy get a few yards ahead of him.

As the line of passengers headed for the air-terminal buildings, Mori, who had fallen completely to the rear, also noticed a man in a black trench coat. Something about the way this man took in everything without apparently looking at anyone signaled that his presence in Zurich was somehow connected with Folco's own purpose.

Unaware that he himself was being watched, Rico Gatto was secretly amused to find that his prey, Italo Volpone, was being stalked, even before he landed in Switzerland, by some kind of shadow—probably the fuzz. Dave Cavanaugh stood head and shoulders above most of the passengers, and it was all he could do to keep from letting his eyes rest on Volpone's back. Rico Gatto, who had a good sense of humor, felt that the tall guy wouldn't be around long if Italo or his bodyguard spotted him. Gatto himself, however, was only here to keep score and to report on it to Ettore Gabelotti. At least for now.

When Babe Volpone and the gargantuan Bellinzona hopped into a taxi, the setup was as follows: Dave Cavanaugh was tailing Volpone and Pietro Bellinzona. They were all being watched by an amused Rico Gatto, who himself was being spied on by Folco Mori at the end of the file. Mori walked side by side with Patrick Mahoney, but neither of them suspected that they were both in Zurich for the same purpose.

"To the morgue!" Italo Volpone told the taxi driver.

That establishment, in the next few hours, was to be more crowded than the local museum.

Orlando Baretto was pacing back and forth on Stampfenbachstrasse, keeping a close watch on the front door of the Zurich Trade Bank. Twice he had gone by the building, which was not yet open for business, dawdling before the window of an underwater-hunting shop, pretending to be fascinated by the compressed-gas harpoons, the bright red diving outfits, the strange shapes of the shiny daggers in their black rubber sheaths. It was five minutes to nine.

He walked past a little Italian café again and had a terrible yearning for a cup of strong coffee, but he couldn't go in without losing sight of the bank door. The fleeting reflection of a head of blond hair caught his eye. The girl's back was to him, and all he could see was the golden hair, a tan traveling coat, and her long delicate hand, with two fingers through the handle of the coffeecup. The man facing her seemed to be vehemently explaining something to her, leaning across the table to make his point. He had the face of a loser, a worried little weasel's head with prying eyes.

Porca madonna! Lando exclaimed inwardly.

His heart beating wildly, Lando recognized Mortimer O'Brion. He quickly retraced his steps and took up a stance in a doorway recess where there was a tiny showcase display of assorted watches. A fine kettle of fish! The guys

73

in Milano hadn't told him the legal eagle would be with a broad! What if she intended to go into the bank with him? Lando kicked himself for having come alone. But he couldn't phone for further instructions without running the risk of losing O'Brion and the girl. He didn't know what to do. There wasn't a chance in a thousand that O'Brion, whom he had seen only once two years before in New York, would remember him. Couldn't he just go into the café, discreetly stick his Mauser in O'Brion's belly, and lead him away?

The noise of a door slamming made him turn. O'Brion had just come out and was heading for the bank. Lando fell in beside him, speeding up a little to get ahead of him. There was no more time for wondering. Lando was five yards ahead of O'Brion when he got to the three steps leading up to the main door of the bank. Its two heavy bronze panels were still closed. Lando glanced at his watch. Nine sharp. A shadow appeared behind the ground-glass pane and there was the click of keys inside a lock. Lando turned around: Mortimer O'Brion was already up two of the steps.

"O'Brion?"

"Huh?"

The little man stepped back.

"I'm a friend, Mr. O'Brion. Please come with me."

"What is this? Who are you? Let me through!"

Before Lando could raise his little finger, the lawyer had turned around, livid, and started running as fast as he could toward the café. A rush of adrenaline came into Lando's mouth. In his racket, success meant survival; failure was a one-way ticket to the morgue. With the wild-animal agility that in his professional-soccer days had made his reputation, in three long strides he caught up to O'Brion. One or two passersby turned around. You don't see a respectable man running through the street in Zurich, any more than in Lausanne or Geneva. And surely not two—one chasing the other.

Lando tripped O'Brion so deftly that not one of the witnesses could see what made the smaller man fall. The lawyer seemed to fly into the air, come down on the sidewalk, slide about a yard, and then come to a dead stop, his forehead against the concrete, his eyes closed. Lando knelt and grabbed him by the armpits, giving a reassuring smile to the people who had stopped to take in the scene, even twisting the end of his nose to indicate that his poor friend had himself a snoutful. Then, picking him up like a straw man, he rapidly dragged him toward the Beauty Ghost, which was parked around the corner.

"Hey, you! What do you think you're doing?"

Lando turned around. The broad from the café was in front of him.

"What's going on here?" she said in a strained voice.

"He took ill," Lando stammered. And for the passersby now bunching around them he added, "You can see how drunk he is!"

"What do you mean, drunk? We didn't even have coffee!"

"Don't just stand there! Come on! Help me get him in!"

But she remained motionless, leery, terrified. When Morty went out of the café, she had kept her eye on him, furious because he wouldn't let her go into the bank with him, suspecting he had some dirty trick up his sleeve. In the time it had taken her to get up and walk around three tables, there was this big guy bending over her unconscious boyfriend.

"Get him in where? What did you do to him?" she said.

Lando was beginning to feel panicky. Not only hadn't he been told about the broad, now she was threatening to have hysterics in the street. And Zurich was not Chicago. He had to put an end to this.

"Come closer, I want to show you something."

He almost pasted himself against her to keep the bystanders from seeing the Mauser that he dug savagely into her ribs. Then, holding Mortimer upright with his left arm, he groaned into her ear in a muddled staccato, "Either you follow me without saying one word, or I'll drill your guts for you!"

If she reacted badly, if she screamed, the jig was up. Sooner or later, Lando would be a goner. She opened her two terror-stricken blue eyes as wide as she could, bit

75

her lip, put her arm under the other shoulder of the unconscious Mortimer, and said loud and clear, almost matter-of-factly, "He's out like a light."

"This way," Lando said, and the three of them moved away quickly. When they turned the corner, there was the P9.

"Open the door!" Lando ordered.

He tossed Morty's body into the back of the car and sat down beside it.

"Here are the keys. You drive."

Obediently Zaza turned on the ignition. She had been beaten up by some of her boyfriends, but no one had ever jammed a pistol into her gut. And this huge dark-haired guy sure didn't seem to be kidding! What kind of hornet's nest had that cheesy little Mortimer gotten himself into? Well, she really didn't give a damn—as long as nobody hurt her. What she couldn't understand was why anyone would want to hold him up before he went into the bank, rather than after he came out with his pockets bulging with bread.

"All right. You gonna start?"

"Where are we going?"

"Just drive straight ahead."

She knew nothing about Zurich. Following Lando's instructions, she drove around until they were on a street with an unpronounceable name: Eschwiesenstrasse.

"On the right, at the end, there's a garage. Drive down the ramp into it."

When she braked and was about to head down the garage ramp, the guy in back barked at her, "Step on the gas!"

Blocking the entrance to the garage was a police car, right up against a Pontiac. Two cops were listening to the explanations of a bald little man.

"Straight ahead!" Lando yelled at Zaza.

The gas pump in the garage belonged to a friend of his, a Sicilian countryman. Why the hell did two cops have to happen to be there when he wanted to use it as a hideout? At the back end of the garage was a locked door that opened onto a nine-by-twelve closet of sorts where Lando had decided to stash O'Brion.

"Still straight ahead?" she asked.

"Shut up and keep going!"

He needed to think. The hideout was not operative for the moment; he'd have to think of another place. O'Brion was coming to. He opened his two little terrified eyes, met Lando's, and saw the weapon aimed at his ribs.

"What do you want from me?"

"Clam up!"

"Zaza, what's happening?"

His Adam's apple kept jumping up and down uncontrollably. Without turning around, Zaza snapped, "What's happening is that you got me into some fine pile of shit!"

"Do you want money?" Morty asked Lando, trying to convince himself that that was it. But in a confused way, he knew that this had to be an organization guy, and that they had figured out what he had tried to pull. But how could they have known so quick?

"Zaza, please believe me, I don't know anything about this. I have no idea what's going on."

Without moving his gun, Lando told Zaza, "Now, turn to the right and drive by the garage once more."

She did as she was told. *Porco Dio!* The damn cops were still blocking the entrance.

"If you don't tell me what you're after, I'm going to jump out!" Mortimer exclaimed.

"You gonna shut your trap or not?" Lando threatened. "And you, turn left again at the end of the street."

When he wanted to take the trouble, Lando knew how to handle women. And this bitch must be one hell of a pig to put out for the likes of O'Brion!

"When you get to the bridge, cross it, and then keep going straight ahead."

Now he knew where he was taking them. A wonderfully quiet spot, from which he'd have plenty of time to contact his bosses: Inez's place.

With an awful premonition in his aching heart, Italo Volpone followed the black-clad man down a long corridor. Their steps echoed off spotless white partitions that were inlaid with ceramic tiles. What surprised Volpone about the morgue was not the cold—which he expected—

77

but the absolute absence of smell. There was neither the odor of formaldehyde nor the subtler, sweeter, more cloying one of death.

"If you will allow me, please." The man excused himself.

He went and checked something in a ledger. Standing motionless, staring straight ahead, Italo felt he was living a nightmare. Despite his brother's patronizing attitude, Genco had always been good and fair with him. Everything Italo had, he owed to Genco, even his life, which Genco had saved twice. He clenched his jaw violently as the man pulled out a drawer and stood still.

Suddenly, at the moment of truth, the younger Volpone didn't want to know.

"Here," said the man in black after a long silence.

Italo came over, forcing himself to keep his eyes open. In the huge box, meant to hold a whole body, the leg seemed both tiny and immense. His throat contracted; he had to do violence to himself to be able to bend over to get a closer look. His eyes went from the horrible wound at the top of the thigh, which was sheared off like a side of meat, to the ankle. He saw the tiny scar, now even paler than the dead flesh around it, and he knew he would never again see his brother alive.

When they had fallen off the bicycle as children, and he had seen the blood on his big brother's sock, Genco had smilingly reassured him, "Don't be scared, Babe. It doesn't hurt."

Genco was the one who had affectionately given him the nickname that stayed with him all his life. How the family had laughed over it! Now, when it was spoken, the monosyllable—*Babe*—inspired awe.

"Sir, can you make the identification?"

"Get the hell out of here. I want to be alone."

"Just call me. I'll be out in the hall."

Who could have done this to Genco? Who? And where was the rest of him? With tears in his eyes, Italo was aware that he was being ridiculous, but there was nothing he could do to help it. He started to mumble fervently, "Our Father, Who art in heaven, hallowed be Thy Name. . . . Thy will be done, on earth as it is in heaven."

The rest of the words were lost in the sobs that convulsed his throat, but Italo summoned strength enough to get to the end of the prayer. He took a silk handkerchief out of his pocket and dried his eyes. It struck him that he was thirty-eight years old, about to become middle-aged. Yet before the death of those we love, everything seems empty, devoid of meaning. How would he ever break the awful news to his sister-in-law Francesca and his two nieces?

But what if Genco weren't dead? What if he had survived the accident and was lying someplace, wounded, battered? Just let him be alive. *Porco Dio,* just let him live!

In his fury, he tore the flesh of his palms with his nails. He looked at his hands; each one had four bloody spots. Then, suddenly shaking, his arm outstretched over the open drawer, he started to mumble in a low voice, "Genco, Genco, *fratello mio!* I got no idea who did this to you, but I swear to you on the head of our sainted mother, I'll find out! It may take my whole life, but I'll do it. I'll find out! And when I do, there won't be enough blood on the earth to wash away what they did to you! Whoever it is, wherever he'd hiding, I'll find him and kill him with my own two hands. Him, and his family, and everybody connected with him!"

Swollen with hate, he dashed out of the mortuary room without even trying to hide his tears.

Now he had a sacred mission: to replace Don Genco at the head of the Volpone family and do what death had not left his brother the time to accomplish. They'd find out what Italo ("Babe") Volpone was made of! And, as his first act as the new don, he figured he ought to go right over to the bank.

Ernst Fluegge, a German, was over six foot six and weighed about 260 pounds. Once a month he came from Hamburg to Zurich on business, and once a month he spent two hours with Inez. The first time, after meeting her on a referral, he had been so overwhelmed by her beauty that it was all he could do to rise to the occasion. The perfection of her body made him all the more aware how bloated, awkward, and graceless was his own. Usually he was not intimidated by whores. The money he was paying

79

them washed away his shyness. Although she was nothing but a whore, his two hours with her cost him the eye-bugging sum of two thousand dollars, yet Inez had such a way of keeping at a distance that he felt he ought to say "Thank you, ma'am" when she consented to pocket his money. Ernst never felt he was being ripped off. He got enough ecstasy to last throughout the ensuing thirty days, the memory of that passion helping him to put up with the temper of a shrewish wife, breweries in which his workers went on strike over the slightest grievance, to say nothing of the myriad problems he had to face as a captain of industry. Right now he was stretched out stark naked on the living room carpet, his eyes closed, his breath heavy.

Using a portrait painter's brush Inez was covering his body with long streaks of honey, not missing one square inch of his skin, from the tips of his toes to the roots of his hair, by way of the bellybutton, the ear openings, and the crack between his buttocks. When she was done, she would lick it all off.

"Do you know how much a kilo of honey costs, my big doll boy?"

"Go on, please go on, I beg you."

"It's expensive, very expensive."

"I'll pay for it."

"You'll never pay enough."

"That's true, I know. Never enough," Ernst stammered, dazzled by what lay ahead for his promising erection.

He reached out to touch her between the thighs. The doorbell rang. Ernst shuddered, opened his eyes, and saw a look of surprise in Inez's face.

"Are you expecting anyone?"

She put her finger to her lips. She was wearing a red dressing gown that opened on all sides, not hiding any detail of her magnificent anatomy. Ernst wanted to rise toward her, but she kept him down on the floor.

The doorbell rang again, this time to the accompaniment of loud knocks.

"No one must know I am here!" he whispered.

She motioned to him to keep still, gave him a reassuring twitch of her lips, then got up and went to look through the peephole in the door. For all her composure, she almost had a seizure: it was Lando with another man and a blond girl! Orlando had never presumed to drop in on her without letting her know in advance, and he had never dragged any strangers to her place. This was not owing to his good manners as much as to his appreciation of her professional endeavors, from which he derived a good share of his income.

She could hear him becoming impatient.

"Well, you gonna open, or what? You know that I'm here!"

"I'm busy now. Come back later."

"I can't," Lando demanded. "Open now."

"Don't open it," begged Ernst Fluegge, lying on the carpet, his hands crossed over his genitals—the erection all but disappeared—not knowing whether to jump under the shower to get rid of his film of honey, put his clothes on right over it, or hide in the bedroom until Inez could get him out of this unspeakable situation.

In stark terror he saw her open the door!

"It's my brother," she whispered to him. "I'm sorry . . ."

He expected to see a black warrior nine feet tall. Instead there was a petite blonde whose eyes nearly popped out at the sight before her, followed by an undersized man and a big dark intimidating character.

Fluegge rushed into the bathroom.

"Who's that?" said Lando.

"What right do you have to come here?" Inez answered in an icy tone, as completely in control of herself as if she had not been half nude.

She saw Lando's pistol aimed at the ground.

"Have you lost your mind or what? Get the hell out of here!"

He looked at her with an evil air and threatened in a low voice, "Shut up! Get that fucker out of here, and make some coffee for my friends."

"Make it yourself, and get the hell on out!"

She never even saw the slap come at her, but it made her head swing back and forth like a Ping-Pong ball. Stunned, she brought her hand to her cheek. Lando had never struck her before.

In a toneless voice she said, "That was a mistake, Orlando."

"Make the fuckin' coffee!"

She started toward the kitchen and calmly took the phone from its hook as she went by. Her fingers punched the various buttons.

Lando raised the point of his gun slightly toward her. "Hang up. Two lumps."

Inez hesitated. Then she understood that the man before her had nothing in common with the Lando she knew.

"I don't know what you want, or why you're acting this way, but after you step outside that door, you'll never set foot in here again."

Lando turned toward O'Brion and Zaza, who stood frozen near the door.

"How many you take?"

"What?" O'Brion asked in surprise.

"How many lumps of sugar?" Lando repeated patiently.

"None. No sugar."

"You?"

"No coffee at all," Zaza hissed at him, her eyes darting fury.

A plaintive voice came out of the bathroom, "Inez! Inez!"

She wanted to go to him. Lando stopped her with a gesture, went over to the door, and opened it. Ernst Fluegge, huge and pitiful, was standing in the shower stall, just about to turn on the faucets.

"Can I help you?" Lando asked him courteously.

"Excuse me," the fat man muttered, "but if you could give me my clothes. Please. They're in the living room."

Lando took two giant steps forward, grabbed the German by the arm, and dragged him out, swinging him around in the same motion.

"Get 'em yourself, and fuck off!"

Lando looked at his hand and bawled, amazed and disgusted, "The fat slob is all sticky!"

"It's honey," Inez calmly put in. "Don't you like honey?"

Nonplussed, Lando looked in turn at Ernst Fluegge, Zaza Finney, Mortimer O'Brion, and finally Inez.

"It's what?"

"Ernst pays me for covering him with honey. If that's the way he likes it, what's it to you?"

Lando burst out laughing. At first, no one else joined in. But then, giving way to his nerves, his terror, his exhaustion, O'Brion hummed a slight hiccup that quickly turned into uncontrollable giggles. Zaza, succumbing in turn, tried to hold back by biting her lips, but she couldn't. Holding her sides with laughter, she finally bent over, tears streaming from her eyes. It was a weird spectacle. Like a sad clown, Fluegge was doing his best to get into his undershirt, but the minute it touched his skin, the material stuck to the honey and wouldn't budge.

"Hurry up!" Lando ordered him between hysterical laughs.

When the brewer tried to get into his socks, it was more than Inez could stand. Until then she had kept a straight face, but now she broke into raucous laughter, succeeding only in saying between spasms, "Don't hold it against me, Ernst! This isn't my fault. He's a real bastard. I'll make him pay for it!"

When Fluegge finally got out of the place, accompanied by everyone's jeering laughter, carrying his shoes but feeling lucky to get out without further damage, Mortimer O'Brion turned to Lando and said, with eyes full of tears and terror, "Tell me, are you planning to keep us here long?"

Despite his gut panic, the absurdity of the situation —made up of a honey-drenched colossus, a giant naked black princess, and this guy he'd never seen before threatening him with a gun—sent him off into another fit of hysterical laughter.

Lando, without any transition, stopped laughing; his lips returned to their hard set, thin and mean. He took the phone from the hook and said, "You'll know in a few seconds."

When they were in New York, Moshe Yudelman had taken Folco Mori aside and whispered instructions to him.

"Italo is an impulsive, nervous man. Someone may try to follow him. He won't even notice it. But don't let any-

one spy on him. If you smell the least off-color thing, eliminate it."

"Eliminate it?"

"Do I have to draw you a picture?"

Now, sitting in a rented car a hundred yards from
the morgue in Zurich, Folco Mori felt a slight tingle in
his spinal column when he recognized the tall, bony,
light-haired fellow he had spotted at the airport. The guy
had tailed Italo by cab without realizing that Falco was
tailing him. Now he was pretending interest in the shop
windows on the street while his driver read the newspaper
La Suisse behind the wheel of the taxi. And Pietro Bellinzona, whom Italo had angrily forbidden to come into the
morgue, did not seem to notice that he was being watched.
Italo had barely gone in when fat Pietro rushed into a
nearby pastry shop and came out with a hefty paper bag of
cakes that he was gobbling up as if there were no tomorrow.

Folco realized that he would have to figure out how
to quietly get rid of the tall intruder. Then, if Italo's visit
to the morgue was a matter of any significance, the guy
wouldn't be able to inform anyone about it. Folco scratched
his back and felt the reassuring presence of the knife that
was placed, blade upward, in a sheath between his shoulder blades. All he had to do to get the knife out was slip his
hand down the back of his shirt collar, and he could throw
it straight at its target in a fraction of a second. But this
was broad daylight in Zurich, a city so clean and well kept
that he hesitated to spit on the ground. You couldn't commit
an obvious murder here without running into the worst
kind of troubles. If he could pull the thing off, he'd have
to make it look like an accident.

Folco considered various methods. He got out of his
car, letting his improvisational sense take over. Nonchalantly he went toward the spot where the taxi was
standing, hoping that Bellinzona would not greet him if
and when he saw him. The slightest miscue and the tall
blond character watching Pietro would be tipped off. Before Folco reached Bellinzona, he warned his partner in a
low but perfectly clear voice, "Pietro, this is Folco. Don't
turn around. Don't pay any attention to me."

Bellinzona reacted so perfectly that Mori was afraid

he had not heard. He went right on consuming his pastries as if nothing had happened. When Folco went past him, he crumpled the bag and put it in his pocket, never looking at Folco. For a second, considering the difficulty, Folco felt like simply walking up to the guy and stabbing him, just like that, but that was out of the question.

As he walked on, he desperately tried to think of a way to get rid of this unwanted surveillance. No one must be informed of what Italo was up to. He glanced toward another parked car and caught the glint of a diamond in a signet ring on a hand resting on the steering wheel. He immediately recognized the man in black he had noticed getting off the plane. Was this guy working with the tall blond? Were they a team? Cops? Hoods? The guy was surely too far away to have understood that Folco had whispered something to Bellinzona. Folco knitted his brow; now he had to take care of two interlopers. In order to keep in countenance, he went into a florist shop, selected a bunch of anemones, and handed it to the salesgirl, all the while keeping an eye on the street through the window. When the girl had wrapped the bouquet, he tossed his money on the counter, nodded a thank-you to her, and without waiting for his change, went back out toward his own car.

Bellinzona was still leaning against the wall outside the morgue, distractedly picking his teeth with a toothpick. He paid no more attention to Folco than he had before, and Folco mentally congratulated him. They were on a one-way street that slanted slightly down. Not much traffic. Cars were parked on both sides, so there was not too much room for driving. At one point there was a recess in the sidewalk, and four cars were parked there on an angle. Hidden from the others by a bend in the street, Folco tried opening their doors. The first, a Ford, was locked. So was the second, a green Renault. The third, a Mercedes, opened easily. No one was around, and Folco quickly got behind the wheel, released the hand brake, and noted with satisfaction that the Mercedes began to roll backward. He smiled slightly, set the brake again, and went back up the street a few feet to see whether anything had changed. After a minute or so he saw Italo Volpone come rushing out of the morgue, speak sharply to Pietro Bellinzona, push him into their rented Ford, then hop in himself. The rest happened in a trice.

In three strides Folco was behind the wheel of the Mercedes. Leaving its door open, he released the hand brake while keeping his foot on the brake pedal. A few seconds later, the Ford passed him with a grinding of its mistreated gears and he just had time to see Italo Volpone tensed over the steering wheel, his face livid and hard as stone. Without waiting, Folco Mori took his foot off the brake and jumped from the Mercedes. It started rolling slowly, gaining speed as it crossed the street, until its ton and a half of metal slammed into the right-hand door of a Volkswagen parked on the other side. At the same moment, Folco rushed into the opening of a porte cochere that led to a hallway, and with a screech of brakes the taxi carrying the tall blond guy crashed into the Mercedes, almost immediately followed by the second car telescoping into the taxi's trunk. While the taxi driver got out, swearing, to see what the damage was, Folco went into the hallway, at the end of which he could see another door that opened onto the next block.

Now he had only to return to his own car and quietly go back to his hotel. At least he had knocked those two off Volpone's trail temporarily. He'd have to find more radical means to get rid of them permanently. Until now, any man he fixed his sights on was as good as dead. His honor required that neither of them should see the sun rise the next day.

He was still holding the bunch of anemones. He released his grip and they fell into the gutter.

Folco Mori couldn't stand flowers—except as an offering on the coffin of one of his enemies.

6

"Do you have an appointment?"

"No."

"I don't know whether Mr. Kloppe is in."

The man in the black suit stared at her, not saying a word. Embarrassed, the secretary added hurriedly, "Would you please tell me your name again, sir?"

"Volpone," he said without taking his eyes off her.

Blushing, she disappeared, not unhappy to get away from this strange, upsetting man. He had a kind of ruthless look, and twitches of pain spasmodically twisted his lips into a disquieting artificial smile. In his black suit, shoes and tie, he made her think of the angel of death.

"Sir, someone to see you."

"Who is it, Marjorie?"

"He said his name is Volpone."

Kloppe raised his head, intrigued. He was expecting O'Brion, and now here again was Volpone, instead. Yet the lying lawyer had assured him that Volpone had gone back to the States. Maybe now the matter would be cleared up at last!

"Tell Mr. Volpone I can see him. Show him in in a minute or so."

He made a slight face, part relief, part disappointment. He would be able to let Genco Volpone know what O'Brion had been trying to pull, and now he was doubly glad that he hadn't complied with the attorney's request. On the other hand, he had hoped that the funds temporarily deposited with him might work a bit longer at Schaan, with his friend Eugene Schmeelbling, the "bankers' banker." Mentally he checked back over his figures: in three full business days, his personal profit came to three times $109,588, or a total of $328,764. Not to mention the bank's service charge for the two billion dollar transaction amounting to two and a half million dollars. "Hallelujah!" he whispered to himself.

"Mr. Volpone," Marjorie announced.

Homer rose to greet the man who three days earlier had given him the *abbraccio*, in the Sicilian mafiosi tradition. Holding out his hand, both by way of welcome and to forestall another embrace, Kloppe walked around his desk to meet Volpone.

To his amazement he saw a stranger. That stupid Marjorie had already closed the heavy leather-armored door; it was too late to turn the man away.

"Mr. Homer Kloppe?" the visitor asked as the banker's hand dropped to his side.

"In person," said Kloppe coldly. "But there must be some mistake. My secretary seems to have gotten your name wrong."

"No, it's Volpone, all right. I'm Italo Volpone, Genco Volpone's younger brother." He thrust his hand into his inside pocket. "Here, you can see, on my passport."

The banker took it and checked his identity.

"Right?" Italo asked.

"Please sit down, Mr. Volpone."

But Italo remained standing.

"I suppose you are aware of the awful news."

Homer raised an eyebrow, went back to his desk, sat down in his chair, and looked at Italo with polite attention. Volpone's Adam's apple was rising and falling in his neck as if he were unable to swallow his spit. Making a supreme effort, he blurted, "My brother is dead."

Kloppe hardened imperceptibly.

"He's been murdered!" Italo spat. "Have you seen O'Brion in the last three days?"

"O'Brion?" Kloppe echoed.

"Yes, Mortimer O'Brion. Has he been in touch in any way? Has he tried to see you?"

Kloppe bit his lip and toyed with his fountain pen.

"Well, has he?" Volpone demanded.

"How did this tragedy happen to your brother?" Kloppe asked.

"You read the papers?"

"Well—mostly just the business pages."

"Three days ago, after Genco was here to see you, on the cowcatcher of a railroad engine that came into Zurich . . ."

The Adam's apple started bobbing again, and in the corners of Volpone's eyes Kloppe thought he detected a film that looked like tears.

". . . there was a leg. Torn off. My brother's right leg."

Kloppe gulped, in his turn. "How awful! His leg?"

"Yes."

"But then, Mr. Volpone, if you haven't seen the rest of the body, there's still a chance that your brother . . ."

His face stolid, Volpone shook his head.

"Mr. Volpone," Kloppe went on, "how can you be sure—?"

"I've just been at the morgue," Italo cut him off. "I swear it! I am sure my brother is dead! I am sure he was murdered! And I know O'Brion was the one who did it!"

Kloppe almost shuddered.

"Listen, Mr. Kloppe. My brother cabled me personally in New York telling me he had turned the money over to you. In the meantime, my brother's been knocked off and O'Brion has dropped out of sight. It adds up, doesn't it?"

His eyes downcast, Kloppe went back to toying with his pen.

Volpone inhaled deeply. "Don't you worry, we'll find the little bastard. It's just a matter of hours. In the meantime, I'm taking over. As far as you're concerned, nothing has changed. You will please now complete the transfer of the funds just as my brother instructed."

Homer Kloppe coughed. Then, looking up at his visitor, he said, "What funds are you talking about, Mr. Volpone?"

Italo could not believe what he had heard. "I beg your pardon?"

Looking him straight in the eye, Kloppe repeated with the utmost calm, "I said, what funds do you mean, sir?"

For a second Italo couldn't even react. He looked at the banker as if he were a Martian.

"What do you mean, what funds? Our funds, our money! The two billion dollars my brother left with you for transfer."

The pen in Kloppe's hands stopped moving. In a perfectly colorless voice, without blinking, he said, "I don't know what you're talking about."

"You don't know what?" Volpone roared. "Three days ago my brother Genco and that slob O'Brion were here, weren't they?"

"Yes, I did see those two gentlemen."

"Well, then?" Italo crowed. "All I'm telling you to do is move on those two billion dollars!"

Kloppe spread his hands slightly, to show the quandary he was in.

"I still don't know what you mean."

"What?" gasped Italo.

"I just can't make out what you're referring to."

Italo took a step toward the desk. Homer stood up, his lips pressed tightly together.

"Say that again!" Volpone said in a menacing tone.

"I don't know what you are talking about," Kloppe hammered out.

"What the fuck are you trying to pull?" Italo snapped, his face in complete disarray by now.

"Mr. Volpone, I feel for your loss. But I cannot in any way countenance such discourtesy."

Italo's eyes went to the spot on Kloppe's neck where he would like to dig his thumbs and squeeze, squeeze, in order to get out of this nightmare and back into reality so he could feel the ground under his feet again. His every fiber united in one impulse: to kill!

"I'm asking you for the last time. Where's our dough?"

"You will please leave my office, sir."

Italo stared at the plumpish little man who was daring to defy the Syndicate. "Do you know who you're talking to?" he stammered.

Homer Kloppe did not move so much as an eyelash. "Get out!" he hissed.

Tiny black and purple filaments started dancing in front of Volpone's eyes.

"Look," said Italo. "Listen to me. I don't know what your game is, but I'm giving you a solemn warning. You have until tomorrow noon to transfer our two billion dollars. If it's not done by then, you're offed."

"One more word and I will have you immediately deported!"

"That won't bring you back to life!"

Weaving like a drunk, Volpone took two steps toward the door, then turned back. "You'll be beyond help, believe me. Remember, tomorrow noon is the deadline."

As he went out, he turned and pointed his finger at Kloppe, and, his voice trembling with fury, spat out, "You're beginning to stink already!"

Pietro Bellinzona rubbed his cheek in disbelief. "This was the first time anybody ever slapped me."

"There's gotta be a first time for everything," said Folco Mori.

"Beat the shit out of me, shoot at me, okay. But this! It's—it's—"

"Humiliating," Mori filled in for him.

"That's right. Humiliating! Would you have let him get away with it?"

"Nobody's ever slapped me," Mori said softly, looking away. He was lying full-length on the bed, dressed in his well-tailored black suit, his tie impeccably knotted, his expensive loafers on the immaculate white pillow.

"I shoulda slugged him!" Bellinzona said.

"Why didn't you?"

"Because he's a Volpone!"

"Why the hell did he slap you, anyway?" Folco asked blandly.

"I wish I knew! Does that make you laugh?"

"Not laugh. Just smile."

"In my place, what would you have done?"

"Turned the other cheek."

"What's he got against me?"

"Go ask him."

"Shit!" Bellinzona swore as his fist pounded into the palm of his left hand.

In the three hours they had been in Zurich, Pietro Bellinzona had been the butt of his boss's murderous mood. When Italo came out of the bank, he had headed for the hotel without a word. Bellinzona had followed him into the elevator and down the hall, standing there while Volpone took out his key. Only then did Italo seem to see that his bodyguard was with him.

"What the fuck are you doing here?"

Pietro didn't know what to answer.

"Well? What the fuck are you here for?"

Impressed by his pallor, the wild gleam in his eyes, and the ugly twitches distorting his face, Bellinzona had stammered, "Well, Moshe told me—"

Before he could finish, the slap had resounded on his cheek.

"Get the fuck out!"

"But, boss—what'd I do?"

"You stick out like a sore thumb!" And he had slammed the door in Pietro's face.

"So, you see, Folco, I don't go for that. It makes me sick."

"Forget it!" Mori advised him. "While you were waiting outside the morgue, did you notice anything?"

"Yeah, all that cockamamie business you were doing. What the hell was that for?"

"There were two guys tailing you."

"Shit!"

"The kicker is, they weren't together."

"How far'd they tail us?"

"They didn't. Just to the morgue."

"How'd you stop them?"

"I released a car in the street. They piled up into it."

"Did you tell Babe?"

"Hell, no! We're not supposed to bother him, just protect him."

"You crazy? So he can hit me again?"

"Leave him alone. We're big enough to handle this ourselves. I know how we can get one of the mothers right now."

"Is he here in the hotel?" Bellinzona asked, an excited look in his eyes.

"Uh-huh. So's the other."

"Are they Swiss?"

"Shit. They came out of New York on the same plane we were on."

Pietro ran a hungry tongue over his lower lip, suddenly a thousand miles away from his recent mishap.

"Cops?"

"I don't know. I don't think they know each other. But that's just a hunch."

"What d'you wanna do?"

"Handle the first one first. He's here on this same floor, the other side of the hall, room 647."

"You got an idea?"

"Yeah, and a good one. Here's what you have to do . . ."

Italo Volpone was so beside himself when he got into his hotel suite that he started smashing things: what Genco used to call "kid stuff." He couldn't use his rod to fire at anything, and the wallop he'd given Bellinzona was far from having assuaged his urge to kill.

He dialed his home number in New York. After six rings his wife came on to the line.

"Angela?"

Her voice was so clear, she might have been in the next room.

"Italo . . ."

"Whatcha doin'?"

"Sleeping."

He could see her, rolled in a ball in their king-size bed, lying on the edge in one of those long granny nightgowns she liked. Warm, soft, smooth, defenseless, alone. In America, day hadn't dawned yet.

"Italo?" she asked in an anxious tone.

"Yes?"

"About Genco?"

Volpone swallowed and said, "Yes."

"Are you sure?"

"Absolutely."

He knew she was trying to keep from crying. Less

perhaps over the brother-in-law she had known for only six months or so than for Italo's sorrow. After a long silence, she murmured, *"Non posso crederlo. . . . È terribile. . . ."*

"You better tell Francesca."

"Yes."

"Tell her I'm taking care of everything."

"Okay."

He could hear her sobbing, and he thought he could taste the salt of her tears on the tip of his tongue. His own tears were dimming his eyes.

"I'll call you back during the day."

"Italo?"

"Yes?"

"Nothing."

He put the phone back on its cradle, dried his eyes with the back of his hand, and dialed again. As soon as he heard Moshe Yudelman's voice, he said, "It's me."

If he had been calling the president of the United States, he would have opened the conversation the same way. Italo always identified himself by saying, "It's me." Let the other person figure out who it was.

"Genco?" Moshe immediately asked, and Italo appreciated it.

But he couldn't answer; he was afraid to get himself started again.

"Genco?" Yudelman asked once more.

"Yes," Italo finally said.

"Oh, God! God! . . ." Moshe stammered. "The body?"

"Not yet."

"Any chance that . . . ?"

"None. Don't ask me why. I just feel it. I know it. That's all."

"What are you going to do?"

"I'm taking over."

Silence ensued, and Italo thought they had been cut off.

"Moshe. Can you hear me?"

"Yes. Yes."

"I said I'm taking over."

"I heard."

Yudelman's voice sounded forced.

"You got something against that?"

"No, no."

"You don't sound overjoyed."

"Yes, yes, of course I am. Just, things have been happening so fast . . ."

"I've been to the bank."

"What?"

"I said, I was just at the bank. Are you deaf? There's a snag."

"What kind of snag, Italo?" Moshe asked in alarm.

"That crook of a banker says he never heard of our account."

Back in New York, despite his apprehension over Italo's violent reaction to things, Yudelman protested, "You shouldn't have! If Gabelotti finds out about it, he'll think—that is, he'll imagine . . ."

"What'll he imagine?"

"I don't know. But you're rushing things. Try not to louse everything up."

"Moshe."

"Yes."

"Are you with me or against me?"

"Just listen, Italo. Try to understand—"

"With me or against me?" Volpone cut him off.

"If I were against you, I'd let you foul things up any way you wanted," Yudelman came back. "Do you really think a Swiss banker will answer your questions when you don't even know the number of the account?"

"Fuck the number!" Italo stormed. "I gave him until noon tomorrow to carry out my orders."

"My God!" Moshe moaned.

"It's our bread, ain't it? My brother died for it, didn't he? And you want me to shut up?"

"But you can't do this!"

"Who's gonna stop me?"

"Italo, please listen to me. I beg you. This is too serious a matter! Don't do a thing until I get there. I'll charter a plane right away."

"You think I'm a kid?" Volpone barked.

"Italo, I know how to handle this kind of business. I'm used to it."

"So am I."

95

"Italo. Let me come over."

"If I need you, I'll whistle."

"I'm coming anyway."

"Set foot in Zurich without my okay and I promise you, it's curtains!"

"Italo—we're heading for a catastrophe."

"Then keep out of it."

"At least let me fill Gabelotti in. He's gonna think we're trying to double-cross him."

"Forget that fat pile of shit! When I get done with the banker, I'll take care of him. I don't work slow and easy, the way Genco did."

"Italo, one last time—"

"Shut your goddamned trap!"

"Don't hang up, Italo. Let me make one suggestion. You trust me, don't you? I have a friend in Zurich, a very good friend. He's done a lot of things for Genco in the past. His name is Karl Deutsch. We used him any number of times. For the sake of your brother's memory, let me call him. He knows the banker very well. Let him handle it. I'll ask him to contact the guy right away—"

"Send the Pope if you want, I don't give a fuck. But if I don't get what I asked for by tomorrow noon, I'll handle this my own way."

"It's bad—bad, Italo," said Yudelman. "You won't get anywhere with violence."

"Is that all you have to tell me?" Italo sneered.

"No. What about O'Brion?"

"Nothing."

"He's the only one who can—oh, Italo, those Swiss, they're stubborn as mules. You'll louse it all up."

"Moshe—"

"You have to handle them with care."

"Moshe . . ."

"Yes?"

"You're bustin' my balls."

Italo hung up, furious once again. His eyes darted around the room, looking for what he could destroy next.

And then the phone rang.

In room 647 at Sordi's Hotel Dave Cavanaugh threw his jacket on a chair, went into the bathroom, turned the faucet on full force in the sink, and doused his face with water. He was sore as hell at having lost track of Volpone because some nameless idiot hadn't set his hand brake. By miracle, as he had come through the hotel lobby, his eyes had connected with those of Pat Mahoney, who pretended to be absorbed in a magazine. One blink was enough to inform him that the bird had flown back to the nest.

That was reassuring. At least they hadn't lost him. Still, there was that gap in the minute-by-minute report. In the half hour Dave had been going through the streets of Zurich looking for him, the bastard certainly hadn't been in church. Where had he gone? What had he done? Whom had he met? Captain Kirkpatrick hated such unanswered questions, and Cavanaugh didn't like having to admit to them.

During the few hours they had been in Switzerland, Cavanaugh had been in touch with Mahoney only twice, by fleeting visual signals, so when the phone rang, Dave naturally thought Pat had found some way to call him from the lobby.

"Yes?"

To his surprise, he heard an excited voice stumbling over its words: "The concierge, here. . . . Hurry up, sir. . . . Open your window and look down. . . . Something terrible has just happened!"

Mahoney, he thought. Dave rushed to the window, unlocked it, and leaned out. Six stories down, the terrace over the Sordi's marquee kept him from seeing what was going on below. The tulle curtain, blown by the wind, flew over his face, and at the same moment, he had the feeling there was someone behind him. Right on top of him. As he tried to move the curtain away, he had the awful sensation of being grabbed by the ankles. He attempted to lock his large knotty hands around the window's concrete railing, but it was no use. Despite his desperate effort to resist, all two hundred pounds of him swung over the handrail as his center of gravity moved forward, his legs rising inexorably into the air. He wildly tried to kick, scratching the stone with his bleeding hands, but nothing stopped the deadly thrust that was propelling him out headfirst. In a series of disjointed images he visualized the dive ahead of him, tried to utter Mahoney's name, saw his wife with their youngest girl in her arms, and remembered Kirkpatrick's laugh when he said, "Cavanaugh, when you become a cop, you knew you wouldn't just be twiddling your thumbs!"

When he realized that he was dropping like deadweight down the front of the hotel in a nightmare fall that nothing could stop, his last thought was a question that, like so many others, would never be answered: Am I going to be sick?

Without letting a second go by, Folco Mori made the sign of the cross, an old Catholic habit he never failed to observe when he dispatched one of his fellow humans *ad patres*. Without giving himself a chance to enjoy the results of his work, he came away from the window and quickly frisked his victim's jacket. There was a wallet in it, and the first card he took out of it told him what he wanted to know: David Cavanaugh, NYPD.

Okay—he had just offed a cop. Not the first time. Or the last, he hoped with a vicious grin. He put the wallet back into the jacket pocket and gave an admiring expert's look to the Government Model lying on the bed—but abstained from touching it. He looked cautiously out into the corridor. Still empty, except for a cart loaded with bed linens, brooms, and cleaning fluids, standing outside room 609. He quietly closed the door behind him, covered the twenty yards that separated him from 609, and peeked in. The chambermaid had her back to him and was vacuuming. He calmly took the passkey he had swiped a few moments before and slipped it back into the lock of 609.

A short way off, from his half-open door, Pietro Bellinzona was watching. Folco nodded and Bellinzona gave him a thumbs-up "well done." For all that Pietro might seem like a dope, he had handled his telephone impersonation of the concierge very adroitly. But that didn't mean he was through. Folco had told him to keep on watching after the murder; the cop might have a partner lurking around who would unquestionably surface as soon as word of the "accident" got out. Which meant any minute now.

Folco Mori slipped into his own room, directly opposite Italo Volpone's. He was wondering if everything was the way he had it figured.

"Homer, you're hardly eating," Chimene Kloppe reproached. "Don't you like the soufflé?"

"Yes, it's fine, dear. But I'm just not very hungry," Kloppe replied.

"Don't worry, mother," Renata soothed. "It's springtime getting to him. It's making dad's sap rise!"

"Renata, you should be ashamed."

"Why? It's happening to me, too, isn't it? That's why I'm marrying Kurt."

It was the usual family noontime meal. Only one thing was different: Kloppe's life had been threatened, and there was little he could do about it. Certainly he could not alert the police. As an extreme measure, he could arrange for Volpone's deportation as an undesirable alien, but for now, he resolved, he would not tell that little tramp a thing. As long as Genco Volpone or Mortimer O'Brion did not put in an appearance, the two billion dollars would keep on accruing interest. If Genco Volpone were really dead, as his brother insisted, Homer could only turn the money over to O'Brion, or to someone who knew the identifying code name of the account. And if O'Brion failed to collect, and Italo Volpone sued, Homer could tie him up in the courts for years.

"Papa, if you tell me truly what you're thinking, I'll give you a kiss."

"I'm thinking of a leg," Kloppe answered innocently.

"Aha!" Renata gloated. "I was right! Your sap *is* rising with spring."

"On second thought, Chimene, I will have some more soufflé."

Chimene was in seventh heaven. When Homer enjoyed the food, all was right in her world.

"Ottavio," the voice said.

"It's me," Italo answered.

Ottavio Giacomassi was the Volpone family's *caporegime* in charge of the European side of the Mediterranean basin. He had residences in Rome, Naples, and Milan, but he was never in any of them, although at any given moment his bosses could be informed of his whereabouts. Genco Volpone had spun a web of intelligence so fine that he could be filled in almost instantly on any danger to his interests throughout the world. Such an organization cost a bundle, but that was a drop in the bucket to what it brought in.

"We found your guy," said Ottavio.

Italo shivered with enjoyment. "Alive?"

"Very much so."

"Where is he?"

"He's not alone."

"What the fuck do I care? Where is he?"

"With Orlando Baretto. Go to the corner of Universitätstrasse and Waldenbachstrasse. That can't be far from where you are. Can you go right away?"

"Yes."

"Then go to Number 7 Universitätstrasse, third floor. There's only one door. He'll be waiting for you there."

"Ottavio?"

"Yes?"

"Thanks."

Italo Volpone hung up and rubbed his hands with a demented look of glee. Now he'd find out what actually happened to his brother, he'd get the number of the Swiss account that kept those two billion dollars out of circulation; and, mainly, he'd settle the hash of that fucking O'Brion. He'd do it with his own hands, too, as soon as he had made the little turd talk.

He phoned Bellinzona's room. "Pietro, get a hold of Folco. Get your asses downstairs on the double. We're on our way!"

Pat Mahoney had seen the doorman running toward him and everybody on the porch raising their heads. He got half up, his newspaper—which by now he knew by heart—crumpling in his hand. There were shouts outside. The doorman passed him again, running even faster, and started up the stairway in huge leaps. Without thinking, Mahoney fell in with him, unaware of what made him do it when his main assignment was to remain inconspicuous. However, when his muscles began to operate independently of his conscious will, it usually turned out to be important. A kind of animal instinct shared by both cops and crooks who succeed in their callings.

He got up to the mezzanine, where the bar, the ballroom, a small restaurant, public lavatories, and phone booths were located. He saw the doorman stop still and bring his hand to his mouth in a gesture of revulsion. The heads of all the bystanders turned toward him in one sweep. Mahoney caught up with him, looked out at the terrace atop the marquee, and felt like vomiting. His partner, big Dave, lay in a pool of blood between two large tubs of greenery, bits of brain soiling his white shirt. He was not wearing a jacket. Strangely, one of his shoes was near his smashed head, which was at an abnormal angle with his neck· Dave's body was lying on its stomach, but his wide-open lifeless eyes were facing the sky.

Mahoney's professional reflexes returned. Dave Cavanaugh was not one to fall out of a window. Mahoney raced toward an open elevator, got into it, and pressed the 6 button as his Python 357 came out in his hand.

Goddamn it! This was Switzerland. He put his gun back in his pocket, fury in his heart. There was nothing he could do for Dave, but he might still have a small chance to get his hands on the bastards who had thrown him to his death. How could Dave ever have let himself be taken by surprise like that? Mahoney jumped out of the elevator and raced down the length of the corridor, noting that the door to 647 was locked. He called a chambermaid whom he had rushed by on his way. She was eyeing him curiously.

"Do you have a passkey? There's been an accident. Let me into 647."

She left her cart and did as she was told. The room was empty. Dave's holster and gun still lay on the bedspread and his coat was on the back of the chair. Mahoney ran his fingers through the inside pocket and felt the wallet. The window was open. The curtains, blown by the wind, were streaming into the room like bridal veils.

"What's going on?" the woman asked.

"A man fell from this window. Did you see anyone in the hallway?"

101

"Nobody."

"Did you notice anything strange?"

"Nothing."

"No one went by?"

"I told you, no one," she repeated, surprised.

"Stay where you are. The police'll be here soon."

Mahoney went down one floor to his own room. The cleaning woman went back to 609 to get her cleaning cart. Two other doors on the sixth floor opened slightly, and Folco Mori and Pietro Bellinzona gave each other the thumbs-up victory sign. Now they knew who their next target was.

In his own room, Mahoney tried for five minutes to get through to New York. When he realized he wouldn't be able to dial direct to Kirkpatrick, he asked the hotel operator to make the call. He went to the window. Down below, a police car and an ambulance were parked near the entrance. His heart wrenched as he saw white-suited attendants put a stretcher into the ambulance. It was covered by a sheet, but from this height Mahoney could make out every detail of the load under it. He knew he had to avenge the death of his friend and partner. It was bitter irony to think that big Dave would be taken to the same morgue that held the leg that had brought them to Switzerland in the first place. What the hell was taking the phone so long?

With or without the help of the local cops, he intended to find Dave's killer. Too bad for Volpone if he was in any way connected with it! Then he saw the hood leaving the hotel, Pietro Bellinzona at his side, walking right past the ambulance. It took a second or more for Mahoney to realize that he was letting the bastards get away from him. He grabbed his coat and rushed toward the door, making sure his Magnum 357 was in the holster under his armpit. He was hoping he'd soon get a chance to use it.

7

At the sound of the doorbell, they were all startled. Inez had scarcely turned the knob when the door slammed into her face.

Orlando Baretto took a step forward to greet Volpone. But Italo didn't see him. All he could see was Mortimer O'Brion, his colorless skin turning gray and the nerve over his cheekbone twisting the right corner of his mouth into a hideous grimace.

"Italo, will you please explain the meaning—" O'Brion began to remonstrate.

With lightning motion Volpone grabbed him by the coat lapel, twisting it up around his neck. Then, lifting O'Brion as a bulldog might have done with an old rag, Italo used his free hand to slap him across the mouth. Before O'Brion could make a move or utter a sound, the muzzle of a Mauser was stuck under his jaw.

"Two questions!" Volpone thundered, his eyes wild with rage. "First, how did you go about knocking my brother off?"

"Italo," the terrified O'Brion was whining through the blood on his face and the hiccups that were convulsing him.

"Second, what's the account number? You've got five seconds!"

And he forced open O'Brion's mouth and shoved the point of the gun down his throat.

"One . . . two . . ." he began to count.

After Volpone said, "One," but before he could say "three," terrified though he was, O'Brion realized that Genco's brother could not kill him before getting the secret number for Operation OUT. Moreover, to give the number to anyone, even to Genco Volpone's own brother, would be to admit he knew the don was dead, a virtual confession that he had done Genco in himself. Keeping quiet was his only means of survival, if only for a while—but it would mean some time in which to breathe, to hope. . . .

"Four!" Volpone said in a dull voice.

But what was the use of planning? O'Brion could see that he was dealing with a madman who would shoot on the count of five, just as he had threatened. Even if it meant never seeing the two billion bucks.

"Boss," Pietro Bellinzona interposed, "please, don't do it here. I beg you!"

"Five!" Volpone said, and he twisted the muzzle of the pistol around in O'Brion's gullet.

Respectfully, but as powerfully as a bulldozer, Bellinzona grabbed the gun out of Volpone's hand.

"Boss, the whole town would be on our heels. We wouldn't even get out of the building if you drilled him here."

"He's right," Lando chimed in, trying to keep pace with the fast-moving developments. "Italo, stop!"

To be on the safe side, he grabbed Volpone's other hand and surreptitiously brought it to his lips. *"Bacio mani, I kiss your hands,"* he stammered.

Bellinzona had already done an about-face, and he had Zaza and Inez covered with his Llama .38 Super.

"Who's the blond tomato?" Italo asked, taking his hand back.

"She's with him," Lando replied.

"And the dinge?"

"With me. This is her place."

"Got a car?"

"Yes."

"Let's load 'em up."

"Where to?" Lando asked, his eyes wide.

"Listen," Zaza was whining, "I've got nothing to do with any of this. Let me out of here!"

"Shut up!" Volpone snapped.

"You're in my home," Inez cut in.

Italo sneered at her, then, turning to Lando, he said, "Take us to some quiet spot. Out in the country. Take the blonde with you. Pietro, you go along with that bastard. I'll keep the whore with me, and we'll follow you."

Lando seemed to be hesitating.

"You heard me. Now, let's go. *Andiamo via!*"

"Boss," Bellinzona suggested, "we can't take them out to the street looking like this." He pointed to O'Brion. "He's all bloody."

"Clean him up."

Pietro grabbed the first piece of material at hand: the negligee Inez was wearing.

"Hands off!" she warned.

"You, apehead, shut your trap!" Volpone swore. "Or I'll knock your fuckin' head off with this gun butt."

Lando did not dare interfere, and Bellinzona pulled at the material. It slipped off Inez's shoulders. She stood there stark naked, gorgeous enough to take your breath away. Pietro tossed the negligee to Zaza.

"Here! Wipe off your pig!"

Zaza shrugged in revulsion and shook her head no.

"Bitch!" Pietro snarled. "You went along for the good times, but now that the going is rough . . ."

He rolled the negligee into a ball and roughly wiped the blood from O'Brion's stunned face.

"Get a move on," Volpone urged.

Bellinzona made a face as he looked at Inez. "We can't take her with us without clothes."

"Time's a-wastin'," Volpone said irritably. "Toss a coat around her ass and let's get out."

Inez looked contemptuously at Lando, who turned his eyes away. She took her black mink coat out of the closet and put it on.

"If anyone peeps, give 'em a shot in the knee," Volpone told Pietro.

Lando was the last one out. He carefully, delicately, closed the door behind him.

A moment's hesitation had made Rico Gatto lose the trail again. When he saw the hotel guests rushing up to

105

the mezzanine, Rico had not been able to resist following them. He was amazed to see that the bloody mess on the terrace was the blond man he had noticed a few hours before at the airport. What a strange coincidence. . . .

Not trying to draw any conclusions for the moment, he went back to his room to call Ettore Gabelotti in New York. He struggled for ten minutes trying to get through, failed, and went back to the lobby to make sure Volpone hadn't slipped through his fingers. From a booth that had a good view of the hotel entrance, he called Italo Volpone's and Pietro Bellinzona's rooms, but neither answered, and he was irritated to think they had gotten away. For the moment, the only solid fact he had was that Volpone had been to the morgue. He went back to his room to take up a watch near the window, smoking one cigarette after another and leafing distractedly through his bedside book, the Old Testament in the Septuagint Greek edition, although it was impossible for him to read with any concentration. He kept thinking about that damned taxi that had blocked his way when Volpone left the morgue.

After three-quarters of an hour, Gatto had seen Volpone come back to the hotel, Bellinzona at his side. He blew on the three-carat diamond in his ring and rubbed it to make it shine.

As Rico saw it, this job was beneath him. He enjoyed tailing people when he knew he could look forward to the pleasure of being able to hit them. Temporarily stymied, he left the window to go to the telephone near his bed. Without saying that he had twice lost track of him, he would let Gabelotti know that Volpone had been to the Zurich morgue. After all, he was bound to come back to the hotel sooner or later. Leaving out details was not lying.

The door to Pat Mahoney's room was barely closed when he heard the telephone ring inside. He had been waiting for his New York call and for just a flash he wondered whether he should risk losing Volpone and go back in and inform headquarters about Cavanaugh. Before giving himself a chance to decide, he was heading down the stairs, and when his car started, he had a bead on Italo's Ford.

The driver seemed to hesitate on which way to turn at different corners, but finally he pulled up in front of a four-story building on Universitätstrasse, right behind a spanking new gunmetal gray Beauty Ghost P9.

Italo and his black-clad bodyguard had jumped out of the Ford and gone in, and luckily, Mahoney found a spot between two pickups twenty yards away.

Mahoney lit a cigarette, his face still tense, unable to forget his mental picture of Dave Cavanaugh smashed on the concrete. There was no hard evidence that Volpone and his gorilla had done it, but Pat would have bet his good right arm that they were in on it.

The closer the FBI and the IRS got to finding out what happened to the huge profits the Syndicate accumulated from all its questionable enterprises, the more the gangs had to grease the palms of thousands of nameless go-betweens—cops, corrupt politicians, unscrupulous lawyers—on every continent on earth. But their machine, fed by huge amounts of fresh money, kept working without a hitch, and no one talked. There was always plenty of money to pay the bail of the most unimportant foot soldier, and legal eagles, protected by their goddamn privilege, would bring the bail in cash, and no questions could be asked.

While this went on, new recruits for the underworld kept arriving in the U.S. Each year, under the sponsorship of Cosa Nostra, a thousand Sicilians came into the country, usually through Canada. They came with legal tourist visas on their passports—at a cost to the mob of less than $3,000—and went to work on the lowest rung of the dirty ladder. If they were not afraid to take chances and they were cruel enough, they rose quickly. Like their forerunners, who had come penniless from Europe, they too dreamed of rising to the top and running the country's economy by way of timeworn methods—bribes, blackmail, murder, extortion, labor-union racketeering. Little did they care that most of the capi had come to bad ends: the other guys were the only ones who got shot down.

However, aside from Vito Genovese, Thomas Gagliano, and Gaetano ("Three-Finger Brown") Lucchese, who had died of natural causes in or out of confinement, all the others had met violent deaths. Lucky Luciano probably died by poison, although it was officially called a heart attack; Albert Anastasia was gunned down in a barber's chair; Thomas Eboli was murdered, as were Philip Lombardo. Steve Ferrigno, Alfred Mineo, Salvatore Maranzano, Tom Reina, Joe Aiello, Philip Mangano, and Joseph Pinzolo. Today the Volpone and Gabelotti families were holding the reins. But if Mahoney could uncover the real purpose of Volpone's trip to Switzerland he was sure he could get him behind bars for many years the way they did Al Capone.

Unless war were to break out between Volpone and the Gabelottis. Unless he'd been involved in Cavanaugh's "accident." Unless he made some other mistake. Unless . . . Oh, shit! There he was coming out of the building. Mahoney saw Volpone walk to his car with an elegant black woman a head taller than he. At the same moment a young blond woman was being shoved toward the Beauty Ghost by a tall Latin-looking dude, and the big gorilla bodyguard had his arms around a little sickly man whom he tossed into the rear seat of the P9. An alarm went off inside Mahoney's head: he knew that little guy. Pictures flashed before his eyes, names rang in his ears. The Latin dude got in behind the wheel—a real European gigolo type, he noted—with the blond girl next to him. and the gorilla got in back with the half-pint. The P9 tooled nimbly away from the sidewalk, followed closely by Volpone's Ford.

Mahoney stepped on his accelerator just as the realization hit him that the little man was none other than Mortimer O'Brion, one of the best-known financial lawyers in the States.

Panic engulfed Mortimer O'Brion once the car reached Zurich's outlying districts. Yet Bellinzona seemed to be dozing, paying no attention; and as for the dude who was driving. he was too busy with the road to be able to do anything. Next to him, Zaza was as still as a statue. Mortimer wondered if he had one chance in a thousand to come back from this ride.

He also wondered how Volpone had found out that

Genco was dead. How had Italo tracked him down so fast? It wasn't possible that the two punks who held the contract on Genco had been identified. He had contacted them direct, without intermediary. No one in New York knew them. There was no way to tie him to them, for not even they had any idea who he was.

Two years earlier, Morty had represented a Polish-American named Stepan Katz, accused of a triple murder, and saved him from the electric chair. In gratitude, Katz had given him the name of two of his buddies who lived in Naples, saying, "Just in case you ever need them for anything. You never know! Just use my name, they'll do anything you want—and I mean anything!"

O'Brion had shrugged, but he had made a permanent note of the phone number Katz gave him, never dreaming he'd use it. Three weeks later, Katz was found strangled in his cell, taking his dreams and secrets to the grave with him, and his strangler was never identified.

Had it not been for Zaza, the idea of the crime might never have come into O'Brion's mind; but he had spent a fortune trying to impress her, and a few bad investments had further reduced his nest egg. Of course, he had a numbered account in Switzerland, but a month ago he had gone bullish on sterling, investing everything he had in the British currency when a colleague with high connections in Washington diplomatic circles had tipped him off that the U.S. Treasury was about to make an enormous injection of dollars into the economy of the United Kingdom. The pound would have to go up sharply when this became known—at least by 30 percent—but five weeks later the pound had been devalued by 20 percent.

At the same time, Ettore Gabelotti had let him in, under the strictest seal of confidence, on the main lines of the agreement he and the Volpones had made. They were going to do something unprecedented. They were going to launder no less than two billion dollars at one swipe.

In the convolutions of such an operation, money was so to speak, decanted, losing a fraction of a percent of its face value at each temporary location. But when it finally came through the last of the many sieves that had refined it, it was virginal, without traceable source, ready to be re-invested in broad daylight in perfectly legal enterprises. Washed clean.

That was just when Zaza had started to up her demands, and Judith, Mortimer's missus, smelling a rat with the incomparable instinct women get from twenty years of shared domesticity, had also insisted tartly on being given greater liquid assets.

In order to have a little peace, and to get rid of his guilt feelings, he had given in. One night he had awakened with a startling thought: if Genco Volpone disappeared, he, Mortimer O'Brion, would be the only one able to collect the two billion dollars! Of course it had only been a nightmare. The idea was absurd and out of the question. No one could expect to get away with taking the Syndicate that way; anyone who had ever tried had met a violent death after unspeakable tortures and mutilations. There was no place in the world where one could find a safe haven from its long arm of revenge.

So Mortimer had dismissed the idea, horrified at even having harbored it. Then, through a game of dialectics, "trying it on for size," he had projected various steps, figuring the consequences at each turn, eliminating the imponderables, forestalling the other side's reactions, calculating the chances of success or failure as if with a computer, allowing for all contingencies. To his amazement, he had come to the conclusion that the trick could be pulled off. True, there were some unavoidable risks, but for two billion dollars, weren't they worth taking?

Morty O'Brion had a deep-seated grudge against life. He had turned out to be dull when he would have wanted to be handsome and irresistible, small rather than tall, colorless where he had dreamed of being a leader of men. His need for vengeance had led him to his decision: he would have Genco Volpone rubbed out.

Once the decision was made, the details of the operation had fallen into place in his mind like the steps of a mathematical progression. He had phoned the two Neapolitan cutthroats, using the name of the late Stepan Katz, thanking heaven that the men were alive and ready to take the contract. For fear that the killers might get cold feet if they realized who their victim was, he had not revealed Genco's identity. Without any assurance that they would do the job properly, he had arranged for $50,000 to be paid to them in Italy. And then things started to happen. Holding Gabelotti's power of attorney, Mortimer O'Brion had landed in Zurich with Don Genco Volpone. Two days earlier, he had let the hit men know that their target was on the way, and he had found himself both scared and excited by the fact that they were ready to carry out their end of the bargain.

He had described Genco, giving them the name of the hotel he would stop at and his schedule. The rest was up to them. Mortimer did not want to know how they did it. On the plane back to New York after the meeting with Kloppe, a moment of lucidity made him see—too late!— that his impossible bluff would never work. He began fervently hoping that Katz's friends would let him down, but he had barely arrived in Nassau when he got the evidence to the contrary: "PLEASE CALL BACK. JUDITH." The telegraphic code that meant that Zu Genco Volpone was dead. Willy-nilly, he had to go along with the implacable unfolding of the details of his plan. The lie he was about to tell upset him more than the murder he had paid for.

Before going to the meeting Italo Volpone had set up in Nassau for the capi and consiglieri of the two families, O'Brion had made his report to Don Ettore Gabelotti.

"The number?" Ettore had demanded after a perfunctory greeting.

"21877."

Gabelotti immediately wrote it down and asked the code name.

"God."

"Very good."

Mortimer was beside himself: for the first time in his brilliant legal career, he had failed to tell a client the truth. The real number and code name were etched in his mind: 828384—*Mamma mia.*

Genco Volpone's body was somewhere near Zurich. And Gabelotti had no reason whatsoever to doubt O'Brion, so his lie could not be given away by anyone. Gabelotti would never again talk to Genco Volpone. Nor to the Zurich Trade Bank. By his nature and calling. Homer Kloppe would remain as silent as the tomb if Gabelotti

—whose name he didn't even know—were to ask him anything. Especially using the phony number and code name.

All Mortimer needed to do was close the account and disappear with Zaza.

He looked warmly at the nape of her neck as they drove along in the P9. The cowardice she had shown toward him came as no surprise. She was weak, calculating, venal, cold, stupid, and selfish. But he loved her. Up to this moment, for all the rebuffs she gave him, she was still the only woman who had ever made him really feel like a man. Was she going to get killed too? Italo had no proof that O'Brion had had Genco knocked off. Could Volpone take the senseless risk of killing him before he found out how to get the two billion bucks? As of now, Mortimer was the only key that could possibly open the bank, and the Zurich Trade Bank would never release the dough if the proper legal conditions were not met.

No one in the world would ever convince Homer Kloppe to cough it up without hearing the account number and code.

A sharp turn into a side road threw Mortimer against Pietro Bellinzona. With a grumble the big guy shoved him back to the other corner.

When it wasn't hidden around a bend, Folco Mori could see the tail of the dark blue Fiat bouncing along the road. It had been rented that morning by the cop who had taken the dive, and now his buddy was driving it. Folco felt glad that he wasn't that cop. That one wasn't going to see the sun set tonight either, so he'd never be able to report to his superiors—that bastard Kirkpatrick, probably—that Italo Volpone had taken O'Brion and his pussy for a one-way drive into the rugged Swiss countryside. Folco wondered if the cop had time to advise his New York bosses about what happened to his partner.

When Volpone and Bellinzona left Sordi's Hotel, Mori had stayed as a rear guard, watching from his Volkswagen, hidden behind a row of prickly shrubs. He had seen the copper take off after Italo and Pietro, and he had hoped that the other unidentified shadow would also show up. Unfortunately, there'd been no sign of him.

Too bad. Folco was dying to know who he was before making it a lucky threesome of corpses.

When they left the airport, after arriving from New York, there had been three guys tailing Volpone. Two were cops—a team, though they pretended not to know each other. The first one was dead; the second, in his blue Fiat, was in Folco's sight. Only the third guy remained an unknown quantity. Either an operative of another government agency or a torpedo for a rival family. Ettore Gabelotti would be the only one big enough to dare keep a tail on Volpone.

As for cop number two, no need for Folco to knock himself out trying to pass his death off as an accident.

The wild countryside they were traversing provided every opportunity for disposing of a body. By the time it was found, a lot of snow would have melted in that valley, and Folco Mori would be far away.

At the next bend in the road, Folco had a panoramic view of the whole horizon. Far ahead, he could see the P9, followed by Volpone's Ford, majestically climbing the side of the mountain. Three hundred yards behind came the cop's Fiat.

"Enjoy yourself, bastard!" Folco said aloud. "Enjoy! You won't have a chance much longer!"

The grade suddenly became so steep that Folco had to shift back into low in order to climb.

"I am Mr. Volpone's secretary," Rico Gatto said.
"Indeed." said the unflappable morgue attendant.
"You know—the man who was here this morning. He asked me to come and see if he lost something here."
"Here? What kind of thing?"
"A watch."
"Where?"
"If you don't mind, I'd like to look around."
"But where?"
"Wherever my boss went this morning."
"I'm sorry, you're not allowed in."
"Why?"
"Because only family are admitted. He'll have to come back himself."

"Mr. Volpone is terribly busy," Rico Gatto said, taking several American bills out of his pocket.

The attendant did not seem to notice. Back home, that bait would have sent his counterpart off like a flash to bring in ten coffins, with or without occupants. But this was Switzerland.

"Here!" Rico said, offering him the money.

The man looked appalled. "For me? Why?"

"For your trouble."

"What trouble? This is what I get paid for."

"Well, then, show me in," Rico said impatiently.

"I told you, no visitors are allowed in the morgue."

"What do I have to do to get in?"

"Like anyone else. Wait until some relative of yours dies, and then make a written request."

Rico gladly would have taken a shot at the guy.

On the phone, Ettore Gabelotti had been speechless with rage when Rico hadn't been able to tell him whose body Volpone had seen in the morgue.

"Didn't Mr. Volpone drop his watch in the coffin?" Rico asked, trying a new tack.

"Well, I don't know," the man said. "When I closed it, I didn't see a thing."

"Are you sure?"

"Absolutely. I certainly wouldn't have missed it, with just a leg in there."

"What do you mean, just a leg?"

The man looked at Rico questioningly. "Well, yes—the leg."

Rico was so taken aback that he gave himself away. "You mean Mr. Volpone just came in to see a leg?" He paused. "Whose was it?"

"What did you say your name was again?" the man asked, now fully on the defensive.

"Listen," Rico pleaded. "Check it again, will you? I'll come back before closing time."

Pat Mahoney was sure that Cavanaugh had been murdered. As he followed the P9 and Volpone's Ford up the mountain trails, he noticed a Volkswagen hot on his own track. He kicked himself for not having considered that one of Volpone's men might have stayed behind to keep an eye on him. They had surely lured Dave to the window and thrown him down. With a chill of ferocious pleasure Mahoney realized they were preparing the same kind of thing for him. He felt the butt of his Magnum. They were hunting him, but he was going to kill the hunter.

For a moment he forgot he was a cop with an assignment. Later he'd be able to find a thousand ways to justify the carnage. One was enough: self-defense.

First he'd try to get that guy tailing him to talk. As soon as he got him to confess, he'd do away with him and, depending on what the guy told him, fire at the rest of them until the terrible fury splitting his temples had been satisfied.

The trail began to wind in and out under a high arch of huge firs and larches that hid the road from the light of day. Their bluish shadow gave a metallic tone to the patches of snow that lay here and there along the way. The closer they got toward the summit, the heavier was the snow, protected by the mantle of the trees and devoid of any tracks except for those of the two cars that had gone before. The road became rough, and it was full of potholes hidden under the snow. The Fiat had trouble getting up one especially steep rise, and no sooner was it at the top of the bump than it flew down a breakneck descent for some thirty yards. Taken by surprise, Mahoney jammed on his brakes. All its wheels locked, the car turned slightly sideways and started to skid, sliding all the way to the bottom of the drop where the forest road made a turn, as if to get a better start up toward the next crest.

Mahoney knew that here, and nowhere else, was where it would happen. Momentarily giving up the chase, he jumped out of the Fiat, which was now across the road, and rolled behind some bushes. Crouching, he climbed a few yards up the hill, bent over, his Police Python 357 at the ready, and hid behind a tree trunk. He waited, panting. The guy in the car on his heels was going to skid at the top of that bump and come down the same way he had. He grinned viciously as he heard the sound of an engine. First he saw the two front wheels of the Volkswagen skate along the top, then its rounded hood come hurtling down. The driver quickly went into a lower gear to brake his drop, and when he saw the Fiat across his path, it was too late to do anything. In three strides, Mahoney was at the door of the VW. He tore it open and with his free left hand he grabbed the man from the wheel and threw him to the ground.

Folco Mori saw the black hole of the Python an inch from his right eye. He was going to raise his head when he was struck by a wrist across his Adam's apple. Gasping, he raised his hands to his throat and rolled over in the snow. Mahoney quickly frisked him, and grabbed his wallet, and took a couple of steps away, his weapon still covering Folco, who was softly moaning as he spat out a mixture of saliva and bile.

"What are you trying to sell up here?" Mahoney demanded.

Folco took a good look at Mahoney. Huge and bony, he was inspecting Folco's passport, which listed him as a traveling salesman. By the way the cop had frisked him, by his tone and his manner, Folco had no doubt: the flatfoot was going to blow his brains out.

In that case, this was the end of the road. Everybody had to pay the price. He wasn't really so sorry to die, just sad not to be living anymore; to be out rotting someplace while other guys were still having fun, fucking, laying in the sun. He had often idly wondered where it would happen to him. Now he knew. In a forest that smelled good, on a patch of snow, in April.

"How did you kill my partner?" Mahoney demanded.

His accent told Folco they had both grown up in the same part of the Bronx.

"You know what I mean," Mahoney shouted, his face fierce with rage.

Mori painfully got up, leaning on his hands, unable to get his breath to come in a regular rhythm. The engine of the Volks, which he hadn't had a chance to shut off, was still purring and spitting. Why should he bother to answer?

"I'll give you three seconds," Mahoney said. "How did you kill my partner?"

Mori could see the cop's finger turn white on the

116

trigger of the Magnum. He shook his head and stepped away. "What the fuck difference does it make?"

That was as good a confession as any. Mahoney raised the muzzle of the Python. He was about to shoot when Folco Mori started to put his hands down toward his pants.

"Hands behind your head!" Mahoney ordered by professional reflex, as he had done a thousand times when he collared city troublemakers.

Mori did as he was told. The two men were facing each other, ten yards apart, Folco Mori with his hands knotted behind his head, Mahoney with his gun at his hip.

Then a truly strange thing happened. Mahoney saw Mori throw one arm out in his direction and roll over on the ground in a desperate hedgehog movement. What did the bum think? That this would keep a bullet from hitting him? Mahoney wanted to laugh, but he felt a lukewarm liquid spurt into his mouth with the strength of a geyser, and he saw three or four Folco Moris jumping in different directions while the trees seemed to be dancing a jig above him and the sky turned alternately black and purple. As he lowered his head, he was amazed to see that he had dropped his Magnum. He wondered what the hell he was doing there, lying on the ground, which was the only solid thing in the dizzily whirling landscape. Then he raised his heavy hand to his throat to find a gaping hole hugging a long blade that went straight through in a flood of blood. He thought, If only my jugular wasn't cut . . .

8

At 4:00 P.M. Marjorie ushered Karl Deutsch into Homer Kloppe's office. The banker rose to greet the "Doktor." After a few courteous remarks, they got to the heart of the matter.

"I hope you won't mind my having barged in," said Deutsch.

Homer magnanimously waved this scruple away.

"I'd also appreciate your forgetting my call the minute I leave here."

"Would you like a drink?" asked Kloppe, taking out his giant bottle of Waterman's ink.

They had known each other for nearly ten years and were full of mutual esteem. Karl Deutsch, an Austrian by birth, had had a hard time getting Zurich financial circles to forget his national origin; despite the use of the same language, they did not look on him as "one of ours." His gifts as a conciliator and his innate sense of helpfulness, not to mention his highly placed international connections, had finally won him acceptance among the local upper bourgeoisie. Even the highest bank officials often came to ask his opinion with respect to new customers. As if by magic, Karl Deutsch always had information handy, and gratis; he had never been known to be wrong about anyone. It was almost enough to make them forgive his lack of devotion in the practice of the Protestant religion he professed.

They also had the greatest respect for the unparal-

leled regularity with which he ushered foreign capital into the country, for he made a habit of spreading such
sums among the various institutions of Zurich, Geneva,
and Lausanne that had won his favor. There was no
business deal he was ever unaware of, no secret he couldn't
fathom, no social circle, however closed, he could not
penetrate. Wealthy individuals, foreign banks, and multinational corporations, as well as some governments that
needed fresh supplies of money or lucrative short-term
investments, all made use of his services. Deutsch speculated in currency exchange, knowing before anyone else
the exact day on which any country's money was going
to be devalued or revalued. He could obtain the address of
a dealer who had Tiger tanks, M-1 rifles, or Sten light
machine guns on hand in quantity. He had ways known
only to him of transferring money to shelter it from
voracious American or European taxes. Naturally, Deutsch
collected his percentage on each transfer. Naturally, the
value of such a talent had not escaped the notice of the
Syndicate. On several occasions Deutsch had been able to
launder huge sums, the source of which he did not question. He enjoyed his ability to outsmart the all-powerful
American IRS. He had even succeeded on occasion in getting high government officials to take on directorships at
fancy salaries, so that, by poetic justice, the ill-gotten gains
of the mob were used to remunerate the very people who
had been in charge of fighting it. Karl Deutsch, af-
fable, loyal, always ready to do a favor or bring together
those who could do one another some good, pulled all the
strings of the huge skein he had woven.

"To your health!" Kloppe said, raising his glass.

"*Prosit!*" replied Deutsch, draining his.

Homer poured him another.

"Well, now," said Deutsch after taking a deep breath,
"I have the greatest respect and esteem for you, Mr.
Kloppe. So I suggest that you make no reply to what
I am going to tell you. And after I've gone, you can
do as you see fit. Of course, this story is purely imagi-
nary . . ."

"Of course," Kloppe chimed in, concerned, but
deeply interested.

"My only reason for telling it to you," Deutsch

119

went on, "is that it may be helpful. You'll decide that. Let us suppose that a huge sum of money had been entrusted to one of the banks in this city, under the cloak of a numbered account." He saw Kloppe's face lose its expression. "And let us suppose also that this sum, which was just in transit, belonged to a group of partners—not necessarily Swiss—but foreigners, say, maybe Americans, whose ways of doing business are rather different from ours. People who, perhaps primitively, feel that papers and signatures mean less than giving one's word or shaking hands on a deal."

Kloppe carefully placed the Waterman's bottle back into his desk drawer. The one thing he would never have anticipated was that Deutsch, of all people, would turn out to be representing the Volpones. But then, wasn't he, Kloppe himself, the custodian of their funds?

"Now, let us suppose that the people who deposited the sum and knew the account number were unable to come and claim it. The duty of a banker would be never to reveal the existence of the money to anyone."

Karl Deutsch cleared his throat. "Unless, of course, Mr. Kloppe, the claimants were madmen or outlaws who would stop at nothing in order to collect. In that case, and in that one case alone, the banker might be better advised to let caution be the better part of valor, to listen to his common sense rather than to adhere to the letter of the law. Do you follow me?"

"Did you receive the invitation to my daughter's wedding?" Kloppe abruptly changed the subject.

"Yes, thanks."

"Are you planning to come?"

"Why, of course."

Kloppe got up, pushing his chair back.

"I think it might be better if you decided not to," he said. "Just forget about the wedding, as I have already forgotten the things you've told me, which I must say I could not quite follow."

Karl Deutsch got up, his face drained of color.

"I am deeply sorry, sir. Most upset by this turn of events. I had hoped you would see that I was speaking to you only as a friend."

"Good day, Doktor," said Kloppe.

"Good day, sir," Deutsch replied, and as he turned away, he felt he had just grown ten years older.

Yet, he had done what he did only to try to avoid the worst.

When Angela Volpone reached the landing, she was hesitant about ringing. Her heart was beating fast, and she wanted to turn and run away. To keep herself from ducking out, she had phoned Francesca a half hour earlier to say she was coming. Now she wondered whether she would have the courage to tell her sister-in-law that Genco was dead.

Francesca opened the door herself. Perhaps because of her simple attire, her lack of makeup, or even the subtle signs of wear and tear in her face, she looked older than her fifty years. Since marrying Italo, Angela had met Francesca on only three or four occasions, and each time, they had found nothing more to say to each other than the conventional civilities. They were far too different, even though they had married brothers.

Angela's healthy twenty-five-year-old urges could not but make her feel ill at ease in Francesca's calm and resigned presence. What could this woman have been through to appear so broken?

"Come in, Angela. Welcome to my home."

The apartment looked like Francesca. Despite its size, nothing broke its dull, quiet air. Everything was gray, soft, a bit faded, timeless. Anonymous. And yet the rustic furnishings seemed to reflect the touch of the man who made them. As if here, on Eighth Avenue, one had suddenly come out into the country.

"Would you like some coffee?"

Angela shook her head. Ushered in by Francesca, she sat down in an easy chair near the window, her hostess on a straight chair facing her.

"Here's the thing," Angela began. "Italo just phoned from Zurich. I have some bad news." Francesca's face contracted almost imperceptibly. "It's about your husband. Genco . . . uh, had an accident."

Unable to look into her sister-in-law's devouring

121

eyes, Angela looked at her own tensed hands, knotted on her tweed skirt.

"An accident?" Francesca inquired. "Is he . . . ? Is he . . . ?" she kept asking as she stood up.

Angela, overcome with emotion, bit her lip and lowered her head. Then, with a burst of sympathy, she got up and threw herself into the older woman's arms. Francesca was sobbing but no tears were coming from her eyes.

"Where?" she asked in a changed and hardened voice as she withdrew from the embrace.

Angela did not know what to answer. Wild as it seemed, Italo had not given her any details.

"I asked you, where is my husband?" Francesca repeated. "What happened to him?"

"I don't know," Angela gulped, holding back her sobs. "Italo is supposed to call me back. He didn't tell me anything more. He's taking care of everything."

Francesca collapsed on the easy chair, bent over herself, her head buried in the cushions, punching them as hard as she could while an inhuman groan spurted from her breast.

"I knew they'd kill him on me! I always knew it! And now they'll kill Italo, too!"

Angela brought her fists up before her mouth to keep from screaming.

Every time Lando Baretto seemed to be slowing down, Volpone honked his horn imperiously, urging him to keep up the pace. Now Lando could see the end of the path, as it led into a clearing where, on one side, there was a main building fitted out with barns, lofts, and lean-tos. He cut the motor, got out of the car, and waited for the Ford to come alongside. Not daring to meet Inez's eyes, he rushed to open the door for Volpone.

"This okay?"

"Make sure there's nobody in there," Italo answered sharply, remaining in the car.

Irked by the mud and melting snow that soiled his loafers, Lando walked toward the buildings. Everything was closed. He knocked on the door several times. Nothing. He walked around the building, saw a partly open door, and shoved it wide. It squeaked as it swung. The mud floor was covered by a deep layer of chips and scraps of wood. Against the retaining walls were various tools—picks, hatchets, steel wedges—and in the middle of the warehouse sat a huge electric saw covered with sawdust and grime. Lando ran his finger over the rusted circular blade.

He went out again and climbed the surrounding rise for a hundred yards or so. From the top, he had a panoramic view of the landscape, hidden from sight in the clearing. In the foreground, diving steeply to the edge of a mountain torrent gleaming below, were several acres of sparsely planted firs, sheared off at the stumps. Farther down, between the stream and the stumps, tree trunks cut into logs lay in piles secured by huge wooden blocks. When the time came, the woodcutters would simply let the logs roll into the water and then collect them downstream. Beyond, among the sharp blacks and whites that faded into bluish grays, was a whole range of hills and snowy escarpments.

Looking back to the clearing, Lando could see the buildings in one corner, completely surrounded by the dark mass of the trees. He went down, fuming at the fact that he kept sinking into snow halfway up his calves.

"Well?" Volpone asked.

"All clear."

"Get the bastards out!"

Lando signaled to Pietro Bellinzona, who came out of the P9 behind Mortimer O'Brion and Zaza Finney. Volpone got out of the Ford, pushing Inez before him. For a moment they all stood still. Bellinzona kept Zaza and Mortimer covered. Italo Volpone, his face cruel and impersonal, was casually holding Inez's arm while she gazed ahead impassively.

The sudden silence that precedes executions fell over the group. At the sound of an approaching motor, Volpone raised his hand slightly; no one else moved. Then Folco Mori's cream-colored Volkswagen came into the clearing. He parked it alongside the other two cars, pulled on the hand brake, and came to join them.

"Where'd you come from?" Volpone asked.

"I was in back."

123

"We didn't even see you," Bellinzona marveled.

"I had to make a stop."

"What for?" Bellinzona asked.

"Never mind."

Volpone gave a signal with his head and they all fell into step behind him. Outside the barn, Volpone said to Pietro and Mori, "Get 'em all inside."

And to Lando, "You stay here."

When Zaza, Inez, Mortimer, Folco, and Bellinzona had gone in, Volpone scratched the snow with the tip of his shoe.

"You know my brother?" he asked Lando, without looking up.

"Yes. I saw him three days ago."

"Where?"

"In town. He had me meet him in the bar of the Continental."

"What for?"

"Don Genco wanted me to take him to the train station."

"Did you?"

"Yes."

"Tell me about it."

Lando looked at him. "What's to tell?"

"Did you take a taxi?"

"No," he replied with self-satisfaction, twisting his head toward the P9. "We went in that."

"Is it yours?"

"Yes, a gift from Don Genco."

"When?"

"When we went past the dealer, he said he wanted to give me a memento. I drove it out and took him to the station."

"Did you see him to the train?"

"No, he didn't want me to. I left him outside."

"You didn't go to the ticket window?"

"He told me to just go on."

"So you don't know if he really bought a ticket."

"No."

"How did he seem?"

"Who?"

"My brother," Italo snapped.

124

"Fine. Relaxed. In a good mood."

"Who followed you?"

Lando looked surprised. "Followed us? Nobody. I guess."

"You know that guy you collared?"

"Mortimer O'Brion? He's a lawyer."

"Did you see him with my brother?"

"No. When I met Don Genco, he was alone."

"Your name Baretto?"

"Orlando Baretto. They call me Lando."

"How long you been in the family?"

"Near nine years."

"You well paid?"

"Sure."

"From now on, you got a raise. Double your old pay."

"But, *padrone* . . ." Lando mumbled in confusion.

"Don't you want it?"

"Sure, sure," Lando came back quickly. "But—"

"Take this," Volpone ordered as he stuffed a roll of bills into Lando's hand. It was ten thousand dollars.

"For me?"

"On account. Did you like my brother?"

Lando vigorously nodded again and again.

"He's dead," Italo said. "You know who got him knocked off?"

Lando's lower jaw seemed to fall completely away.

"That bastard O'Brion did it!" Volpone said. "Now, listen to me. I've got two or three questions to ask him. When I get done with him, he won't be going back to Zurich. Get my drift?"

"Sure," Lando said, having already suspected as much.

"His blond biddy won't, either. You gonna help me?"

"Sure."

"Who's the big bean pole, the dinge?"

"She's my girl."

"You in love with her?"

"Well, I . . ." Lando said, the words sticking in his throat, his voice suddenly hoarse.

"She can't come back either."

"But, boss—"

"I'll make it up to you."

"She didn't do anything. She doesn't know anything about it!"

"Could be. Just tough shit for her."

"But—"

"Look, no witnesses, understand? You'll find another
broad. There's plenty of cunts around."

"Please, *padrone* . . ."

Volpone gave him a venomous look. "I already said
I'd make it up to you."

"I know, boss, I know. But that's not the point. If
she disappears, it'll be noticed. She's acquainted with the
big shots all over town—judges and bankers. You know
the place where you sent me this morning, to collar
O'Brion, that bank—"

"What bank?"

"The Zurich Trade Bank. She turns tricks with the
banker."

"Who?"

"Inez."

"You mean with Kloppe?"

"Yes," Lando hastily assured him, realizing that somehow he had hit a soft spot. "He's crazy about her. Off
his fuckin' nut!"

Volpone's mind was clicking at top speed.

"You say your black girl's fucking Homer
Kloppe?"

"Yes, Kloppe, that's the guy."

"You want to keep her hustling?"

"She's a good kid."

"You wanna take her back to Zurich, huh?"

"If she ever said one word, I'd bump her off myself."

Volpone looked at him with contempt. "You trust a
cunt?"

Lando hesitated only a fraction of a second. "This
one, yes."

"Well, I don't. Unless we can scare the shit out of
her. Now, listen to me, Baretto. If she shoots her mouth
off, you know you'll be held responsible. Okay?"

"Okay."

Volpone gave him a friendly tap on the shoulder.

126

"Don't worry if I push her around a little bit. It'll just be for effect. Just for show, you know?"

Kurt Heinz was embarrassed by his parents. Slow and humble, they would probably end their days in the poorly furnished three-room flat where Kurt was born, never questioning the tradition of mediocrity that had graced their lives. With some bitterness Kurt thought back on his efforts to escape from the cocoon of anonymity. His parents were scandalized by their only son's intention to marry into the ranks of the wealthy and socially eminent.

"Well, what's done is done." His father sighed. "But don't imagine I can feel comfortable about it."

"You're a professor, Kurt," his mother joined in. "If you two do what you're planning, you'll antagonize a great many people."

Kurt shrugged angrily. Deep down, he knew they were right. And he resented that fact all the more. As usual, the idea had come into being as a result of one of Renata's stupid dares. And now it was too late to turn back.

"You don't know how to dream!" Renata had accused him. "What you need is a bit of madness in your makeup, Kurt! You'd never carry me away in a helicopter!"

"Sure, darling, sure I would. Why shouldn't I do it on our wedding day?"

"Why not?" she had retorted, her eyes gleaming.

"Yes, why not?"

"You always said you'd like to dump on the dirty bourgeois of this city. Now prove it. I dare you!"

"I'll take the dare!"

"You won't poop out?"

"Me?"

The stupid thing had started as a game, and with utter seriousness they went on to plan a whole schedule of festivities that would shock the pants off all of dignified Zurich. The theme of the wedding was perversity itself: everything was to be upside down.

Kurt felt ill at ease as he imagined himself in a

flowered gondola, hanging from the helicopter, going up into the sky. There would certainly be a lot of his students out to see the show, which, to the resigned consternation of both families, had been widely publicized in the local press. After that pitiful exhibition, he'd almost certainly have to resign from his job. And do what? Become a bank teller, like his father?

"I'm telling you, Kurt," Joseph Heinz kept saying, "you're putting your mother and me in a very difficult spot."

"You have no sense of humor!" his son chided.

"What if the rope breaks?" Utte worried.

She was big and placid, and she was embarrassed at the idea of disturbing anyone. Her strong thick-fingered peasant hands were made for laundry, for darning, for cooking fondues, for milking cows. At night, she was the last one to bed, checking to see that all the lights were out, the kitchen neat, and the front door double-locked, while Joseph Heinz nodded off to sleep promptly at ten o'clock. No stereotype was missing from their lives, even to the cuckoo clock on the wall that sourly peeped every quarter of an hour, marking the passing of time they had never known how to enjoy.

"You can't understand," Kurt told them. "Renata's a live wire."

"I'm just afraid you'll lose your job," Utte stammered, casting her eyes down.

"What if I do?" Kurt blustered, secretly afraid of the same thing.

"After all the sacrifices we made," Utte lamented. "You know, your father and I, we hoped, that is—we would have liked . . ."

"Liked what?" He was almost ready to scream, You would have liked me to be just like you! but he kept silent when he heard his father's heavy sigh.

"Well, I'll have to be going. Is your gown ready, mother?"

She nodded.

"You'll see. You'll be the prettiest one there!"

He was apprehensive about the moment when she would appear in the Kloppes' great parlor, tall and awk-

128

ward as a derrick, in some hideous thing made of a cheap piece of apple-green material.

"Good-bye, father."

He grazingly kissed the blotchy cheeks of that fragile old child who had never really become a man. But was Kurt himself really a man?

When he saw Italo Volpone enter the barn, Mortimer O'Brion wanted to crawl into a shell. But the certainty of his death and the suffering that would precede it steeled him for a final attempt to save his skin.

"Italo, I swear to you, this is all one hell of a misunderstanding!"

Dreamily Italo let his eyes wander, taking in the sawdust and scraps of wood, the saw, the walls, the spiderwebs, and the huge beams that held up the roof structure. Not far from the saw was a metal plate set on the floor of pounded earth. Volpone signaled to Pietro Bellinzona, who lifted it, revealing a hole about six feet by three, and some two and a half feet deep. In it was the motor for the saw, and there was a large electric meter with a master switch on it.

"Leave that hole open!" he ordered Pietro, who was busy rubbing the rust off his hands.

"Italo!" O'Brion yelled, raising himself to all of his unimpressive height. "I have a right to know what this is all about!"

Volpone turned toward O'Brion as if seeing him for the first time.

"I'll tell you," he answered quietly.

He took him amiably by the arm and led him to the back of the barn, far from the others. During the ride in the car, blood had started to run from Mortimer's bruised mouth again, but he hadn't bothered to wipe it off.

"Okay," Volpone calmly told him. "My brother was murdered."

O'Brion called on the last of his nerve to find the strength not to lower his eyes.

"That can't be true!" he forced out.

"Shut up!" Volpone muttered savagely, tring to contain himself. "I'm doing the talking. You're going to give me the code word and the number of the Zurich Trade Back account Genco deposited that money in."

"Italo, I can't! That would mean betraying Genco!"

In order not to kill O'Brion then and there, Babe Volpone had to shut his eyes, take his own head in both his hands, and squeeze as hard as he could until the marks of his fingers were visible in his limpid flesh.

"Listen to me, you rotten dog. And get this straight! Before I kill you, I'm ready to make a deal with you. Talk right now, and I'll finish you off like a man, clean and fast with a bullet in your head. And I give you my word nothing'll happen to your broad."

"What? You mean to say?"

"If you decide to hold out, you'll talk anyway. But I'll pull your lousy skin off inch by inch, so you can stay alive and enjoy every bit of it. Now, which way do you want it?"

"Italo, I swear you're making a big mistake," Mortimer pleaded. "I swear that—"

"Pietro! Put that metal plate back where it belongs. And take the blonde and stand her up on it!"

"Hey, what's eating you?" Zaza protested. "What business of mine is it if you guys are fighting? I hardly even know this character."

Bellinzona twisted her arm behind her back and shoved her onto the metal plate.

"Now what do I do?" he asked.

"Hang her," said Volpone quietly.

"You bastards!" Zaza screamed.

She tried to kick Pietro, but he overwhelmed her with his big bear's arms.

Inez had an unusual reaction. "How long is all this crap gonna last? I'm cold. I want to get out of here and go home."

"Get over by that fucker," Folco Mori ordered her, pointing to O'Brion.

"I don't know what they've got against you," she said to Mortimer, "but why not talk to them? Can't you see you're dragging all of us down into this shit?"

At a wink from Volpone, Folco picked up a coil of rope and handed it to Lando. Lando held one end and flung the coil up over the beam. Then, as Bellinzona watched with interest, Lando fashioned a noose.

"Put it around her neck!" Volpone told them.

Her eyes bugging out in horror, a look of utter disbelief on her face, Zaza glanced around, trying to find some kind of help.

"Mortimer!" she screamed. "Mortimer, do something!"

"Leave her alone!" O'Brion yelled. "For chrissake, leave her alone!"

With one twist Bellinzona tied Zaza's wrists behind her back while Lando attached the end of the rope to a ring that was welded into the wall.

"Mortimer!" Zaza screamed again, as loud as she could.

She could see him trying to free himself from the arms of Folco Mori, who now had him in a chest lock.

"The plate!" Italo said.

Like a bronco bucking a halter, Zaza, at the extreme of her terror, started to turn on herself in a wild, blind gyration, hammering on the metal with the heel of the one shoe she had on. Bellinzona grabbed the edge of the metal plate with both his hands and pulled it out from under her. Zaza jiggled desperately in space.

"You motherfuckers!" Inez cried.

She bent to pick up a rusted sickle, felt a karate chop on the back of her neck, and fell groaning to her knees, while Folco Mori, who had relaxed his hold on O'Brion just long enough to chop at her, renewed his grip. Inez started to vomit silently, her lips right down on the ground so that she didn't have to see Zaza's eyes pop out of their sockets as her body convulsed through one final spasm.

"Pietro!" Volpone ordered. "Go have yourself some fun with the nigger broad!"

Bellinzona looked sideways at Lando, who had turned pale. His fists clenched, Lando was keeping a weather eye on Italo, whose arm had sprouted a Mauser.

"Baretto," Volpone called without specifically threatening him, "go turn the saw on."

Italo's voice implied so much clear and present danger that Lando did not even flinch when Bellinzona lifted Inez to carry her, half unconscious, behind a stack of sawed wood, where he flung her on a pile of sawdust.

"Baretto!" Volpone repeated. "I told you to do something!"

Lando took a few steps and dropped down into the hole. He had to push Zaza's legs away in order to get at the switch. When he turned it on, a slight hum could be heard, and the blade of the rotary saw started to turn slowly, then faster.

Mainly so he wouldn't hear what might be going on behind him, Lando got out of the hole, picked up a large hunk of wood, and moved it to test the blade. The saw sliced through it as if it were no bigger than a matchstick.

"Bring him over," Italo said to Mori.

Folco pushed Mortimer O'Brion forward, still holding his arms behind his back.

A scream came from the pile of sawdust. Lando stood stock-still. Volpone pretended he hadn't noticed anything. Bellinzona's voice rang out, "Fuckin' bitch!" and there were the heavy thumps of blows being struck and someone fighting back violently.

"Baretto, lay him down in front of the saw, and make sure he holds still . . ."

O'Brion, now beyond terror, wanted to talk. But all he could do was make desperate signs. No sound came out of his mouth. Roughly held by Folco Mori and Lando, he was lying on the steel apron before the electric saw, his neck only four inches or so from the humming metal blade.

Volpone grabbed him by the hair, raised his head, and said, "I'm all ears."

Vomiting a long spew of bile, Mortimer, who wanted to stay alive, succeeded in overcoming his fright long enough to repeat the code words chosen by Don Genco: *"Mamma mia! Mamma mia!"*

But Italo did not grasp the fact that he had just been given half the answer he was looking for. He thought that those words, wrenched from O'Brion's gut as he approached his death agony, were a final appeal for help.

In a second, Italo's face was covered with sweat as

132

dazzling white streaks passed before his eyes. He remembered his brother after he fell from his bike, consoling him. *Don't worry! It won't hurt!* Then he thought of his wife, Angela. His tongue could almost taste her taut nipples. His brother's image rose again, alive, then dead; then he could see only the severed leg.

"Son of a bitch!" he screamed. "You bastard!"

He had completely forgotten who he was, where he was, and what he had come here to do.

When the luminous filaments stopped dancing before his eyes, Babe Volpone saw that he was still holding Mortimer O'Brion's head by the hair. He raised his stupidly staring eyes at Orlando Baretto and Folco Mori, who turned away in embarrassment. He had blood all over him.

Then he noticed that there was no longer any connection between Mortimer O'Brion's head and body. Along with the head, he had just cut himself off from the last link to two billion dollars.

Part Two

IMPASSE

9

Renata Kloppe rang for Manuella to bring her breakfast—strong coffee, chilled grapefruit juice, bacon and eggs, toast, and strawberry jam. Stifling a yawn, she got up, opened a closet, and erased one of the three chalk marks inside the closet door.

"Two to go," she said. "Two to go . . ."

"Good morning, miss. I hope you had a good night. Only two days to go," Manuella chirped.

"Good morning, Manuella," she replied. "Where's the pepper?"

"I'll go for it."

"Manuella, a thousand francs if you can answer this one right: Why am I marrying him?"

"Because you love him."

"Wrong."

"I'll bring you the pepper. Meantime, maybe you'd better take a look at your wedding menu."

"Is it here?"

"On the tray."

And Manuella burst out laughing again before going out. Renata picked up the card with the details of her wedding meal spelled out in fancy script. She could not help smiling over the subversive little masterpiece she and Kurt had so carefully prepared.

April 26, 1979
Grande Fine Champagne 1936

Coffee
Passionate Sherbet
Charlotte au chocolat
Cheeses
Saddle of Lamb with Provençal Aromatics
Striped Bass in Pastry Shell with Tomato Sauce
Pâté de foie gras
Belon Oysters
Apéritifs
Dom Pérignon 1961
Clicquot rosé 1929

Louis Philippon, the world-famous French chef who was due at the Kloppes' the next day with his entire staff, had made no comment when Renata had given him the menu. This upside down and backward meal had left the arrogant Frenchman as cold as ice.

Renata had taunted Kurt to see how far she could push him, and he had finally said no when she proposed that he dress in a bridal gown and she in a tuxedo. When she accused him of turning chicken, he got angry and he swore that he was up to it but that he was worried about the reactions of his students.

"Your pepper, miss."

"Manuella, I know! I know why I'm marrying him! I need a guy whom I can torture—morning, noon, and night."

"Yes, until the day he starts to torture you," her chambermaid answered tartly. "I've laid out your beige suit."

"Thanks, I'll be wearing the sky blue."

"Tough! That's laid out too."

It was Renata's turn to laugh. She adored Manuella and was delighted with the way the maid matched her, thrust for thrust, Renata rewarded her with last season's dresses, which infuriated Kurt.

"You treat her like a servant!" he would storm.

"Manuella! My fiancé says I'm treating you like a servant," Renata relayed.

"Well, I am a servant!" Manuella would burst out gleefully, keeping up her end of the game.

There was one thing Renata really liked about Kurt.

In bed, he was absolutely passive. She could use him as if he were some familiar object to be bent to whatever fantasy she created. In her vast experience around the world, she had gone through the gamut of macho cocksmen who knew just what they wanted; somehow, they always left her peculiarly unfulfilled. Now, having decided that she wouldn't cheat on her husband after she was married, she was sorry she had never encountered the blinding climactic lights some of her girl friends claimed to have achieved.

Were they really telling the truth?

Anyway, she had one chance left. Ranata had determined that, as a final gesture before entering conjugal life and motherhood, she would give herself a proper send-off. On the afternoon before her wedding night, she planned to go out on the street and pick up the first attractive man she saw. Perhaps those very circumstances would at last give her the fulfillment she had sought for so long.

The saw was coming back at him at regular intervals, marked by a disagreeable vibration each time it sliced off a part of one of his limbs. Italo twisted to get away from its teeth, cried out, and opened his eyes. The phone was ringing. He was bathed in perspiration and the light was flooding into his bedroom through the blinds. The night before, he had not even had the presence of mind to draw the curtains. He picked up the phone, which continued ringing in his ears; he belched into the mouthpiece, "Hold the line," got shakily out of bed, went straight to the bathroom, and there tried to piss and douse his face with cold water at the same time. What a way to wake up! He had been asleep only two hours. Before that, he had played solitaire all night, losing every game. Even his miniature roulette wheel had not been able to calm him. None of the numbers he mentally bet on had paid off. He had played the zero 108 times without its coming up, and when he finally dropped the zero for eleven, the ball, as if to plague him, went into zero three times in a row! He hadn't been able to concentrate. All he could think of was O'Brion's bloody head.

Why had he let him die so quickly, so painlessly? He

would have liked to torture the bastard for hours. By dying, O'Brion had played one last filthy trick on him. With Genco dead and O'Brion's head cut off, the thread was broken. Now the two billion bucks belonging to the Volpone and Gabelotti families could only be restored to their rightful owners by the decision of the banker.

He came back and grabbed the phone.

"Hello," he yelled into it as he stretched out on the bed.

"Italo?"

He recognized Moshe's voice and figured he was in for a lecture.

"Italo? Can you hear me?"

"You don't have to yell!"

"What about Genco? Anything new?"

"Not a thing."

"That's too bad. Listen. Things aren't going well. Gabelotti just sent for me."

"You're not going?" Italo raged. "Since when are you taking orders from that tub of lard?"

"Don't forget, we're partners."

"Tell him where he can shove it!"

"He'll want to know where we stand on Operation OUT. That's his right."

"Stall for time! I'll have it settled by noon."

"I thought I told you—"

"Dry up! I know what I have to do!"

"Italo, if Genco were alive, he'd be telling you the same thing. You won't get anywhere that way. Our only way to get out of this in one piece is to find O'Brion."

"Hold the phone," Italo gulped.

Things were moving too fast for him. He didn't dare tell Moshe that Mortimer was no longer in one piece. He needed more time to think.

He picked up the phone again. "That was a guy bringing me some aspirin. My skull's killing me."

"What am I supposed to tell Ettore about Genco? If you agree, I think I better let him in on it. If we don't, he'll find out anyway."

Italo looked at his watch. It was 9:10 A.M. In less than three hours he'd be playing his last trump with Kloppe. The problem was, he couldn't really carry out any of the threats he had made. From now, on, nothing was more precious to him than that goddamned banker's life. The most he could do was scare him shitless.

"Moshe! If you don't do what I tell you, you don't belong to the family anymore."

"Okay. You're entitled. But I still have an obligation to Genco. He didn't want any war! I'll do everything to see that his orders are carried out. For his sake, and for yours—for your own good!"

"Go fuck yourself!"

"Well, if I strike out, you can do whatever you want."

"You're full of shit!"

"Listen to me, don't go back to that bank. At least wait until I've seen Ettore. I just have to talk to him—"

Italo Volpone slammed the receiver down. If he listened further, he might be won over by the consigliere's logic. And he was firm in his decision not be swayed, even though he knew Moshe was absolutely right.

Up to now, no one, not even his brother, had been able to keep Italo from doing as he pleased. No one could start now.

He had warned Kloppe he would be back to see him at noon, and he planned to be prompt.

When Ettore Gabelotti came out of the sauna next to his bathroom, he stepped on the scale and noted that the needle went beyond the highest figure shown. Disgusted, Gabelotti looked down at his body. His stomach was distended, even though the rolls of fat didn't completely hide his powerful muscles. Years ago, when he was thirty, he had been able to pick up two guys, one in each hand, and toss them ten feet away like empty peanut bags. Today he had to leave it to his punks to do that kind of work.

Carmine Crimello and Angelo Barba, his two consiglieri, were waiting for him in the next room. He put on a white shirt, a black tie, and a dark blue suit that made him look seventy-five pounds lighter. Then he sprayed himself with toilet water.

Ettore had not been enthusiastic about the temporary alliance between his family and the Volpones, but he had given in to Moshe Yudelman's persuasion. Over a ten-year period the two dons had inflicted heavy losses on each other, and when they finally realized that their feuds were benefiting nobody but the feds, they had signed a nonaggression pact, carefully defining the spheres of control each of them would have. Still, that didn't mean they willingly pooled their resources! Ettore Gabelotti, who trusted no one, had had a feeling that Volpone would try to screw him. And now it was happening.

When the boss came in, Carmine Crimello and Angelo Barba got up as one man. With a wave of his hand Ettore indicated they could be seated. He opened the refrigerator, poured himself a beer that he laced with a finger of cognac, rolled up two slices of ham and gulped them down, and eyed his two advisers.

"No fun, is it, being pulled out of bed at 3:00 A.M.?"

Carmine and Angelo halfheartedly shook their heads to assure him that it didn't bother them.

"I'm sorry, but I couldn't get to sleep. I miss you boys when you're not here. I feel all alone. I guess you ought to be flattered, huh?"

He downed his boilermaker in one long gulp and then poured straight brandy into his beer glass.

"When I get bored, I start thinking, and thinking— Believe me, it's no picnic."

He swallowed half the cognac.

"Incidentally, anybody heard from O'Brion?"

"Should we have?" asked Crimello.

Ettore didn't answer directly. "Rico Gatto called me from Switzerland," he said. "What the hell business do you boys think Babe Volpone has in Zurich?"

He slowly swished the rest of his cognac around the bottom of the glass.

Crimello and Barba, all too familiar with the way Gabelotti could pretend not to be worried, figured all hell was about to bust loose.

"He went to the morgue," Ettore told them.

"The morgue?"

"Yes, the morgue! After all, anybody might want to go there to pay their respects."

"Who to?" Barba asked.

"A leg."

"Whose leg?" Angelo came back, exchanging a brief look with Crimello.

"If I had smart guys working for me, I'd know," Gabelotti said softly. "That fuckin' Rico Gatto couldn't even tell me. That's a gas, isn't it?"

Crimello and Barba, ill at ease, tried to laugh.

Barba decided to jump in. "Don Ettore, why not just tell us what's bothering you?"

"We been fucked!" Gabelotti yelled as he smashed his glass down on the coffee table. "And if I been fucked, its because I got nothin' but shitheads workin' for me. You boys don't even seem to see anything wrong about it. My partner's brother goes making courtesy calls to the morgue, and at the same time my mouthpiece disappears!"

"O'Brion?"

"Yes, O'Brion! If any of those fuckin' Volpones harmed a single hair on his head, I'll knock off the lot of 'em!"

Carmine Crimello cleared his throat.

"Padrone, what leads you to believe—?"

"Nothin'!" Gabelotti cut him off, furious. "My nose knows! Right now, we are being screwed, left, right, and center, and we're sitting here holding our cocks! It just so happens I haven't heard from Mortimer since he left Nassau. He hasn't been at his office His wife doesn't know where he went. And his cunt is no place around. You want I should draw you a picture? The Volpones are copping our bread!"

"Just a minute . . ." Barba tried to intercede.

Angelo Barba had the greatest respect for the don, but his five years in medical school before he went to work for the family made him think of a diagnosis for what was ailing his boss: paranoia (accompanied by delusions of persecution). "Maybe O'Brion just decided to shack up with his broad for a while?" he said.

Gabelotti eyed him viciously. "While he knows two billion bucks are at stake?"

"I think you're jumping to conclusions, *padrone,*" Carmine Crimello chimed in.

"Oh, you do, do you? Well, if they knocked Morty off, what's gonna keep them bastards from makin' off with the bread?"

"Why, you can, Don Ettore!" Angelo said indignantly. "You have the number. All you have to do is phone the bank and have the money released."

"If it's still there," grumbled Gabelotti.

"Nothing easier than checking that out."

"I just called Phil Diego," Ettore grudgingly confirmed. "He knows the banker. He's on the spot."

"At three in the morning?" Crimello said.

"In Zurich it's going on nine."

Barba was trying to find a way to tell the don, without being disrespectful, that his whole theory was bullshit. But all he found was a stopgap.

"Look, those Volpones may be anything you say, but one thing they're not is crazy! If they pulled something like that, the Commissione would give 'em all the kiss of death."

"First they'd have to find them," Gabelotti stubbornly contended.

"They're not in hiding. You just said yourself that Italo is in Switzerland."

"You're beatin' your gums for nothin'," Gabelotti thundered. "If I tell you there's been a double cross, you can believe me!"

Angelo Barba took refuge in prudent silence. There was no meeting Gabelotti head on, especially when his instinct was dictating rather than his mind. He had to be gotten around softly, little by little, without any set-to.

"And Moshe Yudelman?" Crimello querulously asked.

"Don't think I haven't covered that!" Ettore said. "He'll be here any minute now."

"How about Italo's missus?" said Carmine, as if it were a minor matter. "Is she in town?"

Gabelotti stuck a handful of crackers in his mouth and began to chew. With his mouth full, he looked at Crimello.

"You think we can make a trade with that?" he asked. "When you're playing for two billion bucks, how much is any woman worth?"

"Okay, but is she around?" Crimello insisted.

144

"Yes." Ettore sloughed off the word. "And I got two guys on her tail."

The meeting was notable for its brevity. Marjorie showed Philip Diego into Homer Kloppe's office at 9:01. At 9:04 he was out again.

Philip Diego was not yet forty, but he was one of the most promising lawyers of the younger generation. He had a staff of twenty-three in offices that overlooked the river, hard by the Rathaus, where the Parliament of the commune and the canton met. He also had an apartment in Paris, a hideaway in London, a chalet at Gstaad, an estate at Saint-Paul-de-Vence, and a packet of real estate in the Bahamas. A self-made man, he combined the virtues of charm and experience with physical fitness, a cunning mind, and the touch of thoughtful skepticism that always catches a client off guard.

Kloppe and he had met on several occasions involving international deals in which each of them, delighted with the other's efficiency, had come out with great benefit to himself and those he represented. Now, when he came into the banker's lair, Diego called on all his resources as a man of action.

"My dear friend, I am too well acquainted with the ethics of your business to expect you to be able to answer my question. However, a mere indication would be enough to reassure one of my clients, who also happens to be a client of yours. He just called from New York, and he seems very concerned. His name is Ettore Gabelotti. You know him, don't you?"

Homer Kloppe remained expressionless. All Philip Diego could do was carry on with a smile.

"For one operation—just one, but a very important one—he has pooled his interests with those of Genco Volpone. That's what's rather curious about this whole thing. Gabelotti is terrified of flying. As you can imagine, that's a great drawback when it comes to checking on his various enterprises. As far as you are concerned, he was represented by his lawyer with power of attorney, Mortimer O'Brion. Now, it so happens that his partner, Genco Volpone, has not been in touch with him for three days, nor has O'Brion. Naturally, my client is concerned.

Before giving you the instructions to transfer the funds, he felt he owed it to his partner to have me contact you. He wants to be sure that neither O'Brion nor Volpone has made any move without informing him. My question—that is, his question—therefore, is simply this: Is that sum of money still on deposit with you at the Zurich Trade Bank?"

Homer Kloppe got up out of his armchair, walked over to the bay window that was framed in light wood, looked out at the few white clouds in the pure blue sky, and said in a completely neutral voice, "What a glorious day!"

Diego hid his defeat behind a burst of laughter that was irresistible. Irresistible to anyone but Kloppe.

"At any rate," said Diego, "I'll be able to tell my client that I tried."

"It's been delightful to see you again," Homer said.

"Likewise," said Diego. "After all, Gabelotti has the account number. I'll just tell him he'll have to come over here himself."

"Good day, then, counselor," said the banker.

If Moshe Yudelman had agreed to come to see Ettore Gabelotti at 3:00 A.M., it was only to keep war from breaking out on the spot between the two families. In just a few hours the situation had become so tense that even the slightest misstep might set the powder on fire. When the don heard what Moshe had to say, there was no telling what his reaction would be.

After his phone call to Italo, Yudelman hadn't been able to make up his mind: Should he tell Gabelotti the whole truth; should he try to pacify him with blank reassurances; or should he just give him a few details without the overall picture? A quick review of the alternatives made Moshe decide on the first solution. If Gabelotti wanted to see him, the don already smelled something rotten. Moshe might as well put all the cards on the table.

That Ettore had requested the appointment at such an ungodly hour was worrisome enough. By a reflex as childish as it was useless, Moshe had asked Vittorio Pizzu to go with him. Pizzu had been a *sottocapo* in the

Volpone family for fifteen years, outranking Genco's three *capiregime:* Aldo Amalfi, Vincente Bruttore, and Joseph Dotto.

In the past, these three lieutenants had often come to grips with the Gabelotti family. They got their orders from Vittorio Pizzu and transmitted them to the soldiers, each of whom had authority over several punks. In the old days, when showdowns were frequent, Amalfi, Bruttore, and Dotto had given ample proof of their guts and their loyalty. Before acceding to his high position, Pizzu himself had not been above doing some of the dirty work, in which his natural cruelty, along with a total absence of sensitivity, made him stand out.

Just as their car came to a halt in front of Gabelotti's place, Yudelman had an idea. "Are you loaded?" he asked Vittorio.

"Always."

"Leave your rod in the car."

"Why?"

"To make me happy. We're not at war with them."

"You want to walk out of here?"

"Vittorio, don't act like a kid. If they wanted to get us, it would be easy, with or without your gun. Leave it in the glove compartment."

Pizzu shook his head. "What'd you bring me along for?"

"I want to have a witness. And I want you to back me up, if need be. But not by shooting it out."

"With Gabelotti, I never feel sure of anything. You think he'll be alone?"

"I don't know, but believe me, leave it here."

Grudgingly Pizzu slipped the Smith and Wesson 39 Parabellum out of its holster and put it into the glove compartment under some road maps.

"Some idea!" he commented. "With those faggots in there, it's like my balls was hanging out."

"Come on!"

The two men casually guarding the vestibule did not insult them by frisking them. Vittorio Pizzu felt the worse for it. But when he followed Moshe into Gabelotti's office, he was surprised to see that the don had three of his men with him: Angelo Barba and Carmine Crimello, his

147

two consiglieri, and Carlo Badaletto, who had jumped ship from the Volpones. Badaletto had once been under Pizzu's command, and Vittorio relished the thought that his onetime subordinate had to wear a denture since the time that Italo Volpone had butted his teeth out.

Seeing Yudelman and Pizzu come in, Ettore Gabelotti bowed his head by way of greeting. His bright eyes were underlined by two heavy dark pouches of fat. Yudelman immediately sensed the change in the atmosphere. Three days before, in Nassau, when the representatives of the two clans had gotten together, the climate had been almost euphoric.

"Be seated," Gabelotti said.

Yudelman and Pizzu sat on the edge of their chairs, side by side, facing the don. Ettore wasted no time. "Moshe, I called you here to ask you a few straight questions."

"I'm all ears," said Moshe.

"When Genco cabled us, the money was supposed to be transferred the next day, or at the latest the day after that, out of the Swiss bank. You've let time go by without calling to reassure me, and I expected that a friend like you would at least phone and keep me posted. That, you didn't do. Don Genco didn't either. I must say, I'm disappointed, so I have to ask you right out: Have our two billion dollars been transferred or not?"

"Not yet, Don Gabelotti."

"Why, may I ask?"

"Even if you hadn't called me, I was just about to get in touch with you, so we could discuss it."

"Why did you bring Pizzu with you?"

Moshe didn't dare point out that Gabelotti was surrounded by three of his own henchmen, so he said nothing.

"Were you afraid you wouldn't get a cordial welcome?" Gabelotti asked with pointed sarcasm.

Yudelman only smiled politely, and Badaletto snickered under Vittorio Pizzu's cold gaze.

"I can leave," Pizzu offered, looking at the assembled group.

"Don't move," said Gabelotti. "You're very welcome, Vittorio. After all, aren't we all partners in this?"

Then, without transition, turning to Moshe, he said, "I'm listening."

Moshe gathered his thoughts and clasped his hands in front of him. "There's been a slight delay."

"Why?" asked Gabelotti sympathetically.

"We have had a great tragedy." He saw Gabelotti exchange glances with Crimello and Barba. "Don Genco Volpone is no longer among the living."

The tension in the room increased, evidenced by the quality of the silence.

"That is indeed a very great tragedy," Gabelotti said after a moment. "Tell me what happened."

"Don Genco had an accident in Zurich. His leg was found on the cowcatcher of a railroad engine."

"His leg?" Ettore asked, visibly moved. "But what about him? Where is he?"

"His body hasn't been found. His brother is now in Switzerland investigating."

"How did you find out about the tragedy?"

"We were notified here, by the New York Police Department."

"You mean to say it was the cops who identified Don Genco's leg?"

"Don Genco got his shoes from Biasca's. The Swiss cops sent the shoe over to the cops here. Biasca confirmed that it was one he had made for Don Genco. Unfortunately, after that, Italo was able to identify the leg as really being his brother's."

"This makes me very unhappy, Moshe," Ettore said. "And all of my men, too. Don Genco was a wise man, *un uomo di rispetto*. In the name of all my people, of all my family, I express our deepest and most heartfelt sympathy. When will the burial take place?"

"I guess Italo won't make any decision about that until the rest of Genco's body is found."

"If anyone told me three days ago that such a thing could happen, I wouldn't have believed it," Gabelotti assured him. "Just what did Don Genco die of, anyway?"

Yudelman, not the least bit taken in by Ettore's sympathetic manner, wondered for the merest fraction of a second whether he should go any further.

Gabelotti caught his hesitation. "Go on, Moshe, you

can talk. We're all friends here. Death is waiting for all of us, and we have to help each other whenever we can."

"Don Ettore, for the time being, nobody knows anything much more about this whole sad business."

"What do you mean, Moshe?"

"In spite of the family tragedy, and before he even started to investigate, Italo took steps to protect our mutual interests."

"In what way?"

"He went to the bank where the money had been deposited for the transfer, as we had agreed."

Gabelotti suddenly looked upset. "Italo? What business was it of his? Did someone authorize him to handle my affairs without consulting me?"

"Not at all," Yudelman interrupted. "No, Don Ettore! Italo just wanted to be helpful, so we would not have any loss of time."

"Excuse me, Moshe, but I don't follow you. Did someone ask Italo to step in and be helpful to us? If so, how was he helpful? And who was it that asked him?"

Despite the uneasiness he was beginning to feel, Vittorio Pizzu was doing his best to remain calm. The interrogation was turning sour. If Moshe hadn't forced him to leave his gun in the car, they might have a chance to get out of this hornet's nest alive. Discreetly Vittorio's index finger rubbed against his right thumb, as if it were on an imaginary trigger. Embarrassed, Yudelman cleared his throat.

"Italo was very shook up by his brother's death. I grant that he may have acted hastily, in the shock of the moment, but all he was trying to do was what his brother would have done in his place: get the transfer over with as quickly as possible."

"Did he go to the bank with that in mind?"

"Yes, Don Ettore. To try to move the operation along."

"Without anyone having instructed him to?"

"He must have thought that . . ."

"Thought what?"

Yudelman had a hard time swallowing his saliva. "That inasmuch as Genco was dead, it was up to him temporarily to act as capo of the family."

"And did he inform you, as consigliere of the Volpones, of what he was going to do?"

"He only told me about it after he had done it."

"In what capacity did he go to the bank?"

"As Don Genco's brother and heir."

"And was that enough for the Swiss banker to execute the transfer?"

"No, Don Ettore. He refused."

In the heavy silence that ensued, Gabelotti poured himself a glassful of cognac without offering it to anyone else. He rotated the glass slowly in his fingers, gazing off into the distance. Gabelotti downed the cognac without taking a breath, unthinkingly wiped his lips with the back of his hand, and brought his eyes around to where they were looking directly into Yudelman's. He kept them there for several seconds without saying a word.

"There's one thing that bothers me," he finally uttered in a dreamlike voice. "How could Italo, who was never anything but his brother's brother, and who never represented anything other than himself, have taken it on himself to speak for me? Even sorrow can't explain everything . . ."

"Don Ettore, I may as well tell you the whole thing. Italo thinks someone may have done Don Genco in."

"Done him in? You can't mean it. Who could possibly have had anything against so highly respected a man? He didn't have an enemy in this this world."

"I don't know," Yudelman said lamely.

"Well, you see yourself that it doesn't make sense. But I am grateful to you for filling me in. After all, you are the one who brought about the partnership between our two families, although that doesn't make you responsible for what your padrone's brother may do on the spur of the moment. Incidentally, are you aware that I haven't heard a word from Mortimer O"Brion?"

"No, I wasn't aware of it," Moshe said in a tone that he hoped would reveal no reaction.

"It's a real bother," Gabelotti went on. "As you know, my consigliere was the one who had the number for our account. Have you heard anything about him at all?"

"Me?" Yudelman croaked.

"Yes, you—or Italo?"

"How would I?"

"Yes, of course, you must excuse me. I'm really just thinking out loud, you understand? First you tell me that Don Genco has been murdered, then that his brother has been acting on his own, and along with that my O'Brion seems to have disappeared. What do you make of it, Moshe?"

"I think it's all very puzzling."

"Ah, you see! Well, so do I!"

Moshe was twisting around in his seat, holding back the words that were trying to cross his lips. Should he point out to Gabelotti that O'Brion was the only man in the word who could profit from Genco's disappearance?

"Were you going to say something?" Gabelotti asked.

"No, nothing."

Yet he was dying to talk. If anyone had really helped Zu Genco Volpone come to his sad end, it could only be Morty O'Brion. But how to word that? How could you tell a don that his own trusted counselor tried to double-cross him?

"Go on, Moshe, say what's on your mind. It's the only way we can get things out in the open."

"Well," he began, "considering the size of the transfer, I wonder whether it is just a coincidence."

"What coincidence?"

"That of the three people who can unlock the account, one has died and another has disappeared."

Having spoken, Moshe lowered his eyes and stared at his nails.

Gabelotti shook his head in agreement. "Moshe, you're absolutely right. But tell me. If you were in my shoes, wouldn't you be concerned? I'm the third one of those people. I hope nothing's going to happen to me!"

Carlo Badaletto emitted a mocking laugh. Ettore pretended not to notice.

"Well, Moshe," Gabelotti demanded, "what do you think?"

Yudelman was struck by the possibility that Gabelotti was putting on a show for his crowd, after having himself double-crossed the Volpone family. When Italo suggested that might be the case, had Moshe been wrong in laughing it off? It had seemed out of the questions, but now, as Gabelotti played this cat-and-mouse game, alternating the soft approach with hard sarcasm, Moshe began to appraise his chances of getting out alive, and they seemed minute. With nothing to lose, he might as well go whole hog.

"It was a great misfortune, Don Ettore, that you weren't able to go to Zurich with Don Genco."

"You know very well that I can't fly," Gabelotti replied.

"Yes, I know, Don Ettore, I know. But if he could have had you at his side, Don Genco might still be among us."

"What do you mean by that, Moshe?"

"There would have been the two capi, and no one else."

"Are you trying to say that Mortimer O'Brion didn't do his job right?"

"No, no, Don Ettore! No one faults the competence of your consigliere."

"Then what?"

"Mortimer has always been impeccably moral. But he's only human, after all. He has his weak points, too . . ."

Gabelotti looked at him with feigned surprise and said slowly, "Do you think Mortimer might have double-crossed his *padrone?*"

"I didn't say that!" Yudelman protested. "How could I make such an accusation when I haven't the slightest proof? No. I was only trying to consider every possibility."

Ignoring Pizzu, Ettore looked in turn at his three men: Angelo Barba, Carmine Crimello, and Carlo Badaletto.

"If that were the case, how would you judge the situation?" he said to Moshe.

"I wouldn't, Don Ettore. I wouldn't presume to pass a judgment."

"Come on, Moshe, don't hold back. Let's suppose, say, Mortimer went crazy—because you'll agree with me he'd have to be crazy to try to do anything so impossible! Never mind. Let's suppose he decided he wanted to grab the money . . ." He looked up at Yudelman, extending his chin in a silent question, to make sure Moshe was taking in everything he said.

"Yes, we might suppose he did," Moshe conceded.

"Good. Then how would you imagine he had gone about it? Would O'Brion actually have committed murder to get his hands on our deposit?"

Yudelman remained absolutely motionless.

"You can talk. We're just speculating." Ettore smiled at him. "Could that be possible?"

"It's a possibility," Yudelman prudently admitted.

"Okay, then. At least you don't beat around the bush, Moshe. So, let's say Mortimer had Don Genco rubbed out, grabbed the Syndicate's money from the bank, and disappeared. Is that the picture?"

Yudelman spread his hands to indicate an open mind. "I don't know that any of that happened, Don Ettore, it's just what you're supposing."

Gabelotti jumped out of his seat and his chair whirled back toward the other side of the room.

"What do you take us for? Shitheads?"

Vittorio Pizzu, motionless under the stare of Gabelotti's men, was careful to leave his two hands in clear view on the tabletop, making no gesture that might be thought suspicious.

Speechless, Moshe moved his lips in vain. "Don Ettore, I don't understand," he finally said.

"Well, I'll make you understand!" Gabelotti yelled, his face livid, and he grabbed Yudelman by the shoulders and shook him like a reed. "If Genco is really dead, his fucking brother is the one who offed him. And he knocked O'Brion off, too. He tortured him to get him to reveal the account number. And he's such a fuckin' idiot he thinks he can pin the job on my consigliere! Well, you listen to me! If things did happen the way I just said, your Italo won't last two days more. And he won't be the only one! I can promise you, you'll all get what you've got coming to you, you and the whole Volpone family: men, women, and children!"

Yudelman blanched. The don's interpretation of what happened left him speechless. He was looking wildly at Gabelotti with great round disbelieving eyes. He felt Pizzu tug discreetly at his sleeve.

"Come on, Moshe, let's go," Pizzu said.

Yudelman got up, weak in the knees. Everyone around the table did the same.

The veins in his neck swollen with anger, his fists clenched, Gabelotti spat a final imprecation at him. "You can tell that motherfucker Italo that I know every step he takes. Everything! If he so much as lifts a little finger, I'll have him shot down like a dog. From now on, I'm taking over. And you—be back here in three hours. Now, get the hell out."

When they were in the car, the first thing Vittorio Pizzu did was to get his rod out of the glove compartment.

"I'll move heaven and earth to keep a war from breaking out," Moshe said in a quavering voice, "but Italo's gone crazy, and Gabelotti's crazy, too!"

Pizzu crossed himself. "First you better tell Italo that Gabelotti has a torpedo on his tail in Zurich," he said.

Moshe sighed. From here on in, although he was not ordinarily given to extreme pessimism, all he could anticipate was the worst.

10

After Philip Diego left his office, Homer Kloppe
did something unusual. In spite of the early hour, he took
out his bottle of Waterman's ink, poured himself a glassful, and downed it. Now that he knew there was a third
man, Gabelotti, who had the number of the account, he
finally had all the pieces of the puzzle. He felt in his
bones that the day would not go by without either O'Brion
or Gabelotti getting in touch with him.

In spite of Italo Volpone's accusations, Kloppe
could not imagine O'Brion having someone murdered in
order to be able to embezzle the funds, especially since
Gabelotti, his immediate boss, was no doubt highly placed
in the mob. In case of betrayal, justice would be quickly
dispensed without benefit of trial.

Kloppe had not played his hand with total honesty
when he refused to make the transfer for O'Brion without a signature. If he had followed the letter rather than
the spirit of his profession, he would have released the
money on the spot. But just as priests, in extremely serious cases, may take certain liberties with the secrecy of
the confessional, so bankers, in their souls and con-
sciences, feel they can twist the rules to suit the occasion,
when the customer's own best interests are involved.

Kloppe pressed a button. Across from him a wall
panel swung around, and in its place appeared a
closed-circuit television screen that could be tuned to different areas of the bank. He switched to the main lobby

and spotted the three men he had hired to keep Italo Volpone out of the building. It was now 9:30. If that madman came back as he had threatened, it wouldn't be until noon. The guards Homer hired came from the same agency he usually employed to transport cash. They all had licenses to carry sidearms. In case of trouble, Volpone would have no advantage.

Kloppe rang for Marjorie.

"Yes, sir?"

"I'm going to the dentist's. I do have a ten-o'clock appointment, don't I?"

Marjorie consulted a notebook on her desk.

"Yes, sir."

"I'll be back before noon. It's just a routine check-up."

"Very well, sir. May I remind you that you speak at the Grossmünster at three o'clock?"

"Thanks, I'm aware of it."

Homer was scheduled to give an hour's talk before a privileged group of elders who would have as their guests the members of the various synods' delegations. It would be in the very cathedral in which Zwingli, on New Year's Day of 1519, had begun to preach the Reformation.

He was just about to leave when Marjorie called him back.

"Sir, a telex for you . . ."

"I'll be late, Marjorie. I'll see it when I come back."

"It's from the U.S. About IMC . . ."

"Let me see it!"

It read: EIGHTH ACCIDENT IN LONDON STOP STEERING COLUMN BROKEN STOP AWAIT INSTRUCTIONS STOP MELVIN BOST.

Visibly shaken, he noted Marjorie's eyes on his face.

"Well, what are you waiting for?" he snapped. "Go on back to your office."

Hurt, she hurried out. Kloppe thought back to his meeting with Melvin Bost three days before.

"Are you sure these accidents are not just pure coincidence?"

"Seven accidents for the same reasons can't be coincidence . . ."

Well, now it had happened! A hundred and fifty million dollars to recall and change all the questionable parts on the Beauty Ghost P9s. It could break the Zurich Trade Bank as well as the entire automobile company. But maybe it was just a run of bad luck.

Horribly disturbed, Homer decided to give himself three days before replying. After Renata was married, his mind would be clearer. He rang for Marjorie.

"Sir?"

"I'm on my way. Please let the dentist know that I may be a few minutes late."

Dr. August Strolh had a heavy schedule. And he was the last person in the world Homer Kloppe would want to keep waiting.

Inez lay in bed, her eyes fixed on the ceiling. She had been awake all night, turning an awful truth over and over in her mind: she had been raped!

Two or three generations before, in her native Burundi, it was the custom for nubile young girls to be deflowered by the old women, who broke their hymens with a wooden wand. In their wisdom, the Africans had known that, subconsciously, a girl never forgives the first man who takes her.

Inez, who had known many men, had never been forced to have sex against her will. She swore the pig who had dared violate her so crudely would pay for his pleasure with his life. Nothing less could wipe from her mind the vision of that repulsive face whose lips greedily went after hers while his vulgar hands forced their way between her thighs. After she put up a brief resistance with scratches and bites, he had knocked her out with a karate chop and bulled his way into her half-unconscious body with the brutality of an animal.

She looked over toward Lando, who was sitting in an armchair, and she met his vigilant eyes and turned hers away, her face a mask of sullen indifference. She got up, covering herself with a blanket, and went through the ritual morning movements: squeezing grapefruit juice, putting the kettle on, and laying out a cup—just one—on a tray.

"I'll have some, too," Lando said as he stretched.

Ignoring him, she went into the bathroom and locked

the door. She was as disgusted with Orlando Baretto as she had been by Pietro Bellinzona.

Lando drank the grapefruit juice, rubbed the back of his hand over his unshaven cheeks, and wondered how he ought to behave. He knew that this girl of his was not one to push around. What good would it do to tell her that if he had tried to interfere, Italo Volpone would never have let either of them out of the sawmill alive.

He could still see Italo Volpone, white as a sheet, his clothes soiled with blood, holding Mortimer O'Brion's sawed-off head in his hands while the lawyer's body twitched on the table before falling to the ground, where it took several seconds to stop moving. At that moment Lando knew that Volpone was capable of being enraged enough to take leave of his senses.

He had seemed like a man coming out of a nightmare when Folco Mori took the head out of his hands.

It had taken them about three-quarters of an hour to bury the blonde and O'Brion, separately, with O'Brion's head being held back for special treatment. On some strange whim of Italo's, it had been buried by itself in a deep hole that Lando himself had dug before Inez's wildly staring eyes.

Lando had noticed that Pietro Bellinzona's fly had not been properly closed after his escapade with Inez, and he had resented the fact that the big gorilla had had the use of his girl without having to pay for it. What had followed was even less enjoyable. Volpone had savagely slapped Inez and threatened her in a sugar-sweet voice: from now on, she would have to carry out his orders, whatever they might be, without hesitation or complaint. He had asked her several questions about Homer Kloppe: how he spent his time, what his habits were, what about his sex fantasies. Inez had answered mechanically, revealing details Lando could never have imagined.

Lando turned the gas off under the water that was beginning to boil over. Inez reappeared in slacks and a turtleneck. Seen from the rear, she was as nimble and masculine looking as a basketball pro. Pretending not to notice that he had finished her juice, she squeezed another glassful for herself.

"You gonna give me this silent treatment for long?" Lando asked. "I said something to you."

She poured her coffee and added a lump of sugar that she crushed with a spoon that had once belonged to the Hôtel du Rhône. Just as the cup was about to meet her lips, Lando sent it flying with a swipe of the back of his hand. Despite the embarrassment he felt in her presence, he wasn't about to let her forget he still owned her. She took a sponge from the sink and got down on her hands and knees to wipe up the spot on the rug. Suddenly enraged, Lando grabbed her by the shoulders and forced her to her feet.

"You want me to beat the shit out of you?"

She looked at him. He had no way of telling whether her look was one of contempt or indifference, and she simply muttered, "Bug off."

He snorted. "You oughta thank me for the fact you're still alive, instead of carrying on like this. If my friends didn't rub you out, it's only because of me. You know who Volpone is? Did you ever hear of the Syndicate? Well, that's who I work for. They can smash me like a gnat!"

"That's what you are—a gnat." But she spoke atonally, without aggressiveness.

"If you don't do exactly what you're told, I won't be able to protect you. They can do anything, and they know everything. What are you complaining about? Because that fat slob put it to you a little? So what? You're no fuckin' virgin, are you? You really ought a be kissing my hands for having kept Volpone from offing you the way he wanted to. No witnesses, he said. From now on, you got no choice. You gotta go along with us until they get what they want. And then forget everything you saw and heard."

"I've already forgotten," she said.

"You're not out of the woods yet by a long shot," Lando spat at her furiously. "You know what you have to do this afternoon if they tell you to?"

"Yes."

"You gonna do it?"

"Yes."

"Well, okay, then."

He moved toward her as if to hug her, but she pushed him away. "Don't come near me!"

"What?"

"I'll do whatever I'm told, but I won't let you come near me."

"Okay, okay," he snickered. "Okay already. Just as long as you do as you're told. I got to be going. You're a goner if you try to call the cops. And that goes for trying to get out of town too. First of all, you're being watched. And it wouldn't take them twenty-four hours to catch up with you and slice you into little pieces. Or splatter your pretty face with acid. Don't forget you were a witness and an accomplice in a double murder. You're the one who dug the grave for Zaza. Understand?"

"Yes."

"*Ciao.*"

He had scarcely shut the door when she walked over and pasted her ear against it. She heard his steps fade on the stairs. She double-locked the bolt, went to the phone, and dialed the international code, then an area code and phone number in the United States.

Her little brother Rocky was seven foot two and weighed 290 pounds stripped. Before becoming one of the East Coast's top basketball pros, he had been college decathlon champ, and he had won the Golden Gloves in the heavyweight category. Without even trying. Like Inez's other seven brothers, Rocky was extremely lazy. However, in that family, one was more gifted than the other. And not only in athletics. Rocky was able to figure out the key to any kind of situation in a trice, no matter how complicated it might be. If there was one person in the world who could avenge her and get her out of the hornet's nest into which that dirty pimp of a Lando had gotten her, it was Rocky.

"Rocky?" she said. "Is that you? It's Inez."

Captain Kirkpatrick was thoroughly disgusted.

"How can you drink that stuff so early in the morning?"

"Your health!" Scott Dempsey saluted with an amused smile.

He dipped his lips into the glass of Coke while Kirkpatrick downed his whiskey.

A small, jovial man, Dempsey was a member of the

Securities and Exchange Commission, capable of sowing terror among the toughest wheeler-dealers of the Syndicate. He would stalk suspicious characters with infinite patience, waiting for the slightest slip, and his victims might well find themselves saddled with heavy fines or put behind bars for years.

"Well?" Kirkpatrick asked him greedily.

"You had it figured right. The dough slipped out right under our noses."

"Have you got anything on them?"

"I might, with your help. Provided they screw up the least bit in Zurich. Is there anything new?"

"Not yet. I have two men over there tailing Volpone."

"I've checked out the investment accounts of all their foreign subsidiaries, their annual reports, and their audits. Believe me, that Yudelman is a sharp operator. Tops!"

Kirkpatrick and Scott Dempsey had been working together for the past decade, and the collaboration had been good for both their careers. The captain kept Dempsey informed of the movements of important members of the Syndicate, and the SEC man kept Kirkpatrick abreast of the mob's complicated financial structures.

"If my men report that Italo Volpone went to call on any of the banks, will that do?"

"Sorry, no. He could always say he just went in to use the crapper."

"What about the bankers?"

"Swiss bankers are tighter than clams. Even the new agreements we have with them haven't made them talk. It's not that they refuse to cooperate, but they stall around, and they insist on our showing them proofs. It's a vicious circle. Without proof, we can't get them to testify. And without them, how the hell can we get the proof?"

"One hell of a mess," Kirkpatrick agreed angrily. "All the loot from narcotics, prostitution, loan-sharking, and gunrunning gets processed through Geneva or Zurich."

"Oh, if they didn't have Switzerland, they'd find another place," said Dempsey. "It used to be Lebanon; and there's always Bermuda, Cyprus, Costa Rica, Monaco, Panama, and the New Hebrides. When Hong Kong gets taken over by the Reds, they'll be able to carry on in the Caymans, Liberia, the Dutch West Indies, Campione d'Italia, Jordan, Nauru—who knows where else."

"What about Volpone?"

"A major part of the income is claimed under the heading of an American corporation, Electrical Ltd. The sums appear very legitimately among its assets. At least on the face of it."

"But you know it's a front," Kirkpatrick said. "Why can't you collar them?"

"Take it easy, old man! Moshe Yudelman knows the regulations better than we do! All of Electrical Ltd.'s dough goes into documenting the operations of supposed export-import firms; and all the deals are strictly kosher on paper, even if the export and import of goods never takes place."

"Jesus," Kirkpatrick groaned. "It's gettin' so you can't be a cop without a degree in higher mathematics, law, and economics, to say nothing of all the languages they work in. Okay, go on," he said. "What do you mean the export and import never takes place?"

"I mean they don't export or import a thing. The whole business is merely a paper operation. Let's say you contract to buy a thousand tons of wheat. Naturally, they don't deliver it to you in bushel baskets. The fact is, you never see it at all, even though the legal papers covering the transaction with foreign companies list the name of the carrier, the port of departure, destination, and the quantity and description of the product allegedly transported. In reality, there is no wheat. The loading and unloading of the cargo took place theoretically in free ports in countries whose authorities don't have to give any information to our investigators. Millions of pounds of coffee, sugar, or grain keep moving around the world—without anyone ever seeing one ounce of it. You get my drift?"

"No. Maybe those tons and pounds are imaginary, but the money involved has to go someplace, doesn't it?"

"Right. It's written off as a loss."

"What kind of loss?"

"Oh, on the Stock Market or the Commodity Exchange. It takes a little doing, of course, but for the hundreds of millions of bucks involved, it's worth going to a little trouble to arrange losses like that."

"Are you trying to make me feel like a dumb cop?"

"Look, the Syndicate deals a lot in futures. They buy the same amount of the commodity they already sold short—that is, without actually having had it—when the price was low so it worked in their favor."

"Come on, Dempsey, spell it out a little better."

"Okay. Volpone controls several legal gambling casinos out West. And he's not the only one who does, incidentally. Let's say the take from his other illegal operations is a billion dollars. He can't turn up with that much money at his disposal, so he makes as if that unexplained billion was taken in at the casinos. Meantime, he invests it in one of those export-import companies I was talking about. It so happens that the companies in question, by way of interlocking directorates, are actually other fronts for the Volpone family. So all he has to do now is make their commodities speculations so disastrous that he loses the whole billion. That way, there's no profit to pay any taxes on and nothing to explain."

"Yeah, but what happens to the goddamn billion bucks during that time?"

"It ends up with other foreign export-import companies that also belong to him. But as far as the American government is concerned, it has disappeared."

"And your outfit holds still for all that?"

"We have no choice," the SEC man said. "Volpone's legal gambling enterprises can prove that they invested their profits in joint ventures with an American corporation. To make it look better, the export-import company, which has also been speculating on the commodity futures prices, has advised in its market reports—"

"The same company puts out the reports?"

"Sure. Otherwise, how could it advise investors to expect big profits from speculating in those commodities?"

"Some days, brother, I dream of the days when I was a simple flatfoot back pounding the pavement. Just a big dumb mick. It was easier. Then what happens?"

"Child's play. The import-export firm is in the clear because it can prove that it also speculated on the commodities it recommended and that it took those huge losses. That proves its good faith. Even though the casino investors lost their shirts. In fact, the firm itself may have lost a lot more than the investors. So everything is clear and logical."

Kirkpatrick poured himself another glass of whiskey, dipped a finger in it to dab on his temples, and downed the rest.

"Look, take pity on a mentally underdeveloped cop. You eggheads always think that ordinary people can keep up with you. I told you about a chopped-off leg, Volpone being in Switzerland, and like that. That stuff's easy to understand. How about your telling me in words of one syllable—what the fuck was Genco Volpone doing in Switzerland?"

"He was transferring funds. He had to launder the dirty money so there wouldn't be any SEC investigation. And how does he do that? By diversifying abroad, finding tax shelters, and keeping all his money available there through foreign corporations we can't touch. Why Switzerland? Because it's a banking paradise where you can find competent, discreet men to manage your holdings at a tax on capital gains of only 8½ percent instead of 33!"

"But if Genco Volpone did transfer that money, we have no proof it's going to stay in Switzerland."

"No, we don't. How could we? What we do know is that when it comes back here it'll be through some apparently legitimate economic channel, in broad daylight, and neither your nor I will be able to find anything wrong with it."

"But why does Volpone have to knock himself out going through all that gambling-casino business, instead of just chartering a plane to fly his loot out?"

"That would be too risky. If he were caught exporting securities bought with unaccounted-for money, he'd be headed for the slammer, no two ways about it. To say nothing of the 100 percent and more outright loss. After paying the fines involved, he wouldn't be able to afford a stick of chewing gum. But that gambling-casino/export-import/nonexistent-commodities circuit is foolproof. Nobody can check it out. The price quotations depend on complicated political developments that bring about all

165

sorts of huge rises and drops. In two years, the price of coffee has gone up 500 percent. To take a good loss on that, all a foreign company would have had to do was to sell at the price two years ago and have to buy now to cover the obligation. No problem in that when both the buyer and the seller belong to the same conglomerate. Now, do you get it?"

A plainclothesman came into the office and handed Kirkpatrick a telex. The captain looked at it casually, then read it a second time. Scott Dempsey watched the blood drain from his friend's freckled cheeks.

"Trouble?"

Without answering, the policeman ran his hand through his hair and then handed the message to Dempsey. It read: "CAPTAIN KIRKPATRICK NYPD NEW YORK PLEASE IMMEDIATELY CONTACT LIEUTENANT BLESH ZURICH CANTONAL POLICE RE DEATH OF DETECTIVE DAVID CAVANAUGH STOP"

"One of your two guys?" Scott Dempsey asked.

"Yeah," Kirkpatrick answered as he picked up his phone. "The younger one. He had a wife and three kids."

There were two places in Zurich where Homer Kloppe felt really at home: his own office and that of Dr. August Strolh.

Herr Professor Strolh, as he was known, was fifty-two, rather portly, and imbued with a boundless fascination for everything connected with teeth and dentistry. Twice a year he made trips to the United States to bone up on the latest techniques. His wife was a delightful young brunette, also a dentist. She had the deepest professional admiration for her husband, who was easily old enough to be her father. The fact was, he had been Ingrid's professor before he became her husband. Neither six years of marriage nor the birth of their two little boys had in any way dimmed the esteem and passion they felt for each other. Their work together was so expert that they had become very selective about what patients they took on. Throughout Zurich, everybody who was anybody wanted it known that the jaws they wore were "by Strolh."

August often told Homer Kloppe that he had gone

into the wrong profession. The banker evinced such interest in the research and practice of prosthesis that the dentist assured him, "You would have made a wonderful stomatologist." On other occasions, he would congratulate Homer on the perfect state of his teeth, saying, "If all my patients had teeth like yours, I'd soon be out of business."

The office was done in lavender and black, in a harmony that prompted relaxation. And the minute a patient sat down in the leather dental chair, the spotlights went on and Ingrid Strolh spoke softly: "Just relax now, just relax completely." The only possible thing for a patient to do was to open his mouth and let August Strolh's expert hands massage his gums, while Vivaldi was playing somewhere in the background.

"How are you feeling?" Dr. Strolh asked Kloppe.

"Fine, just fine," the banker said with an expression that bespoke the exact opposite.

When Ingrid came in, Homer was struck once again by how pretty she was, by the long lithe line of her body under her white surgical smock. Had she been six inches taller and had black skin, she would have reminded him of Inez. August noticed how he looked at her. Far from taking offense, he felt proud, delighted to have his excellent taste confirmed by the admiration every one of his male patients openly showed for his wife.

"Just relax, Mr. Kloppe, relax completely," Ingrid said.

Homer opened his mouth. The two doctors looked inside.

"Look, darling," August was saying. "Have there ever been more magnificent teeth?"

"Don't forget I'm due for my monthly prophylaxis tomorrow," Homer said.

Just above his head, on the material of the smock, he could make out the tiny bulge of Ingrid's nipples.

"Just relax," she was saying. "Let yourself go . . ."

Without saying a word to Pietro Bellinzona, Italo Volpone slammed the door of the Ford and bounded up the three steps leading into the bank. It was exactly noon.

He had spent the morning getting organized. If by any misguided inspiration Homer Kloppe decided not to obey his ultimatum, Italo had prepared a series of artfully planned reprisals, each tougher than the previous one. Orlando Baretto, Pietro Bellinzona, and Folco Mori knew just what they had to do.

Volpone's heels rang on the marble floor of the main banking hall. He veered to the left, passing employees and customers who paid no attention to him. Today he didn't have to ask anyone for directions to Kloppe's office on the third floor. He got to the rear of the main area, where there was a door leading to the upper stories; behind it, in the hallway, were the elevators, and just as he was about to go through the door, he felt a discreet tug at his sleeve.

"May I help you, sir?"

He pushed the intruder away and went on. The stranger took two quick steps and then courteously but firmly blocked Volpone's access to the corridor.

"I'm sorry, sir, but this part of the building is off limits."

Volpone gave him a murderous look. "I have an appointment with Kloppe."

"In that case, sir, please follow me. I will have you announced."

Italo grabbed the other man's arm and felt the hard ball of solid muscle. The guy didn't budge an inch.

"You gonna get out of my way, or do I have to bust your head in?" Volpone snarled.

"Please, sir. Let's not make any fuss here."

Suddenly two other huskies appeared. "Having trouble?" one of them asked.

With a gesture that to anyone but Volpone might have seemed casual, the man put his hand on Italo's shoulder. It was enough for Italo to know the nature of the man's job and that he weighed well over two hundred pounds.

"I'm telling you, Kloppe expects me."

"Why, certainly, sir. We'll let him know you're here," the guard said.

"Watch out, don't wrinkle the gentleman's clothes," the third one cut in.

As if to smooth Volpone's jacket, he frisked him quickly, front, back, and sideways, just the way airport inspectors do before letting certain passengers board a flight. Italo was not carrying a weapon.

"Would you please give me your name, sir?"

Italo had no chance of breaking through their line. He made a mental note that the banker would pay extra for this additional insult. Babe Volpone might have tolerated being shot at, if the occasion arose, but the idea of being pushed around by strong-arm men was more than he could bear.

"My card," he said.

His left hand went into his inside coat pocket. The man holding his arm let go. Italo's right hand flew out toward the man's underbelly. Through the material of his pants, Italo could feel the mass of his genitals, and he grabbed at them and squeezed the man's testicles as hard as he could, twisting savagely while he did. In the same fraction of a second, his left knee flew up and caught the second guy smack on his penis. The third one miraculously evaded Italo's other hand, which was flying like an arrow, two forked fingers extended, toward his eyes. When Volpone recovered from that hand having met no target, he found himself staring into the muzzle of a big-caliber Mauser.

On the floor, the first two guards were twisting and turning, their hands grabbing at their painful scrota. Panting, his heart beating hard, Volpone glared at the one who had him covered.

"Shoot, you fucker! Go on, shoot! What the hell you waiting for? I dare you!"

"Get out," the man ordered him. "Now!"

Homer Kloppe had clearly told them he did not want any fuss made inside the bank. "If this gentleman appears," he had said, "just throw a scare into him and get him to leave."

The guard looked down at his two sidekicks and leaned back against the elevator door. Italo saw the one he had kneed get up on all fours, shake his head like a groggy boxer trying to come to, and slowly rise by holding onto the wall. Then he took out a Mauser and aimed it at Volpone.

"That hurts, doesn't it, soft-balls?" Italo jeered at him.

The guard on the ground vomited. Italo turned and

walked out of the bank, his head high. Apparently not a soul in the crowded establishment had been aware of the altercation. He looked at his watch: it was 12:06. His ultimatum had been ignored. The war was on.

11

Lieutenant Fritz Blesh owed his brilliant rise in the cantonal police force to his typically Swiss qualities: flexiablity, efficiency, stubbornness, and sense of duty.

In any given twenty-four hours, as many violent or bizarre happenings took place in Zurich as in any of the great European capitals, but with this difference: a stranger always had the impression that nothing unusual was going on.

Zurich police did not wield nightsticks. Its students and workers did not demonstrate in the streets. And when two cars bumped into each other, their drivers got out, apologized to one another, and then had a drink together while the wreckers towed their vehicles away. The army, made up of citizen volunteers, was not infiltrated by any kind of subversive group, and the New Left comprised only a few overheated intellectuals who at night went quietly back to their well-appointed apartments.

That was just where the skill of the police came in: Within the limits of decency, everything was tolerated, provided it did not offend the public order. Swindlers were quietly escorted across the border, would-be murderers were discreetly disposed of, and jealous husbands had the good taste to commit their crimes of passion in places like Hamburg, London, Rome, or Paris. In Switzerland, everybody loved everybody—in four languages. Since all the basic needs had long since been within everyone's means,

171

the superfluous alone now seemed indispensable. Every day, the borders opened to flocks of foreigners coming in to deposit their currencies. And the banks showed no prejudice, treating everyone alike.

Obviously, the local authorities didn't like foreign nationals to come into the Confederation to settle their personal quarrels. Fritz Blesh was there to see to that. On the pretext of wanting to discover the secret numbered accounts of the Mafia, American police agents had, it seemed, made a breach in the Helvetic system. In cases of large-scale underworld activities, it was agreed that they could ask for certain specific information, but this was by no means an open license to lead their own investigations on Swiss soil. Appropriate authorities had to be notified.

Fritz Blesh had been quick to comprehend the relationship between the severed leg in the local morgue and the American detective who had fallen out of his window at Sordi's Hotel three days later. It did not take much investigating to find out that another American citizen, Patrick Mahoney, who had come in on the same plane, had also disappeared from the same hotel without paying his bill. The management was holding his valise. His rented car was never found. And a routine check further revealed that Mahoney, like Cavanaugh, was one of the regulars on Captain Kirkpatrick's antirackets squad in the New York City Police Department. Blesh deduced that there was something afoot. American detectives were bypassing him in his own bailiwick, and he didn't care for this one little bit.

When Blesh was informed that Captain Kirkpatrick was on the line from New York, he wondered whether his American colleague was ready to come clean. The captain was courteous enough to start by asking whether Fritz spoke English. Yes, he did.

"How did it happen, lieutenant?" asked Kirkpatrick.

"All we have been able to determine so far is that it was an accident."

"Do you believe that?"

"Until I have evidence to the contrary, I have to. At any rate, please accept my condolences."

"Thank you."

172

"Perhaps you can help me, captain. Was David Cavanaugh here in Zurich on official business?"

"Yes. Just a routine matter."

"May I ask you to be more specific?"

"Surveillance."

"Ah. May I ask whom he was surveilling?"

"An Italian-American who we think is a big cog in the Syndicate."

"His name?"

"Look, lieutenant—David Cavanaugh left a wife and three children. I've broken the news to her. It was awful. Could you take care of having his body shipped home?"

"As soon as the autopsy is completed, captain."

"When will that be?"

"I'll have the coroner's report tonight. I'll see to all the rest."

"Thank you so much."

"Captain . . ."

"Yes?"

"Did you have only one man here in Zurich?"

Kirkpatrick hesitated only the briefest second. "No, two."

"Detective Mahoney?"

"That's right."

"Has he returned to New York?"

"I beg your pardon?"

"I asked, is Patrick Mahoney back in New York?"

"I don't believe so. I really don't know where he is."

"Well, I don't either, captain. Your man has disappeared."

"How did you find that out?"

"He left his hotel without paying the bill," Fritz Blesh said in a voice of righteous condemnation.

In Switzerland, that is just not done.

Once out of the bank, Italo Volpone hopped into the Ford and barked at Pietro Bellinzona, "Take off!"

Italo was bubbling over with thoughts of revenge. Once he had his hands on his money, he'd settle that banker's cookies. Not right away, though. He'd give him a little time to forget, to think it was all in the past, that he could go on enjoying life. And the day when he least expected it, he'd get a bullet in his skull, or his car would blow up, or he'd be poisoned in some restaurant or run down by a truck as he was crossing the street.

"Where to?" Bellinzona asked.

"Shut up! To the hotel."

Pietro swallowed whatever he was about to say. He gave a squint into the rearview mirror and saw a gray Opel take off from where it was parked on the street. Behind the wheel was the guy who had been trying to tail them since they got to Zurich, the one Folco Mori had spotted at the airport. Bellinzona didn't know whether he should mention it. Folco had asked him not to tell Volpone that, aside from O'Brion and Zaza, they had also done away with two American dicks since they got here.

"It'll be time enough to tell him when he hasn't got so much on his mind," Folco had decreed.

Pietro had been impressed by the fact that Folco was willing to keep quiet about their accomplishments, but he was afraid it might not be good to keep them secret too long. Babe Volpone's reactions were sometimes unpredictable—and almost always hostile. Having seen the look of despair that came over Italo's face after he shoved O'Brion under the saw, Pietro realized that Italo knew he had done something wrong. Wouldn't he himself be doing wrong if he kept this information from Volpone?

"*Padrone . . .*"

Italo did not seem to hear. Bellinzona had to swerve sharply to miss a woman who was backing up to get into a parking place.

"*Padrone . . .*" he repeated.

"What the hell is it?" Italo barked.

"Somebody's tailing us."

"Where?"

"In a gray Opel."

"How do you know?" Italo asked, curbing his impulse to turn around and look.

"Folco tagged him when we landed. He was on the plane with us."

"Idiot! I've got a cop on my ass and you don't tell me!"

"Not a cop, *padrone*."

"How the hell do you know?" Volpone exploded.

"Folco'll explain it to you. You were so busy. But during that time, we didn't just sit on our asses."

"What does that mean?" Italo asked, knitting his brow.

"Folco'll explain it to you," Bellinzona repeated, trying to get off the dangerous ground he had ventured onto. "Folco thinks the tail is a torpedo Gabelotti pinned on us. Anyway—could be."

"Take the first turn to the right," Volpone ordered, "and just keep driving. I gotta think."

He turned around, pretending to look for something on the back seat, and cased the Opel.

"Where's Folco right now?"

"Behind—tailing that guy."

"Turn left!"

Pietro drove around the traffic circle under the peaceful eye of the traffic cop.

"Still see him?" Italo asked.

"Yep. Want me to cut him off?"

"Just drive along the water's edge and keep quiet. When you get to the park, turn left and head for the Commodore."

The Commodore was a huge new hotel Volpone had passed the day before.

"Drop me off in front, and make like you're taking off. Park the car wherever you can. I'll stay in the lobby for three minutes. After that, all you have to do is tail the guy when he starts following me."

"You got something in mind?"

"Watch the road!"

They were in view of the big hotel, its thirty stories towering over the high greenery of the park. Bellinzona slowly braked to a halt on the gravel drive, and a footman dressed in an admiral's uniform rushed to open the door for Volpone. Bellinzona took off again, following a series of arrows that brought him to an outdoor parking lot. He had to wait until a couple of lovers kissing in an Austin condescended to let him have their space, and he ran back to the main entrance of the hotel, just in time to see

Folco Mori hand a tip to the admiral, who was sitting behind the wheel of Mori's cream-colored Volkswagen. They exchanged a short look and, without apparent connection, went on into the hotel.

Italo Volpone was pacing in the lobby, checking his wristwatch like someone waiting for his date to arrive. Twenty yards away, the torpedo was pretending to study the menu posted outside the door of one of the three Commodore restaurants. Bellinzona walked over and riffled through some travel folders at the main desk. He took one with him, walked over to Italo, and pointed to a picture of hunters on their way back from a safari in Kenya. "It's the guy reading the menu," he whispered.

"Who told you to come and talk to me?" Volpone hissed.

"Padrone, he saw that I was the one who was driving you. If he doesn't see me with you, he'll know I'm following him. Folco's here."

"Where?"

"In front of the bookstall."

"Go ask some information at the desk."

"What?" said Bellinzona.

"Any goddamn thing. Just go and talk to the clerk, and then come back and bring me some information."

Pietro walked lumberingly away. Volpone saw him talk to the clerk, who then turned away to take care of the next customer. When Bellinzona got back, he told Italo, "It's twelve-thirty on the nose."

"Come with me."

They crossed the lobby.

Rico Gatto, who was watching them through the mirror on which the menu was posted, decided they were on their way to meet someone. He wanted to make up for his half-assed job at the morgue. Gabelotti had been furious that he had had nothing new to report about the mysterious leg. Rico saw Volpone and Bellinzona lift up a drape behind an imposing marble column at the end of the lobby. As soon as they disappeared, he headed in the same direction. Folco Mori nonchalantly turned away from the bookstall and began walking.

Behind the drape was a large French door leading into a banquet hall with tables all set and decorated with floral pieces. A small flowered dais had a lectern on it, ready to be used except for the carafe of water and glass for the speaker. He would arrive later. So would the crowd. For the time being, there was no one in the hall. This made Rico Gatto nervous. He wondered whether he had once again lost Volpone. Then an idea hit him: if Italo had deliberately ditched him, that meant he knew he was being tailed. And that changed the whole picture. Volpone would be trying to lure him into a trap and knock him off.

The palm of Rico's hand slipped over the Beretta lodged in the holster on the left side of his chest. With his hand under his coat, he walked toward the dais, trying neither to hide nor to muffle his steps. When he was about fifteen feet from the dais, he darted two bounds to the right, gun in hand, but no one was there.

Very carefully he turned the knob of the door that had been hidden from him by the dais. It started to open. Rico kicked it and jumped back. He moved cautiously down a long, dimly lit corridor. Some twenty yards along, there were two more doors. He quietly opened the one on the left. It led to a concrete spiral stairway. If Volpone and Bellinzona had taken it, he could stop here. It was too late to pick them up again.

The other door was marked Danger. It was a metal door, which he thought would be locked, but it opened easily. Steep iron steps led down to a platform over a huge cave that seemed as large as the entire ground surface of the Commodore. Intertwined with tresses of varicolored pipes, the internal machinery of the big hotel had a life of its own that was pulsating to the muffled hum of its generator.

Rico smiled slightly. It was his kind of terrain. If Italo and his gorilla tried to trap him in here, they would have some surprises in store.

He stayed absolutely motionless for half a minute, listening for the slightest noise. He forgot that Gabelotti only wanted to be kept informed on Volpone's comings and goings, and, caught up in the chase, he jumped out into space, his hand on the stair rail, and landed on the

177

platform fifteen feet below. He leaped again, rolling through the stairs to lie flat behind a boiler, the dull vibration of which filled the place with its waves.

All his senses at the ready, he stayed there for at least two minutes. Nothing happened.

He suddenly felt a little ridiculous. What if Volpone and Bellinzona were gone? What if there was no one else in this engine room? Maybe he was playing war all by himself, for nothing.

But he had to make sure, and to do that he had to risk his life. He would have to cross an open space of some thirty yards, go over a catwalk about ten yards long, and take refuge at the other end of the room.

Very close to him, on his left, someone whistled the first eight bars of "Colonel Bogey's March" from *The Bridge on the River Kwai*. Rico rolled over on himself, instinctively firing three blind shots in the opposite direction. He could hear the tight staccato of several projectiles whining and ricocheting off the stairwell's metal guard. One of them hit the very spot on the boiler where his head had been half a second earlier, and a powerful jet of boiling steam came spurting out of the pierced metal, tracing a straight line as far as the eye could see.

Still trying to keep covered Rico swung to his left and got off a couple more shots. Then, to his amazement, he realized that he was letting the gun slip out of his hand, and his shoulder felt the impact of a sledgehammer blow. Someone grabbed his head from behind and violently banged it against the boiler.

Folco Mori bent over Rico Gatto's unconscious body and with a sharp twist pulled out his dagger, which had penetrated up to its hilt in the flesh of the shoulder muscle, piercing it clean through. He saw Bellinzona rush over to Italo Volpone, who was tottering toward them, his face haggard.

"*Padrone,* you're wounded . . ." said Pietro.

Italo shook his head and tried to motion him away. With horror, Pietro then noticed the small black hole in the boss's coat, right over his heart. Bellinzona opened the coat, expecting to see a horrible wound, but Volpone's shirt was intact. Not a drop of blood.

Before Italo thought of stopping him, Pietro slipped

his hand into his boss's inside coat pocket and pulled out the deck of cards Volpone always carried with him. The top card was the ace of hearts, and the hole in it was right in the middle of the heart. The bottom card, which he didn't bother to look at, was intact.

Pietro wanted to shout, to give thanks, to say a blessing, proclaim a miracle, but all he did utter was, "Goddamn . . ."

"Who is he?" Volpone asked Mori, making no comment as he grabbed the deck of cards out of Bellinzona's hands and stuffed it back into his pocket. Although he had been shaken by the bullet, Italo had not forgotten what had brought him into this engine room.

Mori handed him the passport. Blood was gushing through the dark material of Rico's jacket.

Italo looked at the name page: *Enrico Gatto, Real Estate Agent, 256 Washington Avenue, Miami, Florida.*

Rico opened his eyes. He saw three threatening figures bending over him, and he knew his time had come.

"Who sent you?" Volpone demanded.

Rico Gatto put his hand over his wound but said nothing.

"Help me," Italo said.

In a second Rico was brought up on his feet. Italo made a sign to Bellinzona to keep him from yelling.

While Pietro was holding Rico Gatto's mouth shut with his huge paws, Volpone used all his strength to shove him against the boiler plate from which the geyser of live steam was spurting so that Rico's body would come right into the stream of boiling steam. Gatto, his eyes bulging with pain, tensed all his muscles to try to get away from the jet that was searing his flesh through his clothes, so powerful that it all but overwhelmed the three men shouldering him like three football linemen.

"Who sent you?" Volpone repeated.

Rico's eyes rolled up into his head. "Gabelotti," he spat out in terror, knowing he had nothing more to lose.

Volpone grabbed his mouth with both his hands and spread his jaws as wide as possible. Shielding himself with Gatto's body, he shoved him up against the boiler again, face first, and kept his face pressed against the metal, the deadly jet aimed right down his throat. Rico Gatto's skin turned purple, then livid, like cooked meat. He was long dead by the time Volpone, pulled off by Folco and Pietro, let the lifeless body drop and then jumped back to get out of the way of the steam.

"Your blade," barked Volpone.

Folco Mori gave him the dagger. Italo knelt over Gatto's body, but his position kept Folco and Bellinzona from seeing what he was doing. He kept his back to them one moment longer, wrapped something in his handkerchief, and then got up.

"Are we getting out of here?" Pietro asked.

"Just a second," Italo said. "Grab him and follow me."

Bellinzona and Mori picked up the body.

"You got his passport?" Volpone asked Folco.

"Yes."

"Lemme have it," Volpone said.

They were in front of a circular lid about three yards in diameter, the top of which was at ground level. On the side of the cover was a butterfly that Volpone unscrewed until a rectangular opening appeared.

"Drop him in there!"

Bellinzona and Mori came forward, their faces singed by the intense heat coming up from the hole. Quickly they shoved Rico Gatto's corpse into it. Volpone himself closed the trapdoor and screwed the butterfly back on.

Then he spoke the eulogy: "Just what he deserved. A garbage incinerator."

Steam was beginning to fill the engine room, but they managed to reach the concrete stairs that led out the rear exit without meeting anyone.

Later, when they were back at their own hotel, Volpone handed some money to Bellinzona, who was getting ready to put the car away.

"Go buy me a watch and bring it up to my room," he said.

"What kind of watch?"

"A watch—any kind. And some paper, too—wrapping paper."

"Okay," Pietro answered, sufficiently familiar with

the new *padrone*'s ways to know that it was better not to ask questions.

Chimene Kloppe heaved a sigh. In order to keep her word to Renata, she was going to have to leave her own apartment for forty-eight hours. No one, not even she, was to know what was being done there to prepare for the celebration.

In less than an hour a squad of men would come in and wreak havoc with her well-ordered arrangement and move her Pissarros, Renoirs, and Manets around.

This wedding was going to be incongruous, shocking, yet, for fear of what her daughter might do by way of reprisal, Chimene had not dared object. Renata had her father's iron will: when she got an idea into her head, heaven help those who tried to stop her! To keep her mother in line, and to reassure her, Renata had whispered sweetly, as ingratiatingly as she knew how, "Look, *Mutterchen,* I'm not asking for any queen's dowry! All I want is to be able to fix the place up to suit myself—that can be your wedding present to me."

It was a treacherous request, and it might well cost them the respect of the city's leading citizens. Some people, who didn't appreciate the idea of coming to a wedding at three o'clock in the morning, had already sent their excuses. Of course, there were others who had been delighted, viewing it as an amusing diversion.

In the meantime, for two days, Chimene was going to have to live like a displaced person in the stuffy little four-room flat they owned on the upper floor. She had always wanted to rent it out, but she had never quite dared, lest people think the Kloppes needed money.

She made a mental check to see that she had put all she would need into her overnight bag. Her maid had already moved three trunks "up there." Homer had made no comment, but on two or three occasions she could read in his eyes that he was being made to drink the hemlock.

The doorbell rang, and when she opened it, holding her overnight bag in her hand, two husky hulks were standing there.

"Is this Mr. Homer Kloppe's place?"

"Yes, it is."

The man must have taken her for a servant. Otherwise, how could his tone of voice be explained?

"Well, you're right to be getting out. Things are gonna be hoppin' in here."

Pietro Bellinzona, Folco Mori, and Orlando Baretto were curiously watching Babe Volpone tie the last golden string around his package. It was a small package, in tan wrapping paper. Italo felt it and then pasted on the gummed address label.

"Folco," he said, "I want you to take this to the airport. Put it on the next plane for New York. You make sure that they understand it is to be delivered only to the addressee. Got that?"

"Okay, but who do I give it to?" he asked. "I don't know no one here."

"Baretto?" Volpone queried Lando.

"Go to the freight office," Lando told Folco Mori. "Ask for Elizabeth. She'll know what to do."

"It's nothing to be concerned about," Italo said. "Just a souvenir. A watch. A little gift. Thing is, I don't want him to have to pay no duty on it."

"*Padrone*," Bellinzona protested, "an eighty-dollar watch couldn't cost much duty."

"You, mind your own business!" Volpone said; then he said to Falco, "Come back here and see me when the package is sent off. I'll have a couple of things for you to do."

Folco raised an eyebrow and said, "Okay."

Italo turned back to Bellinzona.

"Go down to the lobby," he said, "and get me two decks of cards. Fifty-two-card decks, right?"

"On my way."

Then Italo started giving instructions to Baretto. "Go to a real estate agency and rent an apartment or a house. Whatever looks best. Pay 'em six months' rent in advance. Tell 'em it's for some diplomats or something, whatever you feel like, but I want to be sleeping there tonight, get it? Hey, wait a minute. You got cash on you?"

"Some."

"Some ain't enough. Here, take this."

He stuffed a fat roll of bills into Lando's hand. "Don't have to bother counting. It's ten grand. Now, tell me about that broad of yours."

"She did everything you wanted, everything."

"Tell me."

"I just talked to her on the phone. She called him at his house."

"When?"

"Just before he sat down to lunch."

"What did she say she wanted?"

"To see him."

"Does she usually call to ask to see him?"

"No, Kloppe's the one who tells her when he wants her."

"Didn't he think it was strange that she called?"

"No, Inez didn't think so. She found out his whole schedule for tomorrow."

"Is she ready to go?"

"Yes."

"She knows she's living on borrowed time?"

"Yeah, she knows."

"Okay, now, beat it."

Lando wasn't sure whether he should ask the question that was on the tip of his tongue.

"What's on your mind now?" Volpone asked him.

"You did say pay six months' rent, didn't you, *padrone?*"

"Yeah, so what? I just happen to like this town. Okay?"

"Okay, sure, boss."

Italo waited for him to close the door before taking his little roulette wheel out of a drawer. He decided he'd see whether he could hit the zero in six tries.

As far as he was concerned, he'd had it with this hotel. It'd be better to go someplace else. At worst, he'd only be in Zurich three more days. Considering what he had in store for Homer Kloppe, that should be more than time enough. But what did it matter if he wasted ten grand on a phony rental? His hand grazed the pocket of his bathrobe, and he felt the hard shape of the deck of cards that had saved his life. He stopped the roulette ball before it had a chance to land on a number. Superstitious, like all

183

gamblers, he had a feeling he'd be tempting fate if he tested his luck again over something inconsequential.

While Italo dialed Angela's number in New York, Folco Mori, riding toward the airport in his Volkswagen, glanced at the package Volpone had given him.

The name Volpone had written on the label in big block letters came as a total surprise: ETTORE GABELOTTI.

There were some twenty people in the audience. Including two women. It was not a mass meeting, and it was customary during these meetings of the elders with the delegates from the synodal assemblies that anyone might interrupt the speaker to make a point about anything questionable. Once or twice Kloppe had been politely reminded that he had misspoken a date.

He had trouble maintaining the continuity of his talk. For the first time in his life, where Zwingli was concerned, his mind was wandering. Yet, the setting was perfect for meditation and concentration: a library in an old crypt alongside the west wing of the Grossmünster, the greatest Romanesque religious edifice in all of Switzerland.

This was where Zwingli had preached the Reformation. But today, his teachings were not taking precedence over the memory of Inez's sensuous voice. She had phoned Homer just as he was about to sit down to the last meal he would have at home before his daughter's wedding. Fortunately, Homer had answered, just making it to the phone ahead of his wife, but then he had had to carry on the conversation under her scrutiny. Inez had never called him at home. Nor anywhere else. He was always the one who called her.

"I'd love to see you . . ."

"That's simply out of the question."

"When, then?"

"Could I call you back," he asked, adding (for Chimene's benefit, although she couldn't see that his hand was over the mouthpiece), "at your office?"

"What're you doing this afternoon?"

"Unfortunately, I'm busy. I'm giving a talk at the Grossmünster at three."

"I miss you. How about tomorrow?"

(She had never told him she missed him!)

"I have such a heavy schedule . . ."

"Tell me about it, then I'll know where you are when I'm thinking about you."

"I have appointments all morning, a meeting early in the afternoon, and then the dentist's at four."

"Later on, then?"

"Sorry, there's going to be a wedding in the family. So many things to be done . . ."

"But when, then? The day after tomorrow?"

"No, no, impossible. My daughter's getting married."

"That's too bad! You know what I'm doing as I listen to your voice?"

"No."

"I'm caressing myself. I'm lying on the bed, stark naked. My legs are spread wide apart."

His face turned scarlet. Chimene, who hadn't taken her eyes off him, gestured to tell him that the fish quenelles were getting cold.

"Listen, I'll have to ask you to excuse me. I'm eating my lunch. Don't you eat lunch?"

"Not when I'm playing with my pussy, little white man. Well, tough luck. *Ciao.*"

After she hung up, he pretended to sign off.

"Very well, then, if you want, my dear fellow. Anytime after the twenty-seventh. Yes, I'll be in at whatever time is best for you. Oh, not at all. Good-bye."

"Would you like me to warm them up for you?" his wife asked. "Your quenelles, I mean."

"No, no, thanks—they're quite warm enough as is." He concentrated on his plate.

"Who was it on the phone?"

"A customer."

"Don't you feel well?"

"Of course I do."

"But your face is crimson!"

"Really? Well, I did have a rather grueling morning at the office."

Three-quarters of an hour before, he had watched on his closed-circuit television while Volpone made his triumphal entry into the Zurich Trade Bank. Owing to a bad connection in the dial of his set, he had not been able to tune the camera to the ground-floor corridor near the elevator entrance. That was where, according to what the guards later told him, Volpone got his comeuppance. At any rate, he'd been able to see the crook stalk out of the bank, and that had been comforting.

"Although Calvin was able to reduce the sacraments to just two," a voice was saying, "baptism and confirmation, and to decree that the flock was to elect its own pastors; and although he rejected the penance and abolished the bishoprics, we must not minimize the major part played in all this by Bèze . . ."

"I beg your pardon?" asked an appalled Homer Kloppe.

Lost in his thoughts, he had completely forgotten the holy place he was in, as well as the people who were there debating a question of theological doctrine at his own instigation. How long had he been absent like this?

"Bèze," his interlocutor was repeating, as all eyes focused on Homer, "Théodore de Bèze, or Theodorus Beza, if you prefer."

A strange thing happened in Homer's mind. The man had somehow been moved to use the French form of Beza's name: *Bèze*. That sounded like *baise*—which, translated, meant "screw." All Homer could see was the shattering image of Inez doing to herself what she had described to him on the phone—her beautiful legs spread wide and invitingly. And for the second time that day, spoken now by a delegate from the synodal assembly, he heard the words, "Mr. Kloppe, don't you feel well?"

"Uh, no, not really . . ." he mumbled.

His audience had its back to the library door. Homer, facing them, saw the door slowly open to reveal Inez's unbelievable silhouette, looking even taller than usual in one of her favorite coats that came all the way down to her ankles. Staring at her as if paralyzed, he tried to wipe away the vision, thinking, This can only be a dream, it can't be real, I'll wake up in a minute.

One by one, every head twisted in the direction in which Kloppe's stare had become set. Some cleared their throats, others moved nervously in their seats. All, without exception, kept observing Kloppe in surprise and embarrassment, as if they expected him to indicate what they ought to do in so unprecedented a circumstance.

They hadn't seen anything yet.

Kloppe tried to take hold of himself. He stammered, if indeed that hoarse voice was his, "Please excuse me. This lady is a friend of mine. I'll be right back. Just go ahead without me."

There she was, some ten yards from him, self-possessed, smiling, as inaccessible as a nightmare. He took three uncertain steps toward her, and she stopped him with a graciously authoritative wave of her hand.

Then, before the assembled group, she quietly spread the flaps of her fur coat. Beneath it, she was totally, absolutely naked, and Homer, for all that he was in an insane situation, could not help for a flash being fascinated by the dark chocolate of her skin, on which, black as the darkest night but shining with a quiet glow, was the vast triangle of her pubic area.

Bemused, but not missing the slightest detail of the show despite their dignified expressions, the witnesses watched it all in deathly silence. Standing solidly on her legs, still smiling, with her proffered body so amply displayed, Inez opened her mouth.

"Oh, Homer, I'm just heartbroken. I thought you and your friends had finished. Just go on. I'll wait for you at home."

She turned her back to the room with the majesty of a queen, swinging her voluminous mink from the rear to the front so that her magnificent buttocks were revealed, thrust out at a striking angle. The speechless audience heard the high heels ring out on the centuries-old slabs of the stone crypt, accompanied by the accelerated breathing of the local elders and the synodal delegates. A carnal burst of her scent wafted across the air, merging its effluvia with the dusty smell of old books and the odor of death arising from the cold stone.

The door squeaked closed, and the vision was gone.

12

In Ettore Gabelotti's New York apartment, Angelo Barba sank into an armchair. Each time Gabelotti went by, Barba could feel the air being displaced by the old man's 275 pounds. The fuming don was pacing back and forth through his parlor, looking furiously at his consiglieri. Carmine Crimello was no cockier than Barba. A little off to the side, Carlo Badaletto was trying to weather the storm.

Anger only seemed to increase Don Ettore's ravenous hunger. A huge platter of buttered delicatessen sandwiches, cut into manageable thirds, was being devoured little by little as Gabelotti absentmindedly replenished his handful each time he walked by.

An hour earlier, Philip Diego had called from Zurich to inform the don of his failure to get anything out of Homer Kloppe. Don Ettore had been so angry that he insulted the lawyer, calling him a fuck-up and saying he didn't know the meaning of tact or diplomacy.

"Why don't you phone him yourself?" Diego had suggested coldly.

"Is that your advice?"

"No. Some things are better not to discuss over the telephone."

"Well, what am I supposed to do, since you're not able to get any information for me?"

There was, of course, one solution they both thought of, but neither mentioned it. Gabelotti, because he never trusted anyone, not even one of his most dependable lawyers; and Philip Diego, because he was afraid the don might say no. Yet, if Gabelotti gave him the number of the secret account, he could immediately instruct Kloppe to make the necessary transfer. Assuming that Italo Volpone had not already made off with the money.

"Why don't you write him?"

"Because that would be stupid."

Diego was well aware of that. Tax evasion and fraud were favorite hunting grounds of the U.S. authorities. Between SEC, IRS, and FBI mail covers, any suspicious correspondence to Switzerland or any other such tax-free paradise constituted an immediate danger to the sender. The mail might get into the wrong hands, with untold consequences.

"It's just too bad that you can't come over," the lawyer interjected nonchalantly.

Gabelotti hung up with a curse. Once again, his fear of flying was keeping him from getting where his business sense said he ought to be. Logically, of course, it made no sense. But in his gut, all the fibers of his body told him he'd die before the plane even took off.

What a hell of a situation! He couldn't write, couldn't phone, couldn't tell anyone the account number O'Brion had given him. Nor could he go to Zurich. Unless he were to go by ship—and that would take at least five or six days, during which time those two billion big ones might move on a dozen times without leaving a forwarding address.

Finally, his nerves and patience gave out, and Gabelotti could no longer stand it. He decided he would take a calculated risk: he would call Kloppe and identify himself by giving the secret account number. Unfortunately, by the time he got the Zurich Trade Bank on the line it was 3:00 P.M. in Switzerland—the very moment when Homer Kloppe was beginning his talk at the Grossmünster.

"When will he be back?" Gabelotti asked.

"Not until tomorrow morning, sir."

"Is there any other number I can reach him at?"

"No, sir. But I could put you through to the assistant director—"

Gabelotti hung up without replying, grabbed another

189

sandwich, and stuffed the whole wedge into his mouth, swallowing most of it without chewing.

"If only Rico Gatto would call in again," Crimello lamented.

Ettore shrugged.

"Listen, Don Ettore," Barba put in, "I think we're losing sight of the most important thing. I understand what you're worried about, and so am I. But Babe Volpone is still in Switzerland, isn't he? If he tried to pull anything, wouldn't he have gone to cover long since?"

"This whole thing is a double cross," thundered Gabelotti. "I don't believe one fuckin' word of what Moshe Yudelman told us. They're just trying to get us to go to sleep. And I'm cut off from the world and can't get any information."

"When is Moshe coming back?"

"Any minute. If he doesn't have anything new to tell me, we'll let them have it."

To get to the Sonnenberg Quarter, Lando had driven past a golf course, then turned left into Sonnenbergstrasse and left again into Aurorastrasse.

"You didn't exactly choose a slum," said Volpone.

"You said you wanted the best," Lando replied, delighted.

The street was lined with magnificent private estates that were hidden behing high walls. "This is known as Bankers' Boulevard," Lando added, waving his arm to indicate the sublime view of the city, the perfect condition of the flower beds seen here and there through the wrought-iron gates.

It was 4:00 P.M., the temperature was mild, and, despite the tension gripping his head, Italo could not help enjoying the aroma of springtime.

"Did you have enough bread?"

"I got a grand left. I had to cough up nine. Not for six months, though, only three."

He glanced at Volpone to see whether the boss was sore.

"These guys in Zurich don't do things halfway, do they?" Italo burst out laughing.

Relieved, Lando let his foot press down on the gas

pedal of the Beauty Ghost P9. Up to now, he'd only had a chance to tease it, but he swore that as soon as things calmed down he'd take it out on the Autobahn and see what he could push it up to. He fleetingly felt the loss of Don Genco, who had given him the regal present. What class he had! Italo was not as much fun to deal with: he was too quick to come to a boil and apt to get sore over next to nothing. But he was a real leader! When Lando had reported on Inez's appearance at the church, he'd felt Volpone's eyes silently congratulating him. Italo had asked for the story to be repeated twice, and he wanted more details on certain especially funny points.

"What did that cold potato look like when she waved her snatch at him?"

"She said his eyes popped out of his head."

"And how about the others, when she shoved her ass under their noses?"

"They were petrified."

Italo had nodded in great satisfaction. Of course, Lando had put it on a little thick. After all, he hadn't actually been there himself. When he tried to get the details out of Inez, she had merely said, "I did what I was told. Now fuck off!" And he had to take her word for it.

"This is the place, boss."

It was a small château, with two stories and an attic that had mansarded windows opening on the gray slate roof. The facade and shutters were white. To enter, you went up a double curved staircase to a landing in front of a heavy black door with a bronze knocker.

"I'll show you around," Lando said.

Italo looked out over the grounds. The grass was as green as a roulette table, and jonquils were blooming at the foot of several giant cedars. This was the kind of place Angela would like. She often told him that all she needed was a supply of good books, a little greenery, and a lot of time to herself.

"What about me?" he'd ask. "Where do I fit in?"

By way of answer, she would cuddle up to him, smile, and play with his earlobe. He swore to himself that once he was out of this pile of shit he'd take her to Sicily on a holiday.

"You first," Lando told him.

Volpone went into a reception hall that was lined with portraits of somebody's ancestors in warrior uniforms. Angela had promised that one day she'd explain to him why old pictures like that were beautiful. He opened a door into a main salon with windows opening out on the greenswards.

"How many rooms?" he asked.

"I forget," Lando answered. "Thirteen or fourteen."

Volpone knitted his brow. "Thirteen?"

"Maybe less, maybe more."

"Go count 'em, and let me know. Does the telephone work?"

"Yep."

"Where is it?"

Lando pointed it out to him.

"There's another extension in your bedroom."

"My bedroom? You telling me where I'm gonna sleep now?"

"It's the best one," Lando said in all honesty.

Italo dismissed him with a wave of the hand. Baretto was obedient and efficient, but that didn't change the fact that he was a pimp. And for some reason Italo had no use for pimps, even though prostitution was one of the mainstays of the Volpone fortune. That was on an abstract industrial scale in which women were counted only as so many head of stock. Wholesalers such as the Volpone brothers had no direct contact with the merchandise.

However, it was Lando's black broad who had hit Homer Kloppe where it hurt most.

But that was only for openers. Babe had figured out an escalating three-stage move to break the banker's resistance. First, his reputation. Then, his person. And finally, his family.

Italo frowned as he looked at the phone. He was going to have to tell Moshe Yudelman that Morty O'Brion was dead. When Italo had a run-in with Genco, Moshe was always the one who had smoothed things out and gotten the brothers back together. The consigliere had an almost paternal affection for the younger Volpone, and Babe knew it. Because of that, he tolerated stuff from Yudelman that he wouldn't take from anyone else. Moshe, aware of this, never beat around the bush with Babe. He was going to have a fit when he heard that Italo had wasted their last chance by excuting Morty.

Nevertheless, Italo dialed Yudelman's number in New York. It rang only once before it was answered.

"It's me," Italo said.

"Goddamn it!" Moshe shouted. "I've been trying to reach you for hours. Where are you?"

"Still in the same place."

"All right, forget it, Italo. That's not important. Things are sour. Come on back."

"That all you got to tell me?"

"Listen to me, Italo. I'm scared. We've done enough stupid things already. One more and the shit'll hit the fan. You're being tailed."

"Not anymore. That's been taken care of."

"Taken care of?"

"I told you, it's all taken care of!" Italo shouted. "You can understand that, can't you?"

"Are you calling from the hotel?" Moshe asked cautiously.

"No, you can go ahead and talk. It's a clean line."

"Gabelotti's gone crazy. He thinks we're trying to rob him."

"And you fall for that shithead's talk? You're losing your touch."

"The shithead is gonna gun us down. Every one of us."

"You don't say."

"He doesn't know what he's saying anymore. He thinks you're the one who had O'Brion knocked off."

"That's not so," said Italo.

"I know it, and you know it. But he doesn't."

Italo took a deep breath. "I didn't have the bastard knocked off. I did it myself."

There was a long silence at the other end. Then Moshe's excited voice came back, "You're nuts! Absolutely nuts!"

"It was an accident. I was trying to get him to talk, and he was making fun of me."

"Oh, no," Yudelman groaned. "I can't believe it. That's just too stupid. You don't seem to understand a thing."

"Stop bustin' my balls!"

"Not the least thing. From now on, who knows what Gabelotti may do. The Commissione will stand behind him!"

"Are you out of your mind?" Italo roared. "Just ask Gabelotti what his friend Morty was trying to pull when we picked him up at the bank. Go ahead!"

"Italo, I've seen Gabelotti. And I can't make out what's going on."

"Well, I can. That fuckin' bastard had my brother knocked off so he could lay his hands on our dough. And now that you've let your pants down to him, he thinks he's got the upper hand and that he'll be able to go right on spitting in my face!"

"Italo!"

"Shut up! Since you're so palsy-walsy with Ettore now, let him tell you why he sent his dear little consigliere to see Mr. Kloppe."

"Italo. Don't you think O'Brion might have been trying to pull that off on his own?"

"You poor sap!" Volpone sneered. "You think this is a movie or something?"

"You're forgetting one thing, Babe. Gabelotti knows the number of the account. He's known it from the start. All he had to do was give it."

"And who says he didn't?" Volpone answered, choking. "Why do you think he sent O'Brion? Huh? Tell me that!"

"Italo, let me tell you frankly, I don't know what to say. There are too many things that aren't clear. We won't get anywhere by bickering. It could cost us too much."

"It won't cost me nothin'. My brother's dead, and his money is probably gone. So what am I worried what it's gonna cost?"

"Look, give me one last chance to try—"

"You just keep out of this!"

"Come back to New York," Yudelman pleaded. "We'll have it out with Don Ettore. We'll lay the cards on the table."

"I wonder why Genco kept you on as long as he did. You're just too fuckin' dumb!"

"Then I'll go by myself," Moshe answered. "In the interest of the family."

"*I'm* the family now!" Volpone shouted.

"Italo, I'm asking you one last time. Come back to New York."

"Go fuck yourself."

"They'll get you," Moshe warned in a low, cold voice. "But I'm not going to let you endanger the lives of Francesca, or her daughters, or Angela."

Italo's eyes opened wide. "What about Angela?" he asked hoarsely.

"If you're not back here in a few hours, heaven protect us all!" Moshe Yudelman said, and he hung up.

Volpone was speechless. He stood dumbstruck, the phone still at his ear. For a moment his brain became paralyzed, and the buzz of the disconnected telephone taunted him. Moshe was right. Angela, of course! He'd have to tell her to hide out—right away!

"It's just wild!" Renata laughed. "They'll have to lie down to get the feeling they're standing up!"

"Terrific," Kurt agreed. "Only the sober ones'll feel they're getting drunk."

They were lying on their backs in what had been a typical opulent parlor of Zurich's upper bourgeoisie. Now, Chimene wouldn't have recognized her pride and joy. The workers had started by taking the paintings and hanging them upside down.

"Just look!" exclaimed the ecstatic Oswald Hepbräuer. "When paintings are masterworks, they're just as fine upside down as right side up!"

In Zurich, Oswald was the last word in decorating. He had been at the Beaux-Arts School in Paris in 1968, and he had stormed the Sorbonne, occupied the Odéon Theater, and made the color bombs that his revolutionary comrades used to write their liberating graffiti on the walls of the City of Light. To the gilded intelligentsia in Switzerland, accomplishments like that made him a hero. Oswald had a double halo as both a man of action and a noncomformist, all of which made him wildly enthusiastic about Renata Kloppe's idea of an upside-down wedding. He had spent three feverish weeks working out the details. Now it was coming to life. His workers covered the whole ceiling with trompe-l'oeil wallpaper to simulate a parquet floor, and a set of upside-down café chairs "stood" up there, held in place by mortises.

"Couldn't we put one of the Louis XV armchairs up there?" Renata asked.

"It's too heavy," said Oswald, "but the Formica table might do very well. Paul! The table!"

"Why not add some refuse to it?" suggested Kurt, not about to be left behind in this drive toward the absurd.

"Obvious, too obvious," Oswald decreed. "You see shit wherever you look, so we have to use it sparingly. It just gets boring—"

"Oswald," Renata cut in, "how about some clothes? As if people had just dropped them on the floor?"

"Let's not get carried away. First things first. The details can be filled in later. But look at the Pissarro! That sky at the bottom. It's too wonderful for words."

He joined Renata and Kurt on the floor, twisting himself into a pretzel shape, his buttocks above and his head peering up through his legs.

"Wait till they see the Leonardo! Can you picture it? A Da Vinci masterpiece ass over teakettle? It's never been done before! All right. Paul, how about that table?"

There were ten of them working. In order not to get her parents too worried, Renata had insisted that the work be finished as quickly as possible.

"You have carte blanche," she had told Oswald. "Use as many men as you need, but work around the clock. After the wedding, get the whole shooting match out immediately."

Hepbräuer was never reluctant to have a go at anything, especially for a price, and this event would make every newspaper in town.

"How about this? Isn't it great?" he asked as a workman came in carrying an electric chandelier with fake crystal pendants pointing up instead of down, skillfully pasted to defy the laws of gravity.

"We'll hang this from the floor—I mean to say, the ceiling." He corrected himself between laughs. "I'm

going to have three or four of them around the room.
Just look. Hubert! Up there, on the left, is the table
ready, with the bottles?"

"Here it is."

Liquor bottles of all brands were glued to the smooth
surface of a chrome and glass coffee table.

"Add a bouquet of flowers to that!" he called. "And
watch out up there. The weight has to be carried by the
sconces."

He turned back and gave the engaged couple a wink
of complicity.

"Well, kids, you've given us quite a job. But it's gonna
knock 'em reeling. They won't get over your wedding for
many a moon!"

Kurt took Renata's hand. The closer their crazy idea
came to realization, the more he felt strangely uneasy
about it. But it was too late to do anything but voice
the fullest approval. To overcome his malaise, he felt it was
best to keep adding suggestions.

"Oswald, how about your ceiling? When are you setting it up on the floor?"

"Later, later. Now look, kids, I don't want to drive
you out, but I've got to get on with the work. You can
come back in two hours, okay? You'll see how far we've
gotten!"

The minute she felt her hand in Kurt's, Renata had
pulled it back unthinkingly. Things seemed to be taking
place without her having anything to do with them. On a
dare, she had set all this in motion. Now that the prison
was being built, she felt caught in a trap.

"You coming?"

"Let's go," Kurt replied.

"Renata," Oswald Hepbräuer called to her as she was
going, "you may think you thought of everything, but I
still have some surprises in store for you. You'll see, kid-
dies! Just wait!"

Moshe Yudelman walked into Don Ettore's office as if
entering a slaughterhouse. Carmine Crimello, Angelo Barba, and Carlo Badaletto stared at him, but Moshe ignored
them. He took two steps toward Gabelotti and said, "Don
Ettore, could I speak with you alone?"

"Out," Gabelotti said to his men, waving at the same time.

"Just a second, *padrone,*" said Badaletto.

He stepped up and frisked Yudelman, who let him do it, eyeing him with something like contempt.

"Out," Don Ettore repeated to Badaletto.

Carlo closed the door behind him. Gabelotti raised an eyebrow and said to Yudelman, "I'm listening."

Moshe felt that his visit would in itself constitute an earnest of good faith. But if he had misread Gabelotti, if Italo had been right, then it was his tough luck: he'd never walk out of there alive.

"Don Ettore," he began, "you asked me to come back, and here I am. Of my own free will. I trust your judgment and your wisdom. I'm not a member of your family, but we are all children of the same mother family, the Syndicate. All of us have been at our jobs long enough to know that there is no need to let things start popping without reason."

Gabelotti listened attentively as he cracked and munched pistachio nuts. The fact that Yudelman had come back to his headquarters was a good sign. His men, after several fruitless attempts, had succeeded in getting Homer Kloppe's home phone number. Unfortunately, Ettore had no more luck there than at the bank. A female voice informed him that the banker was not at home. When he declined to give his name, she had abruptly hung up, so for the time being, the best he could do was to wait and pray that Volpone had not withdrawn the money. Yudelman's presence could only mean reassurance on that account.

"To tell the truth, I have come here against the advice of Italo Volpone."

"Did you reach him?" Ettore asked, trying not to show his anxiety.

"Yes."

"Still in Zurich?"

"Yes."

Gabelotti swallowed a handful of shucked pistachios. He held the can out to Yudelman, who shook his head no.

"Did he tell you what he's doing there?"

"His brother has been murdered," Moshe quietly reminded the don.

"That's what he says."

"Just a minute, Don Ettore. We're all on edge on account of this business. Any one of us may say something more than he means to. A little while ago you made some pretty serious accusations against Italo. I didn't approve of what you said. Then Italo said things about you. I don't approve of those either. What I want to do is get at the truth and end this misunderstanding. It can only bring harm to all of us."

"Since your don is dead, whose name are you talking in?"

"In my own name, and the name of reason, and our mutual interest. However, I must add that, since Don Genco died, his younger brother is, at least temporarily, his successor as head of the family."

"Italo is an irresponsible character!"

"No, Don Ettore. Italo simply is a man who has never had to shoulder any real responsibilities. Unfortunately, he's broken up by the tragedy, he's hotheaded and stubborn, yes. And he's convinced that your consigliere tried to go behind your back and double-cross you."

Despite the cold sweat that was running down his spine, Moshe looked into Gabelotti's venomous eyes. If this giant ever found out that Morty O'Brion was gone, that Italo Volpone had personally killed him, it would mean war without mercy—to the last man alive. And the first one to get an epitaph would be Moshe himself.

"Do you agree with him?" Gabelotti asked in an absolutely neutral tone.

"All men are fallible, Don Ettore. Mortimer O'Brion is no exception. Italo doesn't think his brother died by accident."

"I'm sure of that," Ettore replied in a voice full of undertones. "You want to know how I feel about all this? As long as O'Brion isn't standing before me in the flesh to tell me so himself, no one in the world is going to make me believe he double-crossed me! It's just too convenient to

199

finger a guy who isn't here to defend himself. Much too easy! It doesn't take a brain to see who can benefit from that! Italo Volpone."

"There's one sure way to find out, Don Ettore. And it would clear up this whole mess. There were three people who knew the account number. Don Genco, O'Brion, and yourself. All you have to do is phone Zurich and set the whole matter straight."

"If I didn't do that before now," Gabelotti lied, "it was out of respect for my friend Genco. We were in this together."

"If Babe Volpone made the mistake of going to the bank without notifying you," Moshe Yudelman now lied in his turn, "it was only because his brother's death led him to believe that your consigliere was trying to do you dirt. Now he is asking through my mouth, please call Zurich immediately and give the order for the transfer."

Gabelotti pretended to go along with him. He looked at his watch.

"Too late. It's almost six o'clock in Europe now. The bank'll be closed."

"Well, then, tomorrow, Don Ettore. As soon as it opens."

Gabelotti thought about it.

"Incidentally, do you know where to reach Volpone?"

"Of course."

Ettore pushed the phone over to Yudelman.

"Get him. I want to talk to him."

"Okay," Moshe said.

Hiding his discomfort, he picked up the phone. He had hoped he'd be able to handle things smartly enough to keep himself in the clear, to avoid open conflict, to save two billion dollars, and to spare human lives. He wanted to be the buffer between the two barrels of explosives—to keep them from coming into violent contact. Now he felt a cold sweat between his shoulder blades. He smiled tentatively, in a friendly way, toward Gabelotti, who was watching him carefully.

"Sordi's?" he inquired. "Please let me talk to Mr. Volpone."

"Hold the line."

To his surprise, he found that the answer from Zurich filled the whole room. Gabelotti had connected the phone to the squawkbox. Moshe silently prayed that Italo might be out.

"Mr. Volpone's room doesn't answer."

"Would you let me have the desk, please? . . . Hello, reception desk?"

"Yes, sir."

"Can you leave a message for Mr. Volpone?"

"Mr. Volpone is no longer registered here, sir."

"I beg your pardon."

"Mr. Volpone settled his bill an hour or two ago and checked out."

Yudelman felt himself turning soft in the legs.

"Did he leave any address?"

"None, sir."

Moshe hung up without daring to look at Don Ettore. Well, you can only die once, Moshe told himself.

"There it is, Don Ettore," he said. "You know as much about it as me."

Suddenly he felt exhausted. "Maybe he's on his way back to New York—or he might be calling me at my place . . ."

He slowly got to his feet.

"Where are you going?" Gabelotti asked.

"Home," he replied. "I'll be in touch as soon as I hear from him."

"Moshe," Ettore said, "you look depressed."

He walked around the desk and placed an arm as fat as a ham hock over Moshe's shoulders.

"Do me a favor. Be my guest. Stay here. I might need you on hand when I call the bank in the morning. After all, we're partners in this deal. Go on, take a rest. Simeone will show you to your room. Simeone!" he called.

Simeone Ferro appeared so fast it would seem he had been listening behind the door.

"*Padrone?*"

"Show my partner, Mr. Yudelman, to the guest room. Be sure he has everything he needs."

"Yes, *padrone.*"

201

Moshe, heavy at heart, gave him a sad little smile. "You're right, Don Ettore. I'll take a rest for a while. Believe me, I appreciate your hospitality."

"You're doing me an honor by accepting it," Gabelotti oozed.

As soon as Moshe and Ferro were out of the room, he went to the intercom. In a short imperative tone he barked, "Grab Angela Volpone."

13

When they were seated, there was nothing about the two young black men that would have attracted attention except for the remarkable handsomeness of their faces. One, in blue jeans and a fur coat, sported the studied negligence typical of American college men. The other wore a turtleneck, a tweed jacket, and flannel slacks.

Blood brothers, they were both hereditary princes, direct descendants of the royal line of the Kibondos. The first, named Amadou Tézé, but better known in the U.S. as Rocky, was one of the world's five top-money basketball players. The younger, Kouakou Touamé, was one of the most significant new hopes in the nuclear-physics field, and he was presently involved in giving a series of lectures on high-velocity particle accelerators in France.

Rocky and Kouakou had six other brothers. The tallest was seven foot six. The shortest, at six foot seven, was affectionately known to the family as Runt. Kouakou, standing an even seven feet, and Rocky, who was seven foot two, were in the happy-medium range.

Rocky had phoned Kouakou from New York.

"I'll pick you up in Paris in eight hours. Be ready."

"For how long?"

"A couple of days."

"Where we going?"

"To Zurich. I'll explain. A family matter.

For generations beyond memory, the word *family* was a sacred word among the Kibondos. Anyone who insulted one of them had the whole tribe to deal with. It was this extreme spirit of devotion that had kept the line intact for over two centuries. But times were changing. Five of the eight brothers had gone to college; two, including Rocky, had become professional athletes; and only the youngest boy, Mango, had stayed home with their father, the king. The baby of the family was Inez, born after all eight of the boys.

They all idolized her. She had traveled a great deal in Europe, having settled briefly in Rome, then London and Paris, where her exotic beauty had made her a fixture on the leading magazine covers.

"Just what happened to her?" Kouakou asked Rocky.

"She was treated disrespectfully in Zurich."

The expression "treated disrespectfully," applied to their sister, immediately wiped away all their Western veneer and brought out the tribal reflexes of the Kibondos. That such a thing should happen was intolerable to them, and the less comprehensible since Inez herself was big enough to stand up to anyone.

"Did she get hit?" Kouakou asked.

"I don't know; she didn't say. She just said she needed help. I thought you'd like to be in on it."

"Thanks," Kouakou acknowledged. "I don't suppose we'll have any trouble locating the guy."

"From what I gathered, it's guys," Rocky explained. "I played in Zurich once in an exhibition game against the Globetrotters. It's a nice little place. Unless they skipped out, we'll find them in a hurry."

Angela Volpone was ashamed of the way she had felt the day before. Instead of helping Francesca, she had returned home, unable to tolerate her sister-in-law's grief. She had been a Volpone for six months now, yet she realized she had never fully accepted the family's attitudes and burdens.

Her education, tastes, and life-style all separated her from that narrowly inner-directed clan, in which the women's role was merely to wait and to be resigned. Sicilian families had lived that way since time immemorial. But Angela was not Sicilian; and tragedy was not her cup of tea.

The problem was that she had fallen madly in love with a man whose way of life was worlds away from her own. Something animal, something irresistible had hit her like a knife in the heart when Italo walked into that library in London.

She would never forget the first exchange that sealed their mutual fate. That evening, he'd come back for her. She was the last one in the place, and she locked up. The fifteen pounds sterling they paid her each week wasn't enough to live on, but her father, who had a ship chandler's shop in Amalfi, sent her the difference monthly.

She was twenty-three and, to her knowledge, the only one of her contemporaries to have reached that advanced age still a virgin. Not that she bragged about it. Some of her college chums related sex experiences they'd had as early as their fourteenth year, but when she dated one of her peers, she never let things get very far. Not that her father, or even her mother, had ever laid down any law to her in that regard. Sex was something just not discussed in her family.

Yet Angela was a beauty. She had huge gray eyes, black hair, and sweet, fleshy lips—a young girl's lips in a perfectly oval face that was totally woman. Boys were always overwhelming her with compliments. But, unlike most girls of her generation, she felt that in order to have sex you also ought to feel "something else."

On spring evenings she had often felt the sap rising hotly inside her, urging her to bestow what she had been so jealously guarding, and she wondered whether she wasn't wasting something precious, something as fragile and fleeting as time itself.

Italo took her to a little Italian restaurant in the rather uninspiring neighborhood of the Edgeware Road. She had watched him eat, herself unable to swallow a thing, fascinated by his pale face and hypnotic eyes.

"Aren't you hungry?" he'd asked.

"Yes, I am," she said.

"You haven't touched a thing on your plate. How old are you?"

"Twenty-three."

He had burst out laughing as he continued to devour his scampi.

"Really, only twenty-three?"

"Yes, why? What's so funny about that?"

She was so sure she was going to spend the night with him that she had bought a toothbrush and hidden it in her purse. He was the one, and tonight was the night. This was what she had been waiting for all her life . . .

"You American?" she had asked.

"That's what my passport says. But I'm Sicilian-American."

"*Anch'io son'italiana.*"

"*Lei, da dov'è?*"

"From Amalfi. Did you really shake those two jerks?"

"Yes. What'll you have for dessert?"

"Just coffee."

Later, when they left the restaurant, he held the car door for her, then got in behind the wheel and lit a cigarette.

"What would you like to do?"

"When?"

"Now."

Without hesitating, she had answered, "Whatever you want."

"Well," he had gone on, "something funny, exciting, offbeat, funky, or what?"

"Whatever you want."

"You got some time to spare?"

She had all the time in the world, whenever he wanted. So he had taken her to a place where she never would have imagined going: a gambling club in the West End.

"You're lucky," he told her. "A few years ago your mother wouldn't even have been allowed in here."

For two hours he had concentrated on the gambling tables, paying absolutely no attention to her, his eyes seeing only the cards. He seemed to be known in the club. The bets he made at every deal would have been enough to support Angela for a year. He kept calling, "*Banco! . . . Banco! . . . Banco! . . .*"

"I won eleven thousand pounds," he told her when they left. "You're my lucky charm. We go halves on it."

"But you're mad!"

"Not at all. It's just money. Here, take it."

He tried to shove a huge bundle of currency into her purse. "Come on, don't make such a fuss over nothing. I take things a lot easier than you do. You want it or not?"

They were standing in front of the club, and she looked carefully at him to see whether he was making fun of her. He only seemed irritated by her refusal.

"You really not gonna take it?"

"No."

"It's your share. You really mean it?"

"Yes."

"Well, then. Here goes. Hey, there!"

A ragged panhandler came over to them when Italo called. Her heart sinking, Angela saw him give the money to the beggar. The tramp's jaw fell in amazement, and he backed away, his outstretched hat overflowing with the Queen's currency. When Angela got into the car, her legs were weak.

"When I say good-bye to something, I never take it back," Italo told her.

She was too shaken to answer. She was the kind who saved empty soda bottles in her room and took them back to the store to collect the deposits so she could buy cigarettes. She hated him for what he had just done, and in the darkness she opened her bag and shoved the toothbrush farther down into it.

"Are you angry?" he asked her.

"Yes," she replied. "You insulted that poor man's dignity."

He laughed a cool, spontaneous laugh. "Maybe you'd better go ask him before you tell me something like that."

"Take me home now," she said.

"Okay. But I still want you to know you're entitled to half of what I got. Don't you want it?"

"No," she hissed between clenched teeth.

"Suit yourself. Just wait a minute."

He split his bankroll in two, laid half of it on the car seat, and got out with the other half in his hand. Almost ready to throw up, she saw him give the money to a flower seller who was just about to go into the club. Italo came back carrying one red rose.

"You'll let me give you a flower, won't you?"

She didn't answer.

"Half of it, then?" he asked sweetly. And he carefully tore the rose in two, keeping the petals for himself and handing her the corolla attached to the stem. She pretended not to see what he was doing. He laid it on her lap and drove off.

He resumed in a playful tone. "I still have a bit of cash here that I won at the club. As you know, half of it belongs to you. Don't you want it?"

"You think that's funny?"

Again he split the bills into two parts and handed her one pile.

"Yes or no?"

She shrugged and turned away. He pressed a button, and the window on his side went down automatically. He held his hand out and the bills started floating into the wind.

"If I didn't think I was boring you, Angela," he said a few moments later, "I'd remind you that I still owe you fifty percent of what I have. Don't you want it?"

Her body stiffened, and she looked straight ahead. The bills he had held out to her flew away the way the others had. When they arrived at her door, all he had left were two one-pound notes. He showed her one.

"This is your share. Want it?"

She tried to find the door handle. He set fire to the note with his lighter and used the flame to light his cigarette.

She had not said a word since they got in the car, and she was troubled by conflicting emotions: anger, pride, humiliation, scorn, and the undeniable physical attraction that kept her heart pounding no matter how hard she tried to stifle her desire.

"Would you please help me?" she asked. "I'd like to get out."

"Just a minute, Angela. There's one left. Want your half?"

He cut the note in two.

"Just let me out of here," she raged.

He made two little balls of the last remaining pound out of the eleven thousand he had won, and he flipped them out the window.

"You're obviously not willing to share."

He walked around the car and let her out.

"Good night," she said.

"Good night."

For a second, anything had still been possible. They were face to face, unable to stop looking into each other's eyes. She broke off first and turned on her heels. He did nothing to try to hold her back. Smartly, she went up the steps leading to the door of her lodginghouse, then she slowed down, slowed still more, finally stopped, and grudgingly turned around.

Italo Volpone was leaning against his car, completely motionless, his cigarette dangling from his lips, looking thoughtful and serious. When he saw her come back down he made no move.

"What's the matter?" he asked. "Forget your keys?"

"No."

"Can you do me a favor?"

"That depends . . ."

"I don't have a dime left," he said, unable to keep from smiling. "I might get picked up for vagrancy. Could you let me have some loose change?"

"I don't have any with me," she replied.

And then they were in each other's arms, neither of them conscious of having made the first move. They didn't kiss, but joined in a kind of formal way, in which each seemed to be evaluating the other's presence without a word being uttered. He patted her hair as he emitted a raucous little laugh.

"Since you wouldn't accept any of my money, what is it you want?"

"You."

In Italo's suite at the Dorchester, Angela was afraid to tell him that this was the first time she had ever been naked in bed with a man. She didn't warn him. Her friends had told her nice men were put off if they found out that a girl was a virgin. So she had gritted her teeth when he came into her, and then she was carried off on a wave of mingled pain and pleasure so intense that she passed out.

"I didn't want to tell you," she later admitted.

"But why? Why?"

"I was afraid you'd change your mind. Oh, Italo, I wanted you so much!"

The next day she had stayed away from her lectures. In the afternoon she had not gone to the library. When evening came, she was still there, in his bed. From time to time, a floor waiter brought a tray of exquisite food and fine chilled wines as transparent as water. The following night they slept for two hours inside of each other. In the morning, they were still making love. At noon, without discussing it, they agreed not to budge. On the afternoon of the third day, as Angela came out of the shower, she said, "I don't know whether it's night or day. I don't even remember my name."

She collapsed lovingly on his chest. He put an arm around her shoulders and tenderly raised her chin.

"I can tell you your name," he said. "It's Angela—Angela Volpone."

Fifty-eight days later, in New York, they were married. Genco had given her a priceless diamond bracelet for a wedding gift. The wedding took place at the Pierre, and hundreds of people came by to wish them well. When Angela's eyes quizzed him as to who they all were, Italo answered with amused winks. And when they got to their sumptuous Park Avenue apartment, Angela had not been able to keep from exclaiming, "Heavens, where do you get the money to afford a place like this?"

"Oh, Genco and I are into a lot of things. Like wholesale fruit and vegetables. We don't make out too bad."

Sometimes Italo and his friends had poker games at the apartment. All the guests treated her with the most obsequious respect, and little by little, an idea crept into her head that for the longest time she dared not articulate. Then, one evening, unable to contain it any longer, she asked her husband, half jokingly, half seriously, "Tell me, Italo, are you a racketeer?"

He looked shocked, collapsed on the couch, and pretended to fire a six-shooter into the air.

"No, no, a thousand times no!" he kidded her. "The lady knows all! Yes, I confess, I confess! I'm a thug! I cut little boys up in slices and eat them raw with dill pickles and mustard! Please don't turn me in, lady, please, oh, please!"

But when Francesca Volpone collapsed with pain as she learned of the death of her husband, she had spoken the awful words, *"I knew they'd kill him on me! And now they're going to kill Italo, too!"*

Angela shivered. That shriek remained ringing in her ears, and she felt terribly lost in the big apartment. The doorbell rang. She had sent her maid Fiorentina out to get the papers. Nervously she got up off the couch to answer the bell, and at the same moment, the phone rang. Her heart jumped. It would be Italo! She picked it up.

"Angela!"

"Italo!"

Again the doorbell rang. She was irritated, and she said hurriedly into the phone, "Hold on, darling. Fiorentina's at the front door. I'll be right back."

She put the receiver down, and as she rushed toward the door she had a vague feeling that she could hear her husband yelling something at her from across the ocean. She opened the door and, without looking at Fiorentina, turned to hurry back to the phone. Suddenly she felt her wrist gripped in a steel vise. Terrorized, she saw two men, both images of the men who came to play poker with Italo, except that she had never seen these two before.

"Mrs. Volpone? Sorry to trouble you, but you'll have to come with us. There's someone who has to see you."

Angela, trying to control her fear, wanted to pull her wrist away. No way.

When she opened her mouth to scream, one of the men quickly clamped his hand over her mouth, and she felt the muzzle of a revolver in her side.

"Don't give us no trouble, Mrs. Volpone. We don't wanna hurt you. You'll be back home soon enough."

She felt like she had a mouthful of rusty metal. Her eyes blurred, her legs gave way beneath her, and she fainted.

While one of the men held her up, the other went over and gingerly hung up the phone.

Homer Kloppe wished he could sink through the earth. Forgetting that he had taken his car to the Grossmünster, he started to walk, grazing the pavement with an unsteady pace, not knowing where he was going, not daring to look anyone in the eye, trying in vain to obliterate the whole nightmarish scene from his mind. He needed to get hold of himself, to be alone awhile, to try to understand what had moved Inez to exhibit herself before the meeting of the college of elders and the representatives of the synodal assemblies. Valiantly Homer had carried on in a kind of fog, attempting to convey to his peers that the giant black woman—"an acquaintance of my daughter's"—was mad. Mumbling excuses, he asked them to go on without him while he alerted the authorities.

He looked up and noticed that he had instinctively walked toward home. But he couldn't go there now. The invaders commissioned by his daughter must be ravaging the apartment in preparation for the wedding.

He forked to the right in the direction of the bank, feeling that all the passersby were staring at him as if they could see the guilt on his face. And he thought he saw looks of irreversible condemnation.

He went into the bank through the private entrance, but Marjorie knew the minute he was there.

"All kinds of calls for you, sir," she said as she walked into his office.

He looked at her somberly. "I'm not in."

"But, sir—"

"Not to anyone, nor for anything. Now, leave me alone."

She made a face that seemed to say, Nobody knows the burdens I bear, and replied, "I'm sorry if I have to dis-obey you, sir, but they're very insistent. They say it's a question of life and death for you. On line three, a man— he said that Inez told him to call, and that you would know what it was about. At any rate, now I've given you the message."

She slipped out, lips tight, scampering like a scared fowl. Did she know? he wondered.

Trembling a little, Homer pressed the button for line three.

"Yes?" he said, fingering the knot of his tie.

"What happened with Inez is only the first warning. A friendly one. It's just too bad these things have to happen to a man of your standing. Suppose the whole town were to hear about it?"

Homer tensed; he recognized the voice of Italo Volpone. His first reaction was to cut him off, but he didn't. He was too curious. And scared.

"Inez is a little nuts, you know," the voice went on. "She's the kind who'd go around bragging about what she did. Fortunately, I was able to talk her out of going and telling your wife about it."

"What is it you want?" Kloppe spat out in a metallic voice.

Volpone, soft-soaping until now, slipped into a threatening tone.

"You damn well know what I want. If it isn't settled first thing tomorrow morning, your troubles have only begun."

Kloppe took a breath, swallowed his saliva, and hissed back, "Go fuck yourself!"

It was the first time in his life he had ever allowed himself to use such vocabulary.

Gabelotti and the younger of the Volpone brothers had gone to the mattress, as the expression went. By locking up Moshe Yudelman and snatching Italo's wife, Ettore had burned his bridges behind him. The war would have broken out sooner or later anyway. Genco's replacement would be a thorny problem for the other four big New York families.

According to Moshe, Italo had made himself the new capo of the Volpone clan. How could Babe Volpone expect to pull that off when his gambling history would automatically turn all the members of the Commissione against him? That is, if he ever showed up again.

To Gabelotti, Italo's sudden disappearance from the hotel was a bad sign. Either he had realized that he could never get into that bank and was on his way home with his tail between his legs, or he already had the Syndicate's two billion bucks; in which case it might be as hard to find him as it was to collect the dough.

What exasperated Ettore most was that it would take hours before he could know. With the difference in time, it would be the middle of the night in New York when the banks opened in Zurich. What would Kloppe answer when he stated the account number?

Trying to calm his nerves, Ettore opened the small refrigerator that was hidden behind a wall panel. He took out several bottles of beer, a loaf of bread, and some butter. He buttered several slices of bread, wolfing each one down as it was finished. He was on his third bottle of brew. Waiting without knowing threw him into a state of deep depressive fury.

Things were beyond his influence or control. The preventive measures he had taken against Volpone would not mean much if the little jerk had taken off with the money. What did a consigliere or even a wife count for, pitted against two billion dollars?

A little earlier, Thomas Merta and Frankie Sabatini called to tell him that Angela Volpone had come along without making a fuss. He had warned the two men not to hurt her. As for Yudelman, Ettore had been magnanimous enough to tell Simeone Ferro to try to cheer him up by making small talk and giving him whatever he might ask for. Ettore respected the Volpone consigliere. Still, by making it clear that he was stringing along with Italo, Moshe had signed his own death warrant. He had bet on the wrong horse.

To calm the intestinal cramps brought on by his worries, Gabelotti downed two more bottles of beer. But his stomach still kept giving him off-and-on twinges. He had a sour taste in his mouth, and several times he had to make an effort to keep from throwing up. To calm the twinges, he took an especially thickly buttered piece of bread.

How could they expect to convince him that Mortimer O'Brion had guts enough to double-cross him? He bit into the bread and swallowed a huge bite almost without chewing. O'Brion was scared of his own shadow. Ettore half choked on the last hunk of bread, began violently coughing, and leaned against his bedroom wall to catch his breath and be able to spit. He had left his brain trust in the office; they had been sitting in an embarrassed silence that rubbed him the wrong way. Bent double, he uncapped another bottle of beer. There was a knock on the door.

"Yes?" he answered in a furious tone.

214

Angelo Barba peeked through the half open door. "Are you all right, Don Ettore?"

Gabelotti, coughing again, signaled to ask what he wanted.

"A package for you," he said. "From Switzerland."

Gabelotti's cough stopped. With eyes watering, he looked at Angelo.

"Who brought it?"

"A messenger from the airport."

"Lemme have it!"

Warily he took the little package that was carefully wrapped in tan paper. The label on it had his name and address. No sender's name. No stamps or postmark.

"How do you know it's from Switzerland?"

"The messenger said it just came in on the Zurich flight."

Gabelotti weighed the package in his hand. It seemed too light to have any kind of trap in it; nevertheless, he gave it to Angelo Barba with a gesture of unconcern.

"Here, open it."

He turned on his heels and went a safe distance away, to the refrigerator next to his bed. He got down on his knees the better to look for the beer bottles that were right in front of him, well aware that the bed would act as a cushion if there were an explosion. Moving the bottles around on the refrigerator shelf, he tossed off, "Probably just something from Rico Gatto."

He heard Barba tear the paper. Instinctively he hunched as low as his paunch would allow.

"Well?" he asked without looking up or moving.

"Shit!" Angelo exclaimed.

"What?"

"Come and see, Don Ettore."

Gabelotti got up, holding a beer bottle. If there were going to be an explosion, it would have happened by now.

"Did you open it?"

Angelo came toward him, holding the package. Without taking it, Gabelotti looked curiously at the wristwatch circling another small packet that seemed to have the shape and size of an egg. Barba put the package up to his ear.

"It's running," he announced in amazement.

The wristband had a tag on it, with an inscription carefully printed in big capital letters: SOUVENIR OF ZURICH.

Angelo slipped the watch away from the smaller packet, which was wrapped in a wrinkled bluish paper. Dying of curiosity, Ettore took it from Angelo's hands and unfolded the paper, revealing a matchbox, which he cautiously put down on a chair.

Glued to the middle of the piece of wrapping paper was Rico Gatto's picture. It was the identification page of his passport. Gabelotti read: *Enrico Gatto, Real Estate Agent, 256 Washington Avenue, Miami, Florida.*

Barba and he exchanged a brief look of wonder. Then Ettore, setting caution aside, grabbed the matchbox and opened it.

Lying on a thin bed of cotton that had dirty brownish spots was a small piece of bloodred meat with clots of blood that gave off a sweetish odor. Despite his revulsion, Gabelotti looked closer, and he saw that it was a piece of a human tongue.

The tongue of Rico Gatto.

14

Italo Volpone woke up just as the sun was rising. As was usual when he had not slept long enough, he wondered where he was. He didn't recognize the blue velour drapes, the heavily canopied bed, or the outsize pieces of dark furniture. Through the open window he heard a concert of birdsong. The slits in the shutters let in a golden light that made parallel stripes on the carpet, and he stretched, yawned, scratched his head, and looked at his watch: it was 6:30. Then it all started to come back to him.

The evening before, after he had spoken to Angela and the phone had been hung up, he had dialed again and let it ring, but neither Angela nor Fiorentina had answered.

Wild with worry, he had phoned Moshe Yudelman, and had no more success. Feverishly Italo tried Genco's *sottocapo*, the faithful Vittorio Pizzu, who had been identified with the family for twenty years. But Vittorio's Eighth Avenue apartment didn't answer either. It seemed like all those connected with him had suddenly disappeared. Between trying those three numbers over and over again, Italo did succeed in contacting Genco's three *capiregime*, Aldo Amalfi, Vincente Bruttore, and Joseph Dotto.

To his amazement, none of the three knew about Genco's death. Cursing Yudelman for having ignored his instructions, Italo filled them in briefly, saying his brother's passing in no way changed the family's operations. He announced that he was taking over as boss, and he

217

ordered them to mobilize all the soldiers they could and find Angela and Moshe Yudelman.

After that, he tried his home one last time. Fiorentina was finally back. Her mistress had sent her out for the papers, but when she got back, she told him, the apartment was empty. With a lump in his throat the size of a baseball, Italo could only pray that his wife was attending his sister-in-law, Francesca. But Francesca informed him in her hollow mourning voice that she hadn't seen Angela since the day before. Then, changing her tone, she demanded an explanation about what had happened to her husband. Intensely embarrassed, Italo didn't know what to tell her. He certainly couldn't tell her the details he knew. At least not yet.

Sobbing desperately, Francesca begged him to tell her where Genco's body was so that she might go and kneel before it one last time before he was buried. Italo stammered something about calling her back, saying he was taking care of everything. As he hung up, he tried to react against his confused feeling of guilt: he was in no way responsible for what had happened.

On the other hand, what was to come was entirely within his control. Kloppe was going to find out that you couldn't toy with other people's misfortunes. The banker's reply to his threats had completely floored him, filling him with a pent-up rage that he would not long be able to contain.

He opened the blinds, blinking against the sunlight shining on his face. In the garden of the estate, everything was as pure and sweet as on the morning of the Creation. Not a trace of human life on the flower-decorated lawns that were being invaded by bunches of blackbirds. The lilac along the wrought-iron fence swayed imperceptibly as a slight breeze shook the highest branches of the cedars and bent the frail stems of jonquils around which white butterflies were playing.

It wasn't fair for such beauty to exist, for the living pulsation of all that sap to go on while his brother's body was rotting somewhere.

He forced himself to stop wasting his time over the promise of life in the radiant April morning. He needed to keep his hate charged up. He turned his back on the sun, went into the shower, and turned on the cold water, counting to a hundred while the icy jet nipped at his skin.

He put on clean underwear and one of his invariable black suits, and he went down to the kitchen. Everyone was still asleep. He found a canister of coffee, made himself a cup, lit his first cigarette, and was about to take a small walk in the garden when he sensed a presence at his side, although he had not heard a thing.

"I had hoped to be able to make your coffee for you," Folco Mori was saying to him.

"I have to talk to you," Italo answered.

"Me too."

"Well, go ahead."

"Here's the thing. You really have to know about it. Everything's been happening so fast since we got to Zurich. You had so much to do and were so shook up about your brother, the same as we all were, that maybe you didn't see what was going on behind your back."

Folco was speaking quietly. Babe Volpone watched him from behind half-shut eyelids. Mori had always been a mystery to him.

"What was going on behind my back?" Italo asked, puffing on his cigarette.

"I knocked off two guys," said Folco.

"When?"

"Since we got here."

"Why?"

"They were tailing you from New York. They were on the plane with us."

"Gabelotti?"

"No. When I offed the first one, I couldn't know. But, I'm sorry to say, he was a cop. A New York cop."

Italo shuddered. "How did you kill him?"

"He fell from the sixth story of Sordi's Hotel. An accident."

"Accident?"

"No one'll ever be able to prove it wasn't. Bellinzona and me are the only ones who know what happened."

"And the other guy—was he another cop?"

"Yep. Same squad. Kirkpatrick's special brigade. When you went up to the mountains with O'Brion and his blonde, and the nigger broad, he was right behind you."

219

"Where were you?"

"Behind him. He wasn't as easy as the first one. He almost got me. But I lucked out."

"Where's his body?"

"Half a mile from the sawmill. I stashed it in a gulley."

Volpone looked away, concentrating on the tip of his cigarette. Then he enunciated slowly, "You think I ought to congratulate you?"

"I don't think anything. I'm just telling you. That's all."

"Didn't you know the second one was a bull?"

"If I hadn'a done what I did, we'd all be collared already for murdering the blonde and Morty O'Brion."

Italo spat out the butt of his cigarette. It landed on a daisy and burned away the pistil. He sighed as he turned back to Folco. "What you did was right, Folco. You had no choice. Thanks."

He tapped Folco on the shoulder in a friendly manner, and Folco was just about to say something, but Pietro Bellinzona appeared, surprised to find them there. He was bursting out of a dressing gown he had found in a closet.

"Here I thought I was the first one up," he said, forcing back a yawn. His tough, jowly skin was blue with an unshaven beard. He raised his face to the morning sun and said, "I'm hungry."

Volpone looked at him. "I'm only gonna warn you once," he snapped. "If I ever find you doing the least little thing without my approval, you're out of the family."

Taken unaware, the big guy looked bug-eyed at him and whimpered, "What'd I do now?"

"You helped Folco off two cops. And I didn't even know about it!"

Bellinzona looked reproachfully at Mori. If he hadn't mentioned anything to Italo, it was because Folco had insisted he shouldn't.

"I thought—" he started to mumble.

"You don't have to do no thinking for me. I'm the one who gives the orders around here."

"Pietro didn't have anything to do with it," Folco said quietly.

"You—just keep out of it," Volpone stormed at him. "I already told you how I felt about it. You oughta have told me. I expect to know everything. Get that? Everything!"

He stared at them. Neither Bellinzona nor Mori blinked. The birds in the garden, temporarily startled by the noise of the voices, now began singing all the louder.

Italo pointed at Bellinzona. "In two hours," he said, "you're gonna have one helluva toothache."

Worried by what that could mean, Pietro sneaked a look over at Folco Mori, but Mori's face didn't show a thing.

"Folco!"

"Yes, *padrone*."

"You know what I came to Zurich for?"

"In general, yes," Mori answered without hesitation.

"A shitass little banker is trying to hold up the money my brother deposited with him. That bastard has to be offed. But not right away. I want to cut him down little by little. If he croaks too soon, we'll never get the dough. I gotta make him talk. You get my drift?"

"Yes."

"Zurich is gonna get too hot for us. We gotta work fast. Pietro!"

"Yes?"

"How would you feel if you was Gabelotti and somebody offed one of your soldiers?"

Bellinzona rubbed his jaw, the heavy beard squeaking beneath his fingers.

"I'd get me an execution squad and go out to get even."

"Right. And you, Folco, if you was Kirkpatrick and two of your flatfoots disappeared?"

"Same thing. I'd get in touch with the Swiss coppers."

Volpone confirmed both statements with a nod.

"You said it! So that means we're gonna have a whole flock of fuckers on our tail. All the more reason to get done in a hurry and beat it. Everything depends on the lousy banker. He's a tough bastard, but I'm tougher. I'll break him down! Yesterday's warning wasn't enough. Today we gotta make him cough it up."

Folco looked skeptical. "If he knows we gotta keep him alive, he may not go for any bluff."

Italo smiled nastily. "Try that on me in a couple

hours. I'm betting he'll understand, all right. Now listen. At 9:30 I want you to take Bellinzona to 9 Zweierstrasse. You'll go up to the third floor and ring the bell of a dentist, name of Professor August Strolh. His wife, Ingrid, will open for you. She'll say you don't have no appointment, but Bellinzona will be holding his aching jaw. You'll say his wisdom tooth is hurting him so that he's been screaming his head off."

Pietro, finally beginning to catch on, sighed with relief.

"You scared me when you said I was gonna have a toothache, *padrone*. Once we get inside, what do we do?"

A cruel little light flashed in Volpone's eyes.

"Lemme tell you . . ."

"Why should you wait, Don Ettore? Volpone is not only robbing us, he's making monkeys of us besides!"

For the hundredth time since the long vigil began, Gabelotti looked at his watch. It was nearly four in the morning. All the influential members of his family, gathered around him, had talked at length about what was to be done. Carmine Crimello and Angelo Barba thought they ought to wait until the Zurich Trade Bank opened for business, to make sure of what had happened to the two billion. After that, if necessary, reprisals could be set into motion immediately.

Carlo Badaletto was all for taking it out on Moshe Yudelman and Angela Volpone without waiting. And no halfway measures. As he saw it, Rico Gatto's tongue had been the final proof of Italo Volpone's treachery and had also been intended as an open challenge, the unforgivable insult.

"I tell you this Volpone is a fuckin' madman!" Badaletto said. If he feels we're weakening the least bit, he'll take every one of us, one after the other!"

In order to soothe frayed nerves, Don Ettore had had a ten-pound can of caviar sent up to the office. But his men, knowing the boss's pathological need to keep stuffing himself, had hardly touched a drop of it, despite his repeated invitations. By now there were just a few scraps of the fish eggs left in the bottom of the tin, and the don was scraping them up to spread on his buttered rye bread. He chewed it and then washed it down with a shot of vodka followed by a can of beer. Caviar always made him thirsty.

Up to this point he had simply listened without taking sides, merely shrugging when it seemed like Badaletto was getting carried away with his own violence. The fact was, he thought Badaletto was too chicken-livered. What did he care about the lives of Moshe and Angela? If Volpone really had double-crossed him, he would see to it that the whole goddamned family paid with their lives—from the lowest foot soldier right up to Italo himself. And he'd spend the rest of his life searching the bastard out so he could do away with him with his own hands, if that was what it took. No matter how long he had to wait, nor what it cost, he'd get him!

However, business had to come before revenge.

"Carmine, what time?" he asked.

"One minute after four."

Gabelotti's watch said only 3:59, but he had been holding his rage in check for so long that now he could not keep himself from picking up the phone and dialing. In Zurich it was 9:00 A.M. The bank had just opened its doors. On the second ring he got an answer.

"Hello," he yelled, "I'm calling from very far away! I have to talk to Homer Kloppe. I have an account with you. This is urgent—very urgent!"

On his way through the lobby of his bank, Homer Kloppe sensed an undertone of sarcasm in the way his employees greeted him. He couldn't believe they hadn't heard about yesterday's scandal. An event of that magnitude couldn't remain secret in a town like Zurich.

Homer had spent part of the night trying to sort things out, crushed by a feeling of insuperable guilt. Chimene would know about it, his daughter would know, the whole town, the whole country would know! All the little discrepancies between what he considered himself to be and what he actually was appeared grossly magnified by the lens of remorse. How many years did he have left to live? What had he done to warrant salvation? Had he given his only daughter the proper upbringing? If so, how had this imminent marriage come about? And how would Chimene, whom he had so unjustly rewarded for her impeccable faithfulness by deceiving her with a prostitute, react when the scandal splattered over her?

He who had preached virtue, had done evil. He who had judged, stood condemned. He was being punished in his most sensitive spot, his social persona. He would have to pay the price. The very next day, once Renata had become Mrs. Kurt Heinz—at three o'clock in the morning, as if anything could be more unseemly!—he would begin acting only according to his conscience, no matter what effect it might have on his business.

His recent interview with Melvin Bost had left him with a bitter taste in his mouth. Out of weakness (or was it greed?), he had failed to face up to the Intercontinental Motor Cars situation. It was monstrous to let innocent people die, and Homer would no longer permit it. Whatever it might cost him, he would instruct Bost to have all authorized dealers recall every Beauty Ghost P9 on the road.

Kloppe decided to give himself three years to wind up his affairs. He had no son to succeed him, Renata had no interest in finance, and poor Kurt surely could not run the shop. Why try to accumulate capital that was not a means to an end, but only an end in itself? He and Chimene would never want for anything till the end of their days. Even if they went wild, they would never be able to spend one one-hundredth of their wealth.

"It's urgent, sir, very urgent; important and personal. The party is on the line." Marjorie had been waiting for him outside his office door.

Kloppe looked at his watch. It was 9:01.

"Yes?" he said.

"Mr. Homer Kloppe?"

"Yes."

"You don't know me, but I have an account with you."

"I'm listening."

"You met my attorney, Mr. Mortimer O'Brion."

A little light went on in Kloppe's head. This man could only be Philip Diego's client and Genco Volpone's partner, Ettore Gabelotti. Immediately, the banker visualized the number of the account, 828384, as well as *Mamma mia,* the code name chosen by the depositors. Anything over two or three million dollars etched itself into his memory automatically.

"First I'll give you the number. Then I'll have certain instructions for you."

"Go ahead, sir."

"21877, in the name of G-O-D."

Kloppe knitted his brow. His suspicions about Mortimer O'Brion had not been without foundation. The dishonest little man *had* given his employer a fake number. Kloppe was distressed to find that a human being could stoop to such baseness, but, unfortunately, he was not able to be any more helpful to Ettore Gabelotti than he had been to Italo Volpone. He made his voice sound as impersonal as possible.

"I am very sorry, sir. But I have no idea what you are talking about."

"I beg your pardon?" came the choking reply.

"The details you have just given me do not correspond to those of any account we have here in the firm."

"What are you talking about? What are you trying to tell me?"

"I am very sorry, sir. But apparently you've made some mistake. Good day, sir."

He hung up and rang for Marjorie.

"If by any chance that party should call back, please tell him I've gone out."

"Very well, sir."

She walked out stiffly. By force of habit, he started putting some figures down on paper.

It was now five days since Genco Volpone had made the two-billion-dollar deposit at the Zurich Trade Bank. Homer had immediately redeposited that amount with Eugene Schmeelbling at Schaan. Allowing for the interest that Kloppe would—perhaps—have to pay to whomever came in with the right account number, this perfectly ordinary and legal bit of paperwork left him a daily net profit of \$109,588, or, multiplied by five, \$547,940 in all.

Kloppe couldn't dismiss the Latin phrase that kept coming to his lips: *Cui bono?* (Who profits from the crime?). Obviously, this did not apply to him, and, had it not been for the deep remorse haunting him for totally different reasons, he would never even have thought of it.

Yet, there could be no two ways about it. If there was any crime involved, there was only one person profiting—and that was the banker himself!

At exactly 9:30 A.M., on the third floor of 9 Zweierstrasse, a slim man in a black suit rang Professor August Strolh's bell. His hand was on the arm of a husky character who was holding his jaw, a look of extreme pain on his mug.

Ingrid Strolh opened the door.

"Gentlemen?" she inquired.

Folco Mori pointed to Pietro Bellinzona and said, "For the last hour he's been suffering the tortures of the damned."

"Do you have an appointment?" Ingrid asked, making a face.

"We're just passing through. You must have had a call from the concierge of our hotel, the Continental."

"Not at all."

"But I can't let my friend go on suffering."

To back him up, Pietro gave a muffled groan.

"I'm sorry," Ingrid replied, "but we have a full schedule for the day. Would you like the address of someone else?"

"No, no," Folco protested. "My friend doesn't want to go anywhere else. At the hotel they said that Professor Strolh is the finest specialist in all Zurich."

Ingrid hesitated only a second. "Sit down a minute," she told them. "The professor is busy, but I'll see what I can do." And she turned on her heels. For an instant Pietro and Folco admired the sight of her rump.

"You ever have toothaches?" Bellinzona asked Folco.

"No."

"Me neither. Know why? When I was a kid, I was playing ball and got hit in the face with a bat. The roots are mine, but the rest are caps."

Ingrid was coming back in. Bellinzona's hands went to his jaw and he made an awful face and bent his head.

"The professor has a ten-o'clock appointment. If there's a moment between patients, he's agreed to examine you, but he won't be able to do any dental work today."

She handed Pietro a glass of water and a white pill. "Take this. It'll ease the pain."

Bellinzona sniffed at the glass distrustfully.

"Drink it!" Folco ordered.

Pietro put the pill under his tongue and swallowed the water with revulsion. As soon as Ingrid went out, he took the pill out of his mouth and slipped it into his pocket.

At five minutes to ten, she came back. "Please follow me."

She showed them into a room that had so much chrome it looked more like an electric power station than a dental office. Soft music floated on the air.

"I can only give you a quick examination," August Strolh said to Bellinzona. "Please be seated."

"That your old lady?" Folco Mori asked, pointing to Ingrid.

Strolh shrugged in response and exchanged a glance with his wife. "I beg your pardon?" he replied.

"She's got one helluvan ass," Folco said, raising her skirt.

In the same motion, his right hand, holding a razor, went around Ingrid's neck, while Bellinzona pointed a Walther PP into the stomatologist's solar plexus.

"Higher," Pietro insisted.

Folco raised the folds of the skirt a bit more.

"Hey, the pig's not wearing no underpants!" Pietro guffawed.

Under his salt-and-pepper beard, the blood drained out of August Strolh's face, just as it flushed in Ingrid's.

Folco took advantage of the slight pause to get his statement in. "We got nothin' against you. But that won't keep me from slitting her throat if you don't do everything exactly like I tell you."

"You wouldn't like us to slit the throat of your sweet little pig of a wife, would you?" Bellinzona added in false sympathy. "Hey! You know why she don't wear no panties? He must stick it to her between patients."

"That's not it at all," Folco said. "While he's drilling, she spreads her legs. That way, the patient forgets that it hurts!"

227

Bellinzona guffawed again. One of the reasons he liked Folco so much was that terrific sense of humor he always kept, even in the toughest spots.

Despite the fact that he was trembling and his throat was parched and his legs giving way, August Strolh succeeded in saying, "Tell me how much money you want, and go away."

"Won't cost you a cent," Folco said, marshaling Ingrid off to the back of the office.

He raised a curtain and found himself in a cubbyhole about six feet by nine that was lined with shelves holding all kinds of plaster impressions of jaws. Terrified, Ingrid let herself lean against him, limp as a rag doll. Mori turned back toward Pietro and gave him a thumbs-up sign.

"Will it do?" Bellinzona asked.

"Yeah. We can stay in here with her."

"Listen," the professor said in a quavering voice, "in a minute, one of my patients will be here."

"That's just it," said Mori. "He's the one we're here for. While you treat him, just don't forget that we're watching everything you do."

"What are you talking about?"

Bellinzona couldn't repress a delighted little gurgle. He gently ran the edge of his hand across August Strolh's throat in a gesture of unmistakable meaning.

"We'll let you know. And if you don't do as we say— then, your wife—Oops!"

"Not to mention the shot in the belly you'll get, for good measure," Folco added. Then he started to explain what they expected.

Strolh was desperately making signs of refusal, his eyes glowering with indignation.

"If you'd rather watch your wife croak before your eyes, and your patient get rubbed out too, suit yourself," Folco concluded with a fatalistic shrug.

The doorbell rang.

"Go open up," Mori said calmly.

Bellinzona let go of the dentist. "Don't forget we've got our eyes on you," he said. "One word, one look, one questionable move and it's curtains for all of you."

Pressing close against Ingrid Strolh, they disappeared behind the curtain.

"I repeat, it just can't be done," the professor protested one last time. "He'll see through it."

A stifled cry from Ingrid came back as reply. Terrified, August hurried to answer the door.

Three light knocks, and one heavy one. Orlando Baretto opened the door just a crack and Italo Volpone slipped through.

"Where is she?" Volpone demanded.

"Locked in her bedroom."

Volpone went in. Inez was propped up on a pile of cushions against the radiator. She was reading a fashion magazine that she held in her right hand. Her left wrist was handcuffed to the radiator. She put the magazine down and looked blankly at Italo.

"You know how to write?" Italo asked.

Lando gave him a surprised look. How could anyone ask such a question of a girl who had completed three years of college?

Lando hadn't slept much. Following the boss's orders, he had grudgingly chained Inez to the radiator. She had remained stubbornly silent, hostile, scornful, indifferent, and obedient, and Lando had agreed to give her the phone whenever it rang. Volpone felt she ought to answer it so as not to arouse suspicions in any of her customers. Orlando listened in on the extension, and in doing so he got a whole new idea of what his girl's life was like. She had spoken to several women, models, who chattered to her about dressing-room gossip full of sly innuendos. Men, too: a German movie producer and an Italian fashion photographer. Inez had politely turned down an offer to do a top magazine cover wearing a king's ransom in jewelry covering her body. There were also a few words spoken in an African tongue.

"Two of my cousins," she had told him, "who are passing through. Diplomats. They're coming over."

Lando had gotten furious. "All you had to do was say you'd be out!"

"They haven't seen me in two years. They're

229

bringing presents. You don't have to let them in if you don't want to."

"If you say one more word in that language of yours, I'll beat your brains in."

He had a burning yen for her, but he could only express it by exaggerating his irritation. The fact was, all things considered, he felt he had fallen in love with her, and he was sore at himself for having done so.

"Write what I dictate to you," Volpone ordered as he gave her some paper and a pen.

She pointed to the handcuffs. "I can't write with these on."

"Your right hand is free."

"I'm left-handed."

"Take the cuffs off," he told Lando.

Inez rubbed her wrist and stretched with the supple grace of a jungle cat. She started to take the pad and pen.

"Just a minute," Volpone said. "I want a picture of you. Bare-assed."

She went searching through a dresser drawer, got a folder, and found a print for him. Italo took a quick look at it and pocketed it without a word. Inez lay on her stomach on the bed, picked up the pen in her left hand, and placed the pad in front of her.

"Go ahead," she told Volpone without bothering to look at him.

At any other time, Homer Kloppe would have noticed immediately how distressed Dr. Strolh looked, and how limp and unconvincing his handshake was. But this morning Kloppe was too concerned with his own worries.

"Isn't your wife here?" he asked perfunctorily.

"She'll be back soon," Strolh said, making sure he didn't look into the banker's eyes. "Please be seated. I'll be right with you."

He pretended to be busy with his instruments as Kloppe plopped into the heavy leather dental chair.

Suddenly blinded by the strong light that Strolh flashed into his face, Kloppe saw the professor's long white hands move into his field of vision as if they had no connection with the dentist's arms and body. Kloppe, dazzled, could not even make out where the doctor was standing, and he closed his eyes to avoid the thousand little suns that exploded on his retinas. He felt a bib being tied around his neck, and he was surprised by Strolh's silence. Usually the professor told a string of stories, running them one into the other in a dizzying rhythm so that they had a kind of hypnotic effect on the patient.

"Are you all right?" Homer asked him.

"Yes, just fine. Now, let's take a little look at what we have here."

August Strolh would have liked to yell to Homer to get out. To prove to himself that he wasn't dreaming, he looked back toward the curtain where the two men were holding his wife. The curtain parted just the slightest bit, a the circus strong man gave him what was supposed to be an encouraging smile. Next to him, August could see Ingrid, her eyes wide with fear, in the arms of the other man, her head being held slightly back, the razor poised against her throat.

To retain his sanity, August Strolh launched into his professional monologue. But he had to keep it coherent so he wouldn't arouse Kloppe's suspicions. As far as dental theory went, the banker, being the buff he was, knew almost as much as the doctor himself.

"I have the answer to what you asked me the other day," the professor was saying. "Now, bend your head slightly to the left. There. Yes. Thanks. You know, about dissolving the organic base of the enamel. . . . Most unlikely unless the apatite crystals are broken down first . . ."

"Ah?" Kloppe replied.

"Keep your mouth wide open. The organic elements are petrified right into the mineral base. Besides, as you very well know, cariogenic bacteria are not, generally speaking, proteolytic."

Homer Kloppe raised a finger as if asking permission to speak. He felt Strolh's hands release his jaw.

"There's one other possibility: the simultaneous dissolution of both the organic and mineral base of the enamel."

His face bathed in perspiration, the professor could not resist his violent urge to look toward the curtain again. The strong man signaled to him impatiently, and he mechanically answered Kloppe.

231

"Very unlikely, my friend, very unlikely. Of course, all the apatites that are the main constituents of the enamel are soluble. But at pH7, in distilled water, only 1.2 percent of human enamel dissolves in five weeks."

It would never work. Kloppe would smell a rat the minute he started to anesthetize him. He'd ask why. What could he answer? Kloppe knew his teeth were in perfect condition. But if August didn't do it, the others, behind the curtain with Ingrid . . . Strolh had no choice and no time. Under the impetus of the terror in his solar plexus, he gave a fake miserable little laugh.

"I'm going to show you something entirely new. Something wonderful. It's Swedish. Just keep your mouth closed now. I'm going to have to raise your gum slightly to see what's giving you a bit of inflammation. I'll need a closer look."

Homer raised an eyebrow in surprise.

"Just relax, relax," the dentist told him. "Perhaps some irritating agent at the marginal periodontal tissue. That often happens . . ."

As he was speaking, Strolh was readying the mask that was connected by a rubber hose to the tank of nitrous oxide.

"Now, breathe deeply two or three times."

Kloppe tensed. Strolh had examined him yesterday. A serious irritation could not have occurred overnight. He was going to signal that he had something to say when he felt the professor press the mask down over his face.

"Don't move. Breathe deeply. Just relax."

Not understanding why the dentist should be doing this to him, Homer attempted to raise himself. By reflex, as he did, he inhaled deeply. Instantly he felt a strange softening sensation. He raised his arm to protest, gripped Strolh's arm without conviction, and felt a need for air, so he inhaled deeply again. The mask began to feel heavier on his cheekbones; the professor's hand on his forehead became as weighty as a block of steel; and the light shining on him exploded like crystalline rain.

He passed out. For a few more seconds the professor, his hands trembling, held the mask. When he was sure the banker was completely under, he turned toward the two men, his eyes full of tears.

"I can't," he moaned. "I just can't." He wiped the sweat that was running into his eyes and shouted, "I can't, I tell you!"

The big one took four steps toward him and slapped him. "Go on and do it, jerk! You want us to start bleeding your old lady?"

August, his head about to burst, looked at Ingrid. In her bloodless face, only the eyes expressed her terror.

Then he understood that she would die if he didn't do as he was told. Struggling to overcome his intense urge to vomit, he picked up the forceps, opened Homer Kloppe's jaws, and considered the proper angle of attack. He gripped an upper incisor in the pincers and pulled. The banker's inert head came with it. Strolh blocked it by leaning his left elbow against Kloppe's forehead. He loosened the incisor, twisting it first one way, then the other. Then, taking up a sharp surgical knife he split the flesh of the gum, cutting through the ligaments holding the tooth to the bone. Grasping his pincers again, he pulled once more. Something cracked. Under Bellinzona's interested but unfeeling eye, Strolh dropped the bloodstained tooth into the metal tray. And went after another incisor.

When all of the front of Kloppe's jaw was toothless, Strolh, livid and drenched in sweat, looked imploringly toward Bellinzona. But he found no pity there—just the implacable order to keep going.

The molars with their divergent roots gave him the most trouble. Overcoming his nausea, he had to use an elevator that he lodged between bone and root in order to get the teeth out of their sockets.

"Quicker!" Bellinzona was scolding, as the show began to bore him.

Eight minutes later, it was all over. Homer Kloppe didn't have a tooth left in his head. Strolh's eyes happened onto the tray where, in tiny pools of blood, lay the teeth he had just extracted. His eyes glazed over, his nostrils tightened, and, slowly, he collapsed.

Bellinzona looked at Strolh with contempt. He opened the banker's jaw and shoved his finger inside to make sure there was nothing left in the gums. The job, he found, had been thorough. Satisfied, he wiped his soiled finger on Kloppe's jacket.

Folco Mori let go of Ingrid, folded his razor, and put it back in his pocket. The young woman was not very steady on her legs, and passing near her, Bellinzona smiled amiably. His huge hand suddenly unlimbered and with a sharp blow met Ingrid's forehead. She sank softly to the floor. Folco unlocked a back door that led to a service stairway, and they went down calmly after Pietro had closed the door behind them.

A minute went by. In the ravaged office, nothing moved. The tape continued to play Vivaldi. The telephone rang ten times or so, then stopped.

Homer Kloppe began to move. He opened his eyes, instinctively touched his lips with his hand, and saw that they were full of blood. Lowering his head, he saw the motionless body of August Strolh. In pain, he glanced around the room, and then he saw Ingrid Strolh, her smock raised revealingly over her long round thighs.

Giving up any effort to make sense of it all, he tottered to his feet, holding the edges of the dental chair, and took a few steps over to the bronze-framed mirror. He did not know who he was. His face was covered with blood, as was the bib around his neck. Blood was flowing out of the corners of his mouth in a double stream that ran down the sides of his jaw.

His heart beat like a hammer on an anvil as he concentrated what courage was left in him to confirm what he already guessed. He opened his mouth.

His gums were no more than a bloody mess of flesh with nothing in them. A century before, when he had sat down in the dentist's chair, he had had the most perfect set of teeth in the city. Now, in their place, were only holes. Tears ran down his cheeks as he turned from the mirror.

Ingrid, now sitting up on the floor, looked at him, her eyes dilated with horror. The telephone rang. Like an automaton, her vacant eyes staring straight ahead, Ingrid went to pick it up. As she listened, her expression did not change; she did not seem to be hearing. Yet she held the receiver out to Homer Kloppe, who just as automatically took it from her.

Despite his state of shock, the banker recognized

the voice he would never forget—the voice of Italo Volpone.

"That's the second and last warning. If the money is not released within the hour, I won't be responsible for your life or the lives of your family."

Kloppe didn't have the strength to spit out the large glob of blood that had formed against his palate. He pushed it aside with his tongue, tried to control his hesitant breathing, and slowly, in a voice that had been changed by the loss of his teeth, a voice scarcely above a whisper, forced out the words, "Drop dead!"

15

What was happening was beyond her comprehension. For almost seventeen hours now she had been confined in a luxurious bedroom, full of books, a stereo tape deck, a TV set, all varieties of drinks, and a bell that immediately brought a nice fat woman ready to satisfy whatever needs she might have. But no one would tell Angela why she was here, where she was, and how long this would last.

The woman would only answer her questions with smiles, remaining resolutely mute, complying with any request that might make her more comfortable, such as toilet articles and food.

The two men who abducted her had been no more communicative. Somehow, darkly, she felt this kidnapping was connected with her husband. She was sorry now that she had not insisted on knowing more about his business. All day she had paced around her tiny prison-palace, finding no inside knob on the door, nor any way to open the window. The smoked-glass panes let in the light but allowed her to see nothing that would furnish any information.

Apart from the fat woman, no one had come in. Around four-thirty in the morning, after knocking on the door, a huge man finally made an appearance.

"I want to apologize," he told her, "for the way my men brought you here. Do you have everything you require?"

"Who are you?"

"A friend of your husband's. In fact, more than a friend. Italo and I are partners. My name is Ettore Gabelotti. I hope I didn't wake you."

"I want to go home."

"First, let me warn you. I just got back here. My instructions were not carried out properly. I told them they were to explain to you exactly why I invited you over."

In other circumstances his choice of words might have been funny. Angela did not let it pass.

"Invited me over? What do you mean? I was forced to come, with a gun shoved in my ribs!"

"Those men have been punished. Try to understand —Italo is in Zurich. You know that. He is there on joint business for us. Unfortunately, he lost his brother, whom we all held in the highest esteem. And maybe Genco didn't die of entirely natural causes. So Italo was worried. When I heard that some people who have it in for your husband and me had made some threats concerning you, I thought the best thing would be to bring you here, where you would be safe from harm."

"I want to go."

"You can if you want, but I beg you not to. Later, you will thank me for this. *Lei è italiana?*"

"*Sì, io sono, ma—*"

"*Da dov'è?*"

"Look, I was kidnapped early yesterday afternoon, and it's now almost five in the morning. I don't want to overstay my welcome. I will be sure to let Italo know how well I was treated while I was your guest. Now, please have someone take me back home."

"I can see that you are angry with me, but I cannot, as a friend of Italo's, let you run such a risk. Once more, I must insist that you spend the rest of the night here."

Angela felt the tears welling up in her eyes. She bit her lip. Italo was her life in this country. The only one she saw was him. Her own friends and family were either in Italy or in England. All she knew of New York was some restaurants and a couple of museums. Their conjugal bed had been the center of her universe, but now Italo wasn't here, and she felt desperately alone and vulnerable in the face of a terrifying, incomprehensible situation. Behind

this fat man's polite phrases she recognized pitiless determination. She was not the kind of woman to break down,
so she decided, for the time being, to resign herself to her
fate. Frightened as she was, she replied, "I get up at nine.
I take my coffee black without sugar, and I like the bacon
with my eggs very crisp."

Gabelotti bowed as deeply as his huge belly allowed.

"I am very happy that you are staying. You will
have everything as you wish. Once again, I apologize for
the inconvenience."

Everyone in the Volpone family was fond of Moshe
Yudelman, Vittorio Pizzu no less than the others. But he
questioned Yudelman's faith in smooth words and careful
negotiations. From experience, Vittorio knew that there
came a time when you needed weapons to make your
point of view prevail and to safeguard your interests. So
when Moshe told him he was planning to go back into
Gabelotti's grip, Vittorio had tried to talk him out of it.
But Yudelman had been adamant.

"Ducking out of the situation isn't going to settle
anything," he insisted.

"If you're crazy enough to go back there, you'll
never get out alive."

"I'm going. By myself. And I'll come back alive. You
just keep out of it, Vittorio."

Pizzu pretended to agree, but he instructed Vincente
Bruttore to have two soldiers shadow the consigliere.
Vito Francini and Quinto Favara, in jeans, long hair, and
cyclists' helmets, had gone along on a high-powered Honda
that they "stalled" after making careful note of what time
Moshe Yudelman went into Ettore Gabelotti's.

After that, Vittorio had New York honeycombed by
all the available men in the regimes of his three lieutenants,
Aldo Amalfi, Vincente Bruttore, and Joseph Dotto. Even
though every precinct in Manhattan had at least one cop on
the Volpone pad, Vittorio was not yet ready to go that
route. There would be plenty of time for those measures
if and when Angela Volpone did come home on her own,
and Vittorio had his own ideas about that.

It was probable that Don Ettore had snatched

Angela to hold as a future bargaining chip. If so, Italo would never forgive the insult, and the war between him and Gabelotti would go on until one or the other was dead.

Vittorio looked at his watch. Moshe Yudelman had gone into Gabelotti's yesterday at noon. Now, at 5:00 A.M., Moshe had still not reappeared. Either Ettore was holding him hostage or the don had lost his temper and knocked him off. Except for the three hours during which exhaustion had finally made him sleep, Vittorio had had regular calls from Vito Francini and Quinto Favara every half hour to confirm that Moshe was still in there.

Vittorio made a face and picked up the phone to dial Italo's new number in Zurich. It was high time for going into action, but he would never presume to lift a finger without a go-ahead from Volpone. Fortunately, he got a connection right away.

"Hello, this is Vittorio."

"Where you been, jerk? I been looking for you everyplace. What's with Angela, huh?"

"I've had New York honeycombed. No sign of her yet, *padrone*. We're going ahead—"

Even though there were thousands of miles between them, Pizzu was shaken by the violence of Volpone's reaction.

"I want my wife, you got that? I want my wife!"

"Yes, *padrone*."

Trembling with rage, Volpone screamed, "I'll get every one of you if anything happens to her! Every one! Even you. You'll answer for her safety with your life!"

Pizzu had trouble swallowing.

"I had thought maybe—" he tried to say.

"Don't bother thinking, jerk! Just find her!"

"Yes, boss. I'll find her. But I was wondering—Angela can't get along without you—maybe she's on her way to where you are?"

"She would have let me know. She always tells me everything. And if you're such a big thinker, what do you think about Gabelotti?"

"I don't know."

"So? What are you waiting for? Where's Moshe?"

239

"At Gabelotti's."

"That stupid fuckin' bastard! Since when?"

"Yesterday noon."

"You gotta be nuts! All of you gotta be nuts! *Porco Dio di merda!* I'm busting my balls here, and you guys—"

"I was waiting for your orders, *padrone.*"

"You're never there when I want to give 'em! Now hear this: you take Amalfi and Bruttore and Dotto, and you bring back that fuckin' Yudelman. Understand?"

"Okay, boss." Then, to show Italo that there was to be no more misunderstanding about who was running the family, Vittorio Pizzu corrected himself: "Will do, Don Italo."

Since their talk earlier, Captain Kirkpatrick had not called back, and Fritz Blesh was trying to piece together apparently disparate events to find possible cause-and-effect relationships that would let his mind be at ease once again. A leg arrived on the front of a railroad engine; an American cop disappeared without settling his hotel bill; and the cop's partner—who, the autopsy showed, had no trace of alcohol in his blood—fell six floors to his death at Sordi's Hotel. All in the middle of Zurich, in a matter of less than five days.

As Blesh saw it, it had to be some kind of narcotics deal in which the principals, foreign cops and mafiosi, had selected Switzerland for their showdown. The day before, one of his detectives had told him about a shoot-out in the boiler room of the Commodore Hotel. One of the punctured boilers had several bullets in it, and the bullets were being analyzed at the ballistics lab. No one in the hotel had heard a thing. There was blood on one boiler, on one of the walls, and on the floor, but no body was found.

Blesh planned to do his own investigating. In the meantime, there were more urgent things to be done. He checked his listing for the phone number of the head of Immigration. No American with an Italian-sounding name would be allowed into the country without Blesh knowing about it. As for those who might plan to leave, they would be discreetly held up at the border long enough to make sure they were legitimate tourists.

It wasn't the Honda that attracted the attention of Mauro Zullino as much as the two helmeted riders who kept a vigil between their stalled machine and an all-night diner down the block.

Mauro Zullino was a punk in the Gabelotti family. He took his orders from any one of the three *capiregime:* Carlo Badaletto, Frankie Sabatini, or Simeone Ferro, or sometimes from their boss, Thomas Merta, the *sottocapo* himself. Don Ettore's apartment occupied all of the eighth floor of the building. On the floor below was the family reception room, along with all the offices and a guard-room manned day and night by the soldiers responsible for the don's safety. The only way to get to the eighth floor was by a stairway from the seventh, guarded by the soldiers. Except for an occasional lawyer, businessman, or politician who had professional connections with the Syndicate and more specifically with the family, no one went up without being searched.

The building belonged to one of Gabelotti's companies. The second-floor front room commanded a view of the entrance, so the building was guarded like a castle. Nothing that went on in the street could escape the eye of the second-floor watch, who notified the seventh-floor soldiers of any suspicious activity.

For about the sixth time in the four hours since his tour of duty began, Mauro Zullino saw one of the cyclists come out of the diner and say something to the other one, who was working on the Honda's gear case. Zullino thought this kind of cycle repair unusual at five in the morning, and he decided to alert the guy in charge of the seventh floor. He had waited until now, partly because he was watching a western on the late-late show and drinking beer and partly because he was afraid he'd get his ass chewed out if he disturbed the big shots upstairs for something unimportant. He picked up the intercom, made his report, and got his ass chewed out for not mentioning it earlier.

"They're not cops," Tom Merta said. "They're Volpone's punks. After what he did to Rico Gatto, they're just the dish for us."

After Mauro Zullino called upstairs, the two sentries on the seventh floor hadn't even had to wake Merta. Don Ettore and Angelo Barba had gone to get some rest, but

241

Merta had stayed up with Frankie Sabatini, Simeone Ferro, and Carlo Badaletto. A couple of hours earlier, they had witnessed the wildest fit of rage Ettore Gabelotti had ever been seized by—and all they could do was lower their eyes and endure it.

"A phony number!" the don had screamed. "That fuckin' rotten moron, that shit-eating piece of manure O'Brion gave me a phony number. He dared to do that to me!"

Struck dumb, the three *capiregime,* the two consiglieri, and Thomas Merta himself had silently prayed for the storm to pass. Gabelotti was liable to do almost anything, including holding his own people unfairly responsible for what had happened. This time, Carlo Badaletto was the scapegoat.

"A fine thing!" Gabelotti had stormed at Carlo. "You wanted to drill Yudelman! You wanted to take a shot at Angela Volpone! You poor sick fucker! My enemies aren't out there, they're right here, among the bastards on my payroll! No one had to tell me that Italo was too stupid a prick to even think of double-crossing us! If I listened to you guys, by now I would have knocked off the entire Volpone family. You're all a bunch of useless dopes! Now he's gonna feel he has to get even with us for grabbing his wife! And all this time our two billion bucks have been sitting still in Switzerland where some stupid fuckin' flatfoot from the SEC might stumble on them and start trouble. While you guys think you're real soldiers and wanna play war!"

Carlo Badaletto made the mistake of speaking. "Don Ettore, if Italo is as pure as you say, what the hell's he doing in Zurich?"

"Shut your fucking moron mouth!" Gabelotti's jowls trembled as he planted himself squarely in front of his lieutenant. "Well, have you got anything more to say?" he demanded. "You heard me! Go ahead and talk!"

Carlo knew he might get killed if he opened his mouth. He shook his head humbly, put his hands behind his back, and walked over to look at a picture of longshoremen unloading citrus fruit, wondering whether he was about to get shot in the back of the neck. He had seen Don Ettore fire point-blank at a punk who had the impudence to

242

crack a joke while he was being dressed down for not having followed orders properly. The punk, with a gaping hole in his shoulder, had had the presence of mind to get on his knees to apologize and kiss the don's hand before he passed out. He had been taken to the family doctor for treatment, but only that last-ditch show of contrition had saved his life.

"I'm going to go see Angela Volpone and try to get us out of the fucked-up mess you got us into!" Gabelotti snorted as he dashed from the room.

His lieutenants had exchanged embarrassed looks. Was Don Ettore naïve enough to think that the insult could be washed away with a few kind words?"

"Frankie, get the Buick out of the garage," Thomas Merta said. "Drive past them without looking, and then take off. As soon as you're out of sight, go around the block and stop on one side of the side streets facing this one, and don't turn off your engine. From the time you leave here, count seven minutes. Simeone, you get behind the wheel of the Pontiac, and in six and a half minutes come into this street slowly, turn your brights on so they can see you, then head straight at them as fast as you can. They'll jump on their fuckin' cycle and beat it. Frankie, as soon as you see them coming, take off full speed and run 'em down."

He looked at his watch.

"Ready? Okay, Frankie . . . go!"

Quinto Favara walked quickly from the diner, although his cyclist's outfit was not made for fast walking. When he was within earshot of Vito Francini, he called, "We're on our way."

He pulled the visor of his helmet down sharply and hopped onto the back seat. Francini didn't waste time asking him to explain. He started up the Honda, slipped into first gear, and with a twist of his hips released the foot stand. A big black sedan was coming at them from behind, its lights on bright, gaining speed. Vito smiled and gave the bike some gas. No car could pick up speed as fast as his cycle. It would move ahead as if the car were standing still.

Vito accelerated so sharply that Quinto had to lean

243

on him, with his arms around his chest. In six seconds the speedometer was at 100, and the street rushed past beneath them as if they were on a bobsled out of control. It was still well before daybreak. There was nothing on the street. Vito shifted into high gear with a roar, and then, a hundred yards ahead at the first corner, he saw the nose of another big black car slowly coming out of the side street.

It was too late to slow down; he had to get by it. The car was stopped, cutting off about a quarter of the roadway. Vito Francini knew the trick: as soon as the Honda started to head into the open space, the driver of the car would simply lurch forward and make the motorcycle hit him.

In a tenth of a second Vito decided his only chance of making it was to pull a feint. He veered to the left, giving the impression that he was falling into the trap. As he expected, the car moved six yards forward. This was what he had been waiting for, and he thought he had it made when the tip of his stand caught the corner of the car's rear bumper. Francini tensed to try to keep his balance, but he moved just a shade too much. The front tire of the Honda rubbed against the curb on the right. The motorcycle started to sway, and at a speed of almost 120 mph it smashed into a concrete wall that erased the faces of Francini and Favara.

When Gabelotti went to his room after talking to Angela, he tried to get some rest and calm himself. Unfortunately, at 5:30 he was still awake and sullen, ready to kill. However, this wasn't the time for it. On the contrary, what he had to do was soft-soap Yudelman in order to reestablish peace between the two families—at least until there was a favorable resolution to Operation OUT.

Whatever Babe Volpone might claim, Yudelman was, and would remain, the brains of the Volpone family. Italo didn't have the experience or the composure to stay at the head of the clan very long. Behind him, there wasn't a soul who could take over. And that opened all kinds of fine prospects for the day, which would come very soon, when the Commissione convened to determine what to do about Volpone, whose responsibilities as capo presented a real danger for the Syndicate as a whole.

Gabelotti got up and went into the living room. "Go get me Moshe," he ordered.

Thomas Merta handed him a pot of coffee and a pile of buttered bread slices that Carlo Badaletto had prepared in the hope of getting back into the don's good graces. Ettore started to eat them, dunking them into his coffee, and then Badaletto came back with Yudelman. Apparently Moshe had not much more sleep than the rest of them, and the way he moved bespoke discouragement and defeat.

Don Ettore gave him a friendly clap on the shoulder.

"Moshe, excuse me for having gotten you up so early. Won't you have a cup of coffee with me?"

Gabelotti poured the coffee and offered him the tray of bread and butter.

"I guess I'd better start explaining things," Gabelotti began. "I owe you some explanation, Moshe. I hope you'll believe every word of what I'm telling you in front of all these witnesses."

Badaletto and Merta exchanged a look of surprise.

"We're partners now, Moshe. Whatever happens to one of us affects us all; it don't matter what family we're in. This whole business has us on edge. Look at me—I never slept a wink. Why? Because I been thinking everything over. There are things you don't know, things I didn't want to tell you before we had it all settled. Besides, I didn't want to give you no worries. Yesterday two of my men tipped me off that somebody was planning to make a grab on Angela Volpone. You can figure out why. Who would her husband have blamed for it, huh? Me, of course! Don Ettore! Somebody is trying to bring about a split between us, Moshe. There have been leaks. Too many people would like to see our two families at war with each other . . ."

Gabelotti looked angrily at Carlo Badaletto. "Well, how's about some bread and butter? You can see it's all gone!"

Carlo dashed out.

"With Don Genco dead," Gabelotti continued, "there will be a lot of people who get ideas. So when I heard about this kidnap business—I won't lie to you—I was scared. I had only one idea: how could I protect Italo's wife! Right away I sent two of my men to bring her here for safekeeping. You approve, don't you?"

Yudelman concentrated on trying to sip his coffee. When he felt he was sufficiently in control of himself, he said, "There was nothing better anyone could do, Don Ettore. I congratulate you for your prompt action, and I thank you in Italo's name."

"This kind of help is the most natural thing between friends like us," Gabelotti protested, equally unabashed. "During the night, I went in and explained to Angela why this all happened. Of course, she would rather have been at home, and I can well understand it. She is young and headstrong, and, after all, she don't know who I am. That's true. What am I to her except a *rifardu*, a stranger? I had to insist to get her to agree to stay here the rest of the night. But she did. You'll see her as soon as she gets up."

Yudelman might well have asked Don Ettore why he had been kept under lock and key, but he didn't. A new element had crept in, and now it seemed that Gabelotti was trying to smooth things out.

"While I was asleep, Don Ettore, did you get in touch with the bank?"

"I tried, Moshe. I tried," the don lied, looking him in the eye. "Kloppe wasn't in, and I wasn't going to give the number to some subordinate. So I'll call back in a little while."

Gabelotti got up, took a few steps toward the window and glanced down at the street, seven floors below. At the corner, he saw uniformed policemen tracing chalk marks on the sidewalk where some human forms lay, temporarily shrouded in blankets. He turned toward Thomas Merta and asked, "What are those cops doing down there?"

Merta shrugged. "A motorcycle accident, Don Ettore. These kids today, they drive like crazy lunatics . . ."

Vittorio Pizzu made sure to warn his lieutenants: "This job is for us, not for the soldiers. Italo wants it that way, and so do I. This time it's a question of honor. No one touches a member of our family without having to pay for it."

246

Aldo Amalfi, Vincente Bruttore, and Joseph Dotto had concurred fully. Their envied positions as *capiregime* in the Volpone family meant that they more often supervised murder than committed it themselves. Violence and death had been their job in the early apprentice years, and now, sometimes they missed the action.

"They're holding Moshe. And they probably grabbed Angela Volpone too."

"Do we knock off old Gabelotti too?" Amalfi asked.

"We knock off anything that stands in our way. Vincente, send four men over there right away. Dress them as sanitation men. Have them get a garbage truck and start manicuring the sidewalk till we get there. See that they have machine guns and grenades."

Bruttore nodded. At every level of the city's services, the Volpone family made ample year-round payments to men who were always ready to carry out orders without asking why. One of the dispatchers in the Sanitation Department was on their pad.

"I'll set it up," Bruttore said.

Now, Pizzu and the three lieutenants were just a few yards from Gabelotti's building. The car that brought them was standing a short distance away, its driver behind the wheel. His orders were to come creeping toward the building and be on hand as their getaway car.

Vittorio could see the four sweepers lazily running their brooms before the entranceway, pretending not to notice Pizzu, Bruttore, Dotto, and Amalfi coming toward them. Pizzu winked approvingly to Vincente Bruttore. However, he couldn't help shivering when he saw the squad car. It wasn't daylight yet, and the flasher on top of the car hit them intermittently with a hard beam.

Vittorio looked quizzically at one of the sanitation men.

"Motorcycle accident," he mumbled between his teeth without interrupting his work. "You can go ahead."

Vittorio frowned. "You sure you told Francini and Favara to come back in?" he asked Bruttore.

"Sure. Why?"

"Nothing. Okay, let's go."

The Volpone men didn't realize that they had a very lucky break. They had stayed up against the walls of the houses on their way to Gabelotti's building, and the second-floor lookout, Mauro Zullino, had relaxed his attention, having just witnessed the masterful way Don Ettore's men had taken care of those guys on the Honda. It had been enough to make Zullino turn off the TV.

He was lending a distracted eye as the cops put the two corpses into an ambulance and got ready to leave the scene of the accident. The street was perfectly quiet except for a few sanitation men emptying garbage cans and sweeping up the trash on the sidewalk. When Pizzu and his three lieutenants slipped in the front door, Mauro Zullino never saw them.

Amalfi, Bruttore, Dotto, and Pizzu didn't say a word. They knew the elevator opened directly into the seventh-floor vestibule where there were always at least two soldiers on guard. The success of their expedition might depend on those men's reflexes.

The elevator came to a stop with a sigh. The two sentries opened the door without hesitation, assuming that Frankie Sabatini and Simeone Ferro were returning after their punitive sortie against the cyclists. The elevator door was barely opened when Vittorio Pizzu shot them each in the head. They collapsed, their faces bathed in blood, and Dotto, Bruttore, and Amalfi practically knocked Pizzu over as they charged upstairs into the living room, revolvers in their right hands, grenades in their left.

Gabelotti was biting into some bread and butter. Carlo Badaletto, half-stooping, had his hand inside his jacket, as did Thomas Merta, whose gun was almost out. But at the sight of Pizzu and his henchmen, they froze like statues. Seated across from Don Ettore, a livid Moshe Yudelman suddenly jumped up like a jack-in-the-box and shouted to his men, "Don't shoot!"

"You okay, Moshe?" Vittorio asked, the muzzle of his Smith and Wesson 39 Parabellum not moving an inch away from the target it had lined up: Gabelotti's heart.

Moshe nodded. Don Ettore turned toward him and asked with a pained expression, "Moshe, your friends have a very strange way of breaking into people's houses. Did you ask them over?"

He then calmly sat down and took a gulp of coffee.

"It's all a misunderstanding," Moshe said.

248

"Where is Angela Volpone?" Pizzu demanded in an evil tone.

"Asleep—unless you people woke her up. Moshe, please tell them how things stand."

"That's right," Moshe said.

"Go get her!" Pizzu ordered.

"Carlo!" Gabelotti called.

"Going, *padrone*."

"Don't move!" Pizzu hissed. "Aldo, go with him."

Amalfi shoved his gun into Badaletto's ribs and pushed him toward the door.

Ettore Gabelotti was well aware that at this moment his life wasn't worth two cents. Yet, despite the terror that made his legs shake, he pretended to be the one who was put upon.

"Well, now gentlemen, I think you ought to explain right away why you acted in such an unfriendly way."

"We've made peace," Moshe quickly cut in. "Put your guns away."

No one moved.

"Could be," said Pizzu. And then to Gabelotti: "Your two watchdogs wanted to shoot us without any pretext. They're offed."

Don Ettore raised his eyes to the sky and said to Moshe in a reproachful tone, "How unfortunate for them —and for us, too. Those two men were the only ones who knew the names of those bastards who wanted to snatch Angela Volpone!"

After Italo Volpone finished dictating the letter, he chained Inez to the radiator again and went into the living room, Lando at his side.

"If her fuckin' cousins get here, what do I do?" said Lando.

"You leave her loose. And you sit tight. If anything happens, blast away at 'em right through your pocket. Your black bitch is blown. I'm keeping her on hand for a few hours, but what can we do with her in the end? She's not one of us. She'll talk."

Orlando bit his lip. There was no way he could stop her from being executed, but he didn't want to be part of it.

"I've got work for you to do," Volpone went on. "Bellinzona will come and relieve you any minute now. He's finishing a job I gave him. I want you to go on home, shave and change, and make yourself nice and handsome. You have to look your best. I want you to fuck a broad."

"Who, *padrone?*"

"The banker's daughter. Renata Kloppe."

For all the respect he had for Genco's brother, Lando now looked at Italo as if he had just arrived from outer space.

"But, *padrone*, she's getting married tonight. The whole town's talking about it!"

"All the more reason to show me what you can do."

"On the eve of her wedding? Really, *padrone*, what difference could it make whether I fuck her or not?"

"Don't argue!" Volpone replied with a vicious overtone. "You just fuck her. I'll handle the rest."

"Okay, *padrone.*"

He went and looked at himself in a mirror. He hadn't been home since the day before, and he was beginning to look a little hairy, with an unshaven mug and a wilted shirt. And he was supposed to fuck her. He had no idea what the cunt looked like, nor was he in the mood for this kind of caper.

The doorbell rang: three long rings and two short, the usual family signal.

As Pietro Bellinzona came in, he smiled at Lando. "Where's the beauty now? I wouldn't mind another piece of her twat."

"In her bedroom. Chained down. Italo don't want nobody screwing around with her."

Pietro was surprised by Lando's tone.

"You sore at me 'cause I humped her?" he asked.

"No."

"It was on orders. And I didn't do her any damage, you know. Look, no offense or nothin'. I know she's your chick, but with the number of cocks she'd had in her, one more or less don't make much difference."

Lando shrugged. "Okay, forget it. I think two of her cousins may be coming over to see her."

Bellinzona looked at him, incredulous. "Coming here? You must be nuts!"

"Volpone knows all about it."

"And he said they could come here?"

"Right. If they show, you leave her loose, and keep an eye on 'em."

"What kind of dinges are they?"

"They're diplomats."

"Diplomats, my ass! Niggers is niggers. Just what did Italo say? What am I s'posed to do?"

Lando hesitated a second; then he regretfully repeated what he had been told.

"If anything looks off-color"—he laughed self-consciously—"let 'em all have it."

"This goes down, and we'll have every cop in this fuckin' country on our tails! And the New York police are probably sore at us too by now. Those monkeys never should have been allowed to come here."

Lando turned on him, his face tense with anger. "Stop telling me what should or shouldn't be done. Nobody asked me for my opinion! She was the one who talked to them on the phone, not me!"

"Hey, hey," Pietro came back at him, "I think you got it bad there, pal—"

"*Ciao!*" Lando cut him off, taking his jacket off the back of a chair.

"Bye-bye, baby doll," Pietro answered.

"Anybody calls, you let her talk. Just listen on the extension. That's what Italo ordered."

"And if she wants to take a leak, what? Let her piss on the floor?"

Lando gave him the key to the handcuffs. And just then there were great knocks on the door, loud and heavy, accompanied by the sound of laughter and greetings.

"Shit, they're here!" Lando said, shoving his hand into his pocket.

Bellinzona did likewise, but before they could make another move, Inez shouted from her room in a tone of happy surprise, "Okay, boys, I'm coming!"

Bellinzona walked into the room and glared at her as he unlocked the handcuffs.

"Tell 'em you're busy, you hear? I'm givin' you five minutes to get 'em out of here! If you don't, I'll do it myself!"

251

In order to let her know he meant it, he showed her the Walther PP he had in his pocket.

In the living room, Bellinzona took up a position in an armchair near the door, his right hand in his pocket, a magazine in his lap.

Lando settled down on a couch. "Go on, let 'em in," he said.

With no haste Inez opened the safety latch on the door. All that could be seen was a doorful of lilacs. Followed by two unbelievably big characters who had to stoop in order to get through without banging their heads. Nonplussed, Bellinzona looked down at their feet to see whether they were on stilts, but the feet were their own, and they must have been size twenty or twenty-one. For the first time in his life, Bellinzona felt puny.

He and Lando stared at each other. The brothers dropped their bouquets, hugged Inez, and each in turn spun her around for a few dance steps, with bold happy laughter and hearty slaps on the shoulder.

"You dirty Africans!" Inez burst out laughingly, pretending to punch them. "You'll squeeze me to death!"

Suddenly the two giants stopped cold, as if they had just noticed they were not alone with her. The one in the flannel slacks coughed.

"Sorry," said the other one.

Noting her brothers' embarrassment, Inez came to their assistance. Turning to Pietro and Lando, she called out in a sprightly voice, "Let me introduce my two cousins. Kouakou and Rocky."

The brothers smiled broadly. Just as naturally as could be, they took a step toward Baretto and Bellinzona, their hands extended for a friendly shake. Volpone's men, in spite of their congenital mistrustfulness, allowed themselves the reflex of taking their right hands out of their pockets, letting go of their rods, and what happened next was so swift a cobra couldn't have seen it coming.

In perfect harmony Bellinzona and Baretto went flying through space in a lightning curve. Before they could land, one felt a karate chop on the back of the neck, the other a well-placed kick in the solar plexus. The apartment walls shook with their fall. Immediately Rocky

252

and Kouakou were on top of them, and in another instant their weapons were in the giants' hands.

"He the one?" Rocky asked, pointing to Baretto.

"No," Inez said. "The big one."

"What about this one?" Rocky insisted.

She looked at Lando, who was out cold. "Oh, forget him, he's just a shrimp."

"Go pack and stay in your room. We'll call you as soon as we're through," Kouakou told her.

Inez turned on her heels without looking back, and they heard her bedroom door slamming.

Bellinzona groaned, shook himself, and opened an eye.

"Dirty niggers!"

Neither brother bothered to answer as they conferred in whispers for a moment, not even threatening the two floored Volpone punks with the guns they had taken. While Lando was coming to, Bellinzona saw one of them toss a coin in the air.

"Tails!" Kouakou said.

Rocky and he both bent down to check it.

"Shit, you win," said Rocky.

Pietro sneered. "What you tossing for, boys? Your assholes?"

"No, yours," Kouakou replied calmly.

"Fuckin' spades," Bellinzona mumbled.

Kouakou looked at him with surprise. "Hey, Rocky, I think that fat slob is talking to you."

"Naw, not to me!"

"Goddamn black faggots!" Bellinzona spat out.

Rocky and Kouakou broke into a great bright youthful laugh. Pietro began to get to his feet. The two giants let him, leering at him out of the corners of their eyes.

Kouakou tossed the gun down on a couch and came over to stand in front of Bellinzona.

"My sister informed me that you have been disrespectful to her," Kouakou said softly.

"That bitch your sister?" Pietro laughed. "Sure, I fucked her, and she stunk."

Pietro, on his guard and ready for a fight, never saw what was coming; nor did he have time to raise his arms

253

to parry. Three punches, coming from different angles, hit him in rapid succession in the liver, on the jaw, and in the heart, as hard and precise as if they had come from a hydraulic press. Bellinzona gathered his bull neck into his shoulders and butted forward with the full weight of his 215 pounds in a blind attack that had never given an antagonist the slightest chance. His skull was as hard as granite. At eighteen he had liked to show off by butting his way through plywood partitions. Now he charged.

Kouakou merely swiveled, and when Pietro grazed against him, he shoved his leg out. Bellinzona went sprawling with all his weight, and a low coffee table splintered as he crashed against it. At the same moment, Lando savagely hurled himself at Kouakou, whose back was to him. In his hand he held the jagged neck of a glass lamp he had just smashed.

"Son of a bitch," Rocky muttered calmly.

Without getting out of the chair he was in, he extended his arm and grabbed Lando's wrist, wrenching the weapon from it in one twist, at the same time kicking him in the belly. Then he got up. Neither brother was out of breath. Their eyes merely shone with contempt. Kouakou lifted Bellinzona in one hand, like a bundle of dirty laundry, and then he opened the mobster's belt buckle and pulled his pants down. Bellinzona came to just as Kouakou tore off his underpants.

Pietro couldn't believe his eyes, and he tried to get free, but Kouakou swung him forward three times and smashed his head against the stone stand of an abstract sculpture. Meanwhile, Lando, lying prone at Rocky's feet, was shaken with spasms and vomiting bile.

Kouakou leaned over Bellinzona and whispered something into his ear. Pietro, who could only see him through a red haze, shook his head in protest. Rocky was now over in the corner, with his back to them, doing something strange, as if he were urinating and paying no attention to what went on behind him.

Kouakou placed his fingers around Bellinzona's head as if he were grasping a basketball.

"Now, listen to me," he said without raising his voice. "We're gonna do to you what you did to our sister.

You won't be able to call us nigger faggots anymore, because you're gonna be cornholed good and proper."

Bellinzona, in despair, realized that he was unarmed
and now had no more strength than a child. Once again
he shook his head. His huge half-naked body was spread
on the carpet, his bulging buttocks and monstrous thighs
reminiscent of the hindquarters of a pig in a butcher's
display.

His eyes filled with tears. "Don't do that, brother!
Don't do it!" he begged.

Kouakou turned to Lando, who was green in the face
and running with sweat.

"Nothing's gonna happen to you. We just want you to
watch your pal here get cornholed. You know why?
'Cause he'll never forgive you for having seen it. He'll be
too scared you might go around blabbing about it." He
looked at Lando for a second in silence and then added,
"So he'll kill you."

"Don't do that!" Bellinzona groaned. "Kill me if you
want—anything—but not that!"

"Shut up, pig. Rocky?"

"Ready," he answered.

All their heads turned toward him. He was facing
them now, and what Bellinzona and Orlando saw was
more than enough to strike terror into them. From Rocky's
open fly there stood a penis such as they had never seen—
inhuman in size, swollen, and strained erect with such
power that it seemed nothing could ever make it come
down again. Kouakou quickly knelt, pressed down with
all his weight on Bellinzona's shoulder blades, and stuck
the muzzle of Pietro's own revolver into the back of his
neck.

"Go on, shoot, you bastard!" Bellinzona yelled.

Kouakou grabbed him by one ear and slammed his
forehead on the floor. Lando, in a daze, tried to close his
eyes, but they immediately popped open again. He saw
Rocky stretch out on top of Bellinzona, who was sobbing
like a kid as his nails tried to scratch into the floor.

"Not that! Not that!" he was howling.

"Shitty bastard!" Rocky muttered as he rode him.

For one moment his hips waved hesitantly as his

muscular fingers dug into Pietro's soft white flesh the better to spread it apart. Here in this soft, feminine room, in the center of Zurich, the savage rites of primitive tribes were suddenly reasserting their dominance.

There was nothing about either of the brothers that bespoke the nuclear physicist or the champion athlete. They were two wild-eyed animals, panting, rutting, and roaring, following the age-old law—an eye for an eye, a hole for a hole.

However desperately his victim tried to buck, Rocky succeeded in shoving his hips forward. And thrust home.

As Bellinzona roared with pain, there echoed a victorious shout that seemed to come from the depths of the ages.

16

"What's wrong?" Chimene Kloppe asked. "You're pale." She put her hand on her husband's shoulder. "Is it on account of Renata?"

Homer patted her hand, but his eyes remained distant and absent.

"Do you want some tea?" she inquired.

He shook his head no.

"Don't worry. I know it's a hard thing for a father to go through. But it won't last all that long. Look at me a minute."

She took his chin in her fingers and lifted it. "Smile at me."

Mechanically Kloppe's lips opened to reveal his perfect teeth.

"I like it when you smile," his wife told him.

Four hours before, Homer had been lying limp in Dr. August Strolh's office. He was the only one who had been subjected to physical torture, yet it was he who had brought the dentist around, helped by Ingrid, who was still not very solid on her legs.

The professor had cried, tears mingled with protests. "They forced me to do it, Mr. Kloppe. I didn't want to. This is an abomination! . . . They held a razor to Ingrid's throat. I'll never forgive myself for this. Never!"

As the dental couple succumbed to total nervous collapse, the banker's courage rose. He had to grit his teeth and take hold.

Even as he formed the thought, he realized how absurd it was. He had no teeth left to grit. The nauseating taste of blood still filled his mouth, a clot still dangled from his upper gum. His fingers went to the soft lump and, as he pulled it off, the hemorrhaging resumed, strong as a geyser.

"Take care of me, you fool, instead of sniveling like that!" he stormed, shaking Strolh angrily, forcing him out of his dazed state.

"Yes, get into the chair. You're right. Take care of you, of course. I'll do it. Ingrid! Compresses—coagulant . . ."

His professional reflexes were returning. He would repair the damage. He had genius enough to reconstitute exactly what they had forced him to destroy.

"My daughter's getting married tonight," Kloppe reminded him, "and I want to be able to greet all the guests, you among them. With all my teeth showing."

Despite the awful hissing of the sounds that came out of Kloppe's mouth, Ingrid and August had no trouble understanding him. They looked at each other. Could they possibly put temporary dentures in over those raw bleeding gums?

"Let's get on with it!" Kloppe encouraged them with a twist of the lips that was supposed to be a smile but served only the better to show the wounds that lined the inside of his mouth.

It took three hours. The professor outdid himself. For different reasons, none of the three made any comment whatsoever about what had caused the attack. Kloppe, because he knew. Ingrid and August, because they didn't and were still in shock.

When the banker looked at himself in the mirror, he saw that he appeared almost normal again. His swollen jaws possessed a full double set of teeth, except that they were no longer his own.

"I'm going to press charges," Strolh said.

Homer looked at him. "Do so, if you wish," he said. "That's your right. But, for the time being at least, I forbid you to connect my name in any way with this affair."

"But why? Why?"

Kloppe merely took the pills, the disinfectant, and

the healing powders Ingrid was holding out to him. He nodded and said, "I'll see you both tonight. My congratulations. You did a thorough job."

Once again Dr. Strolh felt tears coming to his eyes. He timidly shook the banker's hand.

"Mr. Kloppe—" he started to say.

The banker cut him off. "Yes, I know, I understand. I'll see you tonight."

Much too conscious of the struggle ahead of him, Kloppe lost none of his presence of mind despite all the analgesics and tranquilizers he had imbibed, and he headed straight for the bank to carry out what he had planned to leave until after Renata's wedding.

He sent out a telex to Melvin Bost in Detroit instructing him to advise all owners of Beauty Ghost P9s about the risk of driving their cars in their present condition. This was no time to be concerned about financial stability. The main thing was, he had to be at peace with his conscience. Once and for all.

He also decided to make a clean breast of things, to confess his transgressions to Chimene without glossing over any of the facts, but when he got home he pushed this thought back. Did he have a right to make her share his violent trials? Chimene lived on a pink cloud. Could she stand the strain of it?

"Chimene . . ."

"Yes, Homer?"

Before her full-length mirror, she cooed over the Parma-violet gown she planned to wear that night.

"I have something to tell you," Homer began.

"Do you like this color?" she asked. "Oh, I beg your pardon. What was it you wanted to say?"

Kloppe gave up. His jaw hurt too much.

"Nothing," he said. "It wasn't anything."

Grouped around Ettore Gabelotti, with worried faces, were Carmine Crimello, Angelo Barba, Thomas Merta, Carlo Badaletto, Frankie Sabatini, and Simeone Ferro. That their capo had made no move after two of his punks had been knocked off right under his nose left them deeply concerned. The greatest strength of the Syndicate, everyone knew, was that it never let an insult go without retaliating. Unless Don Ettore had a secret up his sleeve, he was either going soft or he was actually scared of the Volpones.

The bodies of the two guards gunned down by Vittorio Pizzu had been discreetly put in the elevator, taken down to the basement garage, and loaded into a small van.

The Gabelotti family had a mausoleum large enough for some thirty departed in a small outlying cemetery. When a demise occurred under less than explainable circumstances, the body of the victim was taken there without having to go through the usual red tape of morgue, autopsy, and police. The people who ran the place were dependable, their loyalty well paid for. Don Ettore, like any good Sicilian, knew that even the worst of his killers wanted to be buried in consecrated ground and not walled into a cement block to be dropped into the high seas, and it was this kind of thoughtfulness that made his men so devoted and respectful.

The don smiled sweetly at his chiefs of staff.

"You know what the situation is now," he said to them. "Morty O'Brion tried to take us to the cleaners. I don't know if he's dead or alive, or where the hell he is. My own opinion is that our partner"—and he stopped after that word to clear his throat—"our partner Volpone cooked his goose for him. Which, of course, was a wrong thing to do. Because if I had got my hands on him, I can promise you that swine of an O'Brion would have sung his fuckin' heart out. Anyway, our money, so they tell me, is still safe in the Swiss bank. Nobody's got the secret number for it, not Italo Volpone and not me. Babe Volpone means well. But that don't mean nothing. So there's only one way to finish this thing so it don't turn bad. I got to go to Zurich myself."

The men looked at one another askance. Don Gabelotti hated travel. People always came to him. Why should he bother to go to them? His fear of flying was always good for a laugh.

"How are you going, don?" Crimello asked innocently, and just as innocently added, "By boat?"

"What was that?" Ettore asked in a voice pregnant with menace.

Carmine Crimello, realizing the gaffe he had made,

looked around at the others. No one wanted to give him any help. All turned their eyes away from his, and Carmine, dangling alone, had to face the music.

"I didn't say anything wrong, *padrone*. I just know you don't care for flying—so I thought . . ." and he added in a weaseling, cowardly effort, "besides, you're not the only one. I don't care for flying no more than you do."

"Well, from now on, worry about yourself, not me. You'll be flying out of here—tomorrow."

All of them looked up.

"And I will too," Don Ettore went on with ferocious determination. "Of course, we're not all going to Zurich as a delegation. Angelo, Thomas, and Carlo, you go to France; not Paris, but someplace else, Lyons perhaps. From there you take the train to Switzerland. Frankie and Simeone can fly to Milano and then take a train up north. You, Carmine, as long as you're so scared, you can fly with me right to Zurich." He stopped to give him another look. "I'll hold you in my arms so you won't piss in your pants."

A few laughs greeted this sally, but they quickly dried up.

"When we're over there, we'll meet with Volpone's men. But the first one of you says a thing about what's been happening back here gets sent right home, understand? As long as we ain't got our hands on our dough, we gonna have peace, absolute peace. You understand?"

"And after?" Angelo Barba inquired.

"After what?"

"After we get the dough back, then what?"

"There'll be plenty of time then to talk things over with *Don* Italo Volpone," Gabelotti answered.

The word *Don* came out of his mouth as if it were a big sloppy oyster of spit.

For Italo Volpone, things couldn't be worse. Angela had yet to be found, Gabelotti was putting spokes in his wheels and holding Yudelman hostage, Vittorio Pizzu didn't know how to do a fucking thing on his own, and Homer Kloppe didn't show any signs of cracking.

Once more Italo cursed himself for his lack of self-control. He had blown his chance with Morty O'Brion.

That runt of a lawyer wasn't any Swiss banker. Morty would have given him the secret number that had already been responsible for so many violent deaths.

Italo wanted to find his wife if it meant moving heaven and earth, but he had vowed not to leave Zurich until the money of Operation OUT was theirs again. It was a matter of his honor, his future, his life. He knew that the Commissione considered him flighty and violent. And he *was* all of that. But why couldn't they understand that it was because Genco had been born before him? Even more than their father, it was Genco who had raised him, protected him, taken care of him, made decisions for him. While his older brother's power was continually increasing, Italo had gotten into the habit of living in Genco's shadow. Why should he go out and make it on his own when all he had to do was ask Genco? Why fight when his brother did it for him? Genco was the one who had nicknamed him Babe, and Italo had ended up so identifying with the brother he idolized that he actually thought Genco's victories were his own.

He had only come into his own when he met Angela. With her he was no longer just a little brother, but a full-fledged man, ready to do anything to keep his woman. He had tried to make Genco understand how he had changed, saying that he wanted to play a more active part in the various command posts of the family, and Genco had listened with great attention.

"I'm not saying you're wrong, Genco," Italo had told him, "but maybe you're just too good to me. I feel I'm being held back. You're too big for me, and I'm not trying to fight you, but I'd like to use my own wings and try to fly."

Genco had smilingly tousled Italo's hair the way he did when they were kids.

"You're surely right, Babe," he replied, "but don't hold it against me. Maybe I just didn't see how fast you were growing up."

"I'm thirty-eight years old."

Genco himself was only forty-six, but when Italo had been a ten-year-old kid, Genco was already boss over a dozen men. Before he was twenty, important people were coming to him for advice and protection. Those eight years between them set them up as father and son, master and pupil. To Genco, Italo would always be ten years old.

Now, to Babe, Genco would always be forty-six, the age he was when he died.

After Vittorio Pizzu called about the run-in with Gabelotti, Italo went back to the morgue. The attendant had let him look once again at his brother's leg in the casket, and Italo had remained thoughtful for a long time, letting bittersweet tears flow as an overwhelming lust for revenge invaded him.

After that, he had gone back to the villa. Folco Mori was driving him, but they didn't say a word to each other. Italo now knew that he would carry on with his brother's work; it was the only way he could prove himself deserving of the love and kindness Genco had lavished on him. He swore to himself that he would prove worthy of the heavy crown he was inheriting. But in order to get in good with the Syndicate, he first had to complete the financial transfer.

As he walked into the villa's living room, he saw Pietro Bellinzona and Orlando Baretto sitting gingerly on the edge of the couch. He could see immediately that something was wrong; Lando should have been there alone.

"I thought I told you to guard the nigger broad," he shot at Bellinzona.

He noticed the big guy's bruised face.

Pietro lowered his head in distress. "She's gone."

Italo felt the blood drain from his cheeks. Inez was still scheduled to play a big role in his plans.

"Her cousins snuck up on us," Lando added hastily.

"Shut up. I'm asking Bellinzona."

Folco Mori looked out at the garden as intensely as he could. Bellinzona spread his arms in a gesture of powerlessness.

"Well?" Volpone barked.

"There was two of 'em," Bellinzona began in a hoarse voice. "We kept a sharp eye on 'em when they came in. I had my finger on the trigger of my rod. So did he. But then . . ."

"Then what?"

Bellinzona stared at the tips of his shoes.

"I don't know what to say, *padrone* . . ." He let the sentence hang, then tried to go on, but in his shame could only repeat, "We got taken."

"Two unbelievable giants," Lando chimed in.

"A giant with a bullet in his head ain't no giant anymore—he's just shit!" Volpone exploded. "And you two're a couple of shits yourselves. A couple of double-dyed fuckin' idiots! I need that broad. Where the hell'd she go?"

Lando and Bellinzona didn't dare look at each other. Lando was terribly worried. He would have given anything not to have been there to see Bellinzona get fucked in the ass. "Why should we do anything to you?" the two giant black men had told him. "Your pal'll take care of that for us. He'll kill you!"

"I'm talking to you!" Volpone screamed. "Where is she?"

They were both silent.

"Lando, get the hell out of here. You got a job to do. And if you know what's good for you, you'll do it right."

"*Sì, padrone.*"

In his depressed condition, what chance did he have to make out with the banker's daughter? Even if he got to meet her, even if he could keep his face from looking haunted, even if she noticed him and thought she liked what she saw. Even then, what? He still had to have a free mind to be in top sexual shape. Since witnessing Inez's brother's display of erectile power, his idea of his own virility had shrunk to an all-time low. But if he let Volpone down a second time, it would be curtains for him.

"Folco, check the airport, see what's going on at the railroad station! Three giants like that just don't disappear! Pietro, you go with him. Get your asses out of here before I start gettin' mean!"

Bellinzona got up awkwardly. As long as he lived, he would never be able to shed his humiliation unless he got to kill the ones who hurt him. He was almost sorry that Volpone had not decided to rub him out there and then for his fuck-up. He fell in alongside Folco Mori, who was smart enough not to ask him what went wrong.

In exasperation over this new snag, Volpone rushed to his bedroom to phone New York; he could no longer stand not knowing what had happened to Angela. The first words he heard from Vittorio Pizzu made his chest swell with relief.

"Your wife is home, *padrone,* and she's just fine. I'll put Moshe on. He can fill you in."

When Moshe Yudelman left Gabelotti's with Angela Volpone, Vittorio Pizzu, and the three lieutenants, he wondered at length how to act now. It was just as dangerous to tell Babe the truth as it was to keep it from him. Moshe had not been taken in the slightest bit by Gabelotti's pious lie. Despite the imaginary threats on Angela's safety Don Ettore claimed to have heard, he had snatched them and kept them prisoners, no two ways about it. He wasn't trying to protect them, as he had sworn, but had been holding them hostage to have something to dangle over Italo's head. The fact that he had not reacted against the offing of his two men didn't prove that he had forgotten the incident. Gabelotti was one who never forgot and who forgive nothing. The don had simply let the two-billion-dollar ante take precedence; he'd settle accounts later on.

But, Moshe thought, the real danger was Italo Volpone himself. His fear of not being taken seriously added to his easily piqued pride. He was still too sensitive, too unsure of himself to be able to take it without flinching and dish it back out with interest. Yudelman was going to have to handle him with as much care as if he were defusing a bomb. He sent a silent prayer to the gods of improvisation and took the phone from Vittorio Pizzu.

"Everything is fine, Italo, it's all straightened out," he said.

"Where's Angela?"

"I'll tell you all about it, Italo. We can really be grateful to Don Ettore. Without him—"

"What? What are you talking about?" Volpone cut him off.

"Gabelotti got us out of one tight spot. He heard that someone had been making threats against us. So, out of friendship for you, he brought us to his place for safekeeping."

"Huh?"

"Yes, Italo. He played host to us."

"To who?"

"Angela and me."

"My wife went to that fat slob's? Did he lay a hand on her? Tell me that!"

Yudelman felt his self-assurance melting away. "This whole business is just one big misunderstanding, Italo."

"What about Genco? Was he a misunderstanding, too? And O'Brion? You go kissing the ass of that fat pig when I don't even know if he hasn't snatched our bread."

"Listen to me, Italo—"

"Shut up! You got nothing to tell me. Did he get the tongue I sent him?"

"The tongue?"

"Yeah, the tongue of the little smart-ass he had on my tail right out of JFK. Some friend you've got! It was Rico Gatto's tongue. I sent it to him wrapped up in Gatto's passport. Now, where the hell is Angela?"

"At your place."

"Who's watching over her?"

"Four men from Vincente's regime."

"Put on four more! If she as much as got scared, I'll kill you with my own hands, Moshe!"

"Okay, so you can kill me. Can I get a word in?"

"No! You still don't know that my guys had to off a couple of flatfoots."

"Swiss?" Yudelman choked out.

"American. Kirkpatrick's pricks. What difference does that make?"

"Oh, my God—no!"

"Yes," Italo said; "and that fuckin' banker still won't cough up the dough. Zurich is lousy with cops and stoolies. I'm moving heaven and earth. And while I'm doin' that, my right hand is gettin' palsy with the bastard who kidnapped my wife after having my brother knocked off."

"That's not true!" said Yudelman. "You're making a mistake. If Gabelotti was guilty, he'd never have let us go!"

Moshe bit his tongue, but it was too late. The cat was out of the bag.

Volpone exploded, "You dirty fuckin' lyin' bastard! Did you hear what you just said to me?"

This was it. Now, no more alliance was possible.

"Okay, okay," Yudelman conceded in a colorless voice. "You want the whole story, here it is. I went back to Gabelotti's. And then he wouldn't let me go. On account of you, Italo. He asked me to call you. You had checked out of the hotel, so he got suspicious. You would have done as much in his place. He sent two of his punks to pick up Angela—"

"The bastard!"

"This morning, at five o'clock, he told me we were free to go. He apologized and explained why he acted the way he did. According to him, someone was threatening to kidnap your missus—"

"Who?"

"I don't know. He said he was protecting us from them. He said we were partners and had mutual interest . . ."

"And you fell for that?"

"I didn't have a choice. Especially now that you tell me about that tongue. He could've knocked off the both of us. Then Pizzu busted in, following your orders, with Aldo, Vincente, and Joe. They knocked off two of his men on guard at the door, and that didn't make things any simpler."

"You expect me to leave my wife snatched and locked up and not do nothin' about it?"

"Don't try doing anything else, Italo, please, I beg you. You're cutting the ground out from under me. You have to understand that Gabelotti's in the same boat as us. He's just as worried because he hasn't been able to get the money transferred either."

Volpone was quiet for a moment. Yudelman knew he had gotten through.

"But why couldn't he? He has the account number!"

"Nope. For some reason that I don't know, he hasn't got it. If he did, the transfer would be done. Italo, listen to me. Genco is dead, and you're gonna be the family capo. There's a lot of objections on the Commissione—lots of guys don't want you, they're afraid of what you did in the past, you're in their way. . . . One misstep, and they'll have you offed, Italo! If you listen to me, we got a good chance—"

"Button up, stinker! Gabelotti never woulda dared snatch *Genco's* woman!"

"Right! But your brother never would have waved a red flag in his face! He would have reassured him instead of scaring the shit out of him like you did. You know who's making the profit from all this fuck-up? The banker! Your enemy is that Kloppe guy, not Ettore. You don't know what those banker types are like, Italo! They're legal crooks that are worse than dogs. They're strong and evil and vicious, and they never let go! They're a lot tougher than us. They knock off governments, win wars, send chiefs of state to the firing squad! They're more dangerous than a dozen armies. They fuck up the whole world, and they make the laws 'cause they've got control of the mazuma. If we don't give 'em that fuckin' number, we'll never get a sniff of our two billion again. We have to make an alliance with Gabelotti, Italo, and pool all our resources. It's the only way to win."

"What can Gabelotti do that I can't, if he ain't got the number either?" Italo asked with mounting venom.

"You'll find out when he gets there."

"What's that?"

"Don Ettore'll be in Zurich tomorrow."

What should she wear to bury her bachelor life?

Renata ran her fingers over the dresses and outfits that filled her closets. Some had never been worn. Just owning them was enough. If she felt low, she would go into a shop and pick up some little thing by Dior or Cardin the way other women stuff themselves with pastries. Actually, Renata was confident enough of her affluence to have worn virtually nothing but the same pair of jeans for the past three years.

She finally selected a sky-blue man's-cut flannel suit. She got into it, looked at herself in the mirror, and made a face. The idea of a last fling suddenly struck her as silly. Why should she go and lay some unknown guy a few hours before getting married?

She tried to analyze what it was that had moved her to this last challenge of single life. Would it make up for the absolute faithfulness she had sworn she would observe as long as she was married to Kurt?

Frau Heinz—Renata Heinz. . . . She shrugged, lit a

cigarette, put an old Beatles record on the stereo, and sat on the floor with her back to the wall, to think.

Manuella came in and whistled admiringly. "That blue is very becoming, miss. Is it new?"

"Old as my worries."

"Mr. Kurt will like you in it."

"I didn't put it on for him."

"Oh? Who for, then?"

"I don't know yet. The first guy I can latch on to."

Manuella glanced at her. With her mistress, she never knew how to take things. In order not to make any mistakes, she was shrewd enough to give indirect answers to all questions that didn't directly concern her job.

"Will you tell me about it?"

"Certainly not! It'll be my last girlhood secret. Is my gown pressed?"

"Not quite finished. I'll go back to it."

Renata put her butt out in the ashtray. She burst out laughing at the scene that popped into her head. In her fantasy of her last "bachelor fling," she would walk down the street and accost (or be accosted by) the first guy who was not too unappealing. In her most charming way she would ask him point-blank, Will you sleep with me? So far, so good. But suppose the guy were to turn her down? After all, there are heels everywhere, even in Zurich.

Laughing aloud, she picked up her handbag and headed out into Bellerivestrasse, on the lookout for her last unmarried affair.

She didn't have long to look. There he was, and he was the first one she saw. He was tall, slim, definitely Latin-looking, and impeccably dressed in a wonderfully tailored blazer. He wore a blue woolen tie on a pinstriped white shirt, and was leaning against a sparkling gunmetal-gray Beauty Ghost P9 convertible, watching her come at him as if he had been waiting for her since the dawn of time, as if he had known about their date, which up to now had existed only in Renata's mind. She took a few steps toward him, her heart pounding, still wondering whether she was going to have the guts to go through with her planned escapade.

When she was within his reach, she stopped. Close up,

he was handsome, with a bony but even-featured face, slightly pale, his eyes somewhat strained. She looked especially at his fine, strong, well-groomed hands, now slightly tensed on the car body.

"What's your name?" she said.

His hard mouth opened slightly in a smile. "Orlando," he said.

"Mine's Renata. I'd love to make love with you."

"And I with you," he replied, and he opened the door of the car for her.

17

"No!" Renata begged. "Please—no!"

"Shove it!" Lando commanded.

She went up another step. No one had ever handled her this way. From the start, Lando had given her silent, brutal treatment, to which she responded with a bewildering mixture of pain and pleasure. They had not spoken on the way to his apartment, and once through the door, Lando didn't waste a minute with drinks or music. Shoving the door shut with his foot, he backed Renata up against the door and, without so much as a caress, pushed her flimsy panties down her thighs and rammed into her.

"Take me to bed," she had moaned.

He didn't bother to answer but went on with his pistoning, alternating quick jabs with long slow drives, at times remaining motionless when he felt she was about to come. For an hour he brought her closer and closer to climax, backing off each time just as she was about to let go. He knew exactly how to bring her to that point of no return. He saw himself as a tool provoking her to a debauch of sensuality; he couldn't share in it himself. He was carrying out Volpone's instructions to the best of his ability, that was all.

"Lando!—Lando, I beg of you!"

Once again he stopped short as she was about to go over the brink, but he was a fraction of a second too late; Renata had gotten away from his control. Despite himself, he moved as one with her, his pubis riveted to her as they shook together in a series of heady convulsions. Renata became like a rag doll in his arms.

She had always considered herself the expert in love, but now she realized that she had known nothing. She gazed at Lando with faraway eyes and mumbled, "Thank you."

But the lesson was just beginning. Lando fell to his knees, holding her body with his two arms around her buttocks. Very gently he began to lick the insides of her thighs, soft and warm as the underside of a dove's wing. He held her solidly against him, burying his head in Renata's fleece. As his tongue lingered between her legs, his hands explored her body, and when the muscles of his mouth began to hurt, he let her come a second time.

As she slid down into his arms, he pulled her up and whispered into her ear, "Let's go to bed. That's what you wanted. Now you're going to get it." She tottered toward the stepladder that led to his loft-bed. When he brutally penetrated her once more, her exhaustion gave way to a wave of desire that swept through her body, wetting her thighs, pushing out the nipples on her breasts. He held her there until she reached orgasm, her body ravaged by the onslaught. Every inch of her skin, every fiber of her body exulted in the violation and she came again.

"You're going to kill me," she moaned.

But all he could think of was that Volpone would kill him if he didn't follow orders. He held her there until she reared with the strength of a wild mare, screaming in an agony of delight.

Then, without giving her time to come back to her senses, he forced her up the ladder and entered her from behind.

"Christ!" she protested. "Not that!"

Cruelly he bit her on the nape of the neck as he hissed into her ear, "You'll have your bed, little girl. All you have to do is make it up five more steps!"

"It's me," Volpone said, trying to keep his voice under control.

"Italo, oh, Italo!" Angela said.

He was glad she couldn't see how overcome he was.

He clamped his jaws, gritting his teeth in an effort to hold back the tears.

"Angela, darling, tell me what happened. Did they hurt you?"

Angela had been instructed at length by Moshe Yudelman, who, until then, had never said more than a pleasant hello to her.

"Angela," he had said, "we're playing for heavy stakes. I can't give you all the details, but I have to warn you: if you complain to Italo, everything will fall through."

"What will fall through?" she had wanted to know.

"Your husband's nerves are on edge. His brother's death has saddled him with enormous responsibilities. He now has to carry through a deal that was set up by Genco, and it's a very tough deal. You know Italo loves you more than anything in life, but he's half a world away from us. He might misunderstand why Gabelotti invited us over. Italo doesn't have much use for Gabelotti. But he's wrong. Gabelotti was only acting in your own best interests, to protect you . . ."

"From what?" she persisted in surprise.

"Don't ask me any questions, Angela. I'm your friend. Don't make things harder for me than they have to be."

So she decided she would make it all sound like nothing.

"No, my love, nobody hurt me. The only thing that hurts is how much I miss you."

"I miss you, too, Angela. If only you knew."

"Do you want me to come to you?"

"No, no! I'll only be here another day or two."

"Can't I help you?"

"Yes. By telling me you love me."

"*Ti amo*, Italo . . ."

"As soon as this is over, I'm taking you to Sicily."

"You promise?"

"You'll see! After that, we'll go and visit your folks. But tell me. Did that Gabelotti say anything to you?"

"Yes, of course," Angela lied. "He was very nice and polite."

"Why didn't you tell me you were going to his place?"

"It all happened so fast. When you and I were talking on the phone, remember? I had to go and open the door for Fiorentina. When I picked it up again, we had been cut off."

"Were you treated all right?"

"Of course, Italo."

"Okay, okay. Only, I was worried, y'understand. Knowing you was alone with those—those—Say, are my friends at the apartment now?"

"Yes."

"How many of them?"

"Four."

"Good."

"Italo . . ."

"What?"

"I'm not being nosy, Italo. But you are my husband. Maybe one day you'll feel like telling me about— You know what I mean?"

"Sure. Don't worry your little head about a thing. Did you see Francesca?"

"It was awful."

She almost blurted out what Genco's widow had said to her—"They'll kill your Italo, too!"—but she held back the words, trying not to spread more oil on what she knew was already a fire. She trusted Moshe. She knew he had been Genco Volpone's counselor for many years, and she had guessed by now, by and large, the kind of affairs he counseled him on. And in case she had any illusions, the four armed men outside her door—she had seen the gun under the armpit of one of them when he bent over to pick up some matches—dissipated them.

"Angela . . ."

"Yes, darling?"

"You need anything?"

"Just you."

"Me too, *amore mio*. Did Moshe come to see you?"

"He was here an hour ago. He left to go and pack."

Volpone knitted his brow, but controlled himself. "To pack? What for?"

"Well, you know, Italo . . ."

"No, I don't," he forced out.

A breath of fury swept through him as he thought of

that consigliere who did whatever he pleased, made up his own mind, and then challenged his orders.

"He's off to join you in Zurich on the first available plane," Angela happily informed him.

Kurt Heinz sneaked a look at his parents. They were standing on the sidelines, looking frightened among all the guests. Clustered in noisy, happy groups, people were exclaiming about the originality of the decor.

Uncomfortable in his black velvet suit and frilled shirt, Kurt kept a sharp eye on each arrival, expecting at any moment to see his fiancée's magnificent salmon gown.

Kloppe, more tense than usual, made an all-too-visible effort to force a smile as he exchanged two or three words with Kurt, and Chimene affected a smile that did not conceal her nervousness. (It was a little past midnight; Renata had not yet arrived.)

"How mad these young people are! Just look what they've done to my apartment!" Chimene crowed to her friends.

Kurt was sick at heart at the thought of undergoing another three hours of this circus. The pastor, who hadn't arrived yet either, was to tie the knot immediately after the meal was served. The helicopter was not due on the roof pad until 3:00 A.M.; they were to be transported to the airport, and then Renata would fly him away in her own plane to Portofino, Italy. There, a yacht with a crew of eight was waiting to take the two of them on a week-long Mediterranean cruise.

Big laugh: a German industrialist in a magnificent tuxedo was standing on his head, doing his best to see the Leonardo masterpiece right side up. His wife was discreetly tugging at his leg.

Kurt's eyes met his mother's. Utte didn't have time to hide her expression. Stiff as a board in her hideous apple-green dress, taller than her husband, she looked like a sad tower dressed for company. Kurt turned his eyes away, both to be free of hers and to avoid his father's gaze.

There was a commotion near the door, with loud cries and people calling to one another. Kurt thought it was Renata coming in, and, at the relief he felt, he realized how upset he was over her not being there.

But it was just some of his old schoolmates rushing over to congratulate him.

"Where's your fiancée? Walked out on you already?"

"Just think what it'll be like after you're hitched!"

"Hey, Kurt! Where you hiding your Renata?"

Kurt wondered the same thing. She should have been here an hour ago. Ill at ease, he parried more jokes on the subject. A onetime girl friend got up on tiptoe to whisper in his ear, "If she doesn't show, remember me. Always ready to fill in."

Chimene worked her way through the dense crowd. As they moved among the chandeliers of the floor-turned-ceiling, people were grabbing the first glasses of champagne served by white-jacketed butlers.

"Do you have any idea where Renata is?" Chimene asked Kurt in a voice that was supposed to hide her anxiety.

Kurt smiled serenely back at her. "No, I don't. But I'm sure she's just taking her time getting ready. Have you seen her?"

"She went out about three or four this afternoon. She was supposed to go to the hairdresser's," her mother volunteered.

"And you haven't seen her since?"

"No. And I am rather concerned."

"Where's the bride?" called a guest as he raised his glass.

"On her way! On her way!" answered Chimene, who always felt she had to justify the actions of others as well as her own. And she added, "Good Lord, here's the reverend. Kurt, please do something."

She rushed over to greet the pastor, an old family friend who had agreed, much as he disliked the idea, to officiate at this unseemly wedding. Chimene had overcome his scruples by the size of her donation for "the poor in the parish." Which, in Zurich, was just a figure of speech. For the poor in the city were not Swiss, but Italians and Portuguese.

Kurt furtively consulted his watch. It was well past twelve-thirty. Dinner would be served at one o'clock sharp. Feeling drearier and drearier, his throat constricted, he decided to duck out for a few minutes and see whether he could find Renata.

Renata lit a cigarette, exhaled a long puff of smoke, and traced Lando's profile with her index finger. This slight effort made her realize the enormity of her exhaustion. She had no more body, yet at the same time her body weighed tons. From this moment on, her life would not be long enough to think back over the fantastic sensations that, in a few hours, had destroyed her with delight. She had once and for all crossed over a frontier, climbed into the dimension of climax. Or, you might say, the dimension of death. But surely death could never have such intensity.

Yet all she knew about this man was his first name: Lando. And all he knew about her were the six letters of hers: Renata. He was God; no one in the world could be as good as he. And now she had to leave him.

"Lando? What time is it?"

He ran his hand over her breast. "No idea. Midnight. One o'clock. What does it matter?"

She smiled slightly.

"I've got to go."

"Now?"

"I'm giving a party."

"In the middle of the night?"

"Yes . . . A wedding party. My own. I'm getting married at three."

Lando, worn to a frazzle, still had the courage to pretend amazement: "You're getting married at three in the *morning?*"

"Yes," she said, inserting her cigarette between his lips.

He took a long drag on it. "You putting me on?"

"No. It's true."

He had hoped to make her forget the time, but apparently all he did to her hadn't been enough. Galvanized by his fear of Volpone, he gathered his remaining strength to stage another round that would keep her with him. His tongue pained him, heavy and dry like a hunk of cotton waste. No use to him now! As for the other, well . . .

Italo Volpone had minced no words about what he

wanted: "I want to fuck up the whole Kloppe shindig.
Turn this town upside down. Don't rough up the girl, but
get her so fuck-happy that she'll forget her own wedding.
I don't care where you shove your cock, or how, but
make her want it until she screams!"

Lando turned toward Renata and nibbled at her earlobe. She tensed at the memory of his teeth biting into the
nape of her neck when she was screaming in climax and
pain.

"I don't believe a word of it," he said.

She summoned a smile. "Want me to invite you?"

"Why you getting married?"

She thought about that for several seconds.

"To tell the truth, I don't know. What's your last
name?"

He hesitated, but then admitted, "Baretto."

Renata fleetingly tested *Renata Baretto* in her mind.

"Love him?" he asked.

"No."

"Then why you marrying him?"

"I have no idea. But it's too late, Lando. The wheels
are turning."

He shrugged.

"I'm not alone, you know," she said. "The whole
town knows about it. And all those guests. I couldn't do
that to my father."

"What does your old man do?"

"He's a banker."

"In Zurich?"

"Yes. And you—what do you do?"

"I'm retired."

She burst out laughing.

"I used to be a professional soccer player. Now I run
a chain of laundromats in Switzerland, France, Italy. Ex-
panding into Austria."

"There's never been such a stupid marriage. And it's
my own!" She made as if to get out of the bed. "Have to
go now."

He pulled her back and hugged her. "You know, what
happened between us, to me that was something real special."

."To me too," she said seriously.

"Why'n't you come along with me?"

"Where to?"

"Wherever you want."

."Not now, Lando. No can do."

"Car's downstairs. We could just take off."

She looked thoughtfully at him, and he could sense her hesitation.

"You know, you're doing something terribly foolish. You feel good with me?"

She cuddled up to him.

"So?" he asked.

Without looking at him, she whispered quickly, "What you gave to me—no, you'd never be able to understand!"

She pulled away. His mind was churning as he tried desperately to find what would keep her with him. If only he could slug her, how simple it would be! He watched her climb down from the loft-bed, get into her panties, and slip on the skirt of her blue suit. Then he came down after her.

"I can barely stand," she said.

Her legs were trembling, and she had to sit down on the couch. He sat beside her, and she let her head fall into the hollow of his shoulder, her hand caressing the muscles of his chest.

"Lando . . ."

"Don't go!"

If he had kept still, she might not have had the courage to leave, but that phrase spurred her on. She got up with great effort, fastened her brassiere, and mumbled, "What's happening to me is just crazy. Just plain crazy!"

Looking into a mirror, she was startled. "My God! I look a hundred years old! What ever did you do to me, Lando?"

"Nothing—since you're leaving."

"Try to understand."

"No."

Tears welled up in her eyes.

"Lando, tomorrow—if you want—I swear to you, I'll get a divorce."

He held her shoes out to her.

"You'll be late. It's one-thirty."

He had lost: his instinct told him there was no longer any way to make her give in.

"I don't even have time to go and change," she said. "This is awful."

"I'll see you back."

Later, in the car, she said to him, "I'd like to have a picture of you. Do you have one?"

"No."

"Do you want one of me?"

It was almost 2:00 A.M. They were riding slowly along Stampfenbachstrasse, which was now completely empty, its store windows lighted for no one to see.

"Let me out!" Renata said.

Lando braked. She got out and quickly crossed the street. Between two high-class gift shops there was a little Photomaton hut. Renata slipped in and pulled the curtain shut. Lando vaguely noticed her legs in the space between the floor and the curtain.

The electric flash went off four times. Then Renata was back in the car with him.

"Quick!" she said.

Without looking at him, she held out the wet strip of snapshots. He glanced at it, made a face, and leaned over and whispered something in her ear.

Renata looked surprised. "No," she said, "no, not now. Some other time."

Lando whispered a few more words. She hesitated, got out of the car, and went into the photo cabin again. When she closed the curtain, Lando noted that her legs disappeared from his field of vision.

Four more flashes lighted up the night.

Lando turned on the ignition. He smilingly looked at the strip of pictures she was sliding over to him. This time they showed something else, from four slightly different angles: Renata's vulva. Lando slipped them into his pocket and tooled away from the curb.

"Renata," he said, "just in case you change your mind—I'll leave you my car. The keys'll be on the dashboard. I'll wait for you at the apartment as long as I have to."

280

She took his hand, squeezed it very hard, and brought it to her lips.

Toward one o'clock, the eldest among the guests began to sit down around the small tables. They were unaccustomed to staying up so late. Chimene, feeling disaster on the horizon, wrung her hands and stormed toward her future son-in-law, who had just reappeared.

"Kurt! Did you find her?"

"No, ma'am. No, I couldn't discover a thing. She doesn't seem to be anywhere."

"Oh, heaven! What will I ever tell the reverend?"

"I'm not worried about the reverend, but about Renata!" Kurt answered her. "Everybody's here—except her. And she's the bride! Listen, didn't she give you any clue?"

"Not the slightest."

"You were the last one who saw her."

"I thought you had seen her after I did."

"Not at all. We left each other at noon."

"What can we do? Oh, Lord! What can we do?"

"Where is your husband?"

"Homer? I'm not sure. He was here just a minute ago."

"This entire thing isn't normal. Maybe Renata took ill . . ."

"But where, if she did?"

"I'll telephone the police."

"But—but—what about all these people?"

"Let them sit down and eat. They seem to be doing that already anyway."

"I'll go ask the reverend what he thinks we ought to do."

"If you wish, ma'am. But he certainly doesn't have your daughter in his pocket."

As Kurt turned, he was grabbed by a group of young friends.

"All right already! So where's the Frau? We're getting hungry!"

"Go eat!"

He went his way, looking for Kloppe, whom he found

281

at the far end of the living room, in conversation with two middle-aged men. Barely apologizing, Kurt pulled the banker away by his sleeve.

"I can't figure out what's going on. Renata still hasn't arrived."

"Have you tried our place upstairs?"

"Yes. She's not there either."

"What did Manuella say?"

"She hasn't seen her since four this afternoon."

Kloppe was getting sharp pains in his jaw, which immediately made him suspect that Volpone had staged another assault.

"We have to call the police," he said.

As long as only he had been attacked, Homer Kloppe had stood his ground, refusing to involve the police in personal problems that were mere extensions of his banking business, but this time Volpone had gone too far. Even if it resulted in a public scandal, Homer now felt he had been all too slow to call in the authorities.

"Phone the cantonal police headquarters right away. Ask for Lieutenant Fritz Blesh. Tell him to start hunting for her!"

Chimene caught up with them, her face tense with worry, although by reflex she was still able to smile and wave kisses to those of the guests who were making friendly signs to her.

"What's going on?" she demanded. "Where's Renata? What've you decided to do?"

"Just keep calm," Homer told her. "Kurt is going to alert the police."

"But, Homer—all these people . . ." Two hundred formally attired people, glasses in hand, were standing around in small groups, and a rumble of impatience was beginning to be heard.

"Is anything wrong?" Joseph Heinz politely inquired. A couple of inches behind him, like his very shadow, was his wife, Utte.

"No, father, nothing," Kurt told him. "Everything's just fine. Take mother over there and sit down."

He looked at his mother, who seemed to hold him somehow responsible for the fact that his fiancée was late.

"Your son is right, Frau Heinz." Chimene said. "Do go and sit down. I'll instruct the staff to start serving."

"I haven't had the pleasure of seeing Renata yet," Joseph Heinz put in.

"Look, father, to tell you the truth, neither have I. But there's no time to talk about that now. Just go and sit down."

"You mean your fiancée isn't here yet?" Utte asked with a woeful look, and Kurt suddenly hated her for that green dress.

Chimene grabbed one of the butlers. "Have the dinner service started immediately."

After a few too many glasses of bubbly, several smart alecks, claiming that the decor had made them seasick, were lying on their backs, inert among the upside-down chandeliers, their eyes staring at the furniture hanging from above. A bell rang to announce dinner, and the first people to get seated and read the menu burst out laughing, imagining that the printer had made a mistake. But the waiters were already bringing in trays of steaming hot coffee and bottles of Grande Fine Champagne cognac.

For just a moment the guests seemed to hesitate. How were they supposed to react to this flouting of convention?

"Great!" someone cried out. "We'll have the oysters for dessert!"

The idea caught on and succeeded in unbending those guests who appeared to have swallowed their umbrellas —mostly invited by the elder Kloppes. The coffee was very welcome, partly owing to the numerous glasses of liquor that had been imbibed. While the passionate sherbet was being served, Chimene worried about how her guests would like eating the charlotte au chocolat next, followed by the cheeses.

Chimene didn't recognize her own apartment. Even her prized paintings, hung upside down, seemed unfamiliar after thirty years of peaceful coexistence. This whole thing was maniacal, nightmarish, not to be believed. She didn't know which was more terrifying: Renata's prolonged absence, or the frightful panic she felt at the idea of Zurich's entire upper crust brought out in the middle of the night to attend a wedding that couldn't take place because the bride didn't show up!

"Kurt! Where are you going?" people were asking.

He was rushing among the tables, unable to get away from the outstretched hands, trying to put on a good face and pretending to laugh at the jokes coming at him from all sides. He patted a shoulder here, winked knowingly there, trying to make it appear that he was the one who knew the real secret and had the key to the mystery. At the beginning, Renata's absence had not been so noticeable, but now whispers were running from table to table, all sorts of knowledgeable nods suggesting some unforeseen *coup de théâtre.* Just as he was about to reach the steps to the vestibule, Kurt found himself face to face with Pastor Lustz.

"Professor Heinz!"

"Yes, reverend?"

"Where is your betrothed?"

"On her way. I'm off to get her."

He pushed the man aside, ran down the steps, and grabbed the phone.

"Get me the police!" he shouted into it.

He was craning his neck to be able to see beyond the stacks of coats and keep an eye on the door. The three women working the cloakroom looked at him curiously.

"Let me talk to Lieutenant Blesh! Emergency!"

Just then he saw the front door open, and Renata entered.

"Do you have an invitation?" one of the cloakroom ladies asked her.

Kurt was struck by her strange absent look. Her face was pale, taut, her hair unkempt. She was not wearing her salmon-colored gown, but a lavender-blue afternoon suit that looked unpressed. Was she even wearing makeup?

"Renata!" he called, as he hung up the phone, his fear suddenly turned into anger. "Where have you been? You've kept everybody waiting! Your parents are beside themselves! I was just calling the police!"

The three women were all ears. "You, mind your coat business," he barked at them.

He took Renata's arm and pulled her into a corner. She was eyeing him as if she had never seen him before.

"Will you tell me what this is all about? Why, you're not even properly dressed! Renata, I'm talking to you!"

She noted his sweat-gleaming face, tight with exasperation: this guy was a stranger. She was going to marry him, of course, but no later than tomorrow she would start divorce proceedings.

He shook her violently. "Are you high on drugs, or what? Renata! Where the hell have you been?"

Wearily, she freed herself from his grip. "Kurt, do you expect me to marry you?"

"What are you saying?" he stammered.

"Well, if you do, just fuck off! Don't ask me any more questions!"

Floored, he took a step backward.

"But you can't . . . The way you look . . ."

"If you don't take me up there right now, I'm going away again!"

She started up the stairs, and he followed her, barely catching up to her as they reached the landing. He was just able to take her arm with a conquering, possessive air as they crossed the threshold of the grand salon.

"Here she is now!" someone shouted.

Renata summoned a smile as an ovation greeted her. The women whispered as she went by, wondering what was the significance of the lavender-blue suit at such an hour. After all, maybe she *had* intended it that way—everything was strange about this whole affair. Decidedly, Zurich wasn't Zurich anymore!

Renata sat at the table with her future in-laws.

"Problems?" Joseph Heinz quietly inquired.

"I'll tell you later," Renata said.

An overzealous waiter made a point of bringing her all the things she had missed since the dinner began: cognac, coffee, sherbet, charlotte, cheeses, and a slice of saddle of lamb. He leaned over to her and knowledgeably whispered, "You're s'posed to start with the coffee. And hurry up, the bass in pastry shell is on its way!"

"Take it all back," Renata ordered.

"Aren't you hungry?" Joseph asked her.

"Renata, oh, Renata," Chimene was saying.

Chimene had come over from her own table to find out how things were. The blue suit hit her in the solar plexus.

"But—what happened to your dress?" she asked.

Renata sweetly put her arm around her mother's neck and hissed into her ear, "Mom, if you don't get back to your own table, I'm getting up and leaving."

Chimene, shocked and hurt, beat a hasty retreat.

Right after the dessert—Belon oysters on the half shell—a bit of news circulated through the room that excited all the guests: an Italian banker, having gone to the men's room, had looked every which way for a urinal. Finally, he located it where he least expected to find it—hanging from the ceiling. All the male guests rushed in to see this eighth wonder of the world—and to speculate on how it might be used.

Paster Lustz discreetly signaled to the engaged couple, their witnesses, and their parents. All together, they went into a room that had remained off limits to the assembled guests. Usually it was an office. This night, with benefit of clergy, it would be turned into a chapel.

The pastor read all the customary phrases. Then he asked, "Kurt Heinz, do you take Renata Kloppe to be your wife?"

"I do," Kurt said.

Chimene bit her lips to keep the tears back.

"Renata Kloppe, do you take Kurt Heinz to be your husband?"

"I do," said Renata without raising her eyes.

"I now declare you man and wife."

The doors opened wide and all the guests started flocking into the tiny room to smother the newlyweds with kisses and hugs. At the same instant, the wave of sound that swelled from their congratulations was drowned in the powerful noise of a motor: the copter was coming in.

Everyone began to rush toward the stairway leading up to the terraced roof. Pushed by those behind, the people in the front were shoved into violent gusts of wind that hit them like slaps in the face. Some of the women in evening dresses began to shiver, cuddling up against their escorts, who opened their tuxedo jackets as if they could afford protection. But there was no going back down; the stairway was jammed.

The terrace was illuminated by floor-level lights that showed everyone's legs while leaving their upper bodies and faces in darkness, and spotlights converged on the helicopter, catching it in harsh, raw rays. The pilot was keeping his craft hovering some fifty feet above the roof, and on the terrace itself stood a wicker gondola entirely garlanded with lilies and roses. It was connected to the helicopter by a fine steel cable that snaked up into space and got lost in the darkness.

"Let the newlyweds through!" chanted a chorus of guests.

Those on the stairway hugged the walls to make way for Renata, whom Kurt was propelling forcefully ahead of him. By the time they got to the roof, she was livid. Her hair was flying wildly in the wind, and she looked around with dismay at the scene she herself had conceived, unable to believe she had been able to imagine anything so absurd and provoking. Sensing her hesitation, Kurt tugged her after him and moved forward between a double hedge of humanity cheering them on. He clenched his teeth, anxious to have it over with, apprehensive about the dizziness he knew would grab him by both temples the minute the gondola took off into the cold night. The main thing was not to let on to all these nabobs who were probably waiting for some failure of nerve on his part: that young upstart who was marrying the heiress.

"Renata! Renata!" shouted Chimene at the top of her lungs, trying to be heard over the rotors. She was grabbing her daughter's arm with all her weight, trying to slow her progress. From the crowd, jeering laughter could be heard.

"She doesn't want them to be alone for their wedding night!"

"Let her get in!"

"Chimene, go with them! They need a chaperone!"

And all the guests, most of whom were carrying their own bottles of champagne, started chanting, "Chap-e-rone! Chap-e-rone!" between swigs.

"Renata, don't go! Don't get in that machine! Please, do it for me. I had a dream that was an evil omen!" her mother was muttering to her.

Kurt shoved his mother-in-law away, and she landed in the arms of the front row of spectators, who greeted her with jokes in varying degrees of good taste. Kurt jumped bravely into the gondola, only to become terrified at how tiny it was. All he would be able to do would be to lie down on the bottom of it, hide his head, and puke up his guts.

Then two things happened simultaneously. In the midst of the awful confusion, Chimene wrenched free and grabbed Renata, who was just about to vault over the flower-decked side of the gondola. In a far corner of the roof there was a man with a red spotlight, which he was to turn on as a signal that the couple were aboard and ready for takeoff. When a guest handed him a glass of bubbly, he inadvertently let his light go on.

A red beam snaked up into the night. Up above, the pilot was hard put to keep his machine in one place because of the violent gusts. Half-blinded by the other spotlights playing on the whirlybird, he was more than a little relieved to see the red light at last. Obeying instructions, he gracefully lifted his machine some thirty feet or so, and the gondola floated into the air—with only Kurt aboard!

The shouting of all the guests drowned Kurt's scream. But the pilot couldn't hear any of it. Dazzled, bothered by the lights, he swung his machine around, faced in the direction he wanted, and moved forward, the gondola dangling just above the rooftops of the city. "The bridegroom's flown the coop!" someone shouted. Nonplussed, her mother still dragging her back, Renata saw Kurt swinging his arms, hovering between heaven and earth in the flowery gondola that vanished in the night. There was some hesitation on the terrace. Sobered by the cold, all the guests were now looking at Renata. She forced her mother's hands away, shoved back her father, who was trying to restrain her, and made a path for herself through the crowd of wedding guests. Deaf to all their voices, she rushed down the stairs.

In the deserted street, Renata looked about for a taxi. She wanted to get to the airport at the same time as Kurt. She was too properly brought up to jilt him now, in spite of the sudden scorn she felt for him. Then she remembered Lando's car.

"Renata!" Homer Kloppe called from the doorway of the house, his stocky silhouette sharp against the light.

She stopped still for a second.

288

"Listen to me, Renata," her father called as he came toward her.

"Later, daddy, later!"

She ran to the corner, slipped behind the wheel of the Beauty Ghost P9, and found the keys where Lando had said they would be.

When Renata started the motor, she looked around for the button that would raise the convertible top. She couldn't locate it, and she turned the heater on full blast, reversed for a few feet, and swung out practically on the hubcaps down Bellerivestrasse. She drove along the banks of the Limmat, turned sharply into Ramistrasse, zoomed across Kunsthausplatz, and then turned right again into Zurichbergstrasse. As soon as she got beyond the midtown traffic lights, onto the highway, she gave it the gas, her long hair flying in the wind.

She planned to talk to Kurt right away. Obviously they had made a mistake, for which neither of them was to blame. He would understand.

As she came out of a sharp turn, flying along at a neat seventy-five miles an hour, she heard a heavy click, and the wheel began to shake in her hands, no longer responding. She didn't have time to panic. All she could think was, I'm going to be late for Kurt.

The heavy car swung to the left and skittered sideways on the road with the speed of a cannonball. Renata, desperately hanging onto the collapsed steering wheel, jammed on her brakes. The tires shrieked and the front wheels of the roadster hit a low wall that was hidden in the grass on the shoulder of the road. The car bucked and began to fly over the wall. Renata found herself lying flat on the ground, looking into the sky. She could see the two tons of P9 slowly swinging around over her head. Then the steel hulk came down and crushed her.

For Intercontinental Motor Cars, this was the ninth accident caused by a defective steering column in one of the Beauty Ghost P9s that had come off its assembly lines. Of the nine, this was the fifth involving a fatality.

Part Three

OUT

18

Dr. Mellon was unobtrusively testing Gabelotti's pulse.

"You feel all right?" he asked.

"Hell, no," said Don Ettore.

At fifty-four, Gabelotti was taking his maiden flight. Before takeoff, Mellon pumped him full of tranquilizers, which resulted in a bitch of a headache. His every muscle tensed as he desperately held the armrests of his first-class seat, and he mentally reviewed all the plane crashes that had occurred during the past few years. He tried to concentrate on the newspaper, but he couldn't make sense out of it. Why did the captain make such ominous announcements over the loudspeaker? *"We are now cruising at an altitude of thirty-five thousand feet . . ."*

"Richard," said Gabelotti to his doctor.

"Yes, Don Ettore?"

"I'm not feeling very good. Gimme another one of those pills."

"You've had more than enough already."

"I don't care."

"Well, if you insist . . ."

Richard Mellon rang for the stewardess to bring some water. He had had three years of psychiatric experience before specializing in the illness of the affluent, and he understood what fear of flying meant. Gabelotti was paying him the tidy sum of twelve thousand dollars to hold his hand during this three-day trip to Europe. At those rates, he could afford to have someone else look after his other patients—no questions asked.

"This might help you sleep," said Dr. Mellon.

"But I don't want to sleep! I'll dream I'm in a plane and I'll wake up in a cold sweat."

"That's a good one!" The doctor laughed appreciatively. "But don't worry. We'll be in Zurich in three hours."

"If I live that long," Don Ettore lamented.

For the tenth time he checked to make sure the barf bag was handy in the seat pocket. Dying might not be so bad, but throwing up in public was more than he could face.

Chimene took charge of everything. She used all her husband's powerful pull to keep her daughter's body from being taken to the morgue. Instead, Renata was brought home to Bellerivestrasse.

A phone call had taken Chimene away from a group of friends who were talking about Kurt Heinz's amazing solo departure on his honeymoon. Like the others, she had pretended to find it a huge joke, and she was still laughing when a voice on the phone informed her that Renata had had a serious automobile accident. Beside herself, she hurried over to tell Homer, and they slipped away from the reception to rush to the scene of the accident, wild with anxiety.

Homer's first shock had been seeing the Beauty Ghost. The second was seeing Renata's body. The police had not yet moved her. Her neck was broken and her chest crushed by the metal frame of the windshield.

At 4:00 A.M., unaware of the tragedy, the wedding guests were still carousing in the grand salon. When the double doors opened to reveal a group of black-clad men bearing Renata's body on a stretcher, the crowd went limp. The men moved through a sea of half-empty liquor glasses to Renata's bedroom, Chimene, her face glistening with tears, leading the way. Homer Kloppe brought up the rear, his lips pressed together, his face a mask of grief.

Chimene lost no time in waking an undertaker, who sent over a team of his best people. By dawn Renata lay in her bed, dressed in the salmon gown that should have been her wedding dress, her face in repose, as beautiful in death as she had been in life. At each of the four corners of the bed a candle burned, illuminating the kneeling figures of Homer and Chimene who were weeping silently. Manuella had joined them briefly, but, overcome by the stillness of the lovely figure before her, she left the room to bear her pain alone.

Around eight o'clock the door opened to admit Kurt Heinz. The Kloppes did not even glance at him as he knelt beside them and began to pray.

His trip back from the airport had been a nightmare. His cab had run into a police roadblock, and off to the side of the road he saw a gunmetal-gray convertible that was upside down.

"Keep going!" he instructed the driver as he looked away.

Kurt wasn't sure just how he ought to act after what had happened at the wedding. It would all depend on Renata. If she apologized and gave him a reasonable explanation for her intolerable flightiness, he might forgive her. She had turned their marriage into a farce.

"Just a second," the taxi driver was saying. "Boy, that's some accident!"

Kurt's eyes turned toward where the driver was looking, his heart sinking as he spotted Renata's blue suit. He jumped from the cab, devoid of feeling except for the strange taste of rust that seemed to fill his mouth. Five minutes later, the Kloppes had arrived, their evening clothes in cruel contrast to the scene garishly revealed by the headlights of the police cars.

"Did the car belong to the victim?" the police officer in charge asked Homer.

The banker shook his head bitterly. Whoever owned the P9 must be the one responsible for the accident. Why had the Lord seen fit to put his own daughter into this mysterious deathtrap?

"Is the victim's name Renata Kloppe?" the officer had asked.

"Not Kloppe," Kurt put in. "Renata Heinz." And Homer had turned away from Kurt.

Kurt had gone back to his apartment to get out of the ridiculous black velvet suit he was wearing. He had taken a scalding shower and then collapsed in a chair, trying to get it through his head that he was a widower after fifteen minutes of marriage.

Now, as he finished his prayer, he looked over at his father-in-law. At this moment, Kloppe, who was still holding his wife's hand, no longer seemed a stranger to Kurt, but rather a brother to whom he was linked by a common loss. In a very low whisper Kurt asked, "What did we do to the Lord to make Him visit such a misfortune on us?"

Without opening his clenched teeth, Homer Kloppe muttered back, "Leave us alone with our grief!"

"Renata was my wife!" Kurt replied.

"Not your wife; just my daughter," Kloppe decreed. "You have no more business here. Now, get out."

Once more Kurt felt his mouth flood with the strange taste of rust.

Moshe Yudelman watched the birds flutter from branch to branch in the golden sunshine, while Italo Volpone, his upper body bare, walked in circles, drying his back with a bath towel. Each of his movements made his well-developed muscles stand out.

"Who asked you to come here?" he said for the umpteenth time. "Who? Will you tell me that?"

"Nobody," Moshe answered.

"You've done nothing but fuck things up! You let my wife get snatched, and then you play footsie with her kidnapper. You think I'm goin' to welcome Gabelotti with bouquets of flowers?"

Sick of all this sour recrimination, Yudelman turned his eyes away from the rustic scene.

"Listen, quit putting the blame on others. You've been here four days yourself, and how far did you get? Do you have the account number? Of course not. If you wanted to knock off a couple of cops, you didn't have to come to Zurich. Your boys could've done the same thing in New York."

Italo faced him. "If you know what's good for you," he said, "don't you ever talk to me in that tone of voice. You hear me? Never!"

Moshe shrugged. "I'm not interested in what's good for me. What I care about is what's good for you! The

Commissione has its eye on you. If they decide to mix into our business, we've had it."

"You expected me to let Genco get killed and not do nothin' about it! You want me to take Gabelotti's insults and thank him too?"

"There's a time for doing business and a time for settling accounts. I cared for Genco as much as you did. You think it was some kind of accident that he and I worked together for seventeen years, every day, around the clock? You know how he got to be a don? He knew how to bide his time before hitting back."

Italo's anger subsided. Moshe was right—and that was just what galled him. The consigliere was the only one from whom he was willing to listen to the truth.

"You're not some punk, Italo. You're the new capo of our family. And a capo uses his gray matter more than his rod."

"Okay. If you're so smart," Volpone grumbled, "we'll see how you handle it."

"The main thing is to survive. I just got here. I don't know a thing, except that the best we can hope for is that our dough is where we left it. Just what did you do to get even with that banker?"

"Kid stuff. I put him on the spot with a cunt who went and showed him her snatch in a church where he was makin' a speech."

"That all?"

"Then I had all his teeth pulled out."

"What'd he do?"

"Nothin'. Told me to fuck off!"

"That's the wrong approach," Moshe said darkly. "Even if you squeezed his balls off, he'd never talk. You think you're fighting one guy. You're wrong. You're up against all of Switzerland! These goddamn banks never give in to anyone."

"So? What can we do?" Volpone barked.

Yudelman sighed and went back to the window, concentrating on the garden.

"We'll have to wait till Don Ettore gets here," he said.

Italo looked at him. "You mean to say you expect that lard-ass to come up with an idea?"

"No. I just expect him to start acting. Up to now we're the ones who've done everything. If the deal flops, we're the ones who've fucked up. Gabelotti'd have no trouble convincing the Commissione that he let us handle the whole thing our way and we loused it up. If we let him get his feet wet, we'll be in it together. If he's able to get anything done, we'll get our share, all right."

"What makes you think he can do anything I couldn't?"

"Nothing, I'm afraid. But right now that's not our problem. This is a four-handed game, Babe. Volpone, Gabelotti, the banker, and the cops. You lost the first rubber. Let's see what Gabelotti can do in the next one."

"And what do I do meantime? Keep score and scratch my ass?"

"You shut up and let him flounder. We'll see how he goes about it."

"Suppose he flops, too?"

"Then, Italo, you know me: I'll be the first to tell you it's time to take the bull by the horns."

Moshe Yudelman's arrival in Zurich had not softened Italo in any way. He had that worrisome off-day look about him that morning, and his cheeks were blue with an unshaven beard.

"And you let her go and get married, you bum!" Volpone was taunting Lando. "You weren't even man enough to hang onto her!"

"I did everything I could."

"I don't guess you got under her skin that much," Italo sneered. "Here I thought you were the biggest stud of them all."

Lando was zonked. After seeing Renata home, and leaving his car parked, he had hailed a taxi and gone back to his place. The condition of his bed reminded him of the sex performance he had staged to no avail. Renata would not be coming back to him. Too exhausted to sleep, he didn't doze off until 6:00 A.M., and his alarm woke him an hour later. At eight o'clock, he was reporting in to Volpone.

Italo, very busy with Yudelman, had only three minutes to spend with Lando, just enough time to crush him with insults over this latest letdown. Lando was outraged by the unjust criticism, and that made him realize how hungry he was, so he joined Pietro Bellinzona in the kitchen. With fastidious care, Lando set about making himself a salami sandwich while Pietro rummaged in the fridge looking for a bottle of beer.

Lando sat at the rustic kitchen table and bit into his sandwich. Even more than his nightlong sex exertion, the events of the day before were eating at him. Our Holy Mother had seen to it that he escaped the fate those black giants had inflicted on his luckless sidekick, but Lando wondered how a man who had been raped in the ass that way could still look anybody in the eye.

Bellinzona was thinking the exact same thing. He grunted in response to Orlando's desultory conversation. *He'll kill you,* Inez's brother had warned Lando.

"Hey, Pietro, you want me to make you a sandwich?" Lando said.

No answer. Alarmed, Lando turned around. His hair stood on end. Motionless, three feet behind him, Pietro was contemplating the nape of his neck. In his right hand was a long, sharp kitchen knife. For five endless seconds the two mafiosi stared each other down, and Lando was unable to swallow the bite of sandwich in his mouth.

"Why the fuck you lookin' at me like that?" he finally succeeded in spitting at Bellinzona.

Without a word Pietro turned away and began to carve himself a huge slice of bread.

Once the plane landed, Gabelotti felt like getting down on his knees and kissing the ground. For all that his personal croaker had filled him full of tranquilizers, Ettore had remained fascinated during the landing; he watched in panic, the sweat pouring off him, as the runway loomed larger and closer, and he was certain they would crash. The plane was going much too fast to be able to stop without smashing into the hangars at the end of the field. Pretending to wipe his nose, Ettore took out his pocket handkerchief and shoved it into his mouth so he would have something to bite down on.

"Well, there, you see, it wasn't all that bad!" Dr. Mellon comforted him.

Gabelotti looked at Mellon hatefully, tore the safety belt from around his waist, and headed for the exit even before a gangplank had been moved up outside the plane. Carmine Crimello fell in right behind the don, but he knew better than to say a word. Ettore's lifeless complexion was warning enough.

As soon as they were through the passport check, they saw Carlo Badaletto waiting for them.

"Good morning, Don Ettore. Just follow me, if you please."

As instructed, Carlo had flown to Lyons with Thomas Merta and Angelo Barba; Frankie Sabatini and Simeone Ferro had gone to Milan; and they had all headed for Zurich by train.

In Switzerland, Luciano Matarella had been in charge of getting things organized. Matarella was the Gabelotti family's overseer for the Southern European whorehouse network. He supervised a chain of unlicensed brothels, houses of assignation, and roadside motels that stretched across Europe from Bordeaux to Austria, by way of Lyons, Grenoble, Geneva, and Zurich, with a detour to Munich before reaching Vienna. It also covered Barcelona, Madrid, Lisbon, Rome, Milan, and Naples. Seven different countries. Where the ministers of the Common Market had not been able to come to agreement over some petty questions of vegetable prices, Matarella could boast of having "unified the ass of Europe." To be honest about it, his unification was not as firm as Don Ettore would have liked it: Gabelotti had a tendency to downgrade the work of his men and to feel that there was always room for improvement, so when Angelo Barba had called on him to make the arrangements for the don's stay in Zurich, Luciano Matarella had jumped at the chance to make points for himself.

"I'll take care of everything," Matarella had volunteered.

He had never met Gabelotti personally, but he recognized the don as soon as he saw him. He genuflected furtively, and, grabbing the don's wrist, brought Ettore's hand to his lips.

"*Bacio mani,*" he mumbled.

Embarrassed by the public display, Gabelotti withdrew his hand and mumbled the traditional response: "*Alzati, non sei rifardu.*"

A black Mercedes 600 was waiting for them outside the airport building. The chauffeur, in black livery, was holding the doors open.

"Getting in, doctor?" Ettore asked Richard Mellon.

"No, thanks, I think I'll take a cab. You probably have a lot of business to attend to. You know where you can reach me, don't you?"

"Yes, thanks. I'll get in touch a few hours before we're ready to leave. Your ticket will be taken care of."

"Always at your service, sir," Mellon replied. And he nodded, turned, and disappeared into the crowd.

Don Ettore got into the Mercedes with Luciano Matarella, Carlo Badaletto, and Carmine Crimello. He was a respectable businessman traveling with his various administrators. No one should be unaware of where he was going and what he was about to do.

"I reserved suites for you and your men at the Commodore, Don Ettore," Luciano Matarella informed him.

"Good. How about the flowers?"

"In the trunk of the car."

Matarella was about to add something, but he thought better of it.

"How long will it take us?" Gabelotti asked.

"About fifteen minutes," Matarella said.

The don relaxed and looked out at the landscape.

"If you decide to stay for any length of time," Matarella said to him after a bit, "it would be possible to get a house."

"No, thanks," Gabelotti assured him. "That won't be necessary."

And nothing more was said during the rest of the trip.

"Here we are," Matarella announced.

A hundred yards away, a cream-colored Volkswagen also came to a halt: in it was Folco Mori, ordered to follow Gabelotti by Moshe Yudelman, who knew the flight number. Folco saw Gabelotti get out of the car with three men, among whom he recognized Carmine Crimello and Carlo Badaletto.

When Folco saw the chauffeur open the limousine

trunk and take out an enormous floral offering, he thought he knew what Don Ettore was doing at the Zurich morgue. After a few verbal exchanges, the group headed inside the building.

Impressed by the limousine and the air of quiet authority with which Don Ettore lorded it over his entourage, the morgue attendants were ready to dance attendance on him.

"Our colleague will be happy to show you the way. However, insofar as flowers are concerned, sir, may I take the liberty of saying that they are not at all customary in an institution such as this."

Luciano Matarella knew as much when he got the order to have the flowers ready: a morgue is not a cemetery. But, being a discreet man, he had felt it better not to mention the fact on the way over. Following the attendant, they were led into the icy room. Three of its metallic walls were made up of layers of drawers. The attendant delicately pulled out one of them, and there was the leg.

As one long used to human suffering, the attendant went to the farthest corner of the room to allow the visitors their privacy before the ghastly remains. As he leafed through the ledger where he was going to record a signature, he idly wondered whether, when he died, all of his body would be the object of as much attention as this leg had received.

Gabelotti imperiously signaled to Carlo Badaletto. Carlo had spent several years under Genco, and if there was anyone who could identify the bluish limb, it was he. He leaned slightly over the open casket with a look of disgust on his face. Then he shrugged with hands outstretched to show it was beyond him.

Don Ettore had insisted on doing this, and Carlo had agreed, only to avoid fighting the *padrone*. But how could the don have imagined that he, who had come into the Volpone family as a simple soldier, would ever have a chance to see Don Genco's legs?

After a decent interval, Gabelotti started to move. He signed the ledger as requested without the slightest hesitation.

"Our unfortunate ‘relative was a highly respected
302

man," he commented. "I suppose many friends have come to pay a tribute to him."

"Several," the attendant replied noncommittally.

Gabelotti nodded and went toward the corridor, followed by his entourage. He knew no more now in Zurich than he had known in New York. Apart from Italo's assertion, there was nothing to prove that this was indeed Genco's leg. Or that Genco was really dead. Here he was, clowning around in Switzerland, and the Volpones might well be taking him for a ride.

He was out in the street when one of the attendants caught up with him.

"Here, sir," he called out, "you forgot these flowers."

Don Ettore courteously thanked him with a nod. Then he said to the driver, "Put those back in the trunk."

After that, he got into the Mercedes and muttered between his teeth, "If that Volpone is trying to pull a fast one on me, it'll be my pleasure to place the bouquet on his grave in person."

19

Melvin Bost could put it off no longer. The worried, searching eyes of all the company executives were focused on him. He cleared his throat and ostentatiously waved the telex before them.

"Bad news," he announced. "Let me read you what the president just sent me."

Putting on his glasses, he unfolded the sheet of paper that he now knew by heart.

"It's addressed to me, and it reads: USE ALL AVAILABLE MEANS TO ALERT ALL OWNERS OF BEAUTY GHOST P9 RE MANUFACTURING DEFECT IN STEERING COLUMN STOP STRESS DANGER STOP FAULTY PART TO BE REPLACED AT COMPANY EXPENSE STOP. It's signed Homer Kloppe."

Speechless, the executives watched Bost put the paper down. Then a voice cried out, "This is suicide! If we do what he says, we're broke! There are over four hundred thousand P9s on the road. Every car recalled will cost us at least three hundred dollars in parts and labor. You total that up!"

"Didn't you tell us," said the research director, "that the president was willing to take the calculated risk? We were all aware of what the computers forecast."

"This means we're deliberately putting ourselves into bankruptcy," the fiscal head joined in. "No company in the world could withstand a drain like that. It means scuttling our operation."

Melvin Bost lowered his eyes. He wished he didn't have to tell them what Kloppe's right-hand man at the Zurich Trade Bank had told him on the phone ten minutes ago. But, things being what they were, he had no right to hold anything back from them. He raised his arms.

"Gentlemen, gentlemen, may I have your attention, please? When I saw our president in Switzerland last week, he wasn't enthusiastic about the idea of being responsible for even one loss of life. But, to convince him and to keep us in business, I made the following deal with him: if there were no further accidents in the next quarter, we would let things run their course."

"Well?" someone asked. "Has there been another accident?"

"When the president sent us that message, there hadn't. That proves he had changed his mind of his own free will. I thought I might try to get him to change it again, at least to give us a little more time, but unfortunately that idea is no longer feasible, for we've run into an insurmountable obstacle. There's been a ninth defective steering column in a P9."

"Where?"

"In Zurich itself, it so happens."

"Was it a serious accident?"

"Fatal, I'm afraid—and the person at the wheel was our president's only daughter."

"They're all here!"

"All of 'em?"

"Yeah, Gabelotti came over with his whole goddamn staff."

"Who'd you see?"

"Carmine Crimello and Carlo Badaletto were with him at the airport, along with one other guy I didn't know and one more dressed like a chauffeur. Guess where they went?"

"I don't like guessing games."

"They went to the morgue. With flowers, yet."

"And then what?"

"Then they went to the Commodore. I gave the concierge a couple of bucks to see if I could pick up anything else, and he told me there's four other guys registered with them on the same floor."

"Thanks. Come on in now."

That was the telephone conversation that had just taken place between Moshe Yudelman and Folco Mori. As soon as he hung up, Moshe dialed Vittorio Pizzu in New York.

"Vittorio, get ahold of Aldo, Vincente, and Joseph, and join us here. The earlier your flight, the better. Make it snappy. You know where you can reach me?"

When Vittorio said yes, Moshe hung up. With Vittorio Pizzu and the three Volpone *capiregime* on hand, there would be a more even balance between the Volpone and Gabelotti families in Zurich. What remained to be seen was why Don Ettore had felt it necessary to bring his whole administration with him.

Moshe understood that the visit to the morgue, to the accompaniment of flowers and fervent prayers before Genco's mortal remains, was an obvious warrant of peaceful intentions that Don Ettore was holding out to Italo. The truth was, if Gabelotti was making a peace offering to a man he considered less than nothing, it was because he was in no condition to go to the mattress. So Moshe could feel reassured on one point: Gabelotti didn't know anything more about the account number than Volpone did. Obviously, Mortimer O'Brion had indeed doublecrossed his don by giving him a phony number, and now there was only one man who could resolve the impasse: the banker. Unfortunately, after the delicate attentions Italo had shown him, Homer Kloppe was unlikely to hand them the key to the money on a silver platter.

Right now, Moshe had to get his touchy boss to ratify the decisions that had been made in his name without consulting him.

"Italo, Folco Mori just called. Gabelotti's in Zurich, but he's not alone. He's got about eight guys with him."

"So, what you waiting for? Call Vittorio and tell him to get his ass over here with Amalfi, Bruttore, and Dotto!"

"Think we ought to?"

"You rather try to handle all Gabelotti's guys the way we are?"

"Don't get Ettore wrong, Italo: he wants you on his

306

side. His first move was to go to the morgue and pay his respects to Genco."

"He killed him."

"No, it was O'Brion. Now, just let me handle this, and I'll pave the way . . ."

Moshe now had the delicate job of settling the details of protocol for this summit meeting. Neither of the two family heads would call on the other for fear it would be taken as a recognition of some kind of primacy. They had to meet on neutral ground, preferably just the two of them, without witnesses. Yudelman figured they were much more likely to reach agreement if neither had to play for effect before his own men. If Italo pulled any boners, Moshe would be in a position to try to make up for them later.

"What's the matter, Pietro?" Yudelman asked Bellinzona as they drove to the Commodore, where the Gabelottis were staying. The big fellow hadn't opened his mouth all the way. "Is something bothering you?"

"Me? No, nuttin'. Forget it." And he concentrated on dodging traffic.

Moshe had known Pietro from way back: solid, fierce, and faithful to the last drop of his blood. Italo had sketchily filled him in on how Lando and Bellinzona had been beaten up by a couple of nine-foot niggers and fouled up on their assignment with Kloppe's girl friend, Inez. That would be enough to depress Pietro, whose sense of duty was legendary within the mob. Moshe glanced at him: his stonelike face wore a tormented look, and Pietro Bellinzona wasn't usually given to thinking. He drank, ate, and snored like an animal, devoid of preoccupation with higher ideas. As long as he was following orders, he was perfectly happy.

The car swerved around the flowered parterre and pulled up before the hotel entrance.

"Wait for me here," Moshe said.

At the top of the steps he saw Angelo Barba. Protocol being just as important on the level of ambassadors and plenipotentiaries, Barba walked down four steps while Moshe climbed four.

"We were expecting you," Barba said.

"And here I am," Yudelman conceded, nodding.

They went into the lobby together, after Barba, as host, courteously let Moshe precede him through the revolving door.

Now Lando was scared. Lack of sleep didn't account for all of his nervousness. The memory of Bellinzona tenderly fingering that blade behind his back filled him with the jitters. A thousand little details that seemed to have no importance came back to him. Since their encounter with Inez's brothers, Bellinzona had remained silent, turning his back on him, and Lando was relieved to see him go off with Moshe Yudelman.

Pietro and Moshe had barely left when Folco Mori came in. Lando took advantage of his presence to escape from the atmosphere of impending doom around the villa. All he wanted was to get back to his own place and soak in a hot tub.

"Folco, I'm gonna go pick up my wheels and go home and clean up."

"Okay," Mori said.

"Folco . . ."

"Yes?"

"How long you known Bellinzona?"

Folco looked at him quizzically. "Why?"

"No special reason," Lando replied.

He phoned for a taxi and told the driver to take him to Bellerivestrasse. His Beauty Ghost was not where he had left it.

He had no desire to hang around Bellerivestrasse, so he gave the driver his address, wondering whether Renata had taken his convertible. In Switzerland, it's well known that there are no petty thieves. Concerned, but too tired to be upset, Lando paid off the taxi and went into his apartment building. Two guys were leaning against the marble pillar in the lobby.

"Herr Orlando Baretto?" one of them asked, smiling and coming toward him. He showed his police ID to Lando. "You are Herr Baretto, aren't you?"

"Yes," Lando admitted, frowning.

"Would you come along to our office, please?"

"What's the problem?"

The second cop came over. "It's about your car."

Lando kept his composure. "It just happens that it's been stolen," he said. "You may have seen that I came home by taxi. I was just about to report it."

"Don't worry, Herr Baretto. We found it."

"Oh, good. Where?"

"On the airport road. Will you come along, please?"

They were being very courteous, but they took up positions on either side of him.

"I was just going up to get out of these dirty clothes . . ."

"This won't take more than a minute. It's just a formality. Please come along now; Lieutenant Blesh is waiting for you."

After a long preparatory discussion, Moshe Yudelman and Angelo Barba agreed that their two *padroni* should meet on the grounds of the Dolder Grand Hotel. The meeting was to take place on the stroke of noon. Each capo would be allowed only two bodyguards, who would stand fifty yards away from their bosses.

At 11:55 a black Mercedes 600 dropped Gabelotti off in front of the Dolder's parterre. With the practiced nonchalance of a walker in the city, the don took a few steps toward the pool. There were no swimmers, but a few hotel guests, lured by the warmth of the sun, lazed in steamer chairs. The air was full of the sound of buzzing wasps and singing birds, and the sweet-scented wind softly shook the tips of the trees that were just bursting into bloom.

Don Ettore walked down a gravel path bordered by tufts of flowering rosemary. The path veered off between two sycamores, and Gabelotti, with Thomas Merta beside him, could see Simeone Ferro, incongruous in his severe black suit, gazing into one of the smaller pools. Gabelotti suddenly realized that he, as well as Merta, was clad in black. Another black spot, a hundred yards away, caught his eye, and he recognized Pietro Bellinzona attentively reading a paper—or more likely looking at the pictures. Babe Volpone was nowhere to be seen.

Thirty seconds later, Italo's Ford drew up. Folco Mori got out to hold the door for him, and Italo and Mori, also dressed in black, walked up the path. The gravel squeaked beneath their shoes. Italo caught sight of Pietro Bellinzona. Each capo had thus sent one man ahead to reconnoiter the grounds, keeping at his side the one man among his soldiers who was most gifted at hand-to-hand combat. In addition to the Herstal that was weighing down his right-hand combat. In addition to the Herstal that was weighing down his right-hand pocket, Folco was armed with two throwing daggers. One—the one that killed Officer Patrick Mahoney—was, as usual, placed point upward in a sheath between his shoulder blades. The other was kept in place by a complicated set of straps around his left calf, pointed down.

Thomas Merta and Folco Mori discreetly walked away. As Moshe had advised him to, Italo walked straight toward Gabelotti. Since they were of equal rank, it was not unfitting for the younger to take the first step toward his senior, in the traditional way. Babe Volpone came to a halt about a yard from Don Ettore, an attentive but noncommittal expression on his face, his hands hanging at his sides.

"Well, you wished to see me, Don Ettore. Here I am."

Gabelotti smiled paternally, patronizingly, and thanked Italo for having come. But before the younger capo could show any resentment, Don Ettore opened his arms for a fraternal *abbraccio*.

"Let me repeat to you what grief I felt over the loss of your brother, *figlio mio*."

Ettore pulled back slightly, without releasing Italo's shoulders. He kept him at arm's length and looked him in the eye, enveloping him in the warmth of his gaze as if he had just been reunited with an old and dear friend.

"Don Genco was my friend. I had the greatest respect and the most sincere admiration for him."

Then he took Italo by the arm and started to walk. Despite a slight involuntary tensing of his muscles, Italo allowed himself to be swept along. For all their apparent detachment, Mori, Merta, Bellinzona, and Ferro watched the two men like hawks.

"I've heard a great deal about you, Italo, and I'm happy to have this chance to get to know you. I knew your brother from the time he first started out. He used to tell me a lot about you—things I bet you never thought anyone knew."

"Such as?" Volpone asked tartly.

Gabelotti laughed warmly. "Oh, say, how you knocked over old man Bisciotto's grocery . . . See? You're surprised, eh? You musta been—what? Fourteen?"

"Thirteen," Italo corrected.

"That's what I was saying. So, you see! You got a good break in life, Italo: you were born in the shadow of a great man, *un uomo di rispetto.* As luck would have it, we were sometimes on opposite sides in business, but we were always loyal, even as rivals. I shouldn't be telling you this because modesty forbids, but before going to my hotel, I went to the morgue to pay him my last respects."

Overwhelmed by his own magnanimity, Gabelotti stopped talking. Arm in arm, the two capi walked along in silence for twenty yards or so, and from time to time, Don Ettore stretched a hand out to touch a flower. Finally they got to a convenient bench.

"Would you like to sit here? As you know, I'm a few pounds overweight, and a few years older than I'd like. Walking tires me out."

Gabelotti let himself down on the bench with a sigh of satisfaction. Italo sat beside him. Nothing was happening as he had expected. Here he was in a children's playground, surrounded by pink nannies, listening to the conciliatory words of a tired, fatherly man. At the rate things were going, he'd soon be hearing about Don Ettore's arthritis and his digestive problems. But Moshe had begged him to hold his water and let things take their course.

"You haven't said much yet," Don Ettore was saying, "and you may feel that I am being a little too familiar. But I assure you that's only out of trust and friendship. If you have even a share of the esteem for me that I had for your poor brother, please feel at ease with me. And please believe that I sincerely mean everything I have said. I know you must be somewhat distrustful. No, no, don't deny it! I wouldn't believe you if you did. Before men can judge one another, they have to get to know each other. We are full and equal partners in this business here in Zurich. In a short time, you may be the capo of your family."

"I am now."

Again that fatherly laugh, as Don Ettore answered, "Oh, Italo, Italo! Genco had you down pat, all right! Good-hearted but impulsive. You know, becoming a don isn't achieved just for the asking. It has to be earned."

"It can be had for the taking, though," Italo said without raising his voice.

"Well, you're right about that, it can be had for the taking—and I'm sure that in this case the Volpone family is in good hands. Now, let us talk seriously. Do you have any idea why I decided to come to Zurich? My consigliere, Mortimer O'Brion, has disappeared. Your poor brother is dead. I can't stand by while our joint capital lies fallow in a bank. Out of courtesy to you, I didn't want to take any of the steps to get it working again without first advising you. I want your view on the subject. Do you object in any way to my taking our money out of the Zurich Trade Bank and sending it along its way as we had worked it out with Don Genco?"

Volpone could not keep from looking sharply at him.

"You seem surprised," Gabelotti commented. "Do you have an objection?"

"No, none at all. Have you spoken to the banker?"

"Now that you agree, I'll go after our deposit first thing this afternoon."

Volpone could not resist asking the question that was burning his tongue, stupid as he knew it was.

"Do you have the account number?"

Gabelotti seemed taken aback, and he looked at Italo with total incredulousness.

"Why, Italo, if I didn't have the number, who in the world would? I know you tried to make yourself useful to all of us by going to see the banker and trying to push along what your brother didn't have the chance to complete. I can fully understand why you did this, upset as you were. Of course, you ought to have asked me about it first. I would have told you what you must have found out by now: compared to Swiss banks, Fort Knox is wide open. You know, I might have been offended and not even understood that, in your grief, you were doing what you felt was best. To be frank, I could well have thought you were mixing into what was none of your business—either that, or that you were out of your mind over Genco's death. Just put yourself in my shoes—"

"Put yourself in mine!" Volpone cut him off. "My brother turns up dead, and at the same moment your consigliere disappears off the face of the earth!"

"How do you know that?"

"You told me so yourself."

"Correct, I just did. But when you went to the bank, you didn't know it."

"Don't try outsmarting me," Volpone snapped. "Everybody in the organization knows your fuckin' mouthpiece took a powder."

Gabelotti's heavy eyes instantly turned into two shiny, merciless slits in his face. He was at the point of signaling Thomas Merta to open fire. At that range, Merta could hit the center of a playing card. It took enormous effort on Don Ettore's part to control himself. Puffing like a sea lion, he closed his eyes, remembering that Volpone was perfectly right; that son of a bitch O'Brion *had* double-crossed him. But he wasn't ready to admit anything to Volpone. Not yet.

Gabelotti waited for his pulse to resume its normal rhythm; he leaned over to pluck a buttercup and brought it to his nostrils. It had no odor. He crushed the stem and flower in his fingers.

"Now listen to me, Italo, because I never repeat myself. If you want to keep on holding down Don Genco's place, don't let yourself use such abusive language. Out of respect for your brother's memory, I am saying this to you today as an older friend's advice. If you take it, as I hope, I'm willing to wipe the slate clean and forget any differences of opinion that may have cropped up between our two families. I think I'm making you a reasonable offer. The main thing, if you get my drift, is to live to a ripe old age."

"Yeah, that's what Genco used to say."

Gabelotti stood up. "Don't forget what I told you. In a little while I'll go by the bank. I'll let you know the outcome later this afternoon."

And turning on his heels, he walked away.

Fritz Blesh hung up, furious: a few hours more and he'd have Captain Kirkpatrick in his hair. During a long transatlantic phone call, in which each had done his best to get the other to tell everything he knew, Blesh realized that he had met his match.

"Say that again, lieutenant. What did you say?" Kirkpatrick had said.

"I was just pointing out to you that all these people did not come here together. The reports came from different border posts, some from France, some from Italy. Only Gabelotti and Crimello came in direct from New York."

"Listen, lieutenant. I'll come over and explain the whole thing to you."

"I beg your pardon?"

"Yes; if you have no objection, I think I'll hop over to Zurich."

There was nothing Blesh hated worse than other people cutting in on his turf. For any foreign police to move in on his canton seemed to him a personal affront, and he answered only with an extended silence.

"I'll be there as a private citizen, lieutenant, you understand that! I know the men involved. If I can be of any assistance to you . . ." And in a humble, begging tone, he had gone on, ". . . as one officer to another. All I'd like to do is fill you in on the specifically American aspects of this matter, the things you can't possibly know about."

"Just who are these men?"

Now it was Kirkpatrick's turn to mark time. Finally he conceded. "Ettore Gabelotti is the capo of one of the Syndicate families."

"I'll have him deported immediately."

"Please don't do that, lieutenant! Together we could pull off a real coup!"

"*We* could?"

"I'm sorry, I meant to say, you could. But I assure you, I can help you pull it off."

So that his opposite number would not score too many points, Blesh had refrained from informing Kirkpatrick of one new event that he was convinced was connected to the unusual goings-on in Zurich during the past week. A few

314

hours before, between three and four o'clock that morning, Renata Kloppe, sole heiress to one of the wealthiest of all of Zurich's wealthy bankers, had been killed in an auto accident.

The car under which her body was found belonged to another American, Orlando Baretto, a former soccer pro who for the past five years had been living in Switzerland on a visitor's permit renewed every six months. His profession was officially listed as "grain broker," but the foreign residents' dossiers showed no real activity in that line, and Blesh's investigators believed that he had income from something other than trade in cereals, indicated by his close relationship with a very high-priced call girl. Yet he had never been involved in any scandal, and he possessed two very healthy bank accounts.

"Lieutenant," one of the detectives announced as he poked his head through the door, "that man you wanted to see is here. Baretto."

"Show him in," said Blesh.

On the way over, Lando thought out his tactics. There was no way that the cops could find any link between Renata Kloppe and himself. If they could, and some smart little bastard were to find out about the relationship between Volpone and Kloppe, the jig might be up. It was his tough luck that any member of a Syndicate family was considered fair game.

"Come in, Herr Baretto. I'm Lieutenant Blesh. Thank you for coming."

"Your men told me you found my car."

"That's correct."

"I was just getting ready to report it stolen."

"Ah, it was stolen, Herr Baretto? When was that?" Blesh found this gigolo repulsive.

"Probably during the night," Lando said. "When I went to get in it this morning, it was gone. I'm told you found it on the road to the airport, right?"

"Where did you leave it, Herr Baretto?"

"In front of where I live."

"Had you had it long?"

"About a week and a half. Can I get it back now?"

"I'm afraid not, sir. It was involved in an accident."

"What kind of accident?"

"Do you know Renata Kloppe?"

"Who?"

"Renata Kloppe, the banker's daughter?"

Lando shook his head. "Never heard of her."

"Oh, you must have!" Blesh encouraged him. "You've been living in Zurich long enough to keep up with some of our local gossip. Renata Kloppe is the young lady whose wedding took place at three o'clock this morning. The story was in all the papers."

"Could be—I may have read about it. But I don't see the connection . . ."

"There is one, Herr Baretto. Renata Kloppe was killed a few hours ago; and she was driving your Beauty Ghost. Could you explain how she happened to have the keys?"

The smell of danger immediately drove out the feeling of exhaustion that had been dogging Lando since the night before.

"Why, lieutenant," he said with amazement, "how would I possibly know?"

"What did it cost you?"

"What did what cost me?"

"Your car."

"What did my car cost me?"

Lando didn't know how far Blesh had gotten with his inquiry, but he knew he had to hide the truth as tightly as he could, letting it out only a bit at a time, admitting only what his adversary already knew.

"It must have come to some eighteen, nineteen thousand dollars."

"Did you pay for it in dollars?"

"No, in Swiss francs."

"By check?"

"Listen, lieutenant, I don't see what this has—"

"By check, sir?"

"Yes, by check. But not my own."

Lando knew now that he was up to his neck in the trap.

"It was given to me."

"A fine present, indeed!"

"Not exactly a present, lieutenant. It was to pay off a gambling debt. I met a man in a bar, and we got to talking,

316

and after a while we got into a poker game. I won about twenty thousand dollars off him."

"What was that man's name?"

"He didn't tell me."

"And you didn't ask?"

"Why should I, when I was winning?" Lando asked with a fatalistic shrug.

"His name is Volpone, Genco Volpone," the lieutenant said.

"Could be."

"Or rather, that was his name."

Lando felt his palms go moist, but he was able to continue looking politely bored. His jaw set, Lando waited for the words that would tell him he was no longer a free man.

Blesh suddenly looked away. "Thanks for coming in, Herr Baretto," he said in a rough tone. "You'll be able to get your car back as soon as we finish our investigation. I'll just ask you please not to leave the city. We may need you to answer a few more questions."

Speechless, Lando headed out the door, convinced that Blesh was playing a trick on him, that in a minute he would call him back and put him under arrest. But no such thing occurred.

Out in the street, he breathed deeply, repressing an urge to run. He had to let Italo know that the game was over, that he had to get out of Switzerland immediately unless he wanted to spend the rest of his days under lock and key.

Chimene Kloppe begged her husband to leave the room where Renata lay. The prostrate father had not eaten since the night before, but had remained kneeling, insensible to the cramps that had overcome his legs in the intervening hours. Now and then he imagined he saw Renata move ever so slightly in the flickering light of the candles.

"Don't stay here, Homer, I beg you. It's not good for you."

Like a shadow he went out through the apartment. A crew of workmen sent by Oswald Hepbräuer was trying to restore things to normal without making any noise.

317

Kloppe walked through the streets thinking of the ridiculousness of the business deals that had absorbed his whole life. What did they amount to with Renata dead?

Suddenly he was at the bank, without having known he was going there. Marjorie was waiting in the outer office, stiff and embarrassed.

"Sir . . ." she tried to console him.

Homer patted her on the arm as he went by, but he did not look at her. He walked into his office and sat down at his desk, looking at the familiar room as if he had never seen it before. He opened a drawer, took out his bottle of Waterman's ink, uncorked it, and brought it to his lips without drinking. Then he put it back alongside the box of Davidoff's Punch Culebras.

There was nothing he wanted; it was as if he himself had died. He got heavily to his feet and went over to the window, but he didn't really see the landscape. Down below, on the avenue, people were out walking. How could the weather be so fine when a twenty-three-year-old woman had just died? How could the world go on revolving without her, as if nothing had happened?

He returned to his desk, took out a folder, riffled through it without seeing it. Nothing meant anything anymore. . . .

Marjorie slipped into the room.

"Sir, are you in?"

"No."

She was about to go out, but Kloppe called her back.

"Who is it?"

"A gentleman who says he came over specially from America. He says he has to see you. His name is Ettore Gabelotti."

The name of Volpone popped violently into Homer's head. After Renata's accident, he had even pointlessly wondered whether Volpone hadn't . . . But no, the little gangster couldn't have engineered his daughter's death. He himself must take the blame, all on account of a fortune that would never be of any use to him.

"Show him in," he forced himself to say.

Marjorie seemed surprised, but she refrained from comment.

318

Ettore Gabelotti came into the office. "Mr. Kloppe?"

Homer nodded him to a seat.

"Thanks," Gabelotti said. "You know who I am? We have a mutual acquaintance: my lawyer, Philip Diego. He must have spoken to you about me. I'm in a bit of a spot, you see. I have a large sum on deposit with your bank. Two billion dollars, as you know . . ."

Don Ettore glanced at the banker's face to see if it showed any sign of encouragement, but he saw nothing.

"This capital was in transit here, when my partner, who you met, was killed. My friend Genco Volpone. It also happens, by an extraordinary set of circumstances, that my representative, Mr. Mortimer O'Brion, who you met with Volpone when he came here to make the deposit . . ."

Gabelotti stopped, took a deep breath, and then went on.

"It so happens that Mr. O'Brion acted unprofessionally, dishonestly, toward me. He did not give me the true account number for our deposit, as I found out when I phoned from New York to complete that transfer after my unfortunate partner died. Yes, Mr. Kloppe, I was betrayed by the man who had my confidence for many, many years."

Homer reacted to all this no more than if he had been made of cast iron.

Gabelotti twisted in his seat. "I am also aware, Mr. Kloppe, that my partner's brother, Mr. Italo Volpone, took it upon himself to come and see you without consulting me, something he had absolutely no authority to do. I know how awkward he can be sometimes, so I hope you won't feel that a man as honorable as me is responsible for any such actions. I was the one who personally chose your bank for our transfer because I knew your reputation for complete and total faithfulness and integrity. I realize that, with anyone less understanding than you, these very qualities might work against me. For I am not in possession of the number of my own account, Mr. Kloppe.

"As you can see, I'm putting all my cards on the table because I have utter confidence in you. You know that the money deposited in that account is mine. So I am calling upon your long-established business sense, and, man to man, without witnesses, I ask you now to effect the transfer of our deposit to the Panama Chemical, as planned."

For a few seconds a kind of religious silence reigned in the office. For the first time, Homer Kloppe appeared to "see" Ettore Gabelotti. Kloppe stared at him at length, then stood to signify that the meeting was as an end.

"I am most unhappy, I assure you, sir, to have to say that I have not the slightest idea what you are talking about."

20

The immigration inspector scanned their passports without taking particular notice.

The four men all wore dark suits, and each held an important-looking attaché case without which a businessman would only look like what he was: not very much.

"Go on through, gentlemen."

Vittorio Pizzu, Aldo Amalfi, Vincente Bruttore, and Joseph Dotto were swallowed up in the crowd that had just arrived on the New York–Zurich 747. Pizzu had the address of the villa, and Volpone and Moshe Yudelman were expecting them.

"You know the name of the place we're heading for?" Pizzu asked Bruttore. "Bankers' Boulevard. Takes the Swiss to dream up that one."

"I'm hungry," Bruttore replied.

"Where do we get our rods?" Dotto wanted to know.

"Don't worry," Vittorio grumbled.

They piled into a taxi and Pizzu showed the driver a piece of paper that had *Sonnenberg—Aurorastrasse* written on it.

"Ja!" said the driver as he drove them away.

At the same time, the immigration official, having gotten a colleague to take his place, was phoning the central headquarters of the Zurich cantonal police.

"Lieutenant Blesh, please."

"Who's calling?"

"Airport Immigration. Sergeant Glucke."

321

"He's not in, fella, but give me the poop; I know what it's about. Another batch of 'em?"

"Yeah, four."

"Hold it while I get a pencil. Let me have the names."

"Just in from New York. Vincente Bruttore . . ."

"With a double *t?*"

"Yes. Aldo Amalfi . . . Joseph Dotto . . . Vittorio Pizzu."

"Very good. Did you alert our guys?"

"Right away. They're on their tail."

"Thanks again."

"Good-bye."

"So long."

Lieutenant Blesh and Captain Kirkpatrick loathed one another instantly. Blesh couldn't stand redheads, especially when, not satisfied with infringing on him themselves, they brought reinforcements.

"My assistant, Lieutenant Herb Finnegan," Kirkpatrick said.

Blesh dryly nodded recognition.

"And Mr. Scott Dempsey," Kirkpatrick went on. Blesh looked the little man up and down; he seemed to be having the time of his life in his unpressed tweed jacket and his navy blue tie, wrinkled as a dishrag.

"You with the police?" Blesh mistrustfully inquired of Dempsey.

"Not exactly," Kirkpatrick cut in. He cleared his throat and went for broke. "My friend Scott Dempsey is here for the Securities and Exchange Commission."

Blesh frowned. If there was one kind of intruder he had no desire to see in Zurich, it was an SEC bureaucrat.

"I'm truly surprised, captain. I had understood that you were coming alone, purely as a private citizen."

"That's what I said, lieutenant."

"In that case, I don't understand what a full-fledged investigator of the U.S. financial services is doing here."

Scott Dempsey went right on laughing, as if he were not involved in the issue.

Kirkpatrick was upset by Dempsey's lack of concern. "His trip here is on a purely private and friendly basis," he urged.

322

"I'm sorry to have to inform you that it must remain so," said Blesh. "It is difficult for us to permit foreign officials to come investigating on our territory, even when they are from friendly countries."

The "friendly country" bit almost made Kirkpatrick choke.

"We are well aware of those facts, lieutenant," he said, smiling affably. "I can assure you, none of us have the intention of lifting even a finger as long as we are your guests. Just forget who we are and take us on as volunteer informants, won't you?"

Blesh stared at Scott Dempsey and inquired, "May I know, sir, what it was that prompted you to make this trip?"

"I invited him to come along," Kirkpatrick cut in.

"Why?"

Dempsey giggled again, and Kirkpatrick glared at him.

"You see, lieutenant," the captain went on, "the case we are investigating is beyond my competence—"

"I'm surprised," Blesh interrupted. "You assured me when we talked that you were involved in a purely criminal investigation."

"That's correct."

"Well, then?"

Kirkpatrick, accustomed to doing the asking instead of the answering, twisted nervously. He had no intention of letting this pip-squeak lieutenant in on the real reason for the investigation. What could a Swiss understand about how the very existence of the Syndicate affected the life of the United States?

"I don't think you've played fair with me, captain," Lieutenant Blesh remarked icily.

"I beg your pardon?"

"And I must say, I don't like it."

Kirkpatrick's face was now red enough to match his hair. Blesh brought his hand down as if in a karate chop.

"Since the time I informed you of the death of Detective Cavanaugh, sir, you have constantly acted as if I were not all there! You say you want to help me, but I can't believe it. You have tried to get whatever you could

323

out of me, and you have given nothing in return. This is not what we expect from fellow officers."

The last time Kirkpatrick had been chewed out was twenty years ago, when he had been bucking for detective.

"I know as much as you about the case you're investigating, and maybe more," Blesh went on in a peremptory tone. "Volpone, Yudelman, Pizzu, Mori, Dotto, Bruttore, Amalfi—all are here under our surveillance. And the Gabelotti clan as well. Crimello, Barba, Badaletto, Merta, Sabatini, and Ferro." Blesh held out his flat palm and then closed it sharply. "All here! And incidentally, do you know Rico Gatto? No. Have you ever heard of Orlando Baretto? Of course not. Well, there are still a few things I can show you, captain!"

Kirkpatrick rolled with the punch. Herb Finnegan, embarrassed, turned his head away. Even Scott Dempsey looked serious.

"So here's what I propose to you," Blesh concluded, "take it or leave it. Either we put all our cards on the table and loyally exchange information—in which case, if I find you holding back the slightest thing, the deal is off! Or you may prefer not to talk. If so, gentlemen, you are free to leave."

Kirkpatrick bit his lip and glanced at Finnegan and Dempsey.

Finnegan said, "I believe the lieutenant makes sense, captain."

"Just a second," Blesh cut in. "I must add one thing: you have no authority in Switzerland—no police authority and no right to investigate our Confederation's banking activities."

"What does that leave us?" Kirkpatrick asked, swallowing his saliva with difficulty.

"Not a thing! In exchange for certain leads, I will allow you to be present during my investigation. And you may use what you learn in whatever way you see fit— once you are back in your United States!"

"But what if you arrest some of these jokers?"

Blesh made a snide little face. "You're overlooking something, captain. Until proof of the contrary, none of these jokers, as you call them, has so far committed any crime on Swiss soil. What reason would I have to arrest them? What could I charge them with?"

In order not to show how satisfied he was to be able to stick it to his American confrère, Blesh assumed a somber look and paced behind his desk. He suddenly stopped, facing Kirkpatrick, and burst out, "Well? Yes or no?"

Kirkpatrick ran an unsteady hand through his red mop and again sought the approval of Scott Dempsey and Herb Finnegan, both of whom nodded to him.

Kirkpatrick shrugged. "Okay, deal," he conceded.

The lieutenant smiled slightly and pushed a button. A sentry stuck his head through the door.

"Bring some glasses, ice, and scotch."

"Very well, lieutenant."

Fritz Blesh turned toward his guests. "Between you and me, I'd be just as happy if those—fellow citizens of yours hadn't come to Zurich. All I want is to be rid of them. I hope they're not crazy enough to think they can carry on here the way they do in Chicago."

Then he said, "Now, captain, what was it you wanted to tell me?"

At the villa, there was no one in the foyer or in any of the downstairs rooms. Lando bounded up the stairs, four at a time, having forgotten how exhausted he was, concentrating on the task before him: informing Volpone that the Swiss police had pegged them. At the first landing, he bumped into Folco Mori.

"Where's the *padrone*?"

"Not to be disturbed."

"I gotta talk to him, Folco!"

"Pizzu just got here with the three *capiregime*. Italo and Yudelman are reading the riot act to them. You better wait."

"Shit! Will it take long?"

"I don't know."

Knowing family protocol, Lando didn't dare tell Mori that the flames were practically licking at their asses. He had to talk to Italo Volpone first, and to no one else. Frustrated, he went down to the kitchen to get himself a pick-me-up.

He saw Bellinzona's broad back. Pietro was sitting on

a stool at the kitchen table, looking through a comic book. In front of him, there were three or four empty beer bottles. Lando grabbed a bottle of vodka and poured himself a stiff one.

"Pietro, you think they're gonna be long up there?"

"All depends," Pietro said. "Who you want?"

"Volpone."

"They been in there over an hour."

Lando realized something was strange: Bellinzona had started to talk to him again. Reassured, he reasoned with himself that his lack of sleep had made him blow things out of proportion.

"Feeling better now?" he warmly asked Bellinzona.

"What?" the big guy retorted.

"You looked blue yesterday, like depressed, you know?"

If he had dared, Lando would have said that he had already forgotten the scene he had been forced to witness, that he would never breathe a word about the misfortune that had befallen Pietro.

"Sure, I'm okay. Just fine, like."

Pietro got up, went to the refrigerator, and took out another bottle of beer. He twisted off the cap. Downing half of it in one long gulp, he thoughtfully walked toward the door. Lando saw him nonchalantly turn the key and lock it.

"Hey, whatcha doin'?" Lando asked him.

Bellinzona shoved the key into his pocket, and when his hand came out, it was carrying a Walther PP that was aimed at Lando.

"You gone nuts?" Baretto sputtered.

Pietro put a finger to his lips. "Don't make no noise, pal. Can't disturb the guys that're workin'."

"Why you aimin' that at me?"

"I'm gonna kill you, Lando."

Lando felt paralyzed. "What'd I ever do to you?"

Bellinzona scratched his head, embarrassed. "Nothin'; that's just it. Nothin'. I swear I got nothin' against you personally."

"Ain't I your pal?" Lando queried, trying to keep his voice under control.

"Sure," Bellinzona said. "But I still gotta kill ya."

"On accounta yesterday?" Lando blurted. "That's nuts! I didn't see nothin'! I wasn't even lookin'! The same thing coulda happened to me!"

"But it happened to me, Lando," Pietro came back. "And as long as you're walkin' around, I can't go on livin'."

"Pietro," Lando pleaded with him, "you're not gonna do this thing. You can't shoot me. They'll hear you. Italo'd never let you get away 'with it! Forget the whole thing, my man. I forgot it all, I give you my word."

Bellinzona tensed. "Don't look at me like that," he said. "I'm tired of lookin' at your eyes. Turn around!"

"Pietro!"

"Turn around, I said."

"Pietro, don't act like no fuckin' crazy!"

His legs like Jell-O, Lando turned. Without having heard him come near, he felt Bellinzona's breath in his ear.

"I'm sorry, pal. But I ain't got no choice."

"Pietro!" Lando called out.

He wanted to turn around again, but Bellinzona's cuff caught him at the base of the neck, right on the top of the spine, and Lando collapsed on the checkerboard-tile floor. Quickly Pietro moved over to the door and held his ear against it. To make doubly sure, he unlocked it, stuck his head out, then looked around and listened. No one there, no sound. Everyone was still upstairs.

He locked the door again, went to a huge freezer, and took out a chunk of ice weighing thirty pounds or better which he balanced on the edge of the freezer. He went back and, with his foot, turned Lando's body over so he was lying on his back. Then he got the block of ice, and using it like a sledgehammer he smashed it down on Lando's forehead. Shards of bloodstained ice sprinkled all over the kitchen floor. Bellinzona leaned down to make sure that Lando's forehead had been bashed in. Then he got a broom, swept all the ice shards onto a plastic pan, and threw them in the sink. With very precise movements he got up on tiptoe to open a storage closet above the regular cabinets. Before Lando came in, Pietro had made sure to put a large plastic-wrapped loaf of bread up in that closet. In front of the cabinet, he knocked the stepladder over. Then he picked up the block of ice, carried it to the sink, and dropped it in, turning the hot water tap on full

force. The ice began to melt. Then Bellinzona dragged
Lando's body in front of the storage closet, near the stepladder. This time he turned Lando over on his belly, making sure to rub his bloody forehead against the tiling of
the floor. Pietro let Lando's face fall against the floor,
right in the middle of the blood puddle.

Now there were only the final details to arrange, and
the set would be perfect. He took a pile of dishes from the
bottom of the cabinet and placed them up in the closet,
right next to the package of bread. He also took a plate of
cheeses out of the fridge and put it on a shelf halfway up
in the closet, which he could reach only with his fingertips
when he stood on tiptoe. He went to the sink and chipped
off a sliver of ice about an inch thick and a couple of
inches long. It looked something like a prehistoric tool or
an Indian arrowhead, and Pietro slid it under the pile of
dishes that he had placed at the very edge of the closet
shelf. In a couple of minutes, the ice would melt and the
dishes would come crashing down to the floor.

In the sink, the hot water had completely melted the
rest of the ice. The heavy, deadly ice turned into water
had flowed off in waste. Bellinzona looked around one last
time. Obviously Lando had slipped and fallen on his face
while climbing up on that stool to get the bread. What a
stupid way to die. . . .

Pietro opened the kitchen door again. It had taken
him only three minutes to carry out his entire scheme.
Outside the kitchen, things were as quiet as before. He tip-
toed into the foyer, where the heavy carpeting muffled his
steps. The elevator shaft hid him from the sight of Folco
Mori, still on guard upstairs outside Italo Volpone's room.
Bellinzona seated himself in the chair in the corner of the
foyer that was farthest removed from the kitchen. He
opened a newspaper, and called up to Mori. "Hey, Folco!"

The guard looked down over the banister.

"Whatcha want?"

"You think this bullshit can be true?"

"What?"

Pietro pointed to the paper. "It says here they planted
some seeds that was two thousand years old, and they
started to grow."

"Wha' kinda seeds?"

Bellinzona, relaxed in his armchair, was about to answer when they heard a loud noise in the kitchen. Pietro was on his feet in an instant.

"What's that?" Folco called, pulling out his gun.

"Don't move. I'll go see!"

His Walther PP in hand, Pietro crossed the foyer. And Folco Mori heard him exclaim, "Goddamn! I don't believe it!"

Mori swept down the stairs to join Bellinzona, who stood speechless on the threshold of the kitchen door.

Orlando Baretto was lying facedown in a puddle of blood mixed with broken pieces of china. Folco moved in and turned Lando's body over. He bent down so his ear was right against Lando's chest, looked up at Pietro in consternation, and said, "It's too fuckin' stupid. He's dead."

As the undertakers were about to close the lid of Renata's coffin, the funeral director stopped them with a hand signal and went over to Chimene Kloppe.

"Would you like to look at your daughter one last time?" he asked.

Chimene broke into sobs and threw herself into Homer's arms. Kloppe held her tightly, patting her softly on the back of the neck. Over his wife's shoulder he blinked to the funeral director, and immediately came the sound of the casket closing. Flooded with tears, shaken by sobs, Chimene tightened her fists and bit them until they bled. Homer led her through the corridor to her bedroom, struggling all the way, and finally got her seated on the edge of the bed.

"Courage," he said.

He was standing before her with tears in his eyes. Desperately, she held him about the thighs.

"Tell me it's not true," she moaned. "Tell me it can't be!"

"Courage," he repeated. "The Lord will not forsake us."

"He has forsaken us," Chimene moaned again. "Yes, forsaken."

Homer took off his fogged glasses and wiped them

with his thumb. Downstairs, on the street, a large cortege of cars was waiting for the flower-covered hearse to start moving.

"Come on," Homer said to his wife. "We have to see this through."

He helped her stand up. She leaned against him, hiding her face in his shoulder. Homer suddenly stopped as he saw four men walking down the corridor, carrying Renata's casket. Leaning against a wall, Manuella, in mourning attire, stood sobbing. She came over to help Chimene Kloppe, and the three of them made their way down the stairs past the lineup of floral offerings that the mortician's men had not been able to load in any of the vehicles.

When they got down to the street, the bells of Grossmünster were tolling their death knell.

Helena Marcoulis, Chimene's best friend, threw her arms around her in an impulsive gesture. Homer let go of his wife's arm, and that was when he noticed Lieutenant Blesh.

"I am overcome with grief, sir," the policeman said to him. "Please accept my deepest condolences."

Kloppe nodded and made as if to continue walking.

"Herr Kloppe . . ." the policeman said, and the banker looked at him with an expressionless gaze.

"Herr Kloppe," Blesh quickly went on in what was barely more than a whisper, "I know this is neither the time nor the place—"

"No, it isn't," Kloppe said.

"But I'm afraid I have to inform you. Believe me, I would not do this if it weren't for the seriousness of the matter. Have you received any threats lately, Herr Kloppe?"

The undertakers were loading the coffin into the hearse. In the throng of people, Homer made out Utte Heinz. Beside her was her husband, Joseph Heinz, wearing dark glasses. Homer looked around for Kurt, but did not find him.

"Threats? What do you mean?"

"There are some strange things going on in Zurich, sir. And we can't be sure they are not connected with the

330

death of your dear Renata. I have to investigate. Tell me, have there been any threats?"

Homer looked into the eyes of Lieutenant Blesh and said in a colorless voice, "Sir, I don't understand what you are talking about."

Then he turned to help Chimene climb into the limousine.

At four in the afternoon, following the same ritual as they had performed that very morning, Ettore Gabelotti and Italo Volpone met again on the grounds of the Dolder Grand Hotel.

Although his consiglieri, Angelo Barba and Carmine Crimello, did not agree, Don Ettore felt that, considering the urgency of the situation, he had to come clean to Babe Volpone about O'Brion's betrayal. Not out of any love for truth, or because he suddenly trusted Italo so much, but because it would serve his own purposes. He suspected that Volpone already knew all about it; perhaps he had even arranged it! Yet Babe did not have the secret account number. No doubt Volpone had grilled O'Brion to get the information, but obviously he had failed—or he would no longer be where he was.

As for Italo, his mind was completely taken up with the shock of Orlando's death. It amazed him that a mafioso could come to his end by falling off a stool. For the time being, until they could figure out a more suitable and less visible resting-place, Orlando Baretto's body would be stashed in the cellar of the villa. If there hadn't been two witnesses to the accident—Folco Mori and Pietro Bellinzona—Babe Volpone would have refused to believe it. They were all standing around Lando's corpse when Yudelman answered the ringing phone.

"Hello, Angelo Barba here. Gabelotti wants another meeting. Four o'clock, same place. That okay with you?"

Without consulting Italo, Yudelman replied, "Don Italo is agreeable."

By the use of that *don*, Yudelman had made official, to the members of his own family and those of the rival outfit. the title of capo that Italo Volpone had assumed, thereby presenting him to the whole Syndicate as the legitimate successor to his brother. There was no more question about it: The King is dead! Long live the King!

Now it was even hotter in the hotel gardens than it had been at noon. As soon as the two dons caught sight of each other Thomas Merta and Folco Mori discreetly moved off to a distance while Simeone Ferro and Pietro Bellinzona remained stationed about fifty yards from their capi.

This time, Gabelotti made the first move toward Italo. "I have to apologize to you," said Ettore.

Once again he took the younger man by the arm and led him to the same bench.

"You were right. O'Brion double-crossed me. I went to see the banker. The number Morty gave me was a phony."

Italo relaxed slightly.

"I still can't believe it happened," Don Ettore went on, shaking his head. "What bothers me, you see, is that I don't know if that little bastard was able to get the money out of the bank."

Italo concentrated on two blackbirds fighting over a scrap of bread.

"The banker refused to tell me anything at all," Gabelotti was saying. "How do you think we can find out if the money is still safe?"

Gabelotti looked quizzically at Volpone.

"You bet on the one on the left or the one on the right?" Volpone asked, pointing to the blackbirds.

"Look, you and I have to get to the bottom of this. There's no point in continuing to keep after the bank if Morty took off with the dough. If we had the least little information about that, we'd know where we ought to aim our mutual efforts. You were here in Zurich before me. Didn't you find out anything?"

Volpone shook his head.

"I'm really bothered by this, Italo. What do you think we ought to do?"

"Finish what I started," Italo replied.

"Meaning?"

"Keep pushing Kloppe around."

"Apparently that hasn't produced results."

"We been too easy on him."

Gabelotti noted with satisfaction his inclusion in that "we."

"Well, you know his life is precious to us," Don Ettore said. "And he knows it, too. As long as he's sure we can't rub him out, he can go on holding us off for a long time. To say nothing of his possibly calling the cops. *Non siamo a casa nostra*, Italo. The least he could get them to do is deport us—like that!" And he snapped his fingers.

Babe thought it over a moment. Yudelman and he had considered two possibilities: either Gabelotti had the secret number, or he didn't. Obviously, he didn't. Volpone remembered what Moshe had advised him, and in a calm voice he said, "If you're in agreement, I'd like to make a suggestion."

Ettore looked at him. Despite all his feelers, Italo had not in any way reacted to his comments about O'Brion. Not for a second had he seemed to consider it possible that the defecting consigliere had been able to get the money out of the bank. So Ettore came to his own conclusion: Italo had rubbed Mortimer out before he could get any information from him.

"Okay, Italo, let me hear it."

"Do you think we could get Kloppe to give us the number if we could snatch him for a few days?"

"Of course, Italo. But that couldn't possibly be done!"

"Why not?"

"If this Kloppe guy disappears, we've made enough waves in Switzerland by now to have all the cops in the country on our backs. The minute he's reported missing, we'll be collared."

Italo allowed himself to smile easily for the first time.

"I don't think so, Ettore."

He took an envelope out of his pocket. "Would you like to take a look at this?"

Gabelotti, trying to hide his curiosity, slipped the letter out of its envelope. Inside the folded sheet was a snapshot of a statuesque black woman wearing nothing but a bathing monokini, tits proudly displayed, raising her long arms enthusiastically in a winner's salute.

"Who's she?" Don Ettore asked.

"Kloppe's little bed partner. A whore named Inez. He's been screwing her right in the vault of his bank. And look who she addressed the envelope to."

In a free-flowing, typically American hand, the envelope carried the inscription: "Frau Chimene Kloppe, 9 Bellerivestrasse, Zurich."

Gabelotti looked at the Italo in amazement. "Wait a minute! You mean Kloppe's piece of ass wrote to his wife?"

"Yeah. Just exactly what I dictated. Go ahead, read it."

Dear Madam,
     Homer seems to be afraid to tell you, so it's up to me. He and I are going away for a week's vacation—in Sardinia, if you must know. This little recreation is the least you can let him have to make up for thirty years married to you. I'll send him back to you in good shape. He may be a little bit frazzled, but he'll be fine.

                         Not very truly yours,
                         Princess Kibondo

"I'm betting on the one on the left," Don Ettore said.

"You lost. Look."

The blackbird on the right was flying off with the crust of bread in its beak.

"She really a princess?" said Gabelotti.

"She's a royal blow-job. Me, I'm a prince, too, where I come from. You can be sure that if old lady Kloppe gets this love note, she's not gonna run to tell no cops about it. She'll do her best to keep it as quiet as she can. What woman wants people to know her husband's out fucking some Ubangi?"

"Keep going," Don Ettore encouraged him.

"So we snatch Kloppe."

"How?"

"While we got him, I bring some of my guys in from Italy. And we knock over the bank!"

"You really think we could get into their safes and vaults?"

"We don't have to. That's not where our dough is.

334

Old Kloppe has it invested someplace, making a profit for himself."

"So how do we get it?"

"We'll fuck up his business affairs and his private life so good he'll never be able to show his face in Zurich again. He'll be wiped out. And he'll have to come across. The scandal will be what empties his safes and vaults, not us. The customers'll make a run for it and take their bread to a dependable bank."

"What kind of forfeit do you want?"

"Huh?"

"I lost the bet on the blackbirds," Gabelotti said with a forced smile.

"When we're all done, you can buy me a Swiss watch."

"When do we snatch him?"

"This afternoon."

"When do we hit the bank?"

"During the night, if you okay it."

Don Ettore made a face. "I believe in fast work, but let's not overdo it."

"I got ten men coming in from Milan during the night."

"How'll you get them across the border?"

"I got that fixed."

Gabelotti was highly amused. "So the young wolves are working for the old wolves now, eh?"

"Nope, Ettore, all the wolves are working together."

Charged with a new feeling of power, Italo looked at the older don with eyes bright as gushing oil.

"You trust me to do it?"

Gabelotti grabbed Italo's upper arms in both his hands and replied, "Absolutely, Italo. Absolutely! But I'd like it if you filled me in on some of the details."

"Okay."

"You know, Italo. I like being on the sidelines. But not when I got two billion bucks riding on it!"

It seemed as if the whole town had decided to turn out at the cemetery. Floral pieces were crowded on all sides, even decorating the surrounding graves.

Homer Kloppe was much too religious to doubt for a

second that there would be an afterlife for his daughter's soul. God had simply called her home, to a mysterious place where he and Chimene would join her when their own last hour had come. Homer knew with certainty that the Lord had subjected him to this ordeal as punishment for his moral failings, for not running his business with the unbending rigor he professed.

Hidden under dark mourning veils, Chimene shook the hands extended to her. She barely heard the confused litany of whispered condolences. Homer was standing on his wife's left, but he wasn't able to stop Kurt Heinz from coming and standing on her right. The stranger who had been his son-in-law for some ten or fifteen minutes was accepting the affectionate sympathy that rightly belonged only to the father and mother of the dead woman.

As soon as the coffin was in the ground, Kurt slid alongside Chimene as if he were one of the family. The crowd was enormous. People trying to get to see the Kloppes had to stand and wait for half an hour, treading between graves, dancing from one foot to the other before going to join the awful traffic jam trying to get out of the cemetery. An hour later the long line of mourners seemed no shorter. Chimene leaned toward Homer and whispered feebly through her veils, "I'm not feeling very well."

Homer grasped her arm. "Let me take you home."

"No, no," she protested. "Everything's turning around . . ."

"Is something wrong?" asked Helena Marcoulis, standing just behind her friend.

"Let's get out of here," Homer said.

"No," Chimene insisted. "We can't."

"Helena, can you see my wife home?" Homer asked.

"Let me handle it!" she replied, and she put her arm around Chimene's waist, held her up, and nodded unobtrusively to Manuella, standing discreetly a few paces away.

After two hours the line had tapered off, but there were still many groups standing around among the family enclosures, as if this burial place were never to be emptied of the crowd that had invaded it.

"My car is outside," Kurt said to Homer. "Can I drop you off?"

Kloppe turned his eyes away, and at that moment a chauffeur came up to whisper in his ear. "I'm here to pick you up, Herr Kloppe."

"I'm coming along," the relieved banker answered.

The chauffeur cut through the crowd and headed for the exit, and Homer followed him, more than a little grateful that he could escape from the embarrassing presence of Kurt Heinz, whose tactlessness struck him as unpardonable. The chauffeur led him among all kinds of cars, off to a shoulder of the road. He respectfully opened the door of a black Mercedes 600 with tinted panes. Kloppe got in and the chauffeur closed the door.

Inside the Mercedes, there were four men. Two of them, Homer had never seen before. As for the other two, he would have given anything never again to meet them under any circumstances, let alone now.

"I would like you to know," Ettore Gabelotti said contritely, "that you have my heartfelt sympathy in the loss you have suffered."

"Accept my sincere condolences, too," Italo Volpone chimed in.

The banker, his lips pursed, tried the door handle: it would not open from the inside. The Mercedes worked its way out of the confusion of cars surrounding it, turned in the direction of Zurich, and picked up speed. Aware that he had fallen into a trap, Kloppe resolved not to give these hoodlums the satisfaction of seeing him show any reaction. Not deigning to sit back against the soft leather upholstery, he sat erect, hands on his knees, looking straight in front of him. He was not afraid, but angered and bored with the vanity of all human enterprises in general, and this kidnapping in particular.

"I am really terribly sorry, Mr. Kloppe," Gabelotti said to him, "but I think you'll see that this time you do have to pay a little more attention to what we have to say."

21

When she got home, Chimene Kloppe immediately made for her room, where she dropped on the bed, tears pouring down her face. Manuella came in with a cup of tea. Choking on her sobs, Chimene took the maid's hand, squeezing it as if her life depended on it. Weeping copiously, Manuella held her in a tight embrace and then ran from the room, leaving an envelope in Chimene's hand.

Alone, she finally calmed down. She dried her face on the sheet, smearing it with powder and mascara, and sitting up, she opened the envelope. A picture fell out of it, and Chimene rubbed her eyes, immediately recognizing the tall black woman whose pictures she had found in her husband's overcoat pocket. With a heavy heart she glanced over the letter, rereading the words that twisted her insides to a pulp.

The wildest ideas sped through her mind. She looked at the picture again, lingering over the naked breasts. She knew Homer too well to believe for a second that he was capable of deserting his wife, even under normal conditions, and much less so during the horrendous trial the Lord had visited upon them in taking their only daughter.

Shocked into action, she phoned Kurt. She found him at home, and he told her that Homer had left the cemetery about an hour earlier. She thanked him and dialed the bank. Marjorie hadn't seen her boss since yesterday. Chimene called information and asked for the number of the cantonal police headquarters, and just as the connection went through, she hung up. She decided to give herself two hours in which to take action. If, by that time, Homer had still not come home, she would phone Lieutenant Fritz Blesh.

The plane was standing on an alternate runway in a section of the Milan airport that was reserved for taxi-planes and a couple of aeroclubs. On either side of the plane the words FLIGHT SCHOOL were printed in big red letters. It was an MD 315 that the French army had re-tired and sold as surplus. After a heavy case had been loaded on, ten men marched single file up the several steps of the ladder, looking distrustfully at the rust spots around the edges of the door. There were no seats inside. Safety belts were attached directly to the walls of the pas-senger compartment, such as it was. One of the men asked the pilot in a muffled tone, "Say, Morobbia, you sure this thing really flies?"

Amedeo Morobbia shrugged. "Depends on the days, and the wind," he said, "and the Madonna. . . . Go on and belt up; we're taking off."

He turned and went into the cockpit, where he spoke to his mechanic-radioman, Giancarlo Ferrero. "Ready for takeoff?"

"Let 'er go."

Amedeo turned on the contact. The twin engines coughed a bit, sputtered, hissed, and finally decided to purr, imparting a furious shaking to the whole machine, which was neither soundproofed nor pressurized.

No matter. According to Ottavio Giacomassi's in-structions, Morobbia was supposed to practically hedge-hop, navigating by sight as soon as they were past the Swiss frontier, and land on a plateau full of cow pastures between Zug, Näfels, and Schwyz. He would come down in a prairie full of bumps and holes about five hundred meters long, more than enough space to bring the old crate to a halt, for Morobbia had been trained to stop within three hundred meters from touch-down. As the men off-loaded, he was not to cut his motors, and the minute the last one was out, he was to fly toward Zurich, as Giacomassi had instructed him. Giacomassi, once a

Lucky Luciano lieutenant, was now the chief North Italian representative of the Volpone family.

When Amedeo got his idea for the flight school, Ottavio Giacomassi was the one who had grubstaked him. Obviously the few students he had weren't enough to keep Morobbia in business, but his patron paid well for occasional off-the-record jobs such as picking up or delivering packages, and sometimes men, between Switzerland and Italy, always in the Zug-Näfels-Schwyz triangle.

"Flight-school MD 315 requests Runway 9," Amedeo radioed.

"MD 315, the runway is yours," the control tower called back. "Take off."

"Roger. Taking off . . ."

Morobbia give it the gun. The pile of junk rocked and rolled and reluctantly broke free from gravity, rising just enough to clear the repair hangars. It was some 150 kilometers from Milan to their landing area. When it was loaded, the MD could barely get up to 250 KPH at top speed. Making allowances, Amedeo figured it would take them a good forty-five minutes to get there.

He pointed the plane's nose northwest, tapped his mechanic on the arm, and yelled at the top of his lungs, "Giancarlo! Did you check the oil before we left?"

In an iron-gray suit, white shirt, and black tie, neither handsome nor ugly, Cesare Piombino was the archetype of the average man, the kind you might see ten times on the street without paying the slightest attention.

He came into the Zurich Trade Bank three-quarters of an hour before closing time, politely asked the attendant how to get to the entrance to the vault, thanked him, and took the elevator to the third floor. His briefcase under his arm, he sauntered down a hallway, coming to an open area in which three secretaries clad in navy-blue suits were standing and talking near some potted palms.

"Herr Rungghe, if you please."

"Herr Rungghe is not in this afternoon. Did you have an appointment, sir?"

"Yes."

"Would you like to see the person who is filling in for him?"

"No, thanks. It's a personal matter. When will Herr Rungghe be back?"

"In the morning."

"Thank you. I'll come back then."

He was so ordinary-looking that it didn't occur to any of the secretaries to ask his name. Like most of the department heads, Rungghe had gone to the funeral of Renata Kloppe. By the time Cesare Piombino disappeared around the bend in the hall, the three girls had forgotten him.

Cesare Piombino ran an antique-furniture store in the Aussersihl neighborhood, on Zurlidenstrasse. But the antique business was the least of his concerns. He was in reality one of the five Swiss representatives of Ottavio Giacomassi, with whom he had worked back in the war days, when there were Resistance units and surprise attacks to be made. His specialties were derailing trains and poisoning the water supply of the occupying troops.

The job Giacomassi had given him this time was almost as ticklish as the ones he used to carry out thirty years ago. First, he was to get himself locked into the Zurich Trade Bank. Then, if the gods were with him, he was to carry out his mission and, once it was accomplished, get out alive. If he did, he would collect the ten thousand dollars promised him. For the time being, the main thing was to find a place to hide until they closed the bank. Cesare Piombino cautiously opened a door behind the elevator shaft. It led to the service stairway. Taking a firm grip on his briefcase full of dynamite sticks and Bickford fuses, he started to walk up the stairs.

It was a little gas station, like any one of thousands on streets everywhere, located on a Zurich side street called Eschwiesenstrasse. It had three pumps: two for gas, one for diesel fuel for heavy trucks. To the right of the pumps, a concrete ramp led to an underground garage that could hold about thirty cars. This was where Orlando Baretto had originally intended to take Mortimer O'Brion and Zaza Finney when he picked them up outside Kloppe's bank.

The gas station manager, a Sicilian like Lando, occasionally did small favors for the Syndicate, though he wasn't considered a member. But Enzo Priano asked no questions and made no comments when he took the envelopes that paid him off in good hard Swiss francs for those little services he rendered. The most frequent accommodation he provided was the temporary sheltering of certain persons whose identity never became known to him.

At the back of the garage was a huge pile of old tires, against which leaned a heavy worktable. When the tires were moved, a locked metal door was revealed. It opened onto a storage space, about three yards by four, that had a small iron cot, a hole in the ground pretentiously called the "Turkish toilet," a washstand with cold water, and a naked lightbulb hanging from the ceiling by a wire. There was an air vent leading to the garage storeroom; and two stools and a rickety table with a couple of old books and some tattered magazines completed the furnishings.

Ten minutes earlier, a black Mercedes 600 with a tinted windshield had come down the ramp, and Enzo Priano had moved a few tires and opened the door to what he laughingly called his "guest room." Three men had gone in, the smallest one wearing a blindfold, and when Enzo went back up to his gas pumps, the Mercedes was gone.

When Babe Volpone removed the blindfold, Kloppe blinked several times.

"My glasses?" he asked.

Ettore Gabelotti gave them to him. Putting them on, Kloppe saw the naked walls and concrete floor, the iron bed, and the washbasin.

"You can sit down," Gabelotti said.

Homer remained standing. He knew he was still in Zurich, and, from the gas and oil smells that assailed his nostrils, he deduced he was in some kind of garage. In what neighborhood, he had no idea. When the chauffeur at the cemetery had said, "I'm here to pick you up, Herr Kloppe," he had presumed that Helena Marcoulis had sent the car, and he had followed without question.

"Mr. Kloppe," Gabelotti said, "you can get out of this unpleasant place anytime you want. Get out alive, that is. Your dishonest attitude is what forced us to resort to this kind of distasteful measure. You are holding two billion dollars that don't belong to you—for the plain and simple reason that they belong to us. For the last time, are you ready to make the transfer the way Genco Volpone instructed you?"

Kloppe sat on the edge of the cot. He no longer cared about anything. Torture did not scare him, and the idea of dying was inconsequential, perhaps inviting. With Renata buried, the values that had given meaning to his life seemed ridiculous. Except for one: the absolute principles of professional discretion that had created the strength and greatness of his fatherland. Swiss bank employees had not talked when the Nazis tried to force them to reveal the numbers of Jewish accounts that were frozen at the outbreak of hostilities. He, too, would keep still, whatever the consequences. He looked carefully at Ettore Gabelotti and Italo Volpone. The shadow of a contemptuous smile flitted across his thin lips.

"I think he's makin' fun of us!" Italo grumbled.

"I asked you a question!" Gabelotti barked at Kloppe.

The banker calmly shook his head. "I have no idea what you are talking about."

Babe Volpone swung around sharply, grabbed him by the lapels of his coat, and sputtered into his face, "Get this straight, porkface! There's one thing you better think about: what we're gonna do to you and what we're gonna do to your bank and to your wife!"

From the moment Fritz Blesh felt that Kirkpatrick was buttoning his damned lip, the lieutenant had become less aggressive. For over an hour he had questioned his foreign confrères and obtained a lot of useful information, in turn willingly answering the questions they asked him. And little by little, the pieces of this bizarre jigsaw started to fall into place.

Blesh wrapped up the meeting, and Dempsey, Kirkpatrick, and Finnegan headed for Sordi's Hotel, where they dropped off their luggage and cleaned up a bit. Then they got together again in Blesh's office to discuss the disappearance of Pat Mahoney.

"I have a theory," Blesh said, "but it doesn't have much solid information to go on."

"Let's hear it anyway," said Kirkpatrick.

"If, as you think, your detective was done away with, I may know how it was accomplished. Three days ago, there was a gunfight in the cellar of the Commodore Hotel."

"Between who?"

"That, I don't know. No one saw or heard a thing. The staff was alerted when a cloud of steam came up from the machine area. The hot-water pipes had been pierced by bullets in one of the boilers, and my men found traces of blood and picked up several spent cartridges. I went to inspect the place myself, and I am almost certain that a man's body was dragged across the floor and dumped into the hotel furnace."

"You didn't check it out?" asked Kirkpatrick.

Blesh looked at him, irritated. "No, captain. The main burner, which handles the six hundred rooms in the hotel, is an underground cylinder that holds two hundred cubic meters of flaming oil; it also serves as the garbage incinerator. Anything that enters it is consumed in less than ten minutes. If we were to try to let the furnace cool off, captain, it would take at least three days."

"What makes you think it could have been Mahoney?"

"Two men have disappeared in Switzerland in the last few days. Your detective Mahoney, and Rico Gatto, a gangster type out of Florida."

"How do you know this Gatto disappeared?"

"He entered Switzerland. He did not leave. He never paid his hotel bill," Blesh said coldly. "As I see it, the man killed at the Commodore has to be either Rico Gatto or Patrick Mahoney. But I have no way of knowing which until one of the two bodies is found and identified."

"What if neither is found?" Finnegan asked.

Blesh spread his hands in a gesture of impotence.

"Another thing, captain. This doesn't necessarily concern you, but I can tell you that if there's been any capital transaction, it was between the men you are watching and the Zurich Trade Bank. A young woman named Renata Kloppe, the daughter of the owner of that bank, was killed two days ago in an auto accident. She is being

buried right now. And do you know who owned the car
she was killed in? One Orlando Baretto, a Sicilian by origin. And do you know where he got that fancy car?"

He remained silent for a moment, delighted to see how
they turned on the spit, as quiet as model pupils.

"It was given to him by Genco Volpone," he quietly announced.

"Where is this Baretto?" Kirkpatrick gritted out.

"In this city," Blesh nonchalantly replied.

"What! Didn't you have him arrested?"

"He claimed that his car was stolen—"

"Lieutenant," Finnegan cut in, "you have a chance to
make a fantastic sweep, a roundup that may never be
possible again! Why can't you bring the whole bunch of
them in on some pretext?"

Blesh looked shocked.

"What pretext? Has there been a disturbance of the
peace? Has anybody pressed charges?"

Finnegan and Kirkpatrick exchanged an exasperated
look.

"May I ask you a question?" Scott Dempsey said. "Did
Kloppe tell you whether he had been threatened?"

Fritz Blesh pursed his lips.

"Mr. Dempsey, over here the bank is a state within
the state. Our financial consortia are absolutely autono-
mous. They hire their own guards, investigators, experts,
and they have their own security services. Do you think
one of our great bankers would be childish enough to let
our official police mix into his money affairs?"

"Kloppe doesn't know who he's dealing with!" Kirkpatrick exclaimed. "The Syndicate is powerful enough to
bring all of Switzerland to its knees."

Blesh stared him down with infinite compassion. "No
one ever has done that, captain. And do you know why?
Because in our country there is no such thing as a cor-
ruptible citizen," he said. "Captain, do you think Volpone
or Gabelotti would be insane enough to attack a bank in
the heart of Zurich?"

"Why not?" Kirkpatrick spat out bitterly. "If they feel
that justice is on their side?"

Scott Dempsey enjoyed the irony of that and chuck-
led over it.

"That would be more than we could hope for," Lieutenant Blesh mumbled.

"If I understand you," Kirkpatrick began to protest, "you're going to wait until these hoods put Zurich to the torch before you make a move—"

Blesh cut him off sharply. "I know what I have to do."

"Ah, lieutenant . . ." Scott Dempsey sighed. "To think we might be able to chop the head off the whole Syndicate! You wouldn't even have to lift a finger. All I'd need would be a figure, just one little figure . . . The number of those funds that were fraudently exported from the U.S. One word from that banker of ours—just one—and I've got 'em all where I want 'em."

Seeing the threatening look on Blesh's face, Dempsey realized he had gone too far. He prudently turned his eyes away and looked up at the ceiling.

"Listen, lieutenant," Kirkpatrick pleaded. "Far be it from me to tell you what you ought to do, but just the same, considering the circumstances, maybe a little bit of bugging . . ."

Despite his humble tone, Blesh let him have it. "Let's leave Watergate to Washington, captain. This is Zurich!"

Kirkpatrick swallowed his rage. This arrogant little bureaucrat was going to sit there and let the capi of the Syndicate's two most powerful families get away right under his nose. As Kirkpatrick's facial muscles contracted, his Irish physiognomy turned a gorgeous eggplant color.

Blesh could not help but notice it, and, to soften his rude reply as well as to reassure the captain, he said, "You really don't have anything to worry about, captain. I've taken the necessary steps. Two of my men are watching the bank."

The grassy plateau was surrounded by steep hills that were covered with fir trees. Anyone but Amedeo Morobbia would have crashed trying to put the plane down there. It was like landing in the bottom of a bowl. But Morobbia was used to it. His aeroclub deal had been going for three years, and in three years he had made more than a hundred Milan–Switzerland round trips. He preferred to fly by day. Flying close to the tops of the mountains and following their contours, he kept below the radar range. Despite its appearance, his MD 315 had never let him down, unflinchingly responding to his commands. Usually, his passengers—card-carrying aeroclub "student pilots"—hopped off the plane and ran to a forest path where a car stood waiting. Morobbia would then take the return route and report to Ottavio Giacomassi by phone, simply saying, "I'm back. Everything went off as planned."

Today there would be a slight change in the program. He was to land, taxi to the edge of the trees bordering the open field, and then get the plane under cover as much as possible. His orders were to stay there and wait.

"For how long?" he had asked.

"I don't know," Ottavio told him.

"If I don't get back, won't the Milan airport put out an alert?"

"You could have run into mechanical trouble and made a forced landing somewhere."

"Sure, but in that case I have to let them know."

"Okay. I'll take care of that. If you haven't seen your passengers by daybreak, come on back without them."

"Very well."

He spotted the hill he was looking for, hedgehopped up it, got to the top, and let his machine drop into the basin like a rock, keeping it parallel to the incline. The wheels made a brutal impact on the cow grass, and the braking flaps stood out from the wings as the wind from the propellers traced a swath through the pasture.

Giancarlo Ferrero, the radioman, had already gone to help the ten passengers out of their safety belts.

"Shake a leg, there, fellas," he was shouting. "They're waiting for you over behind the rise."

They jumped from the plane. They were all young and properly dressed, with neckties and jackets. Most of them were carrying attaché cases and had raincoats slung over their arms. From the way they ran up the steep hillside, it was clear that these were trained athletes. They soon disappeared into the greenery, and to the cars parked a short way off. By separate roads, in small groups, they were to be dropped off in Zurich, where they would have to kill time until the action started.

"Now what do we do?" Ferrero wanted to know.

"We mark time," Morobbia sulked.

"My friend Italo and I are in full agreement on a number of decisions," Gabelotti was saying. "And we called you all together to tell you about them."

He looked his audience over with a paternal eye. The meeting was taking place in the library of the villa Volpone had rented. Each group of family members sat on its own side of a large rectangular table. On one side was Volpone, flanked by Yudelman and Pizzu, along with Amalfi, Bruttore, and Dotto. Facing them were Crimello and Barba on either side of Don Ettore; then Merta, Badaletto, and Sabatini.

At the end of the table was Luciano Matarella, Gabelotti's representative for Southern Europe, and Simeone Ferro stood guard outside the closed door.

Gabelotti looked very put-upon. "Neither me or Babe Volpone want violence, but you can understand that our interests are at stake as well as the prestige of the Syndicate. What would happen if some little banker could get away with defying the whole organization? So my partner and me decided we can't sit here and take such an insult."

He reached his hand out toward Volpone.

"Italo," he said, "tell our friends what we expect of them."

Don Ettore sat down and wiped his brow. Italo got up. Less than two weeks before, they had been in a similar situation in Nassau. In front of the top council of both families, Italo had read aloud the three letters of his brother's cablegram: OUT. At that point he had not been able to imagine himself as anything but his brother's little brother, a temporary stand-in for Don Genco, a gambler no one took seriously. But Genco's death and the ensuing responsibilities had produced a liberating click in Italo's consciousness, revealing a potential so well hidden that he himself had never suspected it existed. Power was a fine fruit he no longer could do without. Neither Gabelotti nor anyone else would be able to keep him from

348

eating it. One by one, he glanced at each of the men seated around the table.

"We got two things to do," he said. "Get the dough back, and get even. We can't rub out this banker, or we cut ourselves off from the only direct tie to the money. On the other hand, if we go about it right, with different kinds of pressures on him, we can get him to come clean. We got Homer Kloppe where we want him, but we been here in Zurich too long. We got to move fast, make our play, grab our dough, and beat it! Tonight we're going to destroy his bank. We have to make him understand we won't stop at nothing. In Switzerland, they settle this kind of legal rip-off by havng their lawyers fight it out. But that ain't for us. Nobody screws the Syndicate!"

"How about telling us what you're gonna do?" Carlo Badaletto cut in.

Since the day his incisors had stuck in Italo's skull, Badaletto took every chance he got to show his scorn.

Volpone's hands tightened slightly on the table. He lowered his head and muttered, "Shut up! I'm talking."

Moshe Yudelman sensed that the fragile peace that had been restored with so much effort and maneuvering might well come apart before bearing any fruit. Don Ettore also sensed the change in climate. He had made plenty of steps toward reconciliation, and he wasn't about to let anyone spoil this temporary nonaggression pact. His eyes shining with anger, he called his *caporegime* to task rudely: "Carlo, you shut your trap or I'll throw you out myself!"

Carlo Badaletto thereby learned that there had been some changes made in the relationship between the two families, for in normal times Don Ettore would probably have encouraged his remarks. He turned his eyes away in embarrassment and stared down at his hands.

Italo took a long deep breath, as if nothing had interrupted the flow of his speech. Mentally, Moshe congratulated him.

"I brought ten torpedoes in from Italy," Volpone went on. "You're gonna take command of these men and smash that bank."

Thomas Merta politely raised his hand. "I seen the bank," he said. "It's a stone building, six stories high. Unless we drop a two-ton bomb on the roof, we'll only be able to make a little dent in it."

"Not if you go about it the right way," Volpone came back. "The whole success of our plan depends on speed. You do it in four minutes, and the bank is finished, and we win. Don Ettore and me both felt the *capiregime* of our families should be involved in this. In all, you'll be eighteen guys inside the bank: three on each floor. You blow up everything you can and set fires everywhere. You'll have incendiary grenades and army flamethrowers."

"*Padrone*," Pizzu objected, "we can't get the safe doors open with grenades."

"We're not after the safes or vaults," Gabelotti answered amiably. "Don't forget, we're operating out in the open, making one hell of a racket. What we want is to do as much damage as possible. You'll have less than four minutes to burn up all their files and papers. What we're after ain't money, but making a mess, discrediting the bank, turning it into a fuckin' shithouse."

Thomas Merta asked Italo Volpone another question. "You said we'd be eighteen guys in the bank. How you figure we'll get in?"

"By the door—just like that."

"You got keys?"

Italo smiled a tiny tough smile.

"At midnight, on the nose, the big main door will explode and open. One of my men is locked inside the bank right now with a load of dynamite."

"What do we do about cops?" said Vincente Bruttore.

"You won't see none," Volpone assured him. "Between the time the burglar alarms go off and the cops get to the scene—at least eight minutes—you'll be long gone!"

"Long gone where?" asked Frankie Sabatini. "After fireworks like that, how do we get out of this fucking country in four minutes?"

"Don't you worry none about that! Tomorrow morning you'll be drinking your espresso in Italy."

Getting the men out had been Italo's big problem. Since the greater number of men going into the front line were Italo's, Don Ettore had refrained from asking the fundamental question about the pullout. He wasn't too worried about the men the Volpone family might lose. To the contrary, those losses could only strengthen his hand for future purposes. But just a couple of minutes ago Italo had said, "Don Ettore and me both felt the *capiregime* of our families should be involved in this."

Fact was, Don Ettore had not felt anything of the kind. He had not shown surprise when he heard the words spoken, but his mind had speeded up just a little to see if they had any hidden meaning. If the novice Volpone wanted to organize this kind of an expedition at his own expense, that was one thing. But to include Gabelotti's own lieutenants in such a kamikaze undertaking...

Ettore decided he wouldn't agree unless there were some guarantees. As if he were fully conversant with all the details, he said to Italo in a honeyed voice, "Tell the boys just how we're getting them out. I can sense that they're concerned about it."

Volpone was waiting for this opening so he could get another edge on Ettore in public. He smiled sweetly.

"I've thought it all out, Don Ettore. The whole thing."

By speaking for himself alone, he knew that he was depriving Gabelotti of any credit for having found the solution. He had received the solution ready-made from Ottavio Giacomassi, who had set up the entire plan in Milan, but no one needed to know that.

"When you come out of the bank, there'll be six cars waiting, and they'll take off in six different directions, over routes laid out to avoid running into any cops."

"Who'll be driving?" asked Carmine Crimello.

"Friends. They know the town like the inside of their own pockets, and you'll all be taken to the same place outside Zurich."

"Fifteen minutes after the explosion, every road in the country will be blocked," said Thomas Merta. "Do we try to hide out in this goddamn cow country?"

Italo looked at him. "Didn't I say you'd be having breakfast in Italy tomorrow?"

"How do we get across the border?"

"In some milk," Volpone answered quietly.

He let the idea sink in.

"My brother Genco had an interest in a Zurich dairy.

351

Every night, thousands of cans of milk are collected and trucked to our dairy. Three times a week, the fourteen tank trucks from my brother's company make a trip to Milan so that the sweet little Italian babies can drink nice fresh Swiss milk. Every one of those trucks holds close to thirteen thousand gallons. I'm sure you don't hate milk all that much, Thomas."

A few laughs brought some relaxation. Volpone stopped them with a wave of the hand.

"For the past six years, the customs men have watched those trucks go through, so don't sweat it. Eight of the trucks have hiding places inside the tanks. Three or four men fit into each one real easy. You'll be in Milan in less than five hours. And there'll be a welcoming committee to greet you. Good enough?"

Angelo Barba got up the courage to ask a question that had been burning on his tongue. "How about us—if things don't turn out right?"

"Why shouldn't they turn out right?" Italo was surprised. "Tell me, what connection is there between you, a respectable American businessman passing through Zurich, and some crazy anarchists who burn up a bank without stealing a dime?"

"But, just the same, suppose . . ." Barba insisted. "How would we get out of Switzerland?"

Volpone looked at him with an air of indulgent reproach. "Angelo, do you really think I forgot about that?"

22

Folco Mori took in the whole room at a glance.

"This ought to do it," he said. "What do you think?"

Pietro Bellinzona made a face. "I dunno."

"Why not? What's missing?"

Folco looked sharply at Orlando Baretto's corpse. During its stay in the cellar of the villa, Lando's body had completely stiffened. On the way over, they had tried to stuff the corpse into the trunk of the car, but Baretto dead was much less accommodating than when he was alive. No way to get his body to bend, and they had to hurry. So they did the risky thing and hid him on the floor of the car's back seat, disguised, they hoped, under a blanket.

Folco drove with jaws clenched, scrupulously obeying all traffic signals, letting other cars have the right of way, careful not to attract attention. Pietro seemed unconcerned, nerveless. Lando's death was a tremendous relief to him, and now he was certain of never being accused of murder. The only thing was, he still had to live with himself, look himself in the mirror, and try to forget the demeaning thing he had been subjected to. He was not so stupid that he was unaware the Volpone family treated him like the village idiot. He would have liked to brag about how he took care of Lando, to show them how his staging of the accident had fooled the whole lot of them, but he was forced to keep still about it.

In Lando's apartment they staged a similar scenario. When the police or neighbors, alerted by the smell from the corpse, discovered the body, it was pretty certain they would buy the explanation of an accidental death. The living room floor was made of marble, a rung of a chair had been broken, and a pile of gray towels lay in disarray on the floor, just where they had fallen from the top of a linen closet from which Folco, standing on a stool, had shoved them.

"Anyway," Folco said, "what the hell do we care? By the time they find him, we'll be on our way."

"I really liked him," Pietro said.

"So did I," Folco replied. "Really tough luck."

"Yeah," Bellinzona agreed. "Real tough luck."

Hans Bregenz was fed up. He had been on the beat for two hours now, and he knew what was in each window of every shop fifty meters on either side of the main entrance to the Zurich Trade Bank. The wind was beginning to nip his cheeks and he put up his collar as he looked at his watch: 10:00 P.M. He crossed the street, stepped into a passageway, and walked up a few steps into an arcade of stores where there was a bay window facing the bank, making it an efficient as well as inconspicuous observation post.

"Paul, I've had it up to here! When are we being relieved?"

"At midnight," Paul Romanshorn told him.

"I could use a drink right now."

"Anything happen?"

"Happen! What do you expect to happen? Blesh never even told us why he's got us out patrolling in front of this lousy bank. They have their own guards, don't they? Some fucking assignment."

Romanshorn shrugged. The ways of Lieutenant Blesh were mysterious. All he knew was discipline, and he would let his men know only the essentials, since he felt there was no reason to account to them.

"Report anything you consider suspicious or unusual anywhere near the bank," was all he had specified.

Dismissed! Hans Bregenz had mentally added.

He took the walkie-talkie from Paul Romanshorn's hands. "You go walk the street, girlie," he said. "I'm taking five up here."

"Okay," said Romanshorn, and he walked out through the arcade and began patrolling the downhill street, on which a few cars now and then sped by.

There were no passersby to speak of. Zurich is an early-rising town, and that means early to bed as well. Romanshorn wondered what he was supposed to be doing. Swiss banks were sacred. To his knowledge, no one had ever dared try to break into one. Their very names, discreetly posted in gold letters, seemed enough to keep them inviolate from iconoclasts of all kinds. Two more hours to go before they were relieved. . . .

Up in the arcade, Bregenz manipulated the buttons of the walkie-talkie and made contact with headquarters. He recognized the voice of Sergeant Dorner, charge of quarters that night.

"Anything to report?" Dorner asked.

"Yes, papa," Bregenz quipped. "I'm freezing my balls off and getting bored stiff."

Homer Kloppe cupped his hands and took a drink from the tap. He hadn't eaten anything since morning. Before Renata's funeral he had a cup of black coffee, but he wasn't hungry now. Volpone and Gabelotti had threatened him, but he had not been physically harmed.

When Volpone had barked in his face, he had been tempted to tell him yes, he did have the money, but that he couldn't turn it over unless the legal conditions for its surrender were fulfilled. Gabelotti had acted more insinuatingly, switching from threats to promises, from promises to regrets.

"I am most upset, Mr. Kloppe, at being forced to act this way toward you," he said. "But you must admit you don't leave us much choice. You are forcing us to destroy you."

Well, so what? He was destroyed already. The reality of Renata's death was catching up with him. The only thing that mattered now was to be able to hold out, not to give in.

He sat on the iron cot again, his upper body erect, hands on his knees, in what was a familiar position to him. Then he recognized the shuffling sound of tires being moved behind the metal door of his cell. A key turned in the lock, and Ettore Gabelotti came in, followed by Italo Volpone, who locked the door and pocketed the key. Homer didn't move.

Gabelotti opened the verbal fire. "We have come here, Mr. Kloppe, to make a last call on you before certain unpleasant and irreversible events take place. I'll tell you quite frankly what is going to happen, so you can make up your own mind."

Volpone, deathly pale, was sitting on a stool, gazing at a spot on the whitewashed wall. His body was motionless, but his right foot was shaking, striking against the floor in rapid rhythm.

"It is eleven o'clock right now, Mr. Kloppe. In an hour, the Zurich Trade Bank is going to blow up. A squad of men will set fire to everything in the premises. Nothing will remain, sir, not a thing.

"Now, if that little incident is not enough to make you think, tomorrow morning we will kidnap Mrs. Kloppe. I would not be so vulgar as to make you listen to all the things that will be done to her before she welcomes the peace of death, but if you knew them, Mr. Kloppe, you would curse yourself for not having spared her such horrors. As soon as we kidnap her, we will start torturing her, and at the same time we will burn your house down.

"After that, we will turn you over to a crew of brutes who, I swear to you, will make you talk. I believe you are a reasonable man, Mr. Kloppe, a good Christian gentleman. You must realize we are not bluffing. So I am begging you, think about this. Make your decision. There is still time!

"Give us what belongs to us, and you have my word you will be released immediately. You know enough about us now to know who you are dealing with. We go through with everything we plan! I congratulate you on the courage you have shown, but there is a limit to everything. Now your manly stubbornness is turning into criminal folly. This is no longer just a matter of considering yourself, but your wife, too."

Don Ettore stopped. On the concrete floor, Volpone's foot was beating out its rhythm more and more nervously. Don Ettore forced himself to smile.

"There is one thing we have in common, Mr. Kloppe.

356

You certainly have heard of our *omertà*. It is the law of silence. We observe it as strictly as you do. But there is a difference: we observe it for noble reasons, as a matter of honor. You are not doing this for honor, Mr. Kloppe, only for money. And not even your own money. It is ours, as you well know. So I ask you, what's the point? Will you or won't you give the order to transfer our funds?"

Volpone's foot stopped drumming. There was silence in the wretched room, disturbed only by Gabelotti's asthmatic breathing. Then Homer Kloppe turned slowly toward Don Ettore and scrutinized him attentively. This man had brought forth all the convincing arguments in a fine speech appealing to Kloppe's humanity, his intelligence, his reason, with an eloquence Kloppe hadn't thought him capable of. Yet, behind the screen of words, there remained merely his goal, the money he wanted turned over, although nothing in the world proved it belonged to him. Besides, there was his face. Beneath the mask of cordial understanding, Homer could sense cruelty, total absence of pity, something that fleetingly suggested the rage of a wild beast. In order to gain the power he held, this man must have tortured, humiliated, and killed.

The gazes of the two men remained riveted to each other, and for a few seconds Gabelotti had a sneaking hope that he had won. He even thought he saw the banker's lips begin to move, but he was never to find out what words Kloppe might have uttered.

Italo leaped up and jumped on Kloppe. "You're gonna talk, you fuckin' crook! You'll talk, all right!"

Kloppe did nothing to defend himself. He rolled over on the cot under the weight of Volpone grabbing him by the throat. For an instant he hoped this was the end for him.

But Gabelotti seized Italo by the waist, picked him up, and held him with all his strength, shouting, "Italo! Italo!"

"Shut your trap!" Volpone foamed, wrenching loose with the alertness of a jungle cat and turning to aim his gun at Gabelotti.

Don Ettore's face took on a pained expression, meant not for Volpone, but for Homer Kloppe.

357

"Please believe how deeply I regret your attitude, Mr. Kloppe," he said. "You will at least be able to say that what you're getting is what you asked for: all the mourning and the misfortune in store for you."

He turned toward Italo and took his arm in a friendly fashion, as if he had never noticed the Mauser in his hand.

"Come on, Italo, let's go. *Andiamo via.*"

Volpone did not resist. He put his gun back where it belonged, got the key out of his pocket, and opened the door. After it closed again on the imprisoned Kloppe, Don Ettore tried to remember whether any other man who had acted that way towards him had known the good fortune to survive.

The answer was no.

"Hans, don't you think that's strange?"

"What?" Bregenz asked.

"That's the third car stopping on this street."

"So what?"

"Nobody got out of any of them."

"Boy, can't a guy even get a quiet little blow-job on a side street anymore?" Bregenz taunted him.

"Look!" Romanshorn went on. "There's another one!"

Bregenz saw an Opel pull up and park some thirty meters from the entrance to the Zurich Trade Bank.

"That makes four," Romanshorn muttered, his face tense.

Twenty seconds apart, two other vehicles stopped a little farther down.

Bregenz frowned. "What do you think?"

"You know what Blesh said," Romanshorn replied. " 'Report anything unusual.' One blow-job, okay—but six in a row, all at the same time? Pass me the radio!"

He grabbed the walkie-talkie from Bregenz's hands.

"Dorner? This is Romanshorn. Where's Blesh?"

"What's up?"

"Six cars have just pulled up on Stampfenbachstrasse. And nobody got out of any of them."

"I'll contact him," Dorner said.

Romanshorn signed off.

"What do we do now?" Bregenz asked, checking his watch. It was 11:55.

"Nothing. We just wait."

Bregenz checked to make sure that his Colt was in his raincoat pocket. He had never used it except at the range, on training days. Through the bay window he looked apprehensively at the cars parked along the curb, all the lights out. It was peculiar that no one got out.

Lieutenant Blesh was relaxing in his bachelor pad where everything was arranged for the greatest sensual pleasure. Wearing a purple dressing gown, a glass of bourbon in his hand, he was stretched out on a fawn buckskin couch. Enraptured by *Così fan tutte*, his favorite opera, he tried to ignore the ringing telephone. But the noise persisted, spoiling the music for him. Blesh set his highball down and picked up the phone.

"Sergeant Dorner here, lieutenant."

"What do you want?"

"Bregenz and Romanshorn just called in. Six cars have pulled up in front of the Zurich Trade Bank. And nobody got out of any of them."

"So what?" barked Blesh, still somewhat dazed by the music.

"Well, nothing, lieutenant. . . . I'm sorry I disturbed you. But you told me that—"

"Goddamn it!" Blesh swore. "Dispatch two vanloads over there immediately. Block off both ends of Stampfenbachstrasse! And hurry! I'll go straight there myself!"

When he hit the stairs, going down four at a time, it was 11:58 P.M.

The last rendezvous before the attack had been at the dairy, northeast of town, beyond Schwamendingen, on a piece of land slightly off Basserdorf Road. A solid nine-foot wall surrounded all of the buildings and barns, and a huge wooden gate opened onto a central courtyard where the fourteen tank trucks were parked. Millions of gallons of fresh milk were pumped into the tank trucks each day for delivery. At the end of the courtyard an archway led to the processing plant in which the butter and cheese were made. The place was immaculate; nevertheless, as soon as one got past the threshold of the archway, one was assailed by the sourish smell of fermenting milk. Off to the left, covering some twelve hundred square yards, fermentation vats had been dug into the ground, big as swimming pools.

The *sottocapi*, consiglieri, and *capiregime* of both families were all assembled in the office of the Zwiss Milk and Butter Company, five men from the Volpone family and six of Don Ettore's men, aside from the two dons. Vittorio Pizzu, Italo Volpone's *sottocapo*, couldn't get used to the idea that the members of the Gabelotti family were always around. Being with that hated gang, even though now they were so-called allies, didn't sit well with him. Too many years of warfare and too many dead bodies lay between the two families for Pizzu to be able to imagine that an extended truce was possible.

"Your ten men just got in from Italy," Volpone had announced without any other introduction. "Don't let them out of your sight. From here on in, you're in charge of 'em. At 11:15, the eight of you are gonna leave for the bank. In six cars. The drivers know exactly where to go. As soon as you clean out the bank, they bring you right back here, you get into the hideouts inside the tankers, and you'll be in Milan before daybreak. I won't see you again till New York."

Don Ettore had raised his hand in a gesture which, had he been a priest, would have been a benediction. Pizzu noted the phony smile as he mumbled, *"Merda a tutti!"*

Now Vittorio looked at his watch: one minute to midnight. The car he was in had parked on Stampfenbach-strasse four minutes ago. He would be out of it in thirty seconds, as a signal to the rest of the men to take up their places on either side of the main door, sheltered from the imminent explosion. The fireworks should go off in exactly thirty-eight seconds.

At 11:50, Cesare Piombino came out of the broom closet where he had been hiding for more than seven hours. He threaded his way into the main banking hall, alert in the half-darkness. He didn't know what kind of alarm system protected the bank. When he reached the huge wrought-iron door that separated the hall from Stampfenbachstrasse, he sat on the floor, calmly opened his briefcase, and took out his equipment. He had four minutes in which to make it all go bang. He took out the stick of dynamite, patted it gently, and unrolled the Bickford fuse. His survival depended on his ability to estimate the proper length for the wick. It had to burn out in fifty-five seconds, the time it took him to get to shelter behind one of the marble pillars that supported the rear of the banking room. As soon as the door blew out, he would rush into the street and head for his car, parked a short distance away in a cross street called Haldeneggstrasse.

He took a pair of scissors, cut the wick, and put everything he hadn't used back into his briefcase. He lit his trusty old Zippo lighter with one flick of his thumb, and when he saw that the fuse had caught well, he dashed back to the marble pillar and lay down behind it, his head propped against his briefcase, his hands over his ears. And he started to count. When he got to twenty-eight, an unbelievable light filled the bank, followed by an explosion that shook the building to its foundation. A burning-hot draft roared toward him while bits of wood, stone, and steel flew through the air.

Cesare Piombino started running for the street. Where the massive door once had been was a great gaping hole.

The awesome spectacle took place before the disbelieving eyes of Romanshorn and Bregenz. Stampfenbachstrasse, deserted a moment before, filled up in three seconds with silent figures heading toward the Zurich Trade Bank in little groups.

"Shit!" Bregenz exclaimed in a hoarse shriek. "Seventeen of 'em!"

"No," Romanshorn breathed back, "eighteen."

"Paul! What do we do now?"

"Stay where we are. And wait for reinforcements."

Bregenz no longer felt cold. To the contrary, he found he was sweating.

"Look!" Romanshorn warned.

The men stopped on either side of the bank entrance,

361

some fifteen meters away. Bregenz saw them ducking behind the colonnades that held up the portico, standing with their backs against the wall. He was about to ask Romanshorn a question when he was swept away in a whirlwind of red flame and broken glass coming from the arcade's bay window. Deafened by the explosion, he was unable to hear what Romanshorn was shouting at him. All he could see was Paul's outstretched arm begin to spit a sporadic red spark. He painfully got up on all fours, found his Colt Cobra .38 Special two meters from where he'd landed, and crawled toward his partner.

By reflex Romanshorn had lowered his head when the dazzling whirl of fire had blinded him. He felt the breath of it when the window smashed into a thousand pieces and flew above him in a deadly rain of tiny splinters. Sheltered by the wall on which the bay window had stood, he sneaked a look out into Stampfenbachstrasse just a second after the explosion took place, and he was amazed to see a man come hurtling out of a darkened hole where the bank's door had been, while all the men outside rushed in.

The one who came out paid no attention to the men who were going in. And they in turn did not seem to see him. Romanshorn began firing into the bunch at a rapid cadence. In the street, one man fell, immediately retrieved by his comrades. Among those who hadn't entered the bank yet, a moment of hesitation was noticeable. A red light illuminated the inside of the main hall as angry grenade explosions were heard.

"Fire!" Romanshorn was shouting to Bregenz, who had joined him behind the parapet.

Debris from the explosion had not even settled when the two *sottocapi*, Vittorio Pizzu and Thomas Merta dashed into the bank together. They had been squaring off against each other for years, and now, neither one was ready to let the other get ahead. Vittorio pulled the pins on two grenades and pitched them into the rear of the room, behind the tellers' wickets. Merta used his flame-thrower on the rows of file cabinets to his left. Behind them, half a dozen soldiers were attacking in different directions when a yell from Aldo Amalfi stopped them cold.

"The cops are here! Beat it!"

"Upstairs!" Merta ordered.

"You crazy!" Amalfi shouted. "They're holed up across the street and firing on us. One of our guys is hit. There's two vans blocking the street!"

Vittorio Pizzu's presence made Thomas Merta that much more determined.

"Everybody upstairs!" he ordered. "Burn it all!"

"Vittorio!" Aldo roared. "Do something to stop that fool!"

Merta immediately aimed his flamethrower in Aldo Amalfi's direction.

"Say that again!" he challenged.

"Don't move!" Pizzu thundered as he drew a bead on him with his Smith and Wesson 39 Parabellum.

For a second they were on the edge of that mysterious borderline where the slightest movement would be enough to start a massacre.

They could hear reports coming from outside.

"Drop back!" yelled one of the Milanese soldiers. "The place is lousy with fuzz!"

Vincente Bruttore's voice suddenly rose above all the others. "Goddamn it, cut out all this fuckin' around! We blew the job! Let's get the hell out!"

Instantly they were all back in the street, hiding behind the columns. Pizzu took in the situation at a glance: it didn't look good. Harness bulls in safe positions on the second floor of the building across the street had them within range of their automatics. Vittorio pulled the pin from a grenade and sent it flying into the opening of what had been the bay window. At both ends of the block, two police vans, sirens screaming and flashers going, were blocking the exits. Their crews, hidden behind the upholstery, were sniping at the drivers of the getaway cars.

"Get to the wheels!" Pizzu yelled.

The men started running zigzag courses, bent way over; they were covered by Thomas Merta, who shot two scarlet streams from his flamethrower at the vans closing off Stempfenbachstrasse. Vittorio Pizzu aimed another grenade at the closer of the two vans, and as it exploded, he watched two uniformed policemen raise their hands to their faces and collapse as the gas tank went up.

363

"To hell with the vans! Full speed ahead!"

They didn't have a chance in a thousand, but if the odds had been a million to one, Pizzu would have made the try. He jumped into the Ford he came in. The driver was already tooling away from the curb when Vittorio slammed the door shut.

"Drive right into that van down there!" Pizzu shouted.

The Ford speeded up. Pizzu sneaked a look back: the others were following. But thirty yards ahead, down the slant of the street, the van was sitting broadside across Stampfenbachstrasse. Even by going up on the sidewalk, the Ford didn't have a chance to make it past the heavy vehicle.

"We've had it!" cried Aldo Amalfi, who was sitting next to Vittorio.

Pizzu, without answering, flipped the pin out of another grenade. At that moment, the car's tires screeched and it reared up on end and then straightened. Pizzu was violently thrown against Amalfi.

"Your grenade!" Amalfi was yelling. "Get rid of that grenade!"

Hanging on as best he could, Pizzu made a desperate toss, aiming it out the open car window, and it blew up before it ever hit the ground.

Following the incline of Stampfenbachstrasse, there is a small alley between two tall buildings and it opens onto a stairway that ends twenty yards below on the quayside of the Limmat River. Pizzu understood that his driver was skillfully steering the Ford down those stairs. When the car got down to the quay, it swung left on its hubcaps, and then made a sharp right, almost flying across the river on the bridge that was there.

Pizzu was amazed to see that the five other cars in their squad had followed them down the same route.

"We'll be at the dairy in less than five minutes," the driver informed them.

Fritz Blesh took in the scope of the disaster. One police van was in flames, and some officers in uniform were dousing it with fire extinguishers. Three others leaned over two forms stretched on the ground. Just before getting to the flaming van, Blesh jammed on his brakes and jumped out of his car.

"You there!"

One of the cops turned around.

"I'm Lieutenant Blesh. Give me the whole story."

"We have two badly wounded men, lieutenant. Those creeps had grenades."

"Later!" Blesh thundered. "Where did the bastards go?"

"That way," the policeman said, pointing to the alley where the last of the attack cars was disappearing.

"Get in!"

"But, lieutenant—"

"Get in!"

He shoved the man against the body of his Opel and himself jumped in behind the wheel. Hanging on for dear life, the man got in beside him. Blesh went into reverse, then started forward again, maneuvering along the sidewalk in the impossible space between the rear of the van and the building.

"What's your name?" he asked the policeman while he was driving full speed down the steps.

"Schindler, lieutenant," stammered the terrified man.

"Get on the air. Put out an all-cars call. Get headquarters . . ."

Schindler repeated the orders into the microphone he had taken from the dashboard.

"Calling all police cars . . . calling police command post . . ."

"Blesh here!" the lieutenant yelled into the mike.

"Command post here," answered a droning nasal voice.

"Hold that goddamn mike in front of my mouth," Blesh muttered.

Schindler held it up.

"There's been an attack on the Zurich Trade Bank," Blesh reported. "Stay in constant contact with us, and send reinforcements out along the route I relay to you."

"Wilco, lieutenant."

"How many cars you think got away?" Blesh asked Schindler.

"Several—quite a few—I'm not sure, lieutenant."

"Idiot! How many were there?"

"Maybe ten. Maybe twenty."

"You stupid jackass!"

"I beg your pardon, lieutenant?" the voice on the radio droned.

"I wasn't talking to you," Blesh roared. "Stay on! I see one of 'em! Schindler, for crissakes! Gimme the mike! I'm in Museumstrasse, passing in front of the Hauptbahnhof . . ."

"They have flamethrowers," Schindler said.

"I'm going into Limmatstrasse," Blesh hammered out. "Car being followed is a black BMW, or very dark blue . . ."

"Reinforcements have been informed, lieutenant."

"Three? Twenty? A hundred? Come on, Schindler, shit or get off the pot! Wake up. How many cars were there?"

"Five or six, lieutenant."

"Good! The BMW'll lead us to the other ones."

He doused his headlights and slowed a little so as not to be spotted.

"Are you armed, Schindler?"

"Yes."

"Yes, lieutenant," barked Blesh. "Ammo?"

"Twelve rounds, lieutenant."

"Schindler! The mike! Car being followed is going toward Kornhausstrasse. . . . Oh, they had grenades, huh?"

"Yes, lieutenant. And a flamethrower."

"The bastards! The dirty sons of bitches! . . . Gimme the mike. I am now starting down Schaffhauserstrasse."

"Roger, lieutenant. There are four police vans following you, with twenty-four men aboard."

"Weapons?"

"Mauser assault rifles, Sten submachine guns—"

"I'm turning into Hirschweisen . . ."

"Roger, lieutenant. Passing that info on."

"Tell me more, Schindler."

"When we got there, the bank was on fire inside. Then the guys came out and hit us with the flamethrower. We got one of them, lieutenant."

"I'm coming into Winterthurerstrasse. General direction, northeast—toward Schwamendingen."

Five minutes later, the BMW was speeding out on Basserdorf Road. At one point it turned left, and Blesh lost sight of it. When he got around the bend, Blesh found he was on a private road leading to a group of buildings enclosed behind a high wall. The BMW seemed to melt, as if absorbed by the wall. Blesh put on his brakes, went up onto the right-hand shoulder, and took cover under a small clump of trees.

"We've got 'em, Schindler! What is that goddamn factory, anyway?"

"Zwiss Milk and Butter, lieutenant. They also make cheese. I got a sister-in-law who used to work there."

"Order to all police cars: surround the Zwiss Milk and Butter establishment, on Basserdorf Road, on the left coming out of Zurich."

"Roger, wilco, lieutenant. The vans are right behind you. I'll put an all-cars out right away."

"Snap shit, goddamn it! I can't surround the place all by myself!"

He threw the mike down and hopped out of the car.

"Schindler, come with me!"

Schindler got his gun out of its holster and ran through the wet grass behind the lieutenant. When they got to the enclosure, they could hear the sound of heavy trucks revving up on the other side. Blesh dashed over to the wooden gate.

"Gimme a hand!" he yelled.

Schindler gave Blesh a leg up so that Blesh could peer over the top of the gate. What he saw floored him.

Moshe Yudelman had advised the two dons not to set foot again at either the villa or the hotel until they heard the results of the attack and what had followed.

"Things could go wrong, Italo. You never can tell. Let's not underestimate the local police."

Moshe had been in contact with Ottavio Giacomassi in Milan, making sure he could arrange to get them out in case things went too far awry. Swiss territory might become much too hot.

Again on the advice of Yudelman, the capi had holed up in the apartment of a woman called Inez. Vittorio had no idea who she could be, but Babe Volpone, Ettore Gabelotti, Moshe Yudelman, Carmine Crimello, and Angelo Barba were gathered there, with Folco Mori and Pietro Bellinzona standing guard over them.

Moshe's precautions had been well taken, for the entire operation had been an out-and-out flop, and the two *sottocapi*, Vittorio Pizzu and Thomas Merta, knew it. When the time came for settling accounts, they'd have to face up to which one of them had blown it. For now, the urgency of the situation took priority.

The six cars had taken different routes back to the dairy, and according to the guys in them, none had been spotted. Pizzu and Merta rushed to a phone to give their report to Volpone and Gabelotti. As he dialed, Pizzu grumbled, "They said all they wanted was to make a big stink. Well—we sure as hell did that!"

"You think so?" Merta countered. "We barely scratched that goddamn bank. We were supposed to blow it to bits from floor to roof, but all we did was mess up the main hall. If you listened to me, it woulda burned to the ground!"

"If I'da listened to you, we'd all be dead, or in the can!"

"I'll put Don Italo on," Angelo Barba's voice courteously informed him.

Vittorio did not fail to notice the use of the word *don.* Genco's scepter was passing into Italo's hands, and, in a confused sort of way, Vittorio was proud that his young capo was gaining such quick recognition.

"It's me," Italo said into the phone.

"It didn't work, *padrone.* The cops were there waiting for us. There was trouble."

"Where are you now?"

"Back safe."

"The target?"

"Uh, well—part of it. They'll be finecombing the city right now. You'd better be going, *padrone.* It's gettin' hot!"

"*Madonnaccia!*" Thomas Merta was exploding alongside Vittorio. "The bulls are downstairs!"

Vittorio heard a heavy dose of firing.

"*Porco dio! Andate via, padrone! Subito!* Hurry! The

fuzz is shootin' right up our assholes!" he shouted into the phone.

"Vittorio!" Volpone yelled.

But Pizzu had hung up and dashed to the window of the dairy office. The engines of the tank trucks were making a deafening racket. Soldiers were hopping out of the hideouts where they had been concealed inside the trucks. Half a dozen police vans were parked outside the enclosure wall, and any mass exit was impossible.

"Police!" a megaphone-amplified voice was calling to them. *"Come out with your hands up and you won't be harmed! You are entirely surrounded!"*

Pizzu opened a window, pulled the pin from a grenade, stepped back to give himself momentum, and threw it as hard as he could beyond the wall. Its explosion drowned out the noise of the automatic fire. In the courtyard, Ottavio Giacomassi's soldiers, supported by the Volpone and Gabelotti lieutenants, aimed machine gun fire at the top of the wall, where, from time to time, a cop's helmeted head made an appearance.

Pizzu saw one of the cops' armored vehicles swing around to face the gate to the dairy and then back up a hundred yards or so. Yelling to Merta to follow him, Pizzu dashed down the stairs. There was no question of letting themselves be taken. The best they could hope for was life imprisonment.

"This way!" shouted Aldo Amalfi.

The cops had fired tear gas into the courtyard, and the smoke was mixing with the stench of fermented milk and cordite. The gate gave way under the impact of the armored police van, which immediately crashed into one of the tank trucks that had been placed crosswise inside the gate. The police van turned into a torch after ripping open the tanker, which was now disgorging a flood of milk that partly covered the bodies of the wounded soldiers lying in the mud of the courtyard.

Behind the archway near the milk, butter, and cheese warehouses, the men of both mob families flocked around Aldo Amalfi, who was yelling to one of the guys who worked in the factory.

"Quick!" Amalfi shouted to his men. "He knows a way out! Follow him!" he shouted.

They all started to move back under the huge shed over the vats holding tens of thousands of gallons of milk. Every ten or fifteen yards, some of them would turn and fire a few rounds to slow the coppers on their heels.

Aldo Amalfi and Simeone Ferro, bringing up the rear, were suddenly cut off from the group by an unseen sniper on the outside.

"Via! Via!" Vincente Bruttore was yelling at Pizzu, who didn't seem sure about following everyone through a little metal door into which the factory worker had disappeared.

Pizzu pulled the pin from his last grenade and threw it behind the vat of fermenting milk where several of their assailants were hiding. Three uniformed men, wounded by shrapnel, fell off a wall and into the vat. Vittorio pulled a handle that he had seen operated earlier that day. The vat in which the three cops were drowning began to spin. Quickly gaining speed, huge mechanical arms began to turn, tossing the wounded cops like flies inside the giant churn.

Bruttore grabbed Vittorio Pizzu, who wasn't about to run out on his *capiregime*, and shoved him through the metal door and into the slanting hallway, forcing him forward between the concrete walls as they slid down. Then they were on level ground once more, and they saw the first car.

The factory worker was at the wheel. Alongside him, Thomas Merta was signaling wildly and yelling something they couldn't hear. Behind them they saw Carlo Badaletto and Frankie Sabatini. In the other car, with the motor running, sat Joseph Dotto, his eyes darting crazily. Vittorio and Vincente jumped in behind him.

The two cars flew off, going full speed through a stone tunnel. After about three hundred yards they came out facing a metal plaque that formed a dead end.

The factory worker braked hard, jumped out, and ran over to pull a switch in the wall. The plaque swung open, letting them through.

"Put out your headlights," he yelled to Joseph Dotto in the second car.

He got back into his car and in low gear drove

through an empty barn that had steel beams holding up a glass roof through which a vague night sky could be seen.

Once again he got out to open the other barn door. They could hear the distant reports of the firefight still taking place in the dairy between Ottavio's soldiers and the Swiss cantonal police. The fires shot a great red spray into the dark sky.

The worker, whose name was Enzo Cerignola, was a Sicilian, a personal friend of Genco Volpone. Five years before, he had finally convinced Don Genco to dig this subterranean tunnel, and he was the only one who had the key to it.

Walking over to Joseph Dotto, he instructed, "Follow me. Don't put on any lights unless you see me put mine on. God willing, we'll make it to the mountains."

In the shed, Simeone Ferro yelled, "Straight ahead! I've got you covered," to Aldo Amalfi.

Aldo ran as fast as he could, bent all the way over, zigzagging with hare's leaps. A cop who was hidden under the eaves let him have a burst of his Sten gun, and Aldo rolled over and ended up kneeling before the metal door through which Vittorio, Merta, and the others had disappeared. In despair, he found that the surface of the metal had no handle on it. When he turned back toward the cop who had fired at him he saw that the man had no face, just a shapeless, bloody ball. Curiously, that pulp of a head remained lodged against a miraculously unbroken pane of glass, now turned red with the mess that was on it. Aldo looked for Simeone. He lay spread-eagled on his back, and four inches from his chest was the Herstal that slipped from his hands when he got shot. Amalfi understood then that he was alone against all of them, and that he too would have to die.

He crawled behind the stone parapet that surrounded the milk vat. The only protection it afforded him was its height—about eight inches. Bullets whistled past his ears, some hitting the stone, others ricocheting off the surface of the milk with a tiny meow before they crashed dully against the back wall and that forbidden metal door. The cops had come about fifteen yards farther forward, or about the length of one of the vats. Aldo shot at a blond man among them who was not in uniform; the man hit the ground and started to crawl toward him, protected by the parapet of the next-to-last milk vat.

"Get up and come out with your hands up!" the man yelled. "I am Lieutenant Blesh. Surrender, and you will not be harmed!"

Aldo shot three times, and, as the bullets chipped pieces off the parapet, he wondered what kind of slop he was lying in. His belly and chest were all wet. He ran his hand under his body and when his hand came up it was sticky with blood. Afraid to acknowledge the wound, he suddenly sprang up and emptied his clip on the guy in civvies; then a hail of bullets virtually cut him in half, and he fell headfirst into the vat, splashing out a wave of bloody milk as he went.

At the top of the grassy knoll, Don Ettore felt dizzy. Clutching Angelo Barba's arm, he had climbed the hill in total darkness while Folco Mori brought up the rear in surly silence. For an instant Don Ettore had the idea that Italo Volpone had lured him here to get rid of him. He slipped his hand into his pocket and felt the butt of his Luger, his finger going to the trigger.

Italo's voice reached him. "Well, Moshe, what're you waiting for?"

The ray of a flashlight pierced the darkness, and almost immediately there was another flash up ahead, about a hundred or two hundred yards on the right. Their signal was being returned.

"*Andiamo!*" Volpone said.

Behind him were Don Ettore, Moshe Yudelman, Folco Mori, Pietro Bellinzona, Carmine Crimello, and Angelo Barba, all walking in the dark. From time to time Moshe sent a quick flash of light down to his feet, trying to avoid deep holes and unsteady footing.

After Vittorio Pizzu's phone report, Volpone and Gabelotti had held a conference. A very cold and distant one. During the preceding days, for brief moments, the hope of success had brought them closer, but now the failure of their joint enterprise was splitting them apart again.

"I can take you with me," Volpone had said, "if you're ready to go right away."

Gabelotti hesitated. Moshe Yudelman added his weight to the advice of Ettore's two consiglieri, Barba and Crimello, to convince the don that a strategic withdrawal now was the wisest course. A soldier, sent by Ottavio Giacomassi, had come to pick them up, and just before leaving, Volpone had telephoned Enzo Priano, the manager of the gas station where Homer Kloppe was being held.

"Enzo, don't let him go! Wait for orders from me."

Volpone, embittered by the recent fiasco, didn't open his mouth once while the Mercedes 600 headed toward the plateau where Amedeo Morobbia and Giancarlo Ferrero were waiting for them with the plane.

A muffled voice came to them out of the darkness.

"Moshe?"

"Here!" Yudelman replied.

"How many are you?" Morobbia asked.

"Seven."

"Okay. Hop aboard."

With a quick swish of his flashlight, Morobbia showed them the entrance to the plane.

Volpone, Yudelman, Barba, and Mori piled in. Crimello could sense Gabelotti's terror and discreetly shoved him ahead.

"Where is the runway?" Don Ettore asked in a terrified voice.

Pietro Bellinzona, standing still at the foot of the ladder, was waiting for them to make up their minds.

Discreetly Carmine tapped Pietro on the shoulder. Bellinzona understood. He pushed Don Ettore forward, and the radioman, who had guessed what was up, took Gabelotti's hand and pulled him into the plane.

"Here—this way . . ." Ferrero kept repeating as he guided Don Ettore along the inside wall of the cabin and made him sit down.

"Of course, sir, you must be used to first class in 747s," he said laughingly. "And this isn't quite the same kind of luxury!"

He buckled the safety belt around Gabelotti's waist.

"Don't you worry, now. This contraption flies just

fine. In less than an hour we'll be in Milan. The other plane is waiting for you there, a Boeing. We chartered it specially for you. You'll be on your way again without delay."

Ferrero turned back to the door, which he closed and locked from inside the cockpit.

"Amedeo, let's take off!"

The engine noise broke the night silence. Gabelotti scrunched down, calling on all his self-control to contain his terror, digging his nails into the flesh of his thighs. The plane shook from stem to stern and turned into the wind. No one spoke a word as it picked up speed in the darkness and lifted miraculously from the ground.

23

For the first time since he had started to grow hair on his face, Fritz Blesh was not shaved by 8:00 A.M. In fact, he had skipped a night's rest. After the raid on the Zwiss Milk and Butter plant, there had been a great deal to do. Heavy losses were suffered on both sides. Two promising detectives, Hans Bregenz and Paul Romanshorn, had been blown to bits by a grenade near the Zurich Trade Bank. Three men had been shot badly at the dairy, and three more killed, including Officer Schindler, who had found the courage to climb up under the eaves in order to cut off the perpetrators' escape route. Schindler's face was smashed by a dumdum bullet from a Herstal.

As for the gang they had attacked, nine had died—in their pockets, not the slightest bit of identification. Three others had been taken alive: one had a shattered hip and was given immediate transfusions by the ambulance men; another had two bullets in his chest. The doctors at the hospital refused to allow Blesh to interrogate them as long as they remained in critical condition. If they proved as talkative as the third, who sustained only minor wounds, questioning them would be no more useful than the roadblocks had been in stopping the ones that got away.

At 7:00 A.M. Blesh was getting ready to leave his office when Captain Kirkpatrick, Lieutenant Finnegan, and Mr. Scott Dempsey of the SEC dropped in on him unexpectedly. Beside himself, Blesh had thrown them out after a brief, unsavory exchange. Kirkpatrick had had the audacity to say, "I told you so, lieutenant," and Blesh had called in two strong and stready sentries to wish him bon voyage.

By now all of Zurich knew of the shoot-out. The city had been awakened by the unfamiliar music and fireworks—the grenade explosions, the staccato rhythms of automatic weapons, the flashes of flamethrowers, and the crackling of fires.

At 8:00 A.M., Blesh, drunk with exhaustion and rancor, decided to head for home. That was when he got the message that Chimene Kloppe wanted to see him immediately.

"My husband has been kidnapped, lieutenant," she told him when he arrived at her house. "I'm sure of it."

She showed him Inez's letter. "I got this yesterday. But I waited before calling you. I was hoping Homer would come back."

"Do you know what went on during the night, madam?"

"No, lieutenant."

"You didn't hear a thing?"

"Nothing at all!"

"None of the shooting?"

"What are you talking about?"

"A squad of armed men attacked the Zurich Trade Bank," he informed her.

Her reaction took him by surprise.

"Oh—they broke his bank!" Chimene exclaimed as though she were talking about his favorite toy.

"You will have to help me now, madam. Who are 'they'?"

"Why, that's something for you to tell me, lieutenant. How would I know?"

"Has your husband seemed worried or depressed recently?"

He bit his tongue as Chimene looked at him with reproachful eyes, in which tears were welling up. How tactless could he be?

"Please excuse what I just said, Frau Kloppe. I'm truly exhausted—at the end of my rope."

"So am I, lieutenant."

"Perhaps you could give me some kind of lead. The

letter you just showed me was obviously intended to keep you from calling me."

"What is it you would like to know?"

"Did your husband keep you posted about his affairs—at the bank, I mean to say?"

Blesh realized he was out of line a second time.

"Did you get any kind of ransom demand?"

"Ransom?" she asked. "What for?"

"Well, nothing, really, madam. I just wondered . . . There might have been something. May I assume you will let me know if anything unusual occurs? You need have no worry. I'm going all-out on this, alerting every brigade; we'll search the entire city, and I'll keep you posted."

He saluted, as if to leave, but she said, "Lieutenant . . ."

"Yes, madam?"

"My husband is a good man, a very good man. What have they got against him? Why should anyone want to hurt him?"

"I'm sorry to inform you that the Commissione wants me to explain what's been going on," Gabelotti said. He stopped talking, his face icy. No one said a word. Don Ettore let a few doom-laden seconds go by. Without looking at anyone in particular, he went on: "No Syndicate family can be put in danger because somebody in another family makes mistakes."

Jaws clamped, eyes hard, Italo Volpone moved slightly on his chair, but he managed to control himself. Moshe had made him swear he wouldn't let himself get tricked into answering, that he'd remain calm and collected. Unfortunately, he knew his own limits, and he wasn't inclined to put up with Gabelotti's pious-sounding insinuations for too long.

On the long trip back to New York, both Italo and Gabelotti had remained stubbornly locked in their silent hostility. No sooner had Italo arrived home than he threw himself into Angela's arms and dragged her off to the bedroom, locking the door behind them, with total disregard for the fact that Yudelman, Folco Mori, and Pietro Bellinzona were in the living room. After about an hour, Moshe knocked on the door.

"Babe, it's important," he called out.

"Beat it!"

"Angela, please ask him to come out. His safety depends on it."

"Italo . . ." she had whispered.

He had barely taken the time to get her clothes off, furiously grabbing her into his embrace, rolling over on her in the bed, on the rug on the floor, picking her up, shoving her brutally against the wall while she hung onto his muscular shoulders and groaned in happy abandon. He let her go only after he came for the third time. She lay on the floor, out of breath, arms crossed, fulfilled. He pushed his head against her chest and began tenderly licking her breasts. And then Moshe, again . . .

"Italo!"

"You gonna gimme time to take a shower?"

"Hurry up, Italo! Please, hurry!"

He had slipped his arms under his wife's body, picked her up from the floor, and carried her locked onto him into the bathroom, her thighs around his hips, her head bouncing in the hollow of his neck. He turned the water on full force. And there, again, flooded by the soft warm rain that was running down their bodies, he penetrated her.

"Don Ettore's waiting for us, Italo!" she said.

"If he wants to see me, let him come over."

Moshe had not been able to get Italo to change his mind. He had finally called Angelo Barba back to ask him to set a neutral meeting ground, and they met at the Bowl, a Fifty-second Street nightclub that wasn't open at this time of day but whose owner took his orders from the Syndicate.

The two dons got there at the exact same moment. Gabelotti had Carmine Crimello and Angelo Barba, his two consiglieri, with him, as well as two bodyguards who remained with Folco Mori and Pietro Bellinzona on guard outside the club.

Moshe was very concerned. Since their hasty retreat from Zurich, he hadn't heard a thing from Vittorio Pizzu and his *capiregime*, Aldo Amalfi, Vincente Bruttore, and Joseph Dotto. The police assault on the dairy was going to create disturbing waves, and their effects would be felt even in New York. The Commissione could not abide anything that upset its well-regulated routine. The Syndicate was in the habit of settling its internal disputes as quietly as possible, without attracting attention.

"The Commissione," Gabelotti said, "has let me know that it won't tolerate anyone doing stuff on his own to put the safety of all our families in real danger."

Seeing that Italo was about to open his mouth, Moshe rushed to ask, "What did you answer the Commissione, Don Ettore?"

Gabelotti turned a heavy, reproving eye on the consigliere.

"The truth, Moshe, just the truth," he said. "I told them I had to go to Switzerland to clear up a mess I was not responsible for."

"Could I ask you who was responsible for it?" Volpone inquired in a toneless voice.

Disregarding him, Gabelotti continued to look at Yudelman. "The Commissione told me I was slipshod, Moshe. And I had to plead guilty."

"Guilty of what, Don Ettore?" Moshe asked politely, his heart beating rapidly.

Gabelotti answered offhandedly, "Of having let an irresponsible character make this mess."

Volpone jumped up. "You're the irresponsible character!" he shouted.

Only now did Gabelotti appear to notice that Italo was there.

"There are some things a person doesn't say," he commented, "if he expects to live to a ripe old age."

Italo, overflowing with hate, spat at him, "The oldest one is the one that dies first. Just remember that!"

"Gentlemen, gentlemen!" Yudelman cut in. "I beg all of you, let's not get into personal squabbles! There's much too much at stake! Two billion dollars, to be exact."

Ettore Gabelotti now stood up, his face twisted with rage, and pointed a finger at Volpone. "You know what you are? A nobody! All you did was fuck up one thing after another! You took over from Don Genco without any right! From now on, keep your nose out of this deal. When I have it settled, your family's heirs will get the share they're entitled to. Understand?"

379

Volpone stood up now and leaned forward, wild with fury. "You dare threaten me?" he yelled. "After what you did to my brother!"

"I didn't do nothing to your brother!" Gabelotti barked as he banged his fist on the table. "You dirty little louse! You're the one who had O'Brion knocked off!"

"No, I didn't," Volpone shouted back. "I killed him with my own hands—your stinking fuckin' crook of a consigliere!"

"*Cornuto!*" Don Ettore roared. "If he was alive, we'd have the number. You're gonna pay for this!"

"Gentlemen, gentlemen," Moshe said again, trying to make himself heard. "If you stay united, there's nothing lost. We're still holding Homer Kloppe—" Yudelman stopped short. He started to stammer as though he had been struck by lightning.

"Holy shit!" he finally exclaimed. All eyes turned toward him. Then, in a voice that was not his own, he struggled to say, *"I know who has the number!"*

Axel Green downed what was left of his highball and made a face. The ice had melted, leaving the drink flat. He straightened the papers on his desk and looked at his watch. It was well past normal closing time. He tightened the knot of his tie, slipped into his light jacket, and glanced out the window of his office. Bay Street as usual was mobbed with dawdlers in straw hats, going by in a brightly colored stream as they did their window shopping.

Despite its name, the Bahamian Credit Bank was a British bank, and Axel Green was by birth a Londoner; he had arrived in Nassau twenty years before on a business trip and had simply never left, never missing those cold rainy English skies. Today, Green was the head of the foreign accounts department of the bank's Nassau branch, responsible for the huge amounts of capital that passed through the island for brief cleansing stopovers.

Green merged into the flow of tourists, wondering whether he should go home before taking his swim.

"Mr. Axel Green?" a voice asked him.

"Yes?"

"Would you please get in?" a tall man said, pointing to a bottle-green Vauxhall.

"I beg your pardon?"

Another man opened the rear door of the car and pushed him in before he knew what was happening. A third man, at the wheel, started the car moving. Green thought it might be a kidnapping, like the ones that had been taking place recently in Italy. If so, he was done for. The bank would never pay to ransom him. "Where are we going?" he asked.

"To the Beach Hotel. There are some people who have to see you."

"See me? But why?"

"They'll tell you that themselves, Mr. Green."

When the car stopped, the tall man said, "There are two of us here with you, Mr. Green," letting him catch a glimpse of a pistol as he added, without a trace of humor in his voice, "In fact, as you can see, actually three of us. I think you'd do well not to give us any trouble. Get it?"

"I won't give you any trouble."

"Very well, then. Let's go."

Flanked by the two men, he walked through the Beach Hotel lobby where a number of his acquaintances greeted him. It seemed unbelievable that he could be kidnapped in front of a hundred witnesses, without anyone realizing what was going on.

They took the lift up to the top floor, and the shorter of the two men rang the bell of corner penthouse 1029.

A man came and opened. "This way, Mr. Green," he said. "The gentlemen are expecting you."

Green found himself in a huge living room with great bay windows looking out on a breathtaking view. But the five strangers before him didn't care about the view. The man who had opened the door closed it behind him. The five men stood up, and one came toward him.

"Please, first of all, allow me to apologize for the somewhat, shall I say, unconventional way in which we invited you up here, Mr. Green. But this is a real emergency. I should introduce myself; I am Moshe Yudelman."

Something clicked in Axel Green's mind. He had heard Yudelman's name before.

"And this is Mr. Ettore Gabelotti."

The fat man with the heavy jowls acknowledged the introduction with a wave of his chin.

"Mr. Italo Volpone," Yudelman went on, "and Angelo Barba and Carmine Crimello, financial advisers to Mr. Gabelotti."

Green was nonplussed by these formal introductions. Capi of the Syndicate were never known to act out in the open this way.

"Would you like something to drink, Mr. Green?"

"That would be a jolly good idea," he replied.

"Straight or with water?" Barba asked as he poured some scotch into a glass.

"Over one ice cube, if you don't mind," Green requested.

"Please do sit down, Mr. Green."

He sat. Outside of Yudelman and Barba, none of the others had said anything.

"Here's to you, Mr. Green," Yudelman said as he raised his glass. "And to the little business deal we have to conclude."

"You say we have a business deal to conclude?" Green asked with exquisite British courtesy.

"Yes, we do," Yudelman said. "And a very good deal for you, if I may say so. You're going to become a rich man, Mr. Green."

"Nothing could make me happier," Green countered.

Yudelman continued, "Two hundred thousand dollars is nothing to turn your nose up at."

Green gulped his scotch.

"What am I supposed to do to earn these two hundred thousand dollars, Mr. Yudelman?"

"Very, very little. Simply supply us with a bit of information we once had, but have unfortunately lost. We want the number of an account you transferred to Switzerland on the instructions of a depositor, Mr. Genco Volpone. Two billion dollars, Mr. Green, which you forwarded to Switzerland, to the Zurich Trade Bank. Receipt was acknowledged to you by the bank's head, Mr. Homer Kloppe. Will you give me the number of that account, Mr. Green?"

"This is a very embarrassing thing that you are asking me to do, Mr. Yudelman . . ."

"Are you aware of who we are?" Moshe asked him amiably.

"Yes," Green replied.

Yudelman spread his arms in a gesture of resignation. "You see, Mr. Green, I'm afraid you don't have much choice. However, to set your mind at ease about any ethical problem involved, I will tell you something you already know. That money does belong to us. There is not the slightest doubt about that. The two people who had the key to it—Genco Volpone, the brother of Mr. Volpone here, and Mortimer O'Brion, Mr. Gabelotti's legal counsel with power of attorney—are both gone, dead under tragic circumstances, and were not able to give us the number for the account. So, in giving it to us, you are not doing anything dishonest, you are merely acting in the cause of justice, and doing us a favor which, as I told you, we will not fail to appreciate."

Axel Green cleared his throat. "What if I were to refuse?"

"After all I've just told you, I can't really conceive of that," Yudelman said.

"Quite right, I suppose not," Green said, shaking his head.

"Will you accept the two hundred thousand dollars as a token of our friendship and gratitude, then?"

Green ran a hand over his face and stared out at the clear blue sky that was now and then marked by the rapid darting of seagulls. Everything Yudelman had just told him was true. When the order to transfer the money had been given to him, Genco Volpone himself had selected the number under which it would be recorded at the Zurich Trade Bank. Green, who had a fantastic memory for figures, knew it by heart. He had automatically seen the number—828384—as a series of consecutive numbers—82, 83, 84. Child's play.

Axel Green wanted to go on living. He had been in Nassau too long not to know that refusing the Syndicate now would be signing an irrevocable death warrant, not only for himself but for his loved ones as well.

"We know that your son John is ready to enter college," Yudelman went on seriously. "And don't forget you have two more children after him, little Paul and Christine. And Mrs. Green does want the girl to take up ballet. A fine family is a beautiful thing, Mr. Green, but good education doesn't come cheap these days."

"No, indeed, it's quite expensive," he agreed.

"My friends and I feel that the Bahamian Credit Bank is not doing right by you, considering your talents. We are deeply sorry about that, Mr. Green, and that is why we thought it would be nice to reward you properly for this favor you're doing us. Two hundred thousand dollars. Believe me, the figure would have been much lower for anyone less gifted or less worthy than yourself."

"I appreciate that," Green said.

"Well, then, here's the question again: What is the number of that account?"

"Eight hundred and twenty-eight thousand, three hundred and eighty-four," Green said, heaving a deep sigh. "Or, if you prefer it more simply: eighty-two, eighty-three, eighty-four."

"Thank you, Mr. Green," Moshe told him. "I can see that you are a very wise man. The two hundred thousand dollars—in cash—will be delivered to your home tomorrow, at the end of the business day."

A key turned in the lock. Homer Kloppe sat up sharply on the cot, automatically running his fingers over his unshaven chin.

A stranger came in and threw a blindfold down on the bed.

"Put that over your eyes," he instructed Kloppe.

Kloppe shook his head. If he had to die, he was going to do it looking death in the face.

"Hey, what the hell you waiting for? Put it on and make it snappy. We're releasing you!"

As he still did not move, the man went around behind him and tied the piece of black material over his eyes.

"I'm warning you, if you take it off before I tell you, you get a shot in the head."

Kloppe heard the sound of a pistol being cocked.

"Come on, get up!"

Then he was pushed up a step. The noise of a metallic door closing noisily made him realize he was in some kind of truck or van. The motor began to hum. Then there were the noises of the city, followed by the zip of cars going past in the opposite direction, and finally, country silence.

When the brakes went on, he was thrown forward. The man next to him kept him from falling.

"Okay, get out now. The driver's going to move on. I'm staying here with you. Start counting as loud as you can, up to two hundred. After you hit two hundred, you can do whatever you want. Go ahead, start counting."

"One, two, three, four, five . . ."

"Louder!"

"Six, seven, eight . . ."

"Good, keep on like that."

The sound of the car moving away.

"Thirty-two, thirty-three, thirty-four . . ." And Kloppe stopped.

Nothing happened. He took off the blindfold. In the east, the sun was rising; it was as if he were seeing it for the first time. He breathed in the fragrance of the trees, and, to get his bearings, he started walking along a wooded path covered with fragile new grass that gradually led down to a highway from which he had heard the passing sounds of high-speed trucks. Although he was not able definitely to identify it, the place where he was seemed vaguely familiar to him. He set himself up on the shoulder of the road and began trying to hitch a ride. Nobody stopped for him.

From the time it had taken to come out here, he figured he must be about fifteen kilometers from Zurich. But all the drivers who went by seemed to speed up when they came abreast of him, pretending not to see him. The first road marker he saw told him he was moving in the right direction: ZURICH—11 KM.

For the twentieth time, he tried to flag down a car. In a flash, behind the wheel of a Mercedes, he could see the driver turn away. He looked like an elegantly dressed, slightly portly man—who could have been his own twin—and yet the man went by indifferently, just as Kloppe himself would have done in similar circumstances, once upon a time.

A braking sound made him turn around.

"Hi there, pops. You look beat."

There were three of them, two boys, and a girl who looked like Renata, in a tired old jeep.

"Could you give me a ride into Zurich?"

"Sure, hop in. The more crazies in here, the merrier."

When he got to Bellerivestrasse, he found Chimene sitting in the living room. She dropped her teacup and threw herself into his arms.

"Homer, oh, Homer!" she cried. "I was so scared! They didn't hurt you, did they?"

He softly patted her hair, staring into space.

"No, no. Everything is fine. I just need a bath."

She was wearing a robe over her nightgown. She smelled good. Hiding her face against his shoulder, she said, "Homer, you ought to know. They set fire to your bank."

Getting the number from Axel Green didn't relax Gabelotti or Volpone. Since the day before, they had spoken to each other only through their respective consiglieri. The insults and threats they had traded in New York had created an abyss between them that could never be closed, except by the death, sooner or later, of one or the other.

When Green had left, Moshe made a last desperate effort at reconciliation. "Gentlemen, gentlemen! We're in sight of our goal. Nothing is going to stop us from getting our money back now."

Don Ettore grabbed the telephone, connected it to the squawk box so that all of them would be able to hear what he said, and dialed the number of his Swiss lawyer, Philip Diego. When Diego answered, they could hear him as clearly as if he had been in the room with them.

"I have the number we've been looking for," Gabelotti said. "Want to take it down?"

"Of course. Since you left, you know, some unfortunate things have been happening in Zurich. One of our leading bankers, Mr. Homer Kloppe, has disappeared."

"Oh, how I deplore such a thing!" Gabelotti said.

Crimello, Barba, and Yudelman couldn't take their

eyes off him. Only Volpone pretended to be looking out at the sky, as if he weren't involved in what was going on.

"We just don't understand what's been happening," Philip Diego went on. "Mr. Kloppe's bank was raided. The whole police force is on the alert. People have been killed—"

"I don't see what those local problems have to do with us!" Don Ettore cut him off impatiently. "Will you please take down this number and take the necessary steps to have the money transferred?"

"That guy's not going to the bank by himself!" Volpone said suddenly to Yudelman. "Our man has to go with him!"

Gabelotti frowned as he caught those instructions (intended for him—to be sure).

"I'm afraid I don't make myself clear," Philip Diego came back. "All banking operations have been suspended. As I just told you, the banker has disappeared!"

"I understand exactly what you said," Gabelotti barked at Diego. "What makes you think that banker may not be coming home any minute now? And if he does, what's gonna hold us up?"

"Nothing, of course, nothing. Provided you have the number and the secret code name."

Gabelotti looked daggers at Angelo Barba and Carmine Crimello; Moshe Yudelman and Italo Volpone froze.

"The what?" the don roared into the phone.

"You know the money was deposited in the numbered account under a fictitious name: the code name. Do you have it?"

"I have the number, that's enough!" Gabelotti spat at him.

"Oh, I'm afraid not," Diego replied after the briefest of pauses. "If the banker does get back, and I say *if* he does, the slight, uh, misunderstanding we had with him won't make the job any easier for me. You know, he'll stick strictly to the letter of the law."

"What the hell does that mean?" Gabelotti demanded.

The whole thing was just too stupid. They were so close to the goal, and just as they were about to touch it, it started to slip away again.

Moshe signaled to Don Ettore. "Tell Mr. Deigo you'll call him back," he whispered.

"Don't go away from your phone," Gabelotti yelled across the ocean. "I'll be callin' you back right away!"

He hung up, and nobody dared look at anyone else.

Angelo Barba finally broke the silence that engulfed them. "Moshe," he asked, "would you object if we held separate conferences for fifteen minutes or so?"

"That's just what I was going to suggest," Yudelman said.

Barba, Crimello, and Gabelotti left the sitting room, and when Moshe and Italo were alone, Yudelman began to shake his head.

"This is a rough one, all right, Italo. Genco and O'Brion were the only ones who knew the code name. Now neither one of 'em is here to clue us in. Frankly, I don't know where we go from here."

Volpone punched a drape as hard as he could.

"That fucking bastard O'Brion! I was too nice to him —I didn't keep him suffering long enough! His head was right under that electric saw, and instead of talking, the idiot kept calling for his mother, *Mamma mia! Mamma mia!*"

Moshe was hit by a high-voltage charge.

"Say that again! Say it again! What was he calling?"

Italo looked at him carefully. "Moshe? What's with you?"

"What was O'Brion saying when he was under the saw?"

"*Mamma mia,*" Volpone said. "So what? The poor bastard was shitting in his pants with fear. He knew what I was gonna do to him, he knew all right! And instead of answering me, he just kept whining, calling for his whore of a mother!"

Yudelman's lips began to tremble uncontrollably. When he finally could, he said in a toneless voice, "Remember, Italo, O'Brion was an Irishman. An Irishman— you know what that means?"

Volpone looked at him as if he had lost his mind. "What the fuck you talkin' about?"

"O'Brion answered you, Italo. Don't you see? A dying man doesn't utter his last words in a foreign language. If he said *Mamma mia,* that's our code name!"

There were three uniformed policemen pacing up and down on the sidewalk in front of the Zurich Trade Bank. Homer felt as though he had been hit in the stomach when he saw the main banking hall that had been devastated by fire and explosions. The chipped marble pillars were evidence enough of how violent the firefight had been.

Workers were busy cleaning up the debris, and the main attendant, totally unperturbed, was at his post, standing behind an improvised table.

"Victor," Kloppe greeted him.

The attendant bowed respectfully. "Herr Kloppe . . ."

For all his sorrow, Homer's heart swelled with pride. He indeed belonged to a solid, stubborn, hardworking race. All the catastrophes in the world might befall his country, but come what might, banking still went on.

Above the second floor, things were intact. Marjorie, alerted to his arrival, was waiting in the reception room outside his office. She greeted him as if nothing unusual had happened since they last saw each other.

"There have been many calls for you, sir. I've listed them all. Do you want them now?"

"Later," Kloppe told her.

"Should I put any calls through to you?"

"The ones you feel are important."

He was getting his bottle of Waterman's out of the drawer when Marjorie announced on the intercom: "Mr. Schmeelbling is on the line, sir. Will you speak to him?"

"Put him on."

Homer poured himself a couple of drops of liquor. Eugene Schmeelbling was the man who was handling the two-billion-dollar deposit.

His voice came through. "Homer, good Lord, my man! I've been sweating ink worrying over you. What the devil's been going on?"

"The police are investigating."

"What have we come to, tell me. Is there no respect for anything these days?"

389

"That's the way it looks." Kloppe sighed.

Figures started dancing in his head. Between the interest he'd have to pay and the rate he got from Schmeelbling, right now he would be collecting eight times $109,588, or $876,704 in pure profit. Even if he had to foot the bill for rebuilding an even finer facade for his bank, he'd still come out ahead. But, of course, he wouldn't have to pay for that. That's what insurance was for. . . .

"Say, now, Homer," Schmeelbling was saying. "About that deposit you made with me—you know what I mean?"

"Of course."

"What do I do with it?"

"Just keep it working, Eugene. Keep it right on working until you hear from me."

"Fine, just fine. That was all I wanted to hear you say. Please remember me most respectfully to Frau Kloppe, your charming wife."

"I won't fail to, Eugene. I'll talk to you again soon."

"Talk to you soon," he replied.

Marjorie slipped into the sanctum sanctorum and closed the door behind her.

"It's that policeman, sir, Lieutenant Blesh," she half whispered. "He's been here several times already."

"Show him in."

Homer put the bottle of Waterman's back into the drawer and got up to welcome Blesh.

"Ah, Herr Kloppe," said Blesh, "it's so good to see you back safe and sound."

"Thanks very much, lieutenant."

"Your wife let me know you were back. I immediately called off the search."

"Oh, I must apologize to you. I can't tell you how sorry I am to have caused so much trouble. It was unpardonable of me to have failed to notify you."

Blesh's face closed up. "I'm afraid I don't follow you, Herr Kloppe."

"Well, you see, lieutenant, I was so upset by the loss . . . I went off without advising anyone. I needed to be alone, to meditate."

"May I ask where you went, sir?"

The banker faced his visitor with a slight look of

surprise on his face. "I wouldn't think that could be of interest to anyone, lieutenant."

"You're mistaken, sir. Two of my men were killed. Four more are seriously wounded. We had two hours of open warfare in order to protect your property and your person!"

"Well, that's why the citizens of the Confederation maintain a police force, isn't it, lieutenant? You seem to be surprised that you did your duty."

"Not at all, sir. I am only surprised at your answer. Your wife told me you had been kidnapped."

Kloppe retorted with a darkly knowledgeable look, "After all we've been through, lieutenant, you shouldn't be surprised if my wife is a little nervous. I think you might have checked out what she told you before you launched your campaign."

Blesh found it hard to swallow his saliva. "Do you know Italo Volpone and Ettore Gabelotti?" he finally asked.

Kloppe's face grew even more distant as he said, "No, lieutenant."

"Not even their names?"

"I just heard them for the first time."

"Your daughter was killed in a Beauty Ghost P9 that belonged to one Orlando Baretto. Was this Baretto an acquaintance of your daughter's?"

"Renata is no longer here to answer that, lieutenant. Allow me to point out that I received you here today as a friend. I must say, I didn't expect to be addressed in such a tone or subjected to this kind of interrogation."

"I'm investigating, Herr Kloppe. I'm just trying to get at the truth."

"That's what I want you to do, too, lieutenant. And now, if you'll excuse me, I have a great deal of work to catch up on."

Blesh choked down his fury. Kloppe had good connections in high places. If he wanted to stand mute, no one could force him to talk. On the contrary, his peers would secretly applaud his behavior. For the time being, Blesh decided, it would be best to bow to the inevitable.

"I do apologize to you, sir, and I hope you will excuse me if I seemed a bit overzealous."

"Duly noted, lieutenant. You will, of course, understand that I find it hard to accept being treated as a guilty party when, as it so happens, I am the victim."

He got up to indicate that the meeting was over. Blesh did likewise, but he couldn't resist adding, "The slightest lead would be of the greatest help to me, Herr Kloppe. As you see it, who might have assaulted your bank?"

Kloppe eyed him at great length. "Now, that is something I would dearly like to know myself, lieutenant. But if I were a police officer, it seems to me I would start looking among certain troublesome elements that your service permits to gad about Zurich freely."

"What elements do you have in mind, sir?"

"The extreme New Left, lieutenant."

Kloppe took three paces to the door and held it open. "Don't hesitate to come back to see me if you make any progress in your investigation," he said. "I am always fully at your disposal."

Blesh saluted and went out. Waiting in the reception room were two of the city's best-known business lawyers, Philip Diego and Karl Deutsch.

"They don't have appointments, but they are very insistent," Marjorie said to her employer. "Can you see them?"

"Yes," Kloppe replied.

Once inside, Philip Diego was first to open the exchange.

"We heard what happened. Why, that's most unspeakable."

"Unbelievable, unpardonable!" Deutsch chimed in.

Kloppe, sitting rigidly behind his desk, eyed them, his hands remaining flat on the tabletop.

"I am very busy," he said in a glacial voice. "Can you inform me what brings you gentlemen here?"

"Well, yes, this is it," Philip Diego began. "My colleague Karl Deutsch and I jointly represent a client who has a large numbered account here in your bank. This client has instructed us to have that money transferred this very day to the Chemical Inter Trust of Panama."

"Under what name did your client set up his account?"

"*Mamma mia.*"

"What is the account number?"

"828384."

"And the amount of the deposit?"

"Two billion U.S. dollars."

Kloppe picked up the telephone. "Marjorie," he said, "ask Garnheim to bring the *Mamma mia* account file up to you."

For the next five minutes the three men did not move, nor did any of them utter a word. There was absolute silence.

Marjorie came in and set the file down before Kloppe. Homer opened it, leafed through its contents, and took out a paper, which he handed over to Diego.

"Sign on the right-hand side, at the bottom, please."

Philip Diego signed.

"You too, please," Kloppe said to Deutsch.

Karl Deutsch complied.

Kloppe stood up immediately. Philip Diego held his hand out tentatively, but Kloppe appeared not to notice.

"The whole matter will be taken care of before the end of the day," he said.

Once the lawyers had gone, he went to the window and pressed his forehead against the pane. This year, spring had broken out in all its glory, the finest springtime that had ever cast its light on Zurich.

But Homer Kloppe turned his back on it. He returned to his desk, sat down heavily in his chair, and took his Waterman's ink bottle from the drawer.

Epilogue

Between Lausanne and Morges, the railway cuts a hole in the mountain for a distance of a mile and a quarter. At the west end, the tunnel opens onto a landscape of huge fir trees rising up the steep flanks of a valley with an icy mountain stream at the bottom.

On the banks of this stream, the Hummler family had gathered for a picnic. The weather was fair and he had this Saturday off, so Franz Hummler had taken his wife and two children on an outing. Jean-François was eleven, Michel just past nine.

"*Maman,*" Michel asked, "can we go and play?"

"Where?"

"We want to climb up the hillside."

"You didn't finish your cake."

"I don't want any more."

Birghitt carefully wrapped the remnants of their meal in a plastic bag.

"Don't get too far away," she cautioned. "Jean-François, keep an eye on your little brother!"

Michel shrugged scornfully. "I'm just as big as he is."

"Don't get yourselves dirty!" said their mother.

The children ran off, shouting like wild Indians.

"Franz, will you open the trunk for me?"

Franz went over to this brand-new red Volvo, knelt down, wet his finger with saliva, and started to polish a tiny mud spot off the body below the trunk.

"Well, are you going to open it?" Birghitt repeated, trying to keep from laughing.

"What's so funny?"

"You're just like a kid."

"Well, it *is* beautiful, isn't it?"

"Magnificent."

"What about taking a little spin instead of just staying here?"

"Franz, it's very nice here. You'll have plenty of chances to try out the car."

She put the bag in and was about to close the trunk when he put his hand forward quickly, to stop her.

"Wait! Don't touch it. It shouldn't be slammed. Just pushed. Nice and easy . . ."

"Come on!" Birghitt burst out with a laugh. "Let's go back to the monsters."

She grabbed his hand and dragged him along. They had finished off a bottle of Alsatian wine that they had chilled in the stream. The air was warm, very clean and light. They started up the hillside, making their way between the fir trees, at times slipping on the carpet of needles.

"Can you see them?" Birghitt asked.

Franz ran his eyes up the steep slope. It had a sharp break in it at the point where the railway twisted through. Very near the roadbed, somewhat down from the embankment, he saw the red and blue spots of his children's clothes. They were standing motionless in a semicircle of trees.

"Jean-François! Michel!" he yelled to them.

The boys swung their arms in broad signals, asking them to come up. The tree they were standing under had a flock of crows flying over it; it seemed strange. The treetop still had a splotch of snow that the sun had not yet succeeded in melting.

"Come on," Franz said.

He and his wife started to climb again, and when they were within earshot, Jean-François and Michel called out, *"Papa! Maman!* Come and see! Look at the birds!"

"I thought I told you not to get very far away," Birghitt scolded.

"Papa, Jean-François says those are crows."

"Yes," the elder said, "they are crows. Aren't they, *papa?*"

Out of breath, Franz looked up. The crows seemed to be fighting over something in the snow, their wings beating noisily, and hunks of hardened snow were chipping off as they fought.

"What are they doing, *papa?*"

"They're eating," Franz answered unthinkingly.

"Are they eating the tree?"

Franz moved over several yards. He was down below the right-of-way, at the opening of the tunnel, which was just about level with the top of the tree. He looked more closely. In a fork of the tree, stuck between two branches, was a man's body—or what was left of it—lying on its back. Two crows were digging their beaks into the face at the place where the eyes should have been. Others were hopping up and down on the body, waiting to get their turn.

"Go back down to the car," Franz choked out, his voice sounding as though he had a wad of cotton in his mouth.

"What do you see, *papa?*" Jean-François asked as he came closer.

"Go on, beat it!" his father snapped. And he made an impatient gesture to his wife. "Birghitt, take them down!"

She could tell that Franz had just seen something awful, and she did not want to know what it was. She took the two boys by the hands.

"Okay, now, last one down is a monkey's uncle!"

The body was elegantly dressed in a dark suit. The wristwatch it wore reflected the sun's rays in a profusion of fine golden arrows. Even at this distance—fifteen or eighteen feet—Franz could clearly see that the shoe on the left leg was made of luxury leather. The corpse did not have a right leg. At the groin, where the leg had been severed, the flesh was covered with a crust of coagulated blood.

ABOUT THE AUTHOR AND TRANSLATOR

PIERRE REY is one of France's bestselling commercial novelists. He is known worldwide as the author of *The Greek* (over four million copies in print) and *The Widow*, which was translated into fourteen languages. *Out* was a major French novel and to date has been translated into English, Italian, Norwegian, Portuguese, Turkish, Dutch, Spanish, German, and Slovenian.

HAROLD SALEMSON is a former journalist, film correspondent and film company executive. He has subtitled some two dozen foreign feature films in addition to translating over twenty books from French to English.

RELAX!
SIT DOWN
and Catch Up On Your Reading!

Bantam Book Catalog

Here's your up-to-the-minute listing of over 1,400 titles by your favorite authors.

This illustrated, large format catalog gives a description of each title. For your convenience, it is divided into categories in fiction and non-fiction—gothics, science fiction, westerns, mysteries, cookbooks, mysticism and occult, biographies, history, family living, health, psychology, art.

So don't delay—take advantage of this special opportunity to increase your reading pleasure.

Just send us your name and address and 50¢ (to help defray postage and handling costs).